MOUNTAIN MOONLIGHT

Elizabeth Leigh

Zebra Books
Kensington Publishing Corp.
http://www.zebrabooks.com

ZEBRA BOOKS are published by

Kensington Publishing Corp.
850 Third Avenue
New York, NY 10022

Copyright © 1997 by Debbie Barr Hancock

All rights reserved. No part of this book may be reproduced in any form or by any means without the prior written consent of the Publisher, excepting brief quotes used in reviews.

If you purchased this book without a cover you should be aware that this book is stolen property. It was reported as "unsold and destroyed" to the Publisher and neither the Author nor the Publisher has received any payment for this "stripped book."

Zebra and the Z logo Reg. U.S. Pat. & TM Off.

First Printing: April, 1997
10 9 8 7 6 5 4 3 2 1

Printed in the United States of America

PASSIONS AWAKENED

He looked down at her sun-dappled hair, breathed in the sweet scent of jasmine that clung to her, and wished they could stay lost forever.

"And what if I can't find this tree again?" Her voice was whispery hoarse, her mouth so close that the breath of her words tickled his cheek. He couldn't seem to draw enough air into his lungs or stop his pulse from racing out of control.

There was nothing else to tell her, nothing else to think about except the one thing he'd been pushing back: holding her close and kissing her until they were both senseless. *This is insane,* he thought as he found her chin, caught it between his thumb and forefinger, and gently tilted it upward.

I can't believe I want him to kiss me, she thought. *I really am crazy.*

His lips touched hers then, soft as the flutter of a butterfly wing, a tender grazing that took her breath away and left her begging for more. He cupped her face in his palms, but instead of deepening the kiss, he raised his mouth to her forehead and nuzzled her hairline with his nose.

She felt as though he'd allowed her the tiniest taste of the sweetest honeybees ever made, then snatched it away.

He fought for control. It would be so easy to take her, right there in the shady bower of the mountain laurel, but to do so would make him as low as the men who'd taken advantage of her during the war.

YOU WON'T WANT TO READ JUST ONE—KATHERINE STONE

ROOMMATES   (0-8217-5206-5, $6.99/$7.99)
No one could have prepared Carrie for the monumental changes she would face when she met her new circle of friends at Stanford University. Once their lives intertwined and became woven into the tapestry of the times, they would never be the same.

TWINS   (0-8217-5207-3, $6.99/$7.99)
Brook and Melanie Chandler were so different, it was hard to believe they were sisters. One was a dark, serious, ambitious New York attorney; the other, a golden, glamourous, sophisticated supermodel. But they were more than sisters—they were twins and more alike than even they knew . . .

THE CARLTON CLUB   (0-8217-5204-9, $6.99/$7.99)
It was the place to see and be seen, the only place to be. And for those who frequented the playground of the very rich, it was a way of life. Mark, Kathleen, Leslie and Janet—they worked together, played together, and loved together, all behind exclusive gates of the *Carlton Club*.

Available wherever paperbacks are sold, or order direct from the Publisher. Send cover price plus 50¢ per copy for mailing and handling to Penguin USA, P.O. Box 999, c/o Dept. 17109, Bergenfield, NJ 07621. Residents of New York and Tennessee must include sales tax. DO NOT SEND CASH.

*For Mike, Danny, and Chris Barr—
the greatest brothers any sister ever had*

Acknowledgments

Many thanks to Jean Walton, my critique partner, who also served as a sounding board and lent me research material; to Steven Barrett, who told me all about the medicinal properties of the Hercules'-club, brought me an entire limb from the tree, and answered my questions about historic pistols and shotguns; and to Yvette Winstead from Rutledge, Tennessee, who advised me on mountain dialect.

One

Smoky Mountains, Early Spring, 1866

Might near everyone who wandered into Peculiar Cove wanted to know how the settlement came by its name. Course, mountain folks never questioned the "cove" part. What else was a body supposed to call a sheltered valley with a level floor and ringed about by mountains except a cove? That was what it was, pure and simple. But even mountain folks—who themselves had attributed a unique collection of appellations to various local features, employing such outlandish names as Maggot Spring Gap and Hogback Ridge and Charlie's Bunion—even mountain folks asked about the "peculiar" part.

Because mountain folks loved telling and hearing stories about the sources of such entitlements, no one in Peculiar Cove thought twice about elaborating. And elaborate they did. In fact, so many stories had been bandied about over the years that no one rightly knew anymore which story bore even a remote resemblance to the honest-to-God truth. Not that it mattered one whit to most folks in Peculiar Cove.

Since there was nothing truly unusual about the cove itself, logic dictated that the peculiarity of one or more early residents contributed to the original basis of the name. And since the majority of such residents now lay among the grasses and wildflowers near Peculiar Branch, their names carved on slabs of slate at their heads and chunks of granite positioned over their toes, the perpetration of such tales went uncontested.

The most popular story of the day, however, laid the blame—or the credit, depending on who was doing the telling—quite squarely on a living, breathing human being, one Crazy Bets, a woman born in Peculiar Cove long after the valley got its name. This particular fact the storytellers easily overlooked, in light of the thigh-slapping roars the tale usually generated. Indeed, anyone who met Crazy Bets experienced no trouble at all believing everything they'd heard about her and then some, if a body was to believe Uncle Begley, owner of Peculiar Cove's only mercantile and one of the settlement's oldest and longest-term residents.

Being both an only child and a bachelor, Begley wasn't anyone's uncle, but folks had been calling him uncle for so long that no one, including Begley, could recall exactly when or why the title got attached to his name. Perhaps his propensity for taking folks under his wing had contributed to the misnomer. Perhaps his rotund build, round spectacles, and ready smile gave him the appearance of a favorite uncle. More than likely, though, it was the delight he took in claiming kinship to virtually every family for miles around—and his equal delight in recounting everything he knew about both the cove and its residents.

It didn't take much to get Uncle Begley started. A raised eyebrow would do it. When Steele Montgomery, a mountain man himself but a stranger to Peculiar, arrived at the mercantile one crisp, bright Saturday morning, Begley looped a heavy arm around the younger man's shoulders and ushered him into the store before Steele got a chance to explain why he'd come—not that he usually had to. His black broadcloth suit and broad-brimmed black hat usually gave away his calling, but Begley appeared oblivious to everything other than the fact that he had a newcomer in tow.

"This is gonna take a spell, son. Ye might as well set down and git comfortable." The old man practically pushed Steele onto the sagging cowhide seat of a straight chair stationed near a cold wood stove, while he settled his bulk into the plump cushions of a sturdy oak rocker and immediately set in talking.

At first, Begley's words flowed right past Steele, who was more than a little taken aback by the store owner's friendly but domineering attitude. Besides, having to listen to Begley's tale thwarted Steele's purpose in arriving so early, which was to have the entire day to meet as many people as possible before services on Sunday. Even though he was a fairly green circuit rider, Steele had learned the importance of smiles and handshakes before he stepped into the pulpit and lashed out at those same folks. Some called it politicking. He preferred to think of it as soul preparation.

He had another reason, a much darker reason, for meeting as many people as he possibly could. Holed up somewhere in this neck of the woods were three no-account scoundrels whose necks he planned to stretch, assuming he ever found them. He and the Lord weren't presently in complete agreement on this particular matter, but Steele had every confidence that when the time came, God would be on his side.

Eager to get on with both his work and the Lord's, he sat poised for escape, running one excuse after another through his head. But when Begley mentioned the war, Steele perked up, though for the life of him he couldn't have said why. One of his greatest needs was to put the war and all its unpleasant memories behind him.

Begley was saying that folks who knew Betsy Tyler before the War of the Rebellion weaseled its way into Peculiar Cove remembered her as a slender, freckle-faced gal-woman far more opinionated than was considered proper for a female, but otherwise pleasant enough.

"That would a-been before Shiloh," Uncle Begley explained.

Before Shiloh. The phrase snatched at Steele's insides, twisting and squeezing them with the strength of a German washerwoman wringing out a bedsheet. "What was so significant about Shiloh?"

He heard himself ask the question and realized he'd given it no conscious thought. If he had, he would have attempted to steer the subject elsewhere. Doing so, however, wouldn't change the fact that the bloody battle had drawn a dividing line in his life, and a part of him desperately wanted to know how it had done the same to someone who hadn't even been there.

"Hell, where've ye been, son?" Uncle Begley's shaggy gray eyebrows jutted so far forward his forehead resembled one of the brush-grown ledges that marked the Catstairs on Greenbrier Pinnacle. "Even up here in the mount'uns, we heared all about Shiloh."

"I know about the battle." Steele's irritation rang in his ears and he forced a calmness he didn't feel into his voice. "I was wondering how it affected this woman you call Crazy Bets."

"Oh, that." Uncle Begley turned his head, spat at a tobacco-stained syrup bucket next to the wood stove, and missed. Brown-tinged spittle ran down the side of the metal can and puddled on the wood floor. If the old man noticed the mess, he gave no indication. Instead, his bleached blue eyes took on a faraway look and he moved his head sadly from side to side. "She had a brother, ye see, name o' William. Bets doted on him, turned him into a reg'lar sissy-paints after their paw died. Ordered him a mess o' fancy clothes from a outfit in New York City and sent him over to the college in Maryville to learn sumpin called zoo-ology or some such nonsense."

"It's the study of animals," Steele supplied.

"That's what Bets said, though why anybody would want to spend hard-earned money learnin' about critters is beyond me. Course, none o' us ever knowed the Tylers to work at earnin' a nickel, and they always was knowed fer bein' high-toned folk. Hit's a wonder Bets didn't send Willy further away. Phineas Tyler—that'd be their paw— did his studiments way off from here. Some place called Hazard, I think, up north. There's a Hazard in Kentucky. Maybe that's where he went."

"Harvard, perhaps?" A smile tugged at the corners of Steele's lips, but Begley didn't seem to notice.

"Could be. Could be. Anyways, Willy was in Maryville when the war broke out. He must've got hisself all caught up in the heat o' the moment, 'cause he warn't raised political. The Tylers didn' 'pear to keer no more fer the guvmint than most o' us 'round here does. Course, ye prob'ly know all about that."

Steele frowned in confusion. "How so?"

"I figured ye fer a highlander with a bit o' book-larnin'. I s'pose I was wrong."

"I thought you meant I knew about the Tylers. I grew up near White Oak Flats and graduated from Blount College in Knoxville."

Begley grinned in self-satisfaction. "I had ye nailed dead to rights, then. Ye know Radford Gatlin?"

"The one who owns the store in White Oak Flats?"

"That'd be the one. I hear tell he's trying to change the name of the town to Gatlinburg."

"I hear that, too."

"I've been a-knowing Radford fer a long time. He always finds a way to git what he wants." Begley's gaze dropped and fixed itself on Steele's left boot, which made Steele even more uncomfortable than he already was. Self-consciously, he crossed his right ankle over his left. Begley's wrinkled lips pursed up and his eyes narrowed.

"We don' git too many strangers 'round here. Course, mount'un folks is never strangers. I s'pose I art not be callin' ye a stranger, ye bein' from White Oak Flats and all. D'you brang any news 'bout them three devils been spillin' mortal gorm and burnin' down farms?"

Steele's heart lurched, partly from deep-seated anger, partly from hope that Begley knew more than Steele did. "Last I heard, they were in these parts."

The storekeeper shook his head, his gaze never quite leaving the spot on the floor where Steele's left boot rested. "Not for more'n two, three month now. They kilt the whole Porter fam'ly. It was a sad, sad day. What makes folk want t' do thangs like 'at?"

"I don't know."

"We keep hopin' somebody'll kill 'em."

"They'll have their day of judgment," Steele said with conviction.

"I hope ye're right, son." He dipped his forehead toward Steele's foot.

Steele braced himself for the inevitable question.

"I noticed ye was dragging that foot a bit when ye come in here. Ye got a wooden laig?"

"Yes."

"Ye lose it in the war?"

Steele nodded.

"Ye want t' talk about it?"

The circumstances surrounding the loss of his leg fell near the top of Steele Montgomery's list of taboo subjects. "No. I want to hear about Crazy Bets."

Begley spat again—placing the brown stream right on target this time, then adjusted his chaw and set the chair in motion. It creaked a bit, but it was a creak that reminded Steele of home and hearth, a creak that was almost pleasant and would have been quite agreeable had it not suggested matters better left in the past.

"Like I's saying, the Tylers was always diffrent. They

come here not long after I did, and that was nigh on to forty year ago. Warn't many homesteads here then. This land use t' belong to the Injuns, ye know. Most of the settlers was like me, mount'un born, mount'un raised, mostly Scotch-Irish, looking for a place to live that was far removed from the rules of the guvmint. But then, you know about that, ye being from the mount'uns yeself."

Steele was beginning to understand why Uncle Begley said this story was going to take a spell. They'd been sitting and talking for close to half an hour. He'd learned nothing new about the marauders and he still hadn't heard much about Crazy Bets. If he remembered correctly, Begley got sidetracked when he mentioned Shiloh.

"What about Shiloh?" Steele asked, the question catching in his throat.

"Willy was kilt there. The day Betsy got the news . . . she got it from me, ye know, right here in the store." Begley inclined his head toward a wood and iron rack of boxes sitting on the end of the counter. A small sign that read "US Mail" hung from one of the metal crosspieces. "I'm the postmaster, ye see. Anyways, I had to give her the letter. I knowed when I seed it was all banded in black that Willy had gone and got hisself kilt. It didn't help Bets none for me to hand her the letter amongst a crowd of folks, but we don' git mail in here on any kind o' reg'lar schedule, so when it does come, folks flock in. Shucks, I don' even git to use them boxes over there very often."

"I suppose she was upset when she opened the letter."

Begley wiggled in the chair. "That's just hit. She didn't open it here. I reckon she knowed what the black band meant, too, 'cause when she looked at it, she got sorta pale and went all trembly-like, then took out for home. Nobody saw her for a week. Then she come in here one day and tol' me she wanted to buy ever' piece of red and blue yardgoods I had on the shelves, which warn't much. Not just solids, she said. Gingham and calico, too."

"Whatever for?"

"I ast her that myself. 'My brother done give his life fer the Union,' she says, 'and I'm gonna make him a shrine.' Course, she said it a bit more proper-like, her being from such a high-toned family and all. Then she took all the pitchers I had of Union flags and banners, 'long with lotsa sewing thread."

"Did you ever see this shrine?"

The old man cackled. "Did I ever see it? Why, ever'body in Peculiar Cove got a hand-writ invite to come see it. And pert-near everyone come, too. It were on a Sunday evening, best I kin recollect. Bets waited till the parlor filled up, then Auntie Kee struck up a somber tune on the organ and Bets led the crowd up the stairs to Willy's bedchamber."

"Who's Auntie Kee?"

"A woman what lives with Crazy Bets. From the looks of her, she must be half-breed. Nobody rightly knows where she come from. Just showed up one day at the Tyler house—back in the forties, if I recollect right—and they took her in. Been livin' there ever since. She can play the organ, that one can."

Begley's voice trailed off and he seemed to withdraw himself from everything—the story, Steele's company, even the moment. Steele almost wished he hadn't asked about Auntie Kee, but he couldn't deny the pleasure on the old man's wrinkled face. Whoever Auntie Kee was, Begley obviously enjoyed thinking about her. As much as Steele wanted to hear more about the shrine, he didn't want to shatter the storekeeper's reminiscences. After a while, Uncle Begley waggled his head as though to shake off the spell, and picked back up where he'd left off.

"When Bets reached Willy's door, she turned to face the crowd and started speechifyin'. I was too fur back t' make out what she was saying, but folks up front tol' me later she went on and on about her pore brother layin' in a unmarked bury-hole off yonder at Shiloh. Then she flung open the door and we all passed through the chamber. She made us walk one behind t'other and dared us to breathe, let alone tawlk."

"What did it look like?"

"Hit was a sight to behold, I kin tell you. That room was kivered up in Union flags—the bed, the walls, the winders, ever'thang wore a Union kiver of one kind or t'other. Hit'uz the consarnedest thang I ever seed. I had to hold my jaw shut to keep from laughing out loud, but I couldn't keep my sides from shaking. I don' thank Bets seed me, but I've worried about hit 'cause she was serious and I didn't mean no disrespect. I mean, she'd lost her mind right along with her brother. Course, we all figured she'd come around in time. Who knows? She might've, if'n hit hadn't a-been fer shootin' that army feller."

Begley's statement raised all sorts of questions. Steele asked the first one that popped into his mind. "When did that happen?"

"Just a couple days later. The Rebs come in here and set up camp fer a spell. Somehow, they heared about Willy's shrine, which prob'ly warn't too hard. Them that seed it never really quit tawlking about it. One day a bunch of them soldiers got all liquored-up and decided to see fer theirselfs if hit'uz true. They went out to the Tyler place and ordered Bets to let 'em in. Said they was going to burn the house if they fount a single Union flag inside. Bets held 'em off with her paw's brace o' pistols whilst Auntie Kee went upstairs and got rid of all the flags. One of the soldiers got a bit too riled up about Bets not lettin' 'em in. When he tried to push his way past her, she shot him dead."

"I'm surprised the Rebels didn't hang her."

"Prob'ly would've. Lord knows, they wanted to. They

dragged her back to their camp, her screamin' and hollerin' all the way. The next day, she come back home, and nobody rightly knows what they done to her or why they let her go. Course, they's a passel o' speculation."

Steele swallowed hard, glanced around to make sure they were still alone, then lowered his voice to a whisper. "Do you think she was . . ." He couldn't finish the question.

Begley shrugged. "Nobody knows. She ain't hardly come out of that big ol' house since." Begley narrowed his pale blue eyes at Steele. "Ye come in from the west?"

Steele nodded.

"Then ye passed the Tyler place. Hit's that big frame house with the paint peelin' off hit and weeds all growed up around hit. Looks plumb deserted."

"Yes, I noticed it."

"A body cain't help noticin' hit, what with hit bein' the only frame house anywheres around. Hit takes a passel o' money to have milled lumber hauled in here, but Phineas Tyler had money, lotsa hit. Why, he could a-lived anywheres. Me, I always figured Phineas Tyler was runnin' from sumpin'." In the manner of a seasoned storyteller, Begley paused long enough for his observation to sink in. "Mind ye, he never said so, and nobody never come lookin' fer him, but there just ain't no other reason why he'd a-chose to live here in the mount'uns lessen he was trying to hide. He and Rebecca never did fit in here. And those younguns of theirn—Betsy and Willy! They was as strange as their maw and paw. They's a word fer it, but I cain't fer the life o' me recollect what hit is."

"Eccentric?"

The old man slapped the arm of his chair. "That's hit. They was 'centric. A travelin' preacher-parson told me that word onc't on a time."

And it was a traveling preacher-parson reminded you of it.

"So that's why you call Betsy crazy? Because she's a reclusive old maid from a family of eccentrics?"

"Naw. It's more'n that. Like I done told ye, she was pleasant enough before Shiloh. Afterwards . . . after she got word that Willy'd been kilt, after that shrine she made got her in trouble with the Johnny Rebs, she turned plumb twitter-witted. Fergot all her high-toned upbringing. Some folks say she hasn't even warshed herself in a year or more. Others say she's possessed of a demon, like the ancients writ about in the Bible. Right peculiar, that's our Crazy Bets. And that's why this place is called Peculiar Cove."

Steele seriously doubted that Betsy Tyler's plunge into melancholy had contributed to the name of the settlement, which he'd heard about himself as a young child, but he saw no point in arguing about it. "Why do people say she's demon-possessed if they never see her?"

"They hear her. I've heared her myself. Sometimes she screams like a painter-cat. Other times, hit's softer, more like a coon what just chewed hits paw off to get out'n a trap. Either one'll make your blood run as cold as Peculiar Branch."

A shiver traced its way down Steele's spine and goose bumps prickled his upper arms beneath his shirtsleeves.

"Ye chilled?" Begley asked. "I kin start a far if'n ye are. By the time ye git one goin' good this time o' year, it warms up outside and then hit's hot as a fiddler's elbow in here. Takes all day long fer hit to cool off again. But I don' mind startin' a far a bit. This coolish air's got my ole bones to achin'."

"Don't start one for me. I'm fine." He wasn't, but it took more than a fire to warm a soul. Steele Montgomery's had been cold so long he'd almost lost hope of ever knowing joy again.

"Funny," Begley said, a puzzled look on his round face. "I always tell the side-splittin' parts of Betsy's story, never the sad parts. I don' know why I did this time. There's sumpin about ye, though . . ."

The bell tied over the top of the door jingled, cutting off the proprietor's speech. A woman wearing a tattered shawl came in. She carried a baby in one arm and a basket of eggs on the other. The young mother offered a nod and a mumbled how-dee-do in Steele's direction, prompting Uncle Begley to extend a brief introduction.

"This here's Mr. Montgomery, from over White Oak Flats way." Apparently, Begley didn't think Steele needed to know her name.

The old man rubbed his knees, then rose stiffly from the rocking chair and ambled over to a cluttered counter, leaving Steele to a passel of memories he'd sworn never to unearth and an ever-growing list of questions he was determined to have answered.

The best way to do that is by paying Betsy Tyler a visit.

The voice came out of nowhere, as it so often did, gently but firmly urging Steele into territory he'd just as soon not enter. Suddenly antsy, he got up and roamed the store, silently defying the voice, yet knowing all the while that he had no other choice. Not if he was to live with himself. He offered a quick, silent prayer, feeling like a trout twisting on a line and begging to be let off the hook. Instead, divine purpose filled his being. God meant for him to exorcise Betsy's demon and restore her soul to His will. That was why He'd sent Steele to Peculiar Cove. Never had he been quite so eager to perform the Lord's work, but first he owed Uncle Begley the courtesy of a leave-taking.

By the time the old man finished counting the woman's eggs, helping her with her shopping, and adjusting her account, other customers had come in—a young man in worn bib overalls and another young mother trailed by two small children and a buxom daughter with a pimply face. Begley's day as a store owner had started in earnest, leaving Steele with little hope for private words with the talkative old man. There was no sense in waiting any longer to take his leave. The sooner he got it over with, the sooner he could go see Betsy Tyler, whom he refused to call Crazy Bets, even mentally.

He leaned against a bin of winter squash, which put him next to the young man, and cleared his throat. Everyone, including the children, stopped talking and turned to face him, their expressions stony. "Excuse me for interrupting your business, but I need to be getting along. I just wanted to tell you all that I'm the Reverend Montgomery, your new circuit preacher."

Begley's mouth dropped open, and for a moment silence reigned. The woman with the baby, who'd stopped on her way out, spoke first. "Do tell!"

"Why didn't ye say so?" Uncle Begley's voice was accusing.

"Ye prob'ly didn't give the pore man a chance." Laughter trickled through the young man's words. "Let me be the first to give ye a glad-handing." He stuck his right hand out and took Steele's in a friendly shake. "I'm Tom Dickerson. If ye've a mind to go with me, I'll be happy to take ye around and acquaint ye with folks."

Steele groped for a reason to refuse, but none came readily to mind. As much as he found himself liking Tom Dickerson, he wanted nothing more than to head straight to the big frame house with the overgrown garden. Visions of casting out the demon that possessed Betsy Tyler dominated his thoughts, but Tom was waiting for an answer and Steele had no desire to offend the man. Perhaps there was a polite way around the invitation. "I'm obliged to you for offering, but I see no need to take you away from your chores. I'm used to introducing myself."

"Shucks, I got the whole mornin' free. I'd thought to do some visitin' while I was in town. Hit'd pleasure me to do it with ye."

Steele pasted a smile on his face and turned to the two women, who had moved closer. While they welcomed him to the community and told him they were looking forward to his sermon the next day—they used the store for services, they said—Tom gave Begley his order. Within minutes, Steele followed Tom out the door and into the dirt road.

"That yore mule?" Tom pointed to Dusty, Steele's pacing mule.

"Yes. I need to stable him." Taking Dusty's reins, Steele headed west, toward the Tyler house. Tom turned east.

"Liv'ry's thisaway," Tom said. " 'Sides, the onliest person who's to home thataway is Crazy Bets, and ye don' wan' t' meet her."

Yes, I do, Steele thought as he caught up with Tom. *And I will. Today. She'll be right as rain and sitting in church tomorrow, and then neither you nor anyone else can ever call her Crazy Bets again.*

Two

A piercing scream rent the air.

With no small degree of wonder, Betsy Tyler realized the unladylike bellow had come from her throat. It certainly wasn't the first time she'd ever screamed; it simply hadn't happened in a long time. But with her wrists tied securely to the rungs of a kitchen chair, her ankles tied to its legs, and her jaw aching something awful, screaming was the only way she had left to fight.

"Hesh up," Auntie Kee fussed, grasping Betsy's chin in one hand and waving a pair of small pliers in front of Betsy's tear-filled eyes with the other. The dampness fuzzed the image, making the tool appear far larger than it actually was. Betsy closed her eyes and gulped in an attempt to swallow her fear. It didn't work. She opened her mouth to scream again, but the sudden thrust of Auntie Kee's fingers splintered the sound into a series of fragmented gurgles.

"They ain't no way I'm goin' t' be able to fix this here problem with you hollerin' like that."

Betsy blinked back a fresh surge of tears. Talking around fingers and pliers wasn't easy, but she gave it a try. "I-doan-wan-it-fix."

"Yeah, ye do. Ye're jest too stubborn to admit hit."

While a part of Betsy conceded the truth in Auntie Kee's words, a larger part remained focused on denial. What a predicament she'd gotten herself into! If the clove had only worked its numbing magic this time, she wouldn't have ever agreed to this torture. Now that she had, there didn't seem to be an easy way out.

The cold steel clamped down on Betsy's sore jaw tooth, filling her senses with the tastes of metal and strong lye soap and making her gag. In reaction, she tossed her head back and nearly choked on the acrid spittle. Ignoring her, Auntie Kee wiggled the tooth with the pliers. Like a bolt of lightning, intense pain shot through Betsy's jawbone and into her ear.

"E-e-e!" she moaned, trying to say "please" but unable to form the consonants with her lips forced open and her tongue squashed beneath the pliers.

"Hesh up, I told ye!" The older woman's round face was so close to Betsy's that the words tickled the fine hairs on her chin. Auntie Kee wiggled the tooth again, giving it a little pull this time. A wave of nausea washed through Betsy and golden sparks danced before her eyes. "This is only goin' t' hurt fer a secunt. Soon hit'll all be over, and ye'll be obliged to me fer relievin' ye of your misery. Ye'll see."

Betsy couldn't see anything past the misery of the moment—and its reminder of another time when she'd been bound and gagged and unable to fight her way out. The memory jerked at her heart and threw her muscles into spasms. The tears she'd been holding back gushed forth and her voice ripped through her throat in an agonizing wail. Undaunted, Auntie Kee tugged harder on the firmly entrenched tooth.

And then, quite suddenly, the tugging stopped and the slick, cold steel slipped over Betsy's tongue and out of her mouth. Her jaw continued to throb and her lower gum felt like someone had started a brushfire on top of it, but at least the tooth-pulling was a fait accompli.

"Thanks," she muttered, the word coming out on a long sigh. "Let me out of this chair."

"Hit ain't over yet." The pliers clanked on the enamel top of the kitchen worktable. With her eyes still closed and her spine locked, Betsy waited for Auntie Kee to rub in some more of the bittersweet toothache paste the Indian woman had made from snakeweed, burnt alum, and honey. The paste didn't work as effectively as a whole clove, but Betsy couldn't very well bite down on a clove with her mouth open. Instead of applying more paste, however, Auntie Kee gave a disgusted snort and shuffled off toward the front of the house.

"You must be Auntie Kee."

Although there was no denying her heritage—her wrinkled brown skin, high cheekbones, nearly black eyes, and long braids spoke clearly of Indian blood—the woman gawked at Steele in what could only be surprise that he, a perfect stranger, knew who she was. He assumed his most affable pose and pinned her with a smile designed to persuade.

"I'd like to see Miss Tyler, please."

The woman drew up her flagging bosom and pinned him with a frown designed to intimidate. "She ain't to home."

Steele knew better. Well, he corrected, he knew *someone* else was there. He hadn't imagined the screams coming from the bowels of the house. They'd been real, as real as the white paint peeling off the weathered clapboards. As real as the waist-high weeds encroaching the flagstone path. As real as the sagging planks he was standing on. The logical *someone* was Betsy Tyler. Although Steele admired Auntie Kee's fierce protectiveness, he'd come to see Betsy, and by golly, she was going to let him.

"I believe she is."

Auntie Kee planted her fists on what would have been her waist if she'd possessed one, and scowled even harder.

"I told ye she ain't to home. Now git along with ye." Her fist left her side long enough to open up and make a shooing motion. "Go on now. Git!"

Steele got the distinct impression this was the way Auntie Kee would talk to a mad dog. She was definitely a formidable woman, hell-bent on sending him away. But he could be formidable, too. Especially when he'd set his mind to a task. "I'm not leaving here until I see Miss Tyler."

Betsy's eyes flew open. What in heaven's name was going on? The paste sat in a bowl on the table, right next to the pliers. There was nothing in the front of the house the old woman could need, at least nothing that came readily to mind. So why . . .

She heard the knock then, or rather the insistent pounding, and wondered how she'd missed hearing so much racket before. The banging resounded through the house, setting the copper molds hanging from a rack in the kitchen to clinking and threatening to send the framed herb and spice charts flying off their nails. Who could be creating such a disturbance? More to the point, who would want to? No one had come calling at the Tyler house in almost four years, which was the way Betsy wanted it. Whoever had decided to break tradition did so without a trace of shyness or trepidation. There was certainly nothing timid about the knock. A body would think the town was on fire!

Her curiosity about to get the best of her, Betsy pulled against the muslin rags that bound her to the chair, succeeding only in chafing her wrists. Unwilling to give up, she rocked her torso back and forth in short, quick movements that propelled the chair forward in a manner as convulsive as her lurching. Her progress, however, was so slow Betsy figured it would take her an hour or more to reach the front hall. She tried to calm her thudding pulse with the assurance that if anything were truly wrong, Auntie Kee would rescue her.

With that acknowledgment came a little peace, enough to quell the panic that had set her in motion. Too late, Betsy realized she'd stopped too quickly. For a mere hair's breadth in time, the chair teetered on its hind legs. Before she could steady it, the lightweight chair toppled over backwards, jarring her enough to make her teeth rattle.

"Rats!" she muttered, mentally nursing a new pain in her head, this one just below her crown. Already, she could feel a lump forming there, and the spindles cut into her back. To relieve at least part of her discomfort, Betsy rolled hard to the right. It didn't help. If anything, it worsened the situation, for it created an additional pain in her shoulder and arm, a pain that the combined weight of her body and the chair continually worsened.

Thoroughly disgusted, Betsy was attempting to flip the chair back when a man's dusty black boots, their tops covered with black trousers, suddenly planted themselves mere inches from her nose, catching her completely off guard. Shame flooded her cheeks. How awful to be caught tied to a chair! If only she'd borne up under the pain. If only she hadn't behaved like a two-year-old, Auntie Kee wouldn't have been forced to take such drastic measures.

Where was Auntie Kee? She would never have allowed this man entrance . . . unless . . . unless he had . . . unless she had been unable to stop him . . .

A steel-sharp vision of Auntie Kee lying dead in the front hall blinded Betsy to any other possibility. She opened her mouth to scream, but the certainty that this interloper had harmed the older woman begat a tight knot in her stomach that surged upward and lodged in her throat, silencing her voice. The last shred of common sense left to her told Betsy that screaming wouldn't help anyway. If anything, *her* screams kept the townsfolk away, which until that moment had always pleased her.

Maybe someone would come . . . a knight like those in the fairy tales of old, a man large of body but soft of heart, dressed all in white like an angel, swooping down out of the heavens to snatch her away in the nick of time . . .

Strong hands encircled her upper arms and pulled both her and the chair off the floor. Encouraged, Betsy blinked away the glittering illusion—and gasped at the expanse of black broadcloth stretched across wide shoulders. It was Lucifer himself, come to finish what his minions had started those long years ago.

Sheer terror ripped through her, tearing away the last vestiges of hope and plunging her into a darker, deeper abyss of despair than she'd ever thought to know.

Steele held the chair at arm's length, his mind occupied with trying to devise a reason for the horror that gripped Betsy Tyler—a surprisingly clean and attractive young woman—seconds before she went limp. Horror was, perhaps, too strong a word, but he had no other for the irrefutable panic that flashed in her wide, pale green eyes just before they closed.

Was his countenance that unpleasant? None had ever called him handsome, even before the war etched its scourge on his face, but they hadn't labeled him hideous, either. Something about him, though, had terrified her beyond reason. The jagged, nearly white slash of scar tissue that traversed the right side of his face from temple to jaw would frighten the Devil incarnate, but she couldn't have seen that, not through the curtain of long, straight black hair that covered it.

He closed his eyes, attempting to see himself through

her eyes. His nose was overlong and crooked where it had been broken, and he'd always thought his mouth too wide and his cheeks too gaunt, but it wasn't an ugly face. Although he hadn't been smiling, he'd caught himself looking at her with loving-kindness, as a preacher-man should.

Perhaps that was the crux of the problem. Perhaps it was the demon within her that had seen him instead of Betsy Tyler. A demon would have recognized him as a man of God—but if that were the case, then why had the demon caused her to faint? Why not demonstrate his presence first, by having her hiss or spit or something? Maybe the demon was weak or just wanted to regather his forces.

Regardless, there was no longer any doubt in Steele Montgomery's mind that Betsy Tyler's body hosted a demon of some sort. He could think of no other reason for tying her to the chair. Amazing, though, that the woman Uncle Begley called Auntie Kee had managed to subdue her long enough to accomplish such a task. From his limited experience with such matters, Steele knew that the demon-possessed body could—and usually did—exhibit superhuman strength.

"What air ye doin' with her? Put that chair down!"

The sudden vocal intrusion startled him so much he almost dropped the chair. Although he never completely let go of it, he wasn't able to set it down quite as gently as he intended. The jarring brought Betsy out of her swoon. Her eyelids flew open, the same panic he'd witnessed moments before exploded from her pale green irises, and she let out an ear-splitting screech.

"See what ye did?" Auntie Kee demanded, moving between him and Betsy and cupping Betsy's cheek with a soothing palm. The gesture brought the swelling in the younger woman's cheek to his attention. She must have bitten the inside of her mouth when the chair bumped on the floor. He chided himself for causing her more misery—but he wished she'd quit hollering nonetheless. The shrill noise was beginning to play havoc with his good humor. Surely, she wasn't in that much pain.

"I oughter make *ye* pull her tooth."

"What did you say?" Surely, he'd misunderstood the woman, which was perfectly understandable with Betsy Tyler's screaming as accompaniment. He found himself shouting just to be heard above the noise.

Auntie Kee straightened up, planted her fists on her hips, and glared at Steele with her almost black eyes. "I said I oughter make ye pull her tooth. I had her pretty calm 'fore ye come barging in here."

"Tooth?" Steele squeaked in disbelief. "She has a bad tooth?"

She looked at him as though he'd sprouted horns. "Course, she does. Why'd you thank she was tied to the chair?"

"I, uh, I thought—" Steele swallowed hard, but his embarrassment stuck like a pesky fish bone in his throat. "Never mind what I thought."

The woman picked up a small pair of pliers from a nearby table and handed them over. "Right side on the bottom. Almost all the way back. Ye cain't miss hit."

"But"—*Dear God, there must be a way out of this!*—"I've never pulled a tooth before."

"Hit ain't so hard . . . fer a body with some strength in his hands. Mine's gone." She held out her hands for his inspection. "Rheumatiz."

The gnarled, twisted fingers denied argument on that count, but Steele held to his other grounds: inexperience. "Honestly, I really don't know how to pull a tooth. You need a tooth-doctor."

"Ain't got one."

"What if I hurt her?"

"Don' ye hear her cryin'?" How could he not? Now,

however, he noted that her screams had subsided into hiccupping sobs. "That child couldn't hurt much more'n she does already. The tooth's got to come out, pure and simple. Ye got the strength and I don't." When he continued to balk, she added, "Ye told me back at the door that the Lord sent ye here. Did He tell ye how come?"

Steele forced himself to ignore Betsy's moans so he could listen to the calm, soft voice that had intruded upon his thoughts off and on all day. *Go to her*, the voice had said. *She needs your help*. With startling clarity, Steele realized he'd made an assumption, based on Uncle Begley's story, that might not be true. Perhaps the only help Betsy Tyler needed was with her tooth, though Steele couldn't understand why God would send him somewhere to pull a tooth—or to do anything else, for that matter, beyond his realm of either talent or experience. Maybe if he were the only possible choice, but that wasn't the case here. No, there had to be more to it than a simple toothache. There had to be another reason God wanted him to go to Betsy Tyler.

That brought him back to the demon or her insanity or whatever caused her to shut herself away from the world, whatever made her scream so loud folks could hear her from the road. Her obvious physical pain accounted only for the present, while her panic upon seeing him suggested something more complex, something much deeper and far less tangible.

"If ye ain't a-goin' to do hit, give me back them pliers."

If he'd learned one thing about Auntie Kee in the few minutes he'd been around her, it was that she was short on patience. Of course, he might be, too, if he had to live with Betsy Tyler. Nevertheless, the older woman's penchant for butting into his unfinished thoughts frustrated him. He stanched the angry words that tickled his tongue, squatted down in front of Betsy, and prayed. *Lord, if You sent me here for a tooth-pulling, I hope You were aiming to get me through it.*

Although her red, swollen, moisture-filled eyes distorted the image, Betsy believed with all her heart that it could belong to none other than the Devil himself. Only the Devil could have hoodwinked Auntie Kee so thoroughly.

Why the Devil chose this particular day to visit her, she couldn't fathom, especially in light of all the other times she'd been far more vulnerable to his wiles than she was at the moment. Nor could she understand how he'd won Auntie Kee over so easily, but he obviously had. Elsewise, her lifetime companion—whom Betsy knew to be a staunch advocate of the straight and narrow—would never have so blithely handed over the instrument of her present torture: the small but deadly pair of pliers.

"Open up," the Devil requested, teasing her sealed lips with the cold steel, his voice a bit gruff, but otherwise rather pleasant. Well, *she* didn't sway quite so effortlessly. She pressed her lips more firmly together and mumbled "Unh-uh" behind them.

"C'mon now, honey," Auntie Kee coaxed from the sidelines. "Ye know ye need that tooth out'n your head. This kind preacher-man here's goin' t' pull hit fer ye."

Preacher-man! He called himself a preacher-man? No wonder Auntie Kee had fallen so quickly. What a mean, despicable, low-down-dirty trick! Betsy gasped in loathing. Immediately, the pliers were back in her mouth, but they didn't get past her front teeth before she clamped her lips down on them. Lucifer pulled them out.

Betsy grinned despite herself. Battling with the fiend was almost fun. If she were to best him, though, she needed all her wits about her. She took a deep breath through her nose, blinked away the last of her tears, and tried not to think about how her eyes were stinging and her throat was burning and her ears were ringing. Most of all, she tried not to think about the stabbing pain in her jaw and the fire in her gums. With all the willpower she could muster, Betsy shoved her various miseries to the back of her mind and focused all her mental energy on the crooked-nosed, wide-mouthed, dark-eyed demon brandishing the pliers. First the tooth—to gain her trust—and then . . .

She chased away the dull ache surrounding her heart and jerked herself back to her objective, which was to rid both herself and Auntie Kee of the presence of this spawn of hell.

More than anything, she wanted to claw his eyes out, to let into him with the ferocity of a she-lion defending her young, to leave his rugged face riddled with bloody slashes, to fill her nostrils with the smell of his fear. She wanted to see him tuck tail and run like the coward he was, for only a coward would take advantage of two basically helpless females. If only her hands and feet weren't tied to the chair and she wasn't half out of her mind from toothache, what she wouldn't do to him!

"You're lucky I can't get at you, you no-account varmint," she spat, wiggling and squirming, tugging vainly against the muslin ropes. "You're vile and contemptible and . . . and . . . I can't think of a name bad enough to call you."

His face sort of crumbled into a look of pure dismay. "Now, Miss Tyler, is that really fair? I'm only trying to help you."

Help her? Help her right into the stygian depths of hell, that's where he'd help her! For an instant, a sheath of red obstructed her vision, but when it cleared, she found herself gazing into hound-dog-sad eyes. Never had she witnessed such blatant insincerity masked in so warm a face. He was a master at deception.

Cunning struck her with the swiftness of a viper. The sheer brilliance of the notion bubbled in her throat and threatened to explode into hysterical laughter. Betsy squelched it by scrunching up her nose and entrenching her brow in deep furrows. Stretching her skin sharpened the pain in her jaw, lending credence, she hoped, to the agony she portrayed. She even managed a couple of fresh tears, which she squeezed from the corners of her eyes so they'd roll down her cheeks and increase the drama. A final sniffle garnished her performance. Now, all she had to do was hold the pose until either Auntie Kee or Lucifer told her to open her mouth again.

The words weren't long in coming.

"I can't pull your tooth unless you cooperate, Miss Tyler," the Devil said.

"C'mon now, Miss Betsy," Auntie Kee encouraged, "and open up fer the preacher-man."

Betsy milked the moment for all it was worth, allowing first a short time to pass while she supposedly considered the matter, then parting her lips ever so slowly, keeping her gaze glued to the shiny pliers and carefully holding her purpose intact. Little by little, she let her jaw drop, thinking—for some reason totally lost to her—that if she ever had grandchildren, the story of how she'd beat the Devil at his own game would be one she'd tell them over and over. That is, if she survived to tell it.

But then, the Devil didn't take life, she reminded herself. His business was that of wooing souls to the dark side. If he thought he was going to succeed with her, he had another thing coming. She'd lived for a spell in the dark half of her soul, and she intended never to dwell there again. She was ready for him, ready to show him how mistaken he'd been to assume she was such an easy mark. All she had to do was wait for him to stick his fingers back into her mouth . . .

Three

Steele inhaled deeply, fixed his gaze on the bad tooth, and eased the pliers into Betsy Tyler's mouth.

Okay, Lord, here goes . . .

He'd barely launched the silent prayer when she bit him, taking him so completely by surprise that he let out a yelp and yanked his hand back before he fully acknowledged what she'd done. As if biting him hard enough to break the skin weren't sufficient, the little demon bore down on him with her front teeth, scraping his fingers as he extracted them. In shock, he sat staring at the reddened skin, teeth marks, and oozing blood. Then, rage whipped through him with a vengeance and he slapped her hard across her left jaw.

For a moment, she gaped at him, her face a study in incredulity. So, he'd startled her as much as she had him. Exhilaration quickly replaced his rage, but the tears that welled up in her eyes dashed the sensation before he had time to relish it. The rapid swelling in her left cheek and the sight of his handprint, glaring at him in scarlet relief against her blanched complexion, stung his conscience. Never before had he hit a woman. The fact that he'd hit one tied to a chair, completely unable to fight back, sickened him. What kind of monster was he?

One who'd been savagely bitten! an inner voice railed. Such gratitude . . .

"What'd you do that for?" he growled, nursing his injured hand.

"Leave me alone!" She flung the words at him with such intensity he felt their physical force. "Get out of my house and leave me alone!"

He turned to Auntie Kee, who grunted and rolled her eyes. "You better do what she says. When she gets like this, you can't talk sense to her."

She headed toward the front of the house and, like a puppy trotting after its mother, he followed her, his head so full of questions and his heart so full of regret that he didn't realize how complacently he was retreating until the door swung open on squeaking hinges and they walked out onto the porch. Beneath his feet, a board creaked and sagged dangerously close to breaking. As quickly as his wooden leg allowed, he moved down the steps and onto the front walk, which represented safer territory. Auntie Kee stepped back into the doorway.

"Been meaning to have the porch fixed," she muttered.

"No harm done." He held the Indian woman's gaze, unwilling to leave just yet. "What will you do with her now?"

"Untie her, I s'pose."

"I mean . . . about the tooth."

"That child's been sufferin' with that tooth fer nigh on to two year now. Sometimes hit's so bad, she screams with the pain. I reckon she can stand it a mite longer." Although a detached evenness marked the surface of her tone, Steele suspected an abundance of love and sympathy lay beneath.

"Why won't she let you pull it? Doesn't she understand that getting rid of the tooth would more than likely eliminate the pain?"

Auntie Kee sighed and looked off down the road. "I've tried to pull hit before—several times. I just don' have the stren'th. I keep hurtin' her more than she's already hurtin'."

"Surely someone else could pull it, someone in town. Don't you have a barber?"

A wealth of emotions chased themselves across her visage—distress, regret, concern—before she lifted her chin and wiped her face clear of everything except stoic acceptance. "Ain't nobody what'll come here. Even if they would, she won't allow anybody to touch her 'cept me, and I got to tie her down." She shook her head. "I cain't let nobody else see her in her miz'ry."

"You let me."

"Yessir, I did, but ye're diffrent, ye being a preacher-parson and all." She jerked her head around and a combination of fear and maternal watchfulness flickered in her black eyes, reminding him of a female mountain lion protecting her kittens. "Ye ain't gonna tell nobody, air ye?"

That she thought he might go out and gossip about Betsy Tyler cut him to the quick, yet if he were in Auntie Kee's place, he supposed he'd be equally distrustful. "No," he assured her, "I won't breathe a word to anyone except God, and He knows already."

For a moment, he'd forgotten about God sending him to the big frame house, though surely not to pull a tooth. God might work in mysterious ways, but Steele didn't believe that could have been the sole reason to send a man of the cloth here. There had to be something else, something related to the disposition of Betsy Tyler's soul. Who would know about such things better than Auntie Kee?

Steele awarded only brief consideration to his next question before he started speaking. "Do you think she—"

In a flash of insight, Steele realized he dare not suggest that Betsy might be crazy, lest he destroy the tiny bridge of trust he'd built. If he were to help the reclusive and possibly possessed young woman, he was going to need the Indian woman's confidence in his abilities. He changed course with only the slightest hesitation to mark his digression.

"—would let me pull it?"

"Humph! Ye tried, and look what hit got ye. I'm su'prised ye want to try again."

"I don't—but I feel, I don't know . . . compelled to help her. I think she's why God sent me to Peculiar Cove."

The look on Auntie Kee's face made him wonder if she didn't think *he* was insane. "Ye think God sent ye all the way here just to pull a tooth? Doesn't He have better thangs to worry about?"

Steele decided to broach the subject of Betsy's madness after all. "Not only to pull her tooth, but to heal her soul as well."

"Now that I kin believe!" the Indian woman declared. "The Good Lord knows that's what she needs. Only, how ye aiming to heal hit?"

Relief spread through him like wildfire. "We'll start with the tooth. I'm going to pull it if I have to knock her out first. But I don't think such drastic measures will be necessary." He grinned. "I have an idea, and if it works, we won't even have to tie her down to pull that tooth."

Sheer disbelief widened Auntie Kee's dark eyes, but her voice rang with hope. "What ye got in mind?"

"I have to find a Hercules'-club. Some folks call 'em prickly ash. You seen one growing anywhere near here?"

She screwed up her nose. "Ye tawlkin' 'bout one of them devil's wawlkin' sticks?"

"No, they grow straight up. What I'm talking about is a small tree with leaves like an elm. The thorns grow out of lumps, one every hand span or so."

"What ye want a thorny tree fer?" The question dripped with suspicion.

Steele chuckled. "Not to torture her with, if that's what

you're thinking. There's a powerful numbing medicine in the pith beneath the thorns."

Auntie Kee acknowledged his obvious plan with a cursory nod. "I'd fergot all about that tree and hits powerful medicine," she muttered, a trace of a frown creasing her brow as she deliberated silently for a spell. "I cain't tell ye where to find one, though. Hit's been years since I roamed these hills." She glanced back over her shoulder, stepped gingerly onto the rickety porch, and lowered her voice. "I cain't stray too fur, ye see, 'cause o' the way Miss Betsy's been since . . ."

Steele allowed but a small space for her to complete her sentence before he turned to leave. In time, perhaps she'd share her side of Betsy Tyler's story, but for now, he had another, more pressing concern on his mind. "It's getting late. If I'm going to find one before dark, I'd best get started."

She bobbed her chin and he set off down the road, heading away from town and praying for God to guide him straight to a Hercules'-club. He was almost out of sight when a light breeze ruffled his overlong hair, bringing with it a whisper.

"Bless ye, Reverend Preacher-man."

Steele looked back at the peeling clapboards, intending to wave to Auntie Kee, but the front porch was empty.

Betsy couldn't believe her ears. "He's coming back? And you agreed?"

"He wants t' help ye, child!"

"I'm fine. I don't need his help." She winced at the petulance in her voice but refused to succumb to her companion's evident faith in a man who could only be the Devil or one of his underlings.

Auntie Kee finished untying the last muslin strip and heaved herself to her feet. "Ye know that's a lie, Miss

Betsy. That tooth hain't gonna get no better on hits own and I cain't pull hit. Ye oughter be grateful God sent that man to help ye."

"God?" she gasped, rubbing her right calf hard. "Satan's more like it." The memory of warm, sympathetic brown eyes and gentle hands pierced her soul, pricking her conscience and raising the tiniest seed of doubt. Could she be wrong? Quickly, she pushed such a foolish notion aside.

Dismissing Betsy's apprehension with the wave of a gnarled hand, the Indian woman returned to squat in front of the chair. She began to massage the tight muscle in her leg as best she could. "Ye got a charley horse? I'm sorry. I shouldn't a-left ye tied up so long. I got to tawlkin' to the preacher-man on the porch and fergot all about ye bein' so uncomf'table in here."

Thoroughly disgusted with Auntie Kee's ready acceptance of the stranger as a man of God, Betsy nudged her companion away and stood up. "It's better now. I think I can walk it out."

As she hobbled around the table, using its top for support, the older woman moved to the cookstove and stirred the pot of lima beans she'd set to simmering earlier.

"We'll ast the preacher-man to take supper with us," Auntie Kee said.

"No, we won't! That fiend's not coming back in this house, let alone sitting down at the table with us."

"Now, Miss Betsy, don' go gettin' yourself so riled up. Hit ain't becomin'."

"When have you ever known me to concern myself with whether or not my behavior was becoming?" Betsy hurled.

"Never," Auntie Kee admitted on a sigh, "but that don' mean hit's too late to start. Course, I been telling ye that fer most o' yore natchrul life."

Betsy stifled the giggle that threatened to spoil her bad

mood. With Auntie Kee, all lives were "natchrul," but never before had the expression struck Betsy as quite so outlandish as it did now. "Did I ever have another life?"

Auntie Kee stopped stirring the beans, replaced the lid, and turned to face Betsy. "What *air* ye tawlkin' about?"

"Regardless," Betsy said, ignoring the Indian woman's militant glare, "my life couldn't be called natural by any stretch of the imagination." The kink seemed to be gone, but when Betsy put her full weight on her leg, the cramp returned. She sat down and rubbed it again. Talking increased the pain in her jaw, but she made no effort to stop the words. It was high time she and Auntie Kee quit sidestepping the issue. "You know they say this cove's named for me."

"I ain't never heared nothin' so foolish in all my borned days."

"Crazy Bets, that's what they call me in town."

Betsy didn't think she'd ever seen storm clouds as dark and threatening as the ones that clouded Auntie Kee's face. "Who told ye that?"

"A big, fat horsefly. I think he said his name was Dooley."

"Ye keep tawlkin' like that, folks *will* thank ye're crazy."

Betsy released a heavy sigh. "They already do. We both know it, so there's no sense pretending otherwise. I used to want them to think that, but . . ."

"But ye ain't so sure no more?"

The air crackled with expectancy while Betsy pondered Auntie Kee's question. The truth of it was she wasn't so sure anymore. She missed her little jaunts to Uncle Begley's store, missed hearing his stories and picking up her mail. She missed marking the growth of the children and feeling the warmth of a baby's tiny hand clutching her finger. She missed the smell of Miss Gertrude's roses and the pristine white of the picket fence that protected them. She missed the laughter of children at play and the voices of their mothers gently scolding them. She missed being a part of the sluggish little community. When she'd chosen to isolate herself, she hadn't stopped to think about how she was shutting herself off from all those things. She'd been so devastated, so miserable, so very ashamed.

In all the four years since, she'd never once questioned that decision. So why, all of a sudden, was she questioning it now? Because someone besides Auntie Kee had talked to her? Had touched her? Because an outsider had dared step foot in her house?

And he was coming back! Auntie Kee said he'd gone to get something and he was coming back. What was this stranger doing in Peculiar Cove anyway? And what made him think he had the right to interfere in her life, to make her question long-standing decisions she'd been perfectly happy with until just a few minutes ago?

Her sense of justice forced her to consider that he might be a preacher-parson, as he claimed, but she couldn't bring herself to believe it. Preachers didn't have crooked noses and wicked scars. Preachers weren't rugged men with broad shoulders and gruff voices. Preachers didn't wear their hair so long or make your skin tingle when they touched you.

A shiver traced its way down Betsy's spine—a not-altogether-unpleasant tingle. Oh, Lord! Was she subconsciously succumbing to temptation? Did the Devil already have her in his clutches? The suddenly very real possibility sent a nauseating shudder chasing behind the shiver.

She had to act. She had to do something to prevent the man from entering her house again. She'd shot a man before, but she didn't think she could do it again. After all these years, the scarlet blossoming of spilt blood continued to haunt her. Perhaps a simple show of force would scare him away. Unless he truly was the Devil, he couldn't possibly know whether she'd loaded the gun.

And if he were the Devil, it wouldn't matter if she put six bullets in his black heart. You couldn't kill the Devil.

Unfortunately, Auntie Kee—who truly believed the man to be a preacher, heaven-sent to the Tyler house—would never go along with such a plan. Maybe she didn't have to know.

Betsy rubbed her chin, which was about the only part of her face that wasn't sore, while she mentally laid out her scheme. If she could just make it up the stairs to her room, collect one of Papa's pistols, then make it back down again and hide the unloaded gun in the hall tree seat before the man returned—all without snagging Auntie Kee's notice . . .

How much time did she have? she wondered, realizing her heart-thudding panic had wiped out the details Auntie Kee had related as she untied the muslin strips. Betsy knew she'd have to proceed lightly with the older woman, lest Auntie Kee catch on and ruin everything.

"What did you say the preacher-man went to get?"

"Medicine fer your tooth."

That didn't tell Betsy much. Asking for specifics might raise Auntie Kee's suspicions, but the risk was necessary. "What kind of medicine?"

"The natchrul kind—from a tree."

"For someone who takes great pleasure in flapping her jaws, you're being awfully enigmatic."

"Now, Miss Betsy, ye know ye cain't use them big words on me."

Although Betsy suspected her companion was being difficult rather than ignorant, she decided not to pursue the subject. She'd asked more for curiosity's sake than anything else anyway. The tree must be fairly uncommon, else the man would have been back by now.

She moved away from the table's support, taking a trio of tentative steps toward the dining room and experiencing little pain.

"Where ye headed?"

Betsy smiled. Most times, Auntie Kee treated her as though she were six instead of twenty and six. "Upstairs."

"How come?"

"Because I need the necessary."

That seemed to satisfy Auntie Kee, who was dumping yellow meal into a crockery bowl. "Ye want your corn bread baked or fried?" she asked.

"Fried," Betsy replied automatically. She'd always preferred hers fried.

"Fried's harder to chew, and with that sore jaw of your'n—"

"Then bake it, for Christ's sake!"

"No need to swear, Miss Betsy."

"Yes, ma'am." Betsy hoped she sounded duly chastised.

"Tea or cawfee?"

"Tea." Auntie Kee knew that, too. Was the woman deliberately trying to slow Betsy down? Her sore leg accomplished that task quite well on its own. She was almost to the doorway when Auntie Kee spoke again.

"We're out of that kind ye like so much. What's hit called? Dar-jee-ling. Uncle Begley's out, too. I told him t' order ye some, but he said hit might take a spell. All we got's Earl Grey."

Betsy detested Earl Grey tea, which left a bitter aftertaste no matter how much honey she stirred in. "Then make it coffee."

Her suspicions now thoroughly aroused—and she was convinced that Auntie Kee's were, too—Betsy listened closely for the shuffle of the older woman's feet behind her as she half-walked, half-hobbled through the dining room to the front hall. There, she stopped and leaned against the doorjamb, ostensibly to rest her sore leg, which she massaged more for effect than out of necessity. Although her position gave her a clear view all the way to the kitchen door and she could hear Auntie Kee softly humming in the kitchen, she nevertheless stayed put while she counted by thousands. Once she reached the mid-floor landing and started up the second flight, her vision would be blocked and her hearing greatly impaired. If Auntie Kee intended to follow surreptitiously, then the best plan would be to allow Betsy time to pass the landing before starting out after her.

When she'd counted to sixty and Auntie Kee had made no move to follow, Betsy pushed away from the doorjamb and moved as quickly as she could to the stairs. Each step upward strained the already stiff muscle in her calf, but she forced herself forward. By the time she cleared the third tread of the second flight, the pain had become so debilitating that she dropped to her knees and crawled the rest of the way to her room, where she collapsed on the soft wool rug.

For several minutes, she lay still. When the pain eased up a bit, she started flexing her calf muscle, working it a little more with every stretch. After a while, the muscle felt almost normal again. Nonetheless, she hesitated to put her weight on it just yet. Instead, she wiggled her way to the bureau, opened the bottom drawer, and sifted through a mishmash of cast-off underwear and nightgowns until she uncovered one of the pistols.

The second her fingers closed over the grip, her stomach knotted up and she thought she was going to be sick, right there on the rug. She'd forgotten how cold a pistol could be—cold and dangerous, as quick as a rattlesnake, as potent as a dram of arsenic, as deadly as a bolt of lightning. Almost four years had passed since she'd pulled the trigger and sent a living, breathing human being to the grave. In all that time, she hadn't touched the pistols, hadn't so much as looked at them. In all that time, she hadn't dreamed there would come a time when she'd be forced to defend herself again.

But the time had come. Drawing all the inner strength

she could summon, she sat up, laid the pistol in her lap, pulled the cylinder pin out, and removed the cylinder. As she'd expected, it was empty. She started to replace the cylinder, but sheer terror grabbed her and wouldn't let go. What if the stranger was mortal? What if his intentions were far from honorable? What if he had the same despicable act on his mind as the Rebel scum who'd dragged her back to their camp? Could she and Auntie Kee defend themselves with only their meager physical strength to rely on?

No.

The answer slammed into her gut with the power of a physical blow. She rifled through the clothes until she found the tin box that held the caps, wadding, powder, and balls she needed. She was sliding the pin back into place when a shadow darkened the doorway.

"Aha! I cotched ye!"

Betsy looked up to see Auntie Kee, hands on hips and dark eyes blazing, standing just inside the room. She felt like a child caught with her hand in the cookie jar. Denying her guilt might be fruitless, but at least she could attempt to explain. "I wasn't going to load it. Honest."

That was the truth—half of it. Betsy told herself that Auntie Kee didn't need to know the rest of it.

Auntie Kee's shimmering black gaze bored right through her defenses. "Then what was ye aimin' to do with a pistol ye couldn't shoot?"

"Just frighten him. That's all."

The older woman held her hand out, palm up. Betsy started to hand the pistol over, then changed her mind and shoved it deeper into her skirts.

Auntie Kee thrust her hand even closer and her features settled into a mulish glare. "Ye might as well hand it over. I hain't gonna let ye shoot *this* man. Ye'll have to shoot me first."

Four

Betsy returned the mulish glare. "I can be just as stubborn as you."

Auntie Kee's expression dissolved into a condescending sweetness that not only failed to mollify Betsy, but actually increased her irritation. "Now, Miss Betsy," Auntie Kee said, her voice dripping honey, "ye know ye don' want t' shoot me."

"How ridiculous! I wouldn't ever hurt you." Betsy gripped the pistol tighter and buried it in the folds of her skirt. "You don't understand."

This wasn't the first time the older woman had failed to understand Betsy's motives, nor, Betsy was sure, would it be the last. Despite their differences, they had always maintained a healthy respect for each other. However, when Auntie Kee kept her gaze trained on Betsy's lap as she crossed the room, Betsy feared she'd damaged the older woman's trust.

Auntie Kee leaned against the edge of the bed, poised for flight. "Explain hit to me."

Betsy took a deep breath. "The stranger isn't who you think he is."

"Ye met him before?"

"No . . . yes."

"When?"

"In my dreams." As crazy as it sounded, it was true. Partially, anyway. A strange man *did* haunt her dreams, a man who was more vapor than substance, a dark shadow of a man whose phantom image shivered her awake—and whose spiritual essence kept her awake, sometimes for hours. Until this moment, she hadn't connected the dream and reality, but now that she had, Betsy knew in her heart that the two were one and the same.

Auntie Kee threw her arms up and spoke to the ceiling. "She ain't makin' sense again, Lord."

It didn't make sense. If he hadn't grown up in the hills, he might not be quite so convinced that he'd find a Hercules'-club nearby. Of course, Steele reminded himself, little about the tree made sense anyway. When you did find one, it would be all by its lonesome, maybe among a stand of other species, maybe off by itself, but always solitary. Never anywhere around would you find a baby one, which made him wonder how the tree reproduced itself.

Nonetheless, there always seemed to be one within walking distance—as though God had said, "Let's put one here, and another here, and another here . . . so there will be one handy when one of My children has a toothache." The old folks back home sometimes called it a toothache tree. Any of them could tell you where to find one: "Ye know that big chestnut above McDougall's Mill? If ye foller the millrun to the chestnut, then jump the run and go off just a mite to the left, ye'll run smackdab into a toothache tree. Be keerful, now, or ye'll stick yourself runnin' into hit."

Come to think of it, he'd never actually set out to find one. He'd always either been told exactly where to look or just happened upon one. Maybe that was the problem. Maybe he was looking too hard. Steele sat down on an outcropping of granite to assess the situation.

He didn't have long. Already the sun had taken its hiding place behind the mountains. Within a short while, the darkening shadows would prevent his finding anything—perhaps even his way back. Yet, he lingered. Not because he was tired. Not because he was frustrated. But because something tugged at his heart stronger than anything had ever tugged at it before.

That something was Betsy Tyler. He'd expected to find her an unkempt, even downright dirty madwoman. She wasn't. Well, unkempt, maybe, but that was because she'd been suffering with the toothache and fighting Auntie Kee. Actually, she was almost pretty, probably would be with her hair combed and the swelling gone from her cheek, but not the demure kind of pretty. No, there was too much of the earth about her, too much fire within her to ever be demure.

His second expectation—to enter a house cloaked with cobwebs and sheathed in dust—had been shattered as well. But it was the total annihilation of the third expectation—which was to perceive her as nothing other than a subject worthy of his pity—that gave him pause.

Steele couldn't put a name to the emotion he was feeling for Betsy Tyler, but he knew it wasn't pity. Whatever it was, it was new and different and surprisingly pleasant. It gave him warmth against the encroaching chill and somehow lightened the burden he'd carried in his soul for almost a year. It bade him sit for a spell and enjoy the commingling smells of moldy earth and early spring wildflowers. It bade him listen to the lonely cry of the whippoorwill and feel the caress of the evening breeze upon his cheek. It bade him close his eyes and forget for a moment that a world existed beyond the solid rock beneath him and the woods surrounding him.

For the first time since the outbreak of the war, peace settled over him, wrapping around his cold heart like a beaver coat in the dead of winter.

His cold heart . . .

The acknowledgment snapped his eyes open, and the warmth evaporated as briskly as river fog in August. His heart wasn't cold, he vehemently denied. It was broken, which was immensely different. Whose heart wouldn't be broken, given the same set of circumstances? It was his soul that suffered from frostbite, not his heart.

A lone tear moistened one eye, threatening to foster a deluge. That would never do. He'd gone all this time without weeping, and he saw no reason to start now. When a second tear followed, Steele bolted off the rock and ran pell-mell into the trees. His reckless flight sent his hat sailing, but he scarcely noted its absence. Twigs scraped his face and ears, and leaves caught in his hair. Branches tore at his sleeves and briars ripped at his trousers, but still he ran as though the Devil himself were chasing him. He dodged a skinny oak sapling, zigzagged around a massive chestnut, darted between two hickories—and ran smackdab into a Hercules'-club.

By the time Steele found his hat and returned to the Tyler house, darkness had draped its velvety cloak over the cove, bringing with it a heavy blanket of clouds and a cold, bitter wind that pierced to the marrow. Even with the collar turned up, his suit coat offered little barrier against the chill, and his left knee had begun to ache. He shifted his weight to his sound leg, which made the plank beneath his foot creak as it sagged. If someone didn't replace the porch floor soon, the weathered, half-rotten planks were bound to give way. He made a mental note to broach the subject with Auntie Kee—once he'd completed his divine mission at the Tyler house.

As eager as he was to escape the cold, he would have preferred another refuge. Although he was armed with the most powerful toothache medicine around, the prospect of pulling Betsy Tyler's tooth sat like a boulder in his stomach. Even lifting his arm to knock required strength of mind and purpose.

Is your faith so shallow?

The calm quietness of the voice delivered a potent blow, clobbering his defenses—or, perhaps more accurately, diverting them. When Steele allowed truth into the inner sanctum of his soul, he was forced to acknowledge the tattered condition of his faith. Were it whole and hardy, he wouldn't need to ride the circuit, which was the only way, he'd thought, to reweave the damaged fabric of his soul. He wasn't so sure anymore. *You'd think after almost a year that things would have changed . . .*

But nothing had changed. If anything, his soul was colder now than it had been the day he turned his back on the burned-out homestead and the graves of his family. If he could only find the men responsible—whom he'd learned had preyed on other Confederate sympathizers and would most likely continue to do so until someone stopped them—then maybe he could be whole again.

Fortunately, Auntie Kee opened the door at that moment, saving him from a plunge into maudlin self-pity. She offered a brief welcoming smile before propping a finger on her lips and glancing nervously over her shoulder.

"What's going on?" he whispered.

"She's got her paw's gun. I thank hit's loaded."

He stifled the curse that rose to his lips by substituting a prayer. "Lord, help me."

"I tried to get hit away from her."

Only half-listening, Steele bobbed his head in reply. He had an idea, whether divinely inspired he couldn't say, but it was the only solution his mind clung to. He fished one of the peeled Hercules'-club balls from his pocket and handed it to Auntie Kee. "See if you can get her to chew on this, and then we'll worry about the gun."

"Wait here," she murmured, slipping the pithy ball

into her apron pocket and disappearing into the shadows of the dark hall. Steele thought he heard the stairs creak beneath the woman's weight, but the tune the wind was plucking from the deteriorated posts and porch railing made it hard to tell where all the pops and squeaks were coming from. A particularly strong gust slammed into his back, pitching his unbalanced weight forward. He reached for something, anything to grab on to. When his fingers closed around twin pieces of gingerbread trim angling out from each side of the cross-support on the screen door, he expelled a long breath.

A sharp crack obliterated his short-lived relief. The decorative pieces snapped loose, and Steele staggered backwards. With flailing arms and stumbling feet, he tried to regain his balance. The unstable planks turned a difficult feat into an impossible one, especially for a person with a wooden leg that refused to cooperate. When he set his right foot on a sagging plank and felt it start to give way, he leaned to the left in an attempt to prevent a fall.

Immediately, he realized his mistake. The leather straps that held the wooden leg in place slipped loose and the artificial limb wobbled beneath his stump. In reaction, he flung himself back to the right. The additional weight proved too much for the sagging board to bear. It broke.

The events of the next few seconds blurred together for Steele. All he knew was that suddenly his foot was dangling beneath the porch, his shinbone was on fire, and warm blood was oozing down his leg. Could it be . . . Was it possible . . .

No! he vehemently denied. His leg couldn't be broken. It couldn't be. To prove the point, he concentrated all his mental and physical energies on kicking his right foot. But no matter how hard he tried, it wouldn't move. Its refusal to cooperate left him with no other option than to accept reality, yet the agony of losing his good leg, even temporarily, was more than he could bear. It was an intense misery, as deep and sharp and demobilizing as his initial anguish over the amputation of his left leg. He fought back the bile rising in his throat and the tears filling his eyes. *No!* his mind screamed again. It wasn't possible.

And then excruciating physical pain coursed through him, permeating every bone, every muscle, every nerve, every cell, shouting the truth so loudly, so clearly he could no longer ignore it.

"No-o-o," he moaned, pushing the vowels through his tight throat. The low, guttural sound enraged him. He might not be able to move, but by God, he ought to be able to scream.

"No-o-o," he moaned again. This time, the noise seemed a bit louder, encouraging him to persevere. As much as he hated to admit it, he needed help from some quarter, but no one was likely to find him if he couldn't make himself heard.

"No-o-o!" His third cry rose to a crescendo, as loud and as mournful as the howling wind that buffeted the big frame house on the outskirts of Peculiar Cove.

Not satisfied with the bit of havoc it wreaked upon Steele, the mighty gust that spawned his fall snapped a limb off a cedar, then flung it with its brawny breath against a window in Betsy's room.

She was sitting on the rug, completely occupied with conjuring up images from her dreams. The crash of breaking glass obliterated all other concerns, while flying shards sent her scurrying like a frightened rabbit trying to escape a hunter's rifle. She huddled under the high bed—her knees pulled into her chest, her eyes squeezed shut, her entire body quaking, until the warm touch of a hand on her forehead and a familiar soft voice in her ear worked like a balm, soothing away her fear.

"I'm sorry," Betsy murmured, her voice still tight from tension.

"How come?" Auntie Kee asked.

"Because I behave like such a child sometimes."

The older woman hugged her close for a moment. Betsy took nourishment from the pillow of her companion's sagging bosom and the racing heartbeat of one who never showed fear, but obviously felt it. Auntie Kee's words were equally as comforting.

"Bein' sceered of something that's dangerous ain't childish. Ye had a right to be sceered half out of your mind. I don' know when I have seen so much wind—or so many tiny pieces of glass." She paused for a spell, her hand stroking the back of Betsy's head. "Ye didn't get cut, did ye?"

"No."

"That's good. Ye ready to git up and face the mess?"

Betsy nodded against the older woman's chest, then gradually removed her arms from Auntie Kee's midriff. Even with her friend's comforting presence, letting go of her fear wasn't easy, not with the wind still howling like a Banshee and threatening to break another window . . . or worse.

Something about the wind's wail wasn't quite right, though. It was almost as if it had suddenly gained a human voice that protested against its own destructive force. "No-o-o," its cry rang out, loud and long and sad. "No-o-o . . ."

Auntie Kee gasped. "The preacher-man!" She scrambled to her feet, picked up a lamp off the bedside table, and headed for the door.

"What about the preacher-man?" Nothing could have surprised Betsy more than the indisputable concern in her voice or the fact that she'd acknowledged his calling.

"I left him on that rickety ol' porch."

"You don't think—"

"I don' know. I'm gonna see."

"I'm going, too."

That stopped Auntie Kee in her tracks. "How come? I thought ye was a-feared o' him."

In truth, Betsy supposed she was—not because she thought he was the Devil incarnate anymore, but because she knew beyond a shadow of a doubt that he was the man in her dreams, which was almost as frightening, though she couldn't have said why.

"I don't know what made me think he was the Devil," she said, picking her way carefully through the broken glass. "I guess I was half out of my mind with pain. I'm still not so sure he means well, but if he's hurt himself on my front porch, then his injuries are my responsibility."

Auntie Kee shook her head and grinned, exposing the gap in her two top teeth. "Hit sure is good to have ye back, Miss Betsy."

"Back from where?"

"From that place ye go sometimes."

Betsy started to ask what place that was, then changed her mind. There were other, more important, things to do right now than getting into a philosophical discussion with Auntie Kee. She'd meant what she said about feeling responsible for the man's injuries, but despite her revised opinion of him, she still wasn't convinced that he intended no harm. She waited until Auntie Kee left the room, then picked up the pistol from where she'd dropped it on the rug and joined Auntie Kee in the hall.

As they rounded the corner of the landing and started down the lower flight, the plaintive "No-o-o" resounded through the foyer. Never had she heard anything so mournful, so full of despair, and yet so pleading as that single word. Never had she felt quite so impatient or quite so determined to remedy an injustice—and that an injustice had been done was becoming abundantly clear to her. She darted around Auntie Kee, laid the pistol on the hall tree, and snatched open the front door.

Even in the dim light, she could see his misery—but she could feel it as well. That she felt it at all amazed her. That she felt it as keenly as she did left her awestruck. It was as though she and this preacher-man were of a sudden one person. It was as though they shared one maimed body, one crippled mind, one broken heart, one lost soul.

Tears sprang to her eyes and her heart swelled with a combination of grief and sympathy. A part of her consciousness acknowledged that this was a special moment, one she would cherish forever. But that didn't make sense. Why would she treasure a memory that was certain to evoke pain?

"We have to get him inside," Auntie Kee said. She was standing behind Betsy, urging her forward through the screen door and onto the porch.

He lay in a crumpled heap, his left leg twisted behind him, his right leg disappearing into the floor, his back arched forward, his chin lifted heavenward. As Auntie Kee passed the lamp over his head, the light caught the glaze in his dark eyes and the white clench of his bared teeth. The combination gave him an almost feral look, like that of a wolf caught in a trap. Surprisingly, Betsy sensed no danger—only despair of the deepest and darkest sort.

He was a big man. Extricating him from the damaged porch was going to be difficult enough for two women. The prospect of hauling him inside loomed as a near impossibility, yet, they had no choice. Or did they? She could always send Auntie Kee for help. Some of the men would come, not out of consideration for her, the town crazy, but surely for him, his being a preacher-man and all. She started to suggest such a course to Auntie Kee, then realized that meant the men would also take him away. For some reason lost to her, Betsy wasn't quite ready to let go of him.

"I think my leg's broke," he said, jerking her into action. She knelt at his left side and started to reach for the ankle of his twisted leg.

"Not that one." The humorless snort that accompanied his correction confused her, but not as much as his explanation. "If it broke, I'd just replace it."

How did one replace a leg? Unless it was artificial . . .

Her wide-eyed stare must have communicated her question, because she was certain she hadn't verbalized it.

"Lost it in the war," he said, his speech etched with pain. "Shrapnel mangled my foot. Doc took it off at the ankle, then mid-calf, then finally just below the knee."

Betsy tried to imagine how it would feel to have a knife cut into the flesh all the way to the bone and then to have the bone sawed in two. But to have it done three times . . . Just thinking about it made her sick to her stomach. She swallowed hard. "Why?"

"Because gangrene kept setting in."

How awful it must have been for him! How awful it must be now, having to walk on a wooden leg, having folks look at you with pity in their eyes, having to take it off at night and seeing a withered stump where you'd once had flesh and bone. How awful not to be able to run and jump and move with agility. It had to have hurt each time the doctor sawed another part off. She wondered if the loss caused him physical pain now. She'd heard that people who'd lost limbs continued to feel them, just as if they were still there. Did that mean they felt pain, too?

"I'm so sorry."

"I don't need your pity," he snapped, "just your help."

Indignation flared through her. "I'm trying!" The instant the words were out of her mouth, she regretted them. She had, indeed, been pitying him. "Tempers aren't going to solve this problem," she said in a more cooperative tone. "Tell us what to do."

Could this be the same woman he'd met earlier, the one who'd allowed a mere toothache to send her into hysterics? He gave himself a mental shake and concentrated on the best way for her and the Indian woman to assist him.

"Each of you take an arm," he said, straightening his back and stretching his arms straight out from his sides, "and see if you can pull me out of this hole. You don't have to try to lift me, just pull backwards."

As they tugged, it became obvious that neither was very strong, but Betsy's strength proved far greater than Auntie Kee's, evidenced by the fact that all they were accomplishing was to pull him to the right instead of backwards. But bless their hearts, they were working so hard they didn't seem to realize they were getting nowhere.

"Maybe you ought to change sides," he suggested, gritting his teeth against the pain and resolving to help them regardless of the physical cost.

With the women pulling and Steele pushing, they began to make slow headway. Inch by inch, his right leg came out of the hole About midway, something impeded the progress—something that increased the pain, which Steele hadn't thought possible. He clamped his jaw tighter and endured. At long last, his foot cleared the opening. Only then did he allow himself to rest.

"Oh, my!" Betsy declared in chagrin.

"What is it?" he rasped.

"A big ole splinter, sticking out of your leg. Looks real nasty."

"Can you get it out?"

"I think so." Her tone fell woefully short of conviction. "There's not much light, but I'll try."

"Maybe you ought to get me inside first."

"What if your leg's broke?" Auntie Kee reminded him. "I don' know much about settin' bones," she continued. "If there's some secret to hit, you'd best tell me now."

Truth be told, he didn't know much about setting bones either, but they'd cross that bridge later. "You're going to need some splints—and some cloth strips to tie them on."

"We've got some old boards in the shed. I'll git a couple," Auntie Kee said.

"Are they rotten?" Steele asked, visions of splintering wood dancing in his head.

"Could be. I'll test 'em good." Auntie Kee took the lamp and started down the steps.

"I'll get a sheet and tear the strips," Betsy offered, rising.

"Please, hurry back."

Five

Steele couldn't believe the plea had come from his mouth. Moreover, he couldn't believe it had come from his heart. A small part of him didn't want to be left alone on the porch, but the much stronger yearning to have Betsy—and none other—beside him, jolted him to the marrow of his bones. In defense, he attributed the entire feeling to the still stark memory of having been left alone for hours on the battlefield while shells exploded over his head and men cried out in agony . . .

He couldn't think about those things now. He shouldn't ever think about them again, not if he were to retain his sanity. He gave his soul a mental jar and heard Betsy promise to come right back.

Before the screen door snapped shut behind her, Steele had cleared his mind of everything except the faint fragrance of jasmine that lingered in the air. Did the redolent flower bloom somewhere among the wild tangle of bushes and weeds surrounding the house? he wondered. No, it was too early for jasmine. Then where had the suggestion of jasmine come from?

Betsy. It was the only logical explanation. Amazing, he thought, how anyone could think she rarely bathed. Why, she was as clean and fresh as morning dew. If folks around here didn't know that, then it was because they seldom if ever came close to her, which left him to believe that at least the part about her shutting herself off from the community was more than likely true, even if a good portion of Uncle Begley's story wasn't.

She returned then, raggedy-edged muslin strips dangling from her apron pocket, which bulged with something dark and heavy . . . the pistol. Obviously, she didn't completely trust him yet. He didn't suppose he could blame her. He'd have to be careful not to frighten her.

"That was fast," he observed.

"I'd forgotten about the strips Auntie Kee used to tie me to the chair. They ought to serve, don't you think?"

"More than likely."

She squatted down beside him, sitting in the triangle of light spilling out of the hall onto the porch. The golden light set her red hair on fire, while the whistling wind tossed it hither and yon. She wiped a wayward strand off her cheek, tucked it behind her ear, and shivered. "My, it's cold tonight! And just when I was beginning to think spring had finally come."

"You don't have to sit with me," he said, forcing the words past his lips and hoping she would ignore him.

"Oh, I don't mind," she hastily assured him. "Besides, Auntie Kee will be back soon with the boards."

As if they both expected the older woman to round the corner any second, neither said anything else for a spell. In truth, Steele found himself suddenly quite uncomfortable alone with Miss Betsy Tyler, who'd brought the sweet scent of jasmine back with her. The fragrance filled his senses and made him think of things best left to dreams and fantasy. His mind snatched at a subject to discuss, anything to cool the sudden aching desire, for he'd learned that women viewed him with either pity or disdain, but never with longing.

"How's your toothache?"

"It still hurts."

"The Hercules'-club didn't help?"

"Hercules'-club? Is that the natural medicine you went to get?"

He nodded. "Didn't Auntie Kee give you a ball of pith to chew on?"

When she told him no, he fished another of the peeled balls from his pocket and handed it to her. "Put it on the bad tooth and bite down, then gently chew on it. It ought to completely deaden that side of your mouth."

She did as he told her, the swelling combined with the wad of pith in her jaw making her look like a lopsided chipmunk. Gradually, the pinched look around her eyes and mouth disappeared, and her face fairly glowed with what he discerned as a combination of pleasure and surprise. He felt rather proud of himself.

"Hit fworks!"

Even through his pain, Steele couldn't keep from laughing. "But only half of your mouth does."

Betsy's laughter joined his, rippling over him and seeping into his soul. They were laughing so hard when Auntie Kee reappeared that neither of them paid her any heed until she spoke.

"Whatever did you two find to laugh about?"

Betsy sobered enough to mutter, "Toofache's gone."

Auntie Kee's chuckle melded with their dying laughter. When only a trickle of mirth remained among them, Steele asked about the boards.

"Ain't enough good'uns out there to make a coffin, and the best one was too long, so I had to saw hit in two. The saw's done rusted up, so I had to file it 'fore hit'd work. I guessed at the length. Hope I got hit right."

"We'll soon find out," Steele said, gritting his teeth. How odd, he thought, that the pain seemed to have completely vanished as long as he was laughing. But now it was back, stronger and sharper than before. "Do you want to do it here or inside?"

Auntie Kee gave his leg a long moment of scrutiny.

"Hit don' matter t' me. Them britches've got to come off, either way. Ye're the one's got to suffer the cold if we do it out here. Ye say which."

The necessity of removing his trousers was the one thing he hadn't considered. Now that she'd mentioned it, he wasn't the least bit sure he wanted two women performing the task. *Make that one woman,* he amended. Having Auntie Kee see him in his drawers might not be so bad. But Betsy . . . well, that shed a whole different light on the situation.

Why hadn't she realized they'd have to remove his trousers? Betsy caught her lower lip with her top teeth and wondered if maybe they ought to get some of the men from town. She was mentally forming the suggestion when the preacher-man made it himself.

"Maybe you ought to get some help," he said, "not just for setting my leg, but for moving me, too. I'm afraid I'm too heavy for two women to carry."

"That's what I been thanking," Auntie Kee chimed in.

Betsy's spirits plummeted. They'd take him away. She knew they would. She also knew it was for the best, if for no other reason than the preacher-man's immediate welfare. She didn't know why she wanted him to stay, only that she did, which she acknowledged as selfish and thoughtless. She tried to concede, but the words got all garbled on the way out—as much, she reckoned, from her reluctance to say them as from her inability to speak clearly.

"Don' try to tawlk, Miss Betsy." Auntie Kee's voice carried a veiled warning that clearly said, "And don' argufy with me," which left Betsy stunned. Was her reversal that obvious? "I'll just put these boards down," Auntie Kee continued, "and then go see if I kin roust somebody out."

Before she could move, a deafening crash of thunder

shook the house. Betsy snatched up the preacher's hand and squeezed it tight while Auntie Kee jumped straight up, dropping the boards, almost letting go of the lamp, and screeching at the top of her lungs.

The heavens answered with a blinding flash of lightning and an abrupt torrent of rain, allowing them little opportunity to collect themselves. The wind kicked the cold rain up on the porch, drenching them in short order and setting their teeth to chattering. Recovering quickly, Auntie Kee hung the lamp on a wall hook beside the front door, then propped the boards against the wall, safely away from the blowing rain.

"I don' know what made me jump like 'at," Auntie Kee said, her voice full of shame.

And holler, Betsy silently added, hiding a smile behind her free hand, forgetting momentarily that her other hand still held the preacher's—until he squeezed it back. It was a gentle squeeze, one that carried nothing more than a bond of camaraderie, yet Betsy felt its tingle all the way up her arm. She let go of him and fussed with repinning loose strands of hair.

"Don' ye try to move that man whilst I'm gone," Auntie Kee told Betsy.

"Forget going for help," the preacher said. "You'll catch your death in this rain. Just pull that splinter out, tie those boards on my leg, and then get me inside the best you can."

"I thought the 'inside' part come first," Auntie Kee said.

"I'm not thinking too clearly, but I seem to recall the sawbones in our outfit saying you should always splint a broken bone before you move the patient. Something about not causing further injury."

"Then maybe we art to cut them britches off."

"No!" the man objected with more vehemence than

Betsy imagined he possessed. "They're my best pair," he explained, his voice strained but firm.

Auntie Kee nodded. "I'll try to save 'em fer ye. Miss Betsy, ye go git a blanket. If we have to work out here in the cold rain, at least we kin try to keep this here man warm."

The moment she returned with the blanket, Auntie Kee issued further instructions: get scissors, a basin of warm water, soap, and clean rags. By the time Betsy found everything, collected warm water from the stove's reservoir, and returned to the front porch, her breath was coming in short pants and she was quivering so much from both the cold and the exertion she could barely stand up. She leaned against the screen door for support and took slow, measured breaths in an attempt to regain her vitality before helping Auntie Kee move the large man inside.

Intending to pray for the strength of mind and body that task required, she lowered her gaze—and gasped in shock and near revulsion.

The preacher-man's leg lay grotesquely twisted, seemingly unhinged at the knee, his thigh turned in and his foot turned out. The sight raised her bile, and she gagged on the bitterness in her throat. There was no way she could face this task, no way she could participate in straightening that leg. Someone else would have to do it, someone with a stronger constitution than she. If that meant she had to go knocking on doors to find someone who would come, then so be it. She was soaked to the skin already. A little more rain wouldn't matter.

She was almost to the top step when Auntie Kee's voice stayed her. "Where ye going, child?"

"To get some help." Betsy couldn't be sure Auntie Kee heard her over an accompanying crash of thunder, or understood her garbled words, but her aversion to the twisted leg prevented her from turning around.

"Listen to the preacher-man. They's no sense goin' out in this storm. We pulled him out. We kin git him inside."

No, we can't, Betsy mentally argued. *At least I can't.* She took another step, then two quick streaks of lightning stopped her cold. The first slashed through the sky, high above the trees, but the second hurled itself right into a lilac bush near the front gate. The bush burst into hissing flames, which the downpouring rain quickly extinguished. Had Auntie Kee not spoken to her, Betsy figured she would have been opening the gate about the time the lightning struck. The realization sent a shiver coursing through her, but it also served to renew her strength. Better to face a twisted, mangled leg and the sight of a man's drawers than brave exposure to the dangerous, possibly deadly storm. She turned around to confront the repulsive sight of the broken leg.

What she saw startled her all the way to her toes, washing away her extreme reluctance and filling her with pity all over again. It wasn't his broken leg she'd been looking at—it was his wooden leg, which she'd forgotten all about. It had come loose from its moorings at the knee and was hanging loose, with only the preacher's ankle-length woolen drawers to prevent it from falling out. Auntie Kee, who'd wiggled the wooden leg out, set it aside. Betsy watched the movement peripherally, her unwavering gaze fixed on the now empty trouser leg, sympathy colored with a tinge of repugnance consuming her. A part of her heard Auntie Kee speaking, telling her to come and help, but she couldn't move.

"C'mon now and help me with these britches," the older woman pleaded. "This here's a big man. I cain't git 'em off by my ownself." When Betsy neither moved nor replied, Auntie Kee added, "No need to be shy, child. He's got drawers on."

Seeing the preacher in his natural state was the least of Betsy's concerns. She knew she was acting irrationally, but the thought of seeing his stump held her immobilized. Even if she could talk clearly, she couldn't communicate this to Auntie Kee without the man hearing her. Betsy knew only too well how devastating it could be to have your flaws openly aired by those who made no effort to understand.

Was that what she'd been doing? Judging without understanding? Accepting his imperfection had been easy enough so long as his wooden leg was attached. With sudden clarity, Betsy realized her hesitation conveyed her aversion just as clearly as if she'd shouted it from an attic window. Had he noticed?

She tore her gaze from the collapsed trouser leg, traveling it slowly forward until it reached his face. Blessedly, his eyelids were closed. Perhaps he'd paid no heed. Perhaps God was granting her another chance.

"He's done passed out way back yonder," Auntie Kee said, "when I pulled that there splinter out."

"Thank ya, Lor'," Betsy whispered, her speech still distorted from the Hercules'-club medicine, but she supposed the Almighty heard her nonetheless—and knew that her gratitude sprang from not having to remove the splinter as much as it did the preacher's unconsciousness. She watched Auntie Kee unbuckle the preacher's belt and tug it free, then unbutton his fly. Swallowing her trepidation and resolving to keep it suppressed, Betsy pushed herself forward. "Whadda ya need me t' do?"

Auntie Kee folded the blanket so that it covered only his chest, settled herself on one side of his waist, and pointed to the other side. When Betsy was seated, her companion rolled the man's hips toward Betsy. "Hold him here whilst I get his britches down, and then we'll do the same on yore side."

With a great deal of wrestling and tugging and rolling his hips back and forth—causing him to moan louder with each roll, they finally got his trousers off, leaving him in a pair of faded red knit drawers that hugged his legs and hips like a second skin—and making the absence of his lower left leg painfully obvious. Betsy had little opportunity to ponder the kernel of pity the sight evoked, however, for their deed had completely roused him from his stupor. He groaned loudly, muttered something about not taking his leg, and began to thrash at them. Quickly, they moved safely out of his way.

"He's plumb outten his mind," Auntie Kee said. "I s'pose I would be, too, if'n somebody had cut my leg off. But we got to get him calmed down so we kin put the splint on that leg. What are we gonna do?" She rubbed her chin.

Betsy didn't have an answer. Even if she did, she figured she wouldn't be able to make herself understood, not with her mouth all numb on one side. It was a shame they didn't have medicine as powerful as the Hercules'-club ball he'd brought to her. If they could ease the pain in his leg the way the pith had eased the pain in her jaw, he wasn't likely to give them any trouble.

As she readjusted the moistened wad in her jaw, a scathingly brilliant idea struck her, arresting her with the same potent force as the bolt of lightning striking the lilac bush. In a flash, she took Auntie Kee's arm and propelled her back to the spot where the preacher lay. There, she caught his wrists one at a time and pulled them together over his head.

"Hold," she barked, reluctant to pass the task to Auntie Kee, but afraid she'd never be able to make her friend understand what she needed her to do. Thankfully, the older woman complied without argument—and without losing hold of his wrists. Quickly, Betsy moved the items she'd brought closer to his broken leg and set about cutting through the ankle cuff of his drawers and up to the tear the splinter had made. With brisk dispatch, she slipped the knitted fabric over his knee and gently cleaned the wound on his calf, which seemed to make it bleed worse, despite her light touch. It was swelling, too.

"Law, he's li'ble to get the lockjaw," Auntie Kee said.

"Don' let go," Betsy mumbled, waiting for Auntie Kee to nod in acknowledgment before she went inside to get an unlit lamp. Removing the chimney and setting it aside, she hurried back to the preacher-man's side. For a spell, she just sat staring at the gushing wound, working her courage up. There was nothing doing but to cleanse it the best way she knew how, she supposed, even if it did cause him further pain. Better that than the lockjaw.

Heaving a sigh, Betsy unscrewed the wick holder, set it and the dripping wick aside, then picked up the lamp base and held it poised over his leg. With a clean rag in her other hand, she wiped at the wound, pressing down in an attempt to stanch the bleeding a bit. Finally, she was ready . . . she hoped.

"Gon' hurt," she said, certain he couldn't hear her, but feeling better for having warned him. When she poured the coal oil into the wound, he bucked like a wild pony and a heart-wrenching "Aaa-rgh" erupted from his throat. Somehow, Auntie Kee managed to hold onto him.

After a moment, he settled down a bit, and Betsy took the wad of pith out of her mouth and held it against the wound. Gradually, the fight went out of him.

"What are you doing?" he asked, his voice almost mellow.

Betsy let out a long breath she didn't realize she'd been holding. "Tryin' t' stop th' pain." Her lips and tongue were working a bit better now.

"As long as I'm still, it doesn't hurt."

Unconvinced that the Hercules'-club pith hadn't numbed his leg the same way it had numbed her mouth, Betsy left it on the wound, which she hastily bandaged.

"It's time to set the bone," he said, "and then you can put on the splint."

"But we don' know nothin' about settin' bones," Auntie Kee said. " 'Sides, neither of us is strong enough."

The preacher-man was silent for a moment, whether thinking or praying Betsy couldn't say. After a spell, he told them to go ahead and splint his leg. "I don't think it'll make much difference if a day or two passes before someone sets it," he said.

Without conversation, Betsy and Auntie Kee wrapped clean rags around his leg to cushion the splints. When they'd secured the boards, they each took a side, looped their hands under his armpits, and dragged him around until the door was behind him. Auntie Kee let go of him long enough to open the screen door wide and shove the wedge beneath it to hold it open. But the wind was stronger than the wedge. It flung the door back against the wall, then forward until it hit the wedge, then back again. *Crash! Bang! Crash! Bang!* it went. Each time, it shoved the wedge a little bit, therefore widening the space between the door and the wall and making the crashing and banging louder.

Other things were crashing and banging as well, although Betsy couldn't say what they were. Limbs, she supposed, and anything else the wind could break off or pick up. A loud, elongated crack, like that of a tree splitting down the middle, resounded in the distance. The battering storm moaned and whistled, boomed and bellowed, rumbled and pounded, adding its din to that of Betsy's blood droning in her ears and her heart thudding in her chest . . . *ker-thump, ker-thump*. Her racing pulse and quaking arms threatened to rob what little strength she possessed. With determination and true grit, she locked her elbows, took a deep breath, and gave the effort everything she had left to give.

Inch by bone-jarring inch, the two women heaved and tugged, jerked and pulled the big man over the threshold and into the front hall. As soon as they cleared the front door, Betsy dashed back out to release the screen, which she latched before closing and bolting the heavy oak door. She was cold and wet and exhausted, wanting nothing more at the moment than a warm bath, dry clothes, and the comfort of her bed. But they couldn't leave the preacher-man on the rug in the front hall.

Or could they? She didn't have the strength to move him another inch, nor did she expect Auntie Kee did, either. If he could only help them . . .

Auntie Kee had removed her apron and was using it to dry his face and hair. Fortunately, the preacher-man was calm, perhaps too calm, Betsy thought. His dark eyes were glassy, his face was white, and although tiny beads of sweat clung to his forehead, his skin was cold when she touched it.

"He's in shock," she said, surprising herself with the clear flow of words.

Auntie Kee nodded. "Got to git him warm. Go stoke up the far in the parlor whilst I git some dry blankets."

A short while later, Betsy sat cross-legged in the parlor doorway, inches away from the big, dark-haired, dark-eyed man who'd come into her life that day—and who was likely to go out of it come morning. That thought brought a lump to Betsy's throat. She swallowed hard, but it refused to budge.

At least his color was better, his skin wasn't quite so clammy, and his breathing appeared less shallow. Auntie Kee came back from the kitchen with a glass of cloudy liquid.

"What's that?" Betsy whispered around the lump.

"Salt, sodie, and water. Here, hold it whilst I lift his head."

Between the two of them, they got him to drink about half the solution before he collapsed onto the rug.

"Do you think he'll be all right now?"

"He'll live, if that's what ye mean." Auntie Kee jerked

her head toward the kitchen. "I made us some tea. Lord knows we kin both use some."

When the two were seated at the table, Betsy braved another question. "Will he . . ." She gulped down her trepidation and tried again. "Will he be able to walk on that leg?"

"Not 'less it gits set good and proper and then heals right. Somebody in this here place has got to know how to set a bone. I'll go tomarr, see if I kin find somebody."

"No, I'll go."

Six

When the yard rooster announced the dawn, Betsy groaned, turned her face to the back of the horsehair settee, and pulled a brocade pillow over her head. It couldn't be time to get up, not when she'd never gone to sleep.

She couldn't recall when she'd passed such a restless night, but surely not since the black-banded letter had arrived, and even then she'd had the comfort of her bed and the privacy of her room, both of which lent some small measure of solace. No, there was a time after the letter, a niggling voice reminded her, a time when she'd spent days on end jumping at every little sound—and nights on end tossing and turning, fighting sleep in the fear she'd revisit the Confederate army camp, if only in her dreams.

But that was behind her. It was all behind her: the loss of her family, one by one, the . . . *event,* her decision to close herself off from the people and goings-on in Peculiar Cove. *Leave it there!* she commanded the voice. *Leave it all in the past, where it belongs.* Somehow, she'd found the will to go on with her life. Dredging it all up now served no purpose She'd faced it all down and won.

Or had she? What had she honestly gained besides a lonely existence?

Well, that was what she wanted, she argued. That was

what she'd chosen, and she'd live with the decision, thank you very much.

But last night, she'd breached that decision. *No, I'll go,* she'd said. The memory of those words smacked her in the face, pulling her out of her drowsiness with far more success than the grating noise of the boisterous rooster perched on the picket fence.

Whatever had caused her to say that? To volunteer to show her face in town? Like a windbreak of tulip poplars, threats of social injustice lined up in her heart. What if someone laughed at her? What if people turned their heads away when she walked by? What if no one would talk to her?

The prospect of encountering such slights assaulted her pride with devastating force. Betsy pulled her knees into her chest to still her body's sudden quaking, swiped at the hot tears stinging her eyes, and began to shape a plausible excuse that would allow her to renege, while saving face with Auntie Kee. She was too tired. That was it. She expected she looked as tuckered out as she felt. Auntie Kee would know it went deeper than that, but she wouldn't say anything.

"Air ye awake?" A light touch on Betsy's shoulder accompanied Auntie Kee's softly spoken question.

"Never went to sleep," Betsy replied in a voice as scratchy as raw wool in August. She stretched and yawned, moved the pillow off her face, and shoved the heels of her hands into her eyes as she rolled onto her back.

"Why don' ye go on upstairs and crawl in your bed," Auntie Kee said. "The worst of the storm's past, so hit art to be quiet enough for ye. I'll watch out after the preacher-man."

Betsy sat up straight and looked into the hall where he was lying on the floor, but the tears and rubbing had blurred her vision. "Is he awake?"

"He's twitchin', but his eyes're shut. I spec he didn't

rest none too good his ownself, that floor bein' hard and his leg a-achin' and all."

Auntie Kee headed for the kitchen. Betsy sat watching the preacher-man, her mind not on him but on going to town, wishing she'd broached the subject with Auntie Kee, who'd opened the door when she suggested that Betsy go to bed. Maybe in a roundabout way, Auntie Kee was offering to go in Betsy's stead. Maybe she ought to go to the kitchen and talk to the older woman about it.

That required tiptoeing around the preacher-man, who opened his eyes and smiled up at Betsy, taking her by surprise. In reaction, she smiled back. An unaccustomed but not unwelcomed warmth seeped into her core, lending her energy and bolstering her faltering courage.

"How's your toothache?" he asked, sitting up.

"Much better, thank you. How's your leg?"

"Stiff. My whole body's stiff." He wiggled his shoulders, then his torso, then his hips, but his legs didn't move. Guilt sliced through her. How could she be so concerned about something as insignificant as social acceptance when this man had, at least temporarily, lost the use of his only good leg?

"I need to get up," he said.

"Do you think that's wise?"

"Wise or not, I need to. Would you please hand me my leg?"

Betsy knew she'd eventually have to see his stump. She just hadn't thought it would be so soon, nor was she at all certain she was ready for the sight. She supposed she could hand the artificial limb over and then vamoose, but her leaving would clearly indicate her aversion. In all honesty, she silently admitted, she didn't even want to touch the wooden leg.

He must not have noted her hesitation, or perhaps he took her silence for acquiescence. "It's there—on the hall tree."

Pushing back her reluctance—after all, she assured herself, it was only a piece of wood—Betsy plucked the contraption off the base of the hall tree . . . and dropped it on the preacher's lap.

"Oh, my! I'm so sorry," she gushed, mortified at her clumsiness and concerned that she'd caused him further discomfort. "Are you hurt?"

"No. Just startled. It's kind of heavy, isn't it?"

Was it? She hadn't noticed, but if he wanted to think that was why she'd let go of it so quickly, that was all right with her. She picked it up again, taking more care this time to hold it well, and realized it was quite heavy.

"Don't you get tired of dragging this around?" She'd meant the question innocently enough, but once spoken, it sounded callous. The flame of embarrassment burned her cheeks. "I, uh, I'm sorry."

His laughter eased her shame a bit. "Why should you be? Sorry, I mean. It's a perfectly legitimate question. Yes, it's heavy. And yes, I grow weary of having to wear it, but it's better than a peg, and far better than nothing."

Now that she actually held the wooden leg in her hands, Betsy found herself reluctant to let it go, which made no sense at all—but then nothing else she'd done or said or felt since the preacher-man walked into the kitchen made sense, either. She stroked the satin smoothness of the wood and marveled at how the stain matched his skin color.

"It's oak," he said. "Heavy, perhaps, but durable. I didn't want to ever have to whittle another one."

"You made this?"

"Sure did."

"It must have been hard. Not the whittling part as much as . . ." She'd gone and embarrassed herself again. Why did she have this sudden fascination with a piece of wood? But it was more than that. It was a fascination with the man who wore it as well, a fascination that confused and confounded even while it warmed her soul and excited her spirit far more than anything else had before. Betsy hid her embarrassment and confusion behind the action of slipping the faded red leg of his drawers over his thigh, thus exposing his stump, which she refused to look at. Instead, she watched his face, watched him whisk the soul-pain from his eyes and replace it with a detached stare.

"It was hard. I don't deny it. But it was also necessary."

"Surely someone else—"

"Could have whittled it for me," he finished for her. "You don't know how close I came to hiring the job out. Forcing myself to make it was part of the healing."

Had he honestly accepted the loss of his leg—or was his attitude just a facade? she wondered. A couple of times, she thought she detected a trace of bitterness in his voice. She'd be bitter. She *was* bitter about her loss. Maybe losing part of your body wasn't as bad as she'd thought. At least a body part could be duplicated. She'd lost something far less tangible, something a stick of oak and a few leather straps and buckles couldn't replace.

Still refusing to look at his stump, she turned her attention to those leather straps and buckles. Although she understood their function, she couldn't for the life of her figure out how they held the artificial limb in place. "You're going to have to tell me what to do."

The preacher leaned forward and held out his hands. "Give it to me. I'll do it."

There was something in his tone that said, "You don't have to watch," but Betsy did. With quick and efficient dispatch, he slipped the padded leather collar over his stump—so quickly she caught only a glimpse of it, but enough to note that it looked like his lower leg was merely folded backwards, like he was sitting on it. He wrapped two long straps around the collar and buckled them securely, then reached up inside the leg of his drawers and pulled down three straps she hadn't realized were there. These he slipped through buckles sewn onto the collar.

When he'd covered the wooden leg with the bottom of his drawers, he scooted over to the hall tree, set his artificial foot flat on the floor, and laid the palm of his left hand on its base. "Can you support my other side long enough for me to stand?"

"Yes, but I still don't know if this is such a good idea."

"It won't be . . . if my leg's broken."

"If? I thought it was."

"I'm not so sure anymore. See? I can wiggle my foot." He demonstrated. "If I can put my weight on it, then I'll know for sure. But first, I have to get up."

"I'm not so sure about this," Betsy repeated, squatting next to him, "but if you're willing to try, I'm willing to help."

She looked so small, so frail, so childlike with her cloud of tousled red hair and her trusting green eyes. He worried his bottom lip, questioning the prudence of using her as a crutch. He'd have to be careful to throw his weight to the left. That way, should he lose his balance, he'd fall onto the hall tree and not Betsy. He looped his arm around her shoulder and blamed the tingling sensation on languid muscles.

"You ready?"

She nodded against his shoulder.

He took a deep breath, offered a silent prayer, and was standing before he had time to think about how he'd managed it. How *they'd* managed it, he mentally corrected. He hugged her close. She stiffened and pulled away.

"Much obliged."

"You're welcome." Her voice was as rigid as her spine. What had gotten into her? She'd seemed so warm and caring just minutes before . . . so different from most people, who looked at him as though he'd lost something far more important than his leg. He didn't like being a cripple, but life had taught him to count his blessings. He could have lost his life—or the use of both legs.

"Law, ye're up on that leg!" It was Auntie Kee, who was standing just inside the dining room, fists on her hips, her mouth pinched in displeasure.

"And it feels good." It did. A tremendous sense of relief suffused his being, washing away the emotional pain that had kept him awake most of the night.

"But ye shouldn't be puttin' no weight on that leg."

"Not if it's broken, but it isn't." He took a step forward with the splinted leg and almost lost his balance. Betsy grabbed his arm and held on until he'd steadied himself.

Auntie Kee's black gaze narrowed, but Steele thought her mouth softened a bit. "Ye're crazy, the both o' ye." Seemingly finished with her lecture, she turned back toward the kitchen. "Brakefist is done, if'n ye're interested."

How had he missed the commingling smells of honey-cured ham, fried eggs, and coffee? Yes, he was interested. Lord, he was famished!

"Let me help you to the kitchen," Betsy offered, taking his arm, "and then we'll get that splint off and change your bandage."

That sounded good to him, so good he considered asking her to remove the splint right there in the dining room. And he would have, had his gnawing hunger not stopped him. Steele couldn't remember having felt so empty since the war. It was his own fault, of course, for not having eaten much the day before. First, his eagerness to meet the folks of Peculiar Cove and then his accident had abolished his appetite, but now it was back and demanding sustenance.

The lack of food and restless night in combination,

however, had weakened him, forcing him to rest midway across the dining room. Betsy stood by him, taking his weight without complaint, her demeanor as stoic as any he'd ever witnessed. Yet, there was a beguiling innocence about her that was quite feminine and more than a little appealing. Why would anyone call this woman crazy? But they did. Even Auntie Kee had alluded to a shortage of good sense—in both of them.

He might be reckless, but he didn't perceive himself as crazy. How did Betsy view both herself and him? he wondered. He couldn't resist asking her. "Are we crazy, do you think?"

Her tilted chin trembled just a mite, but otherwise she appeared unruffled. "I don't know about you, preacher-man. But I am. I'm as crazy as they come. Just ask anyone for miles around."

Betsy didn't know how accurate her words were. Even in the tiny Hudson's Mill community three mountains, two flats, and a ridge away, folks had heard tales of the crazy woman over Peculiar Cove way. "Bets" was all they knew to call her, and that was sufficient for everyone—except Ty Williams.

At first, he'd vehemently denied the possibility that "Bets" could be his sister. Later, he knew she was. Too many details fit to maintain disbelief. But that didn't mean he had to tell anyone. Quite the contrary, Ty kept this knowledge strictly to himself. It was one of the few things he'd never shared with Lydia, and like the other details of his life he'd kept from her, it was something he hoped he never had to tell her.

Such hope was empty, of course, unless he moved far, far away from Peculiar Cove. Eventually, someone passing through would recognize him, and then everyone would know what a liar he was, among other things. He'd thought about heading west, probably would one day, but not without Lydia. The one time he'd broached the subject with her, she'd looked at him as though she didn't know him at all. That look had scared him good and proper. He couldn't lose Lydia, who'd become more important to him than life itself.

One day, he'd convince her. One day, she'd love him enough to go with him wherever he wanted to go.

Sometimes, he prayed that *one day* wouldn't come too late, but when he did, he felt guilty for asking. He'd never been much for praying anyway, and ever since he'd decided to live a lie, he hadn't cared to expose his inner thoughts too closely to anyone, including God. Which was just plain silly, he told himself from time to time. God knew everything, whether Willy Tyler wanted Him to know it or not. Still, by not actually pushing his thoughts God's way, he managed to maintain a delusion of anonymity.

The more he heard about Betsy, though, the harder it became to keep everything bottled up inside. He loved Betsy. Truly, he did. And he felt sorry for her. But she had Auntie Kee to take care of her. She didn't need him.

And he couldn't afford to need her.

"Would one of you kind ladies please go down to the mercantile after breakfast and tell Uncle Begley to send a wagon for me?"

Following as it did a simple "Pass the biscuits, please," the preacher's request took Betsy by surprise. For one thing, she'd completely forgotten it was Sunday. For another, she'd thought the discovery that his leg wasn't broken, only badly skinned and bruised, automatically negated the necessity of going for help. Apparently, he thought otherwise. The panic she'd experienced earlier gripped her again.

"Surely, ye don' aim to sermonize this morning, Reverend Montgomery," Auntie Kee said, her use of the preacher's last name making Betsy realize it was the first time she'd heard it.

"But I most certainly do. I promised folks a service, and they're going to get one." He spread butter on the biscuit, then spooned on a mound of wild strawberry jam. "This is awfully good eating, Miss— I don't rightly know what to call you."

"Auntie Kee'll do just dandy. And I'll go down to the store fer ye terrectly, after we get that there splint off and change your bandage. I reckon ye'd like to be a-wearin' your britches to sarvice. Miss Betsy can brush 'em good fer ye."

"I'll be much obliged—on all counts."

Betsy was so relieved she didn't have to go to town that she didn't stop to consider the fact that Auntie Kee's absence would put her alone with the preacher—until the older woman knotted her shawl over her ample bosom and walked out the door. That one little click of a door closing set Betsy's nerves to jangling something awful. Suddenly, she wished she'd gone herself. Suddenly, facing the ridicule of the townsfolk seemed far superior to being cooped up with the preacher-man. Something had happened when he put his arm around her in the hall, something strange and wonderful all at the same time, something that was thrilling yet frightening.

The least Auntie Kee could have done, Betsy thought, was wait for her to finish cleaning and rebandaging his wound. Then, she could have excused herself from his presence, if for no other reason than to brush his trousers—a task she could have easily dragged out until Auntie Kee returned. But Auntie Kee had left Betsy with no choice other than to complete the task she'd already begun.

Her fingers faltered, whether from haste or nervousness or concern over the unhealthy color surrounding his wound she couldn't say. Regardless, the damp cloth slipped out of her hand and fell with a plop onto the floor. To cover her agitation, she resorted to inane conversation.

"So tell me, Rev, how you found out about Hercules'-club."

Laughter burst from his lips. *"Rev?"*

Betsy made no attempt to stifle her own laughter. "What do you want me to call you? *Reverend Montgomery* is so formal."

"You might try my given name—Steele."

"Steele? What a cold-sounding word! It doesn't suit you at all." Law, she'd gone and embarrassed herself again. Someone needed to put a rope on her tongue. Or maybe she just needed to pop another Hercules'-club ball into her mouth.

He didn't seem to notice. "Blame it on my mama. It was her maiden name. But thanks for the compliment."

How he'd gotten a compliment out of her stumbling tongue she couldn't fathom, but suddenly that didn't matter anymore. She took one last swipe at his wound, rubbing harder than she had before, just in case she was wrong about the color and it was something that would wash off.

"Ouch! That hurts."

"Sorry." She caught her lower lip in her teeth and finished scrubbing the wound clean.

"Is something wrong?"

"The skin's a mite pink and there's a bit of swelling."

"Pour some more coal oil in it."

"It'll hurt."

"Not as bad as the lockjaw. I can take it."

She reckoned he could. She reckoned anyone who'd had his leg sawed off three times could take just about anything. She reckoned his mother had known what she was doing when she'd named him Steele. He was tough as old shoe leather, but Betsy sensed an underlying softness in him. No, softness was the wrong word, she corrected herself as she collected the coal oil and a pan to catch it in. It was more of a moldy patina that just required the right set of circumstances to polish it to a warm gloss.

"You said you lost your leg in the war?" she asked, voicing her thoughts without stopping to think this might be a sore subject for him.

He nodded, wincing as she poured the kerosene over his wound. "At Shiloh."

"My brother was . . . at Shiloh." She'd almost said "killed," but couldn't quite get the word past her throat.

"Lots of men were there. Many of them didn't live to tell about it. I suppose I was lucky."

She wrapped a clean bandage around his leg. "Willy should never have gone off to war. I don't understand why men think they have to fight each other. Nothing is that important."

"Some things are," he said quietly, "or they seem so at the time. Even lost causes."

Her head snapped up. Was this man a Rebel? The very idea that she might be harboring a man who'd aligned himself with the kind of men who'd attacked her, a man who'd fought against Willy, sickened her. Dizzy and nauseated, she gulped back her revulsion. "What do you mean?"

"The Southern cause was doomed from the outset. Surely you realize that. I wish I had."

Unable to stay and listen to any more, she dropped the ends of the bandage and ran from the kitchen. Once inside her room, she closed the door and locked it, then leaned against it and listened for his footsteps. He'd come after her . . . he'd come after her and try to do unnatural things to her, like the Rebel captain had tried to do . . .

For a long time she listened, but all she could hear was her blood thrumming in her ears. He couldn't move quickly, she reminded herself, not with two gimp legs. Climbing the stairs would be hard. He'd have to move slowly, laboriously, like she had yesterday when she had the charley horse. She imagined him pulling himself up, one step at the time, falling to all fours and crawling when he couldn't stand the pain any longer, just like she had. She'd made it and so could he. And when he arrived, he'd somehow manage to open her door. What would she do then? Screaming wouldn't help. Even if anyone heard, no one paid her screams any mind.

Papa's pistols! How could she have forgotten?

Betsy dashed to the bureau, snatched open the bottom drawer, extracted the pistol she'd put away loaded the evening before, then scrambled onto her bed and pointed the barrel at the door, her thumb on the hammer and her finger on the trigger.

The angle was wrong. She needed to be squarely facing the panel. Off the bed she came, bouncing on the soft mattress, forgetting to employ the caution necessary when handling a loaded gun. Her heel caught in her hem, pitching her off the bed and onto the rug.

Steele was calling himself seven kinds of a fool when the pistol discharged. Terror gripped him, immobilizing him for a moment until he realized the shot had come from upstairs. Nevertheless, he ran his palms over his chest, checking for blood.

If she hadn't intended to shoot him, then who—

No, surely not herself! If she were suicidal, she would have ended her life long ago. The gun must have gone off accidentally, which didn't preclude the fact that she might be lying upstairs in a pool of blood. On the other hand, she could be lying there waiting for him, waiting to pull the trigger again. Dare he take that risk? Dare he not?

He was almost to the landing when Auntie Kee and Uncle Begley burst through the front door.

"Thank heavens!" Auntie Kee exclaimed. "When I heard the report, I thought fer sure—" Her jaw dropped, her face bleached almost white, and she broke into a run. "What'd ye do t' my baby? Git out'n my way!"

Her accusation pierced him to the quick, paralyzing him. How could she think him capable of shooting an innocent woman?

Auntie Kee pushed past him, moving far more agilely than he would have thought possible. He had to go, too. He had to know Betsy was all right. He had to make both her and Auntie Kee understand that he wasn't like the men who'd attacked Betsy, that he wasn't like the ones who'd killed his mother and sisters.

Uncle Begley was right behind. He laid a restraining hand on Steele's shoulder. "Wait, son. Let her see. If'n Bets is alive, she won't shoot Kee."

"And if she's hurt?"

"Kee'll take keer o' her. Never ye fear."

Seven

"Open this door! Let me in!"

Betsy heard Auntie Kee's hollering and banging through a fog of confusion and pain. Her ears rang, her chest ached, her knees hurt, and the heel of one hand throbbed. She couldn't have shot herself in four places with one bullet . . . could she?

As the fog began to dissipate and her eyes refocused, she saw the pistol lying on the rug between her prone body and the door, which boasted a small, round hole in its lower panel that hadn't been there before. So, she'd shot the door. Laughter, born of relief, bubbled in her burning throat, but another thought prevented its release. What if someone had been standing on the other side? What if she'd shot the Rev? Panic gripped her, obstructing her voice as she tried to call out.

"If'n ye don' hurry up and answer me, I'm gonna break this door in!"

A vision of the round-bodied, arthritic Auntie Kee attempting to break a door down would have brought a smile to Betsy's lips, given other circumstances. Obviously, however, Auntie Kee meant to try—and could very well hurt herself in the process. Betsy had to stop her, had to find out if she'd already harmed someone else when she'd accidentally shot through the door. Other than being badly shaken, she seemed to be all right, certainly able to prevent further injury. She dragged herself to all fours, inhaled as deeply as her burning lungs allowed, then by sheer will of purpose stood and walked to the door.

Although the rain had stopped, the distant roll of thunder and a bank of dark gray clouds to the southwest promised more to come. Steele reckoned the weather would greatly reduce the crowd he'd expected at service. Between his injured leg and his sudden reluctance to leave Betsy, he'd lost his own enthusiasm, so he couldn't rightly blame anyone for staying away. Except maybe Betsy.

Thank goodness, she hadn't hurt herself when the pistol fired. Someone ought to take those pistols away from her for her own good, but he couldn't quite imagine anyone being able to. In all fairness, he supposed she did need the weapons for protection. Perhaps this incident would breed more caution in her handling of guns. He certainly hoped so.

Despite Auntie Kee's warning and Uncle Begley's advice, he'd finished climbing the stairs and stood beside the half-breed woman when Betsy finally unlocked the door. He'd been the one she fell against, the one who'd grasped her quaking shoulders and held her while she cried.

"I was so frightened," she murmured. "I thought I'd shot you."

"Isn't that what you intended to do?" he asked.

She nodded against his chest. "But only if you tried to come in. Only if you meant to . . ." Her slender body trembled. "Why?"

Her question brought bewildered frowns to Auntie Kee and Uncle Begley, but Steele understood exactly what she was thinking. "In all honesty, I don't know. Because it seemed the right thing to do at the time. There were many good men who fought for the Confederacy," he added, as much to enlighten their audience as to comfort Betsy. "Adversity always brings out the worst as well as the best in men, regardless of their political affiliations."

"Women, too," she said, standing away from him and swiping at her eyes. "I'm not really so callous."

"I know. You were just frightened. Fortunately, there was no harm done."

He understood perfectly what had happened to her this morning, and he blamed himself for having caused it. He should have known better than to tell her he'd fought for the South. It wasn't as if she'd asked him, and he knew that Willy fought for the Union. He should have known that she hated the South and all who'd fought for it, but he hadn't honestly thought she believed all Confederates were like the Rebels who'd stormed her house and dragged her back to their camp. He'd certainly given her no cause to stereotype him. Apparently, though, she did. He found himself determined to show her that she was wrong—about him and about what was best for herself.

He'd hoped she'd see that rejoining the world was the first step toward healing her soul, just as carving his wooden leg had been the first step for him. Perhaps she understood better than he imagined. As he stood with his back to Uncle Begley's jolt wagon, looking at Betsy, he decided pushing the issue a bit couldn't do much harm.

"You will come to services today, won't you?" Steele watched resolution chase indecision across her upturned face. Had she resolved to go—or to stay home? he wondered.

"Maybe."

Maybe, my eye! You know exactly what you're going to do. His internal voice shouted the argument so clearly he wasn't sure for a moment that he hadn't actually vocalized the words. When she didn't react, he expelled the breath he'd been holding, took her hand in his and squeezed it gently. Auntie Kee, who was standing behind Betsy, indicated her pleasure with a broad grin, exposing the wide gap in her front teeth.

"I expect to see you there," he said, nodding his head at Auntie Kee to let her know he was including her in the invitation.

That, he quickly realized, was the wrong thing to say to Betsy. Her spine went rigid and green fire blazed in her eyes, but it was her voice—lowered to a caustic hiss—that bespoke her anger most eloquently. "And I expect to see you in—"

"Come now, Miss Betsy," Auntie Kee hollered, effectively obscuring the last word out of Betsy's mouth, yet there was no doubt in Steele's mind that she'd finished the sentence with *hell.* His mouth dropped open and he stared at her—bug-eyed, he was sure, but unable to help himself. Ignoring him, Auntie Kee looped an arm around Betsy's shoulders and turned her toward the steps. "The preacher needs to be getting along," she added.

"Amen to that," Uncle Begley called from the wagon seat. "Folks're already gatherin'. Ye need some help?"

Loath to leave, but knowing he had no choice, Steele declined Begley's offer, then stepped onto the mounting box and climbed stiffly into the wagon. With a flick of the reins and a click to the mule, the whippletree snapped up and the wagon jerked forward. By the time Uncle Begley turned the bouncing jolt wagon back toward town, Betsy and Auntie Kee had disappeared inside the house.

Auntie Kee didn't let the door close good before she lit into Betsy. "How come ye to say such a thang to the preacher-man?"

"Don't do this," Betsy asked, certain Auntie Kee would

ignore her plea, but hoping just this once she'd let well enough alone.

She didn't. "How come?"

"Because he deserved it!"

"How d'ye reckon that? He didn' do nothin' to ye, 'cept maybe help ye feel better. That's a good man, only ye're too stubborn to see it. Like he tried to tell ye, not all men are bad 'uns. Ye art to be ashamed o' your ownself."

In truth, Betsy regretted her harsh retort the second it left her mouth. The Rev. Steele Montgomery did seem a very good man, not at all the animal she'd thought every Rebel to be. Yet, the fact that he was a Rebel tainted him. She'd wanted to lash out at him earlier, probably would have had his announcement not shattered her perception of who he was. Later, when he was holding her in the hallway, her relief that she hadn't hurt anyone had temporarily eradicated her bitterness.

Striking out at him when he was on his way to service, however, had been terribly inappropriate. She hadn't intended to. The remark just sort of fell off her tongue, like it had been sitting there waiting for such an opportunity. She supposed she owed him either an apology or an explanation, but neither would be sufficient.

"I done told him how 'shamed I am."

Auntie Kee ashamed? "For what?"

The older woman hung her head. "Begley and me was gittin' out'n the wagon when the gun went off. I thought you'd done gone an' shot the preacher-man. I told Begley I should a-knowed better'n t' leave ye here alone with a man, any man. But when we come in the door, he was on the stairs, so I knowed he was all right. Then I thought 'bout them bad men what folks say is goin' 'round killin' folks, like what happened to the Porters. What if the preacher-man's one of them? I thought. What if Miss Betsy was right 'bout him bein' a devil?"

"But you just thought about it."

"No. I don' recollect now 'xactly what I said, but I 'cused him o' shootin' ye."

How awful he must have felt! First, she thought him capable of attacking her, then Auntie thought him capable of shooting her. Auntie Kee was right. He'd given them no reason to believe such things. If he'd intended either of them any harm, he'd certainly had ample opportunity before this morning. The only way Betsy reckoned they could rectify the situation was to go to the preacher's service, as much as she didn't want to.

"We'll just have to make it up to him." Betsy gave her friend a hug, then broke loose from the older woman's side and headed up the stairs.

"Where ye goin'?"

"To get dressed. And you'd better, too, if you want to make service on time."

They were halfway to the mercantile when Steele remembered he'd left his Bible at the Tyler house.

"Hit don' make no nevermind," Uncle Begley said, leaning over the side of the wagon to spit. "I've got a dozen or more at the store."

"But they won't have my notes in them," Steele argued.

Begley shot him a narrow-eyed glare. "Ye cain't be much of a preacher-man if'n ye need notes. How come ye to want to go and spoil the Good Book like that anyways?"

Steele stifled a grin. "There's nothing wrong with writing in a Bible."

"Says who?"

"Says Bishop Marley, that's who. I need my Bible."

Begley kept the wagon heading straight. "Who's this Bishop Marley? I never heared of him."

"Albert Francis Marley, of the Brooklyn Marleys."

Steele knew he sounded impertinent, but he was beyond caring, had been since Betsy had spouted off at him.

Apparently, Begley took him seriously. "Still never heared of him." He scratched his head and spat again off the side of the wagon. "Seems like I heared tell of that there Brooklyn feller oncet on a time. Kin you tell me more about him?"

This time, Steele couldn't keep from grinning. "Sorry, I never met him, just the bishop."

"Hit shore is nice to have somebody to share funeralizin' and hitchin'-up with," Begley said, confusing the daylights out of Steele, which he was beginning to think was a common occurrence with Begley.

"How's that?"

"I been a-havin' to do it all, me bein' the justice o' the peace, ye see." The storekeeper turned his head and grinned at Steele. "I got me a reg'lar paper from the guvmint what says I am, too. 'Bout the onliest thang the guvmint ever did good fer me, fur as I kin see."

Their arrival at the store precluded further discussion on the matter. Begley turned the mule into a clearing littered with an assortment of carts and farm wagons, found an open spot, and pulled in the reins.

"Lots of people here already," Steele commented. An unexpected knot of anxiety twisted his gut and he broke out in a cold sweat.

"Most Peculiar folks look forward to the Sabbath," Begley said as he set the brake and tied off the reins. "Course, that could be 'cause they's lazy as pregnant possums, the Sabbath giving 'em an excuse to rest and all, like they needed one."

The outlandishness of the old man's vernacular almost relieved Steele's sudden dread—almost, but not quite. A pressing need to be alone with nature, alone with God, alone with his tormented soul, propelled Steele off the wagon. He hit the ground hard, yet barely noted the jolt of pain that ripped through his right leg.

"Yep, folks gen'ly gather early on Sundee," Begley continued in apparent oblivion to Steele's sudden lack of interest, "then sang and pray and eat and pray and sang all day. Havin' a real-live preacher-man to add his sermonizin' to the Sabbath goings-on is shorely gonna be a treat fer Peculiar folks. Yep, a real treat."

With most of his attention focused on finding a quiet spot not too far away, Steele was only half-listening. On the back side of the cleared area, which flanked this side and the back of the mercantile, stood a line of hardwoods, their outstretched limbs bright green with new leaves. Steele thought he heard the babble of a mountain stream coming from that direction, too, which made the site even more appealing.

"Get the singing started," he told Begley. "I'll be back."

"Where ye goin'?"

Steele pointed to the trees. "Just over there. To pray. I never preach without praying first."

Begley frowned. "Jes' don' be too long. Folks'll get antsy, ye know, them expectin' ye and all."

"I won't," Steele threw over his shoulder. He was already hobbling as fast as he could toward the trees, toward sanctuary. The jumbled muddle of his thoughts hobbled with him, sorting themselves out with each awkward step across the rock-strewn clearing.

First, he'd declare himself a sinner and ask God's forgiveness for pushing Betsy too hard. Then, he'd ask for the Lord's guidance in dealing with her. The conviction that God had sent him to Peculiar Cove to redeem Betsy's soul flamed in his heart stronger than ever.

Next, he had to deal with his moment of panic. He'd delivered a dozen or more sermons since becoming a circuit-riding minister without suffering from stage fright.

He wasn't sure why he dreaded this sermon so much, but he suspected his own lack of soul preparation was a strong contributing factor.

All things considered, this particular conversation with the Almighty could take a spell. He hoped the Peculiar folks wouldn't grow too impatient before he returned.

The full-bodied warmth of mountain voices raised in unison sprouted goose bumps on Betsy's arms. She'd forgotten how much these people loved to sing.

There were plenty of things she hadn't forgotten about them though, not the least of which was their capacity to remember. She'd spent the ten-minute walk to the store visualizing the reactions of the townsfolk when she showed up for service. Someone would scream, "Lunatic!" Mouths would fall open, eyes would pop, one of the women would most likely faint, and some of the men would escort her right back out onto the porch and demand that she return home—and stay there. She would be mortified, but she'd get over it. Afterwards, whenever Auntie Kee or the Rev or anyone else suggested she go into town, she would remind them of this day, and that would be the end of that.

But those things hadn't happened. Oh, she'd met a sea of astonished faces, and a chorus of sniggers had broken out among the youngsters. A few people hung their heads—she'd thought there for a spell that Uncle Begley's chin might become permanently attached to his string tie—and others couldn't look her in the eye, but overall, they'd behaved rather civilly. Molly and James Dunbar even scooted over to make room for her and Auntie Kee on a short stack of crates near the front door. People sat wherever they could find a few inches of space—in the few available chairs, on the cold stove, in the open windowsills, on the counter and the floor. Others stood leaning against the walls and shelves.

In pleasant weather folks spread out in the clearing behind the mercantile, but the grass was too wet and the fog was too thick this morning. From her vantage point, it looked like everyone in the cove had turned out, despite the weather. The preacher-man, however, was conspicuously absent—and had been since she and Auntie Kee had arrived almost twenty minutes ago. His absence troubled Betsy more than she cared to admit.

For a moment, her thoughts ran amuck as she created one possible occurrence after another to explain his absence. Without conscious thought, she laid an open palm on the Bible in her lap and offered a silent prayer in his behalf. That was when she remembered the Bible was his. Perhaps he'd simply gone back to her house to retrieve it, never dreaming she'd come to service and bring it with her. If so, he could search forever and not find it.

Just about the time she'd made up her mind to go looking for him, he walked in the door. The singing dwindled to a ragged end. A little girl of some six or seven years piped the last few notes all by herself, then stopped in the middle of a bar and hid her face in her mother's skirts. The same youngsters who'd giggled at Betsy snickered at the child. For a fleeting moment, Betsy wanted to smack them all, but the form and demeanor of the Rev. Steele Montgomery standing in the open doorway might near took her breath away, and banished all other thoughts.

How had she failed to see how handsome he was? Not in the classical sense—his nose was too large and a bit crooked, his mouth too wide, his hair too long—but all together, the ruggedness of these selfsame flaws worked to create a devilishly handsome face. And his eyes! Even the shade from the brim of his hat couldn't dim the mahogany gleam of his eyes. Looking into them conjured up romantic notions the likes of which Betsy Tyler had never entertained before. An unaccustomed warmth coiled in her stomach and wormed its way upward.

The realization that physical desire had put the warmth in her belly caught her unawares, and her palms flew to clasp suddenly hot cheeks. Here she was, sitting in church—it didn't matter how the building was used the other six days, today it was church—having carnal thoughts about a circuit-riding preacher, and one who'd fought for the Confederacy at that. He might never go to hell, but she suspected that was the place she was headed.

A hush settled over the crowd, whether one of reverence for his position or awe at his countenance she didn't know. A drop of water fell from the brim of his black hat and landed with a distinctive plop on the floor, so silent was the crowd. His gaze traversed the room, settling first on one group and then another until it reached those seated on the stack of crates. A fire kindled in his dark blue eyes and a sunny smile creased his cheeks.

With gentlemanly grace, he doffed his hat . . . and exposed a pile of wildflowers on his head.

Immediately, the room erupted with spontaneous laughter that quickly rose to a deafening roar. Old ladies tittered and young children giggled. Men slapped their thighs and each other's backs, while women nudged with their elbows and pointed with their fingers. Sides shook, bellies wobbled, and tears poured from almost every eye. Almost in unison, everyone took a deep breath, and then laughter burst forth again.

Amidst it all, Steele strode right into the center of the room, wearing an air of dignity right along with the wildflowers. Damp, wilted birdfoot violets and snowy bloodroot blossoms drifted to the floor, leaving a purple and white trail. Like drunken butterflies, a few sought temporary refuge on his shoulders, fluttered in the breeze of his passing, then took flight and joined their brethren on the floor. Some actually stayed put on top of his head.

Although she was laughing as hard as anyone else, Betsy marveled at his composure—and couldn't wait to hear the story behind the hat full of tiny, delicate wildflowers.

While Steele waited for the laughter to die away, which took a spell, he offered a silent prayer: *You truly do move in mysterious ways, Lord, and for that I am grateful.*

He wasn't sure why he'd picked the wildflowers, but it wasn't to cause an outburst of unmitigated glee. He'd merely plucked them and tossed them into his hat as he wandered along the banks of the creek and among the stand of hardwoods, thinking only about how beautiful they were, not what he would do with them. When a misty rain started to fall, he plopped the hat on his head and lit a rag to the store, forgetting all about the wildflowers.

How hard he'd prayed for a release of the tension that refused to let go—and all the while he was praying, God was plotting. Steele suspected a bit of tension imbued this new congregation as well, for a new preacher took some getting used to. Amazing, what a hat full of wildflowers could do! He contemplated brushing the remaining ones off his head, then decided he'd leave them there, in the event the relief of tension might again be required.

"That was some mighty beautiful singing," he said. "If your voices aren't too tired, I'd appreciate a little more of it—and I expect the Lord would love to hear some more of it, too. On days as gray and nasty as this one, we tend to forget how truly beautiful God's world is. But you can find beauty even on such drab days, as I did." For emphasis, he removed a handful of flowers from his head and let them dribble to the floor. The youngsters giggled as though on cue. "Do you folks know 'I praised the earth, in beauty seen'?"

At the enthusiastic nodding of almost every head in the crowd, a dainty woman of at least seventy years stepped forward and struck an ancient tuning fork. As the C above middle-C resonated in the small room, a low, slightly discordant hum arose, but those who'd sounded the proper note held it until the others found it. The elderly woman smiled, exposing several missing teeth, and raised the hand that held the small metal wand. A moment of silence prevailed, then the woman dropped her hand and, with amazing accuracy, everyone started singing at the same time, on the same note, and continued at the same tempo without any further direction. Their voices swelled and ebbed with the gentle motion Henry Carey had intended when he wrote the hymn well over a century earlier. It was a shame, Steele thought, that the composer couldn't be there to hear them.

Perhaps he was—at least in spirit. All things were possible to those who believed. And right now, Steele believed with all his heart in the transformation of seemingly insurmountable odds into reality, if for no other reason than Betsy Tyler's extraordinary attendance at service. His male pride basked in the glow of triumph. Yesterday, he'd vowed to get her there, and by dingies, he had.

Immediate contrition pricked his conscience, warning against human arrogance, which had been the Devil's undoing, and reminding him of the power of the all-seeing, all-knowing, all-mighty God. But if God were so powerful, why had He deserted the Montgomery women in their hour of need? Why hadn't He intervened? Why did He allow marauders to pillage and rape, to maim and kill, and then get off scot-free?

Steele had asked these questions of the Almighty many times, but he'd yet to receive a single answer. A pebble of resentment burned in his gut and quickly grew into a massive, fiery brimstone that threatened to consume what little faith he had left. This same bitterness had catapulted him from the devastation at the family farm into the figurative arms of the Methodist Church. The bitterness fueled his search for renewed faith, driving him from one settlement to another and providing the kindling for each sermon.

He'd grown up listening to fire-and-brimstone preachers and wondering from whence they acquired their fervor. Were they, he now wondered, searching for peace, much as he was? And what of the congregation before him? Did they raise melodious voices in song while deep, down inside each and every one of them suffered from a lack of spiritual guidance? Like the vast majority of folks, they were most probably sinners six days of the week and saints only on the Sabbath. And even that concession was questionable. Elsewise, they wouldn't have cast Betsy Tyler from their midst.

In counterpoint to the gentle motion of Carey's hymn of praise, Steele mentally blew on the flame, not in an effort to extinguish it, but rather to goad it into a full conflagration, hoping it would burn the bitterness out of him, leaving not a single ash of remembrance—and praying God would use the fire to light the way to true salvation for him and all the other sinners gathered in Uncle Begley's store.

Eight

The first words out of the preacher-man's mouth and virtually every word thereafter jarred Betsy to the marrow of her bones. Two long, grueling hours later, when he rose from the chair his injured leg forced him to use and called for sinners to come forward and repent, her ears were ringing, her head was throbbing, and her heart was aching—though not from remorse for real or imagined sins. Far from it. Her heart ached for Steele Montgomery, whose preaching had failed miserably, for not one person came forward, despite his extended appeal.

Apparently, he suffered from several grave misconceptions, to her way of thinking, all of which contributed in one way or another to his failure. First, either he thought they were all hard of hearing, or God was. Second, he thought these simple mountain folk were as well-educated as he, when in reality many of them barely knew the alphabet, let alone such words as "idolaters" and "reprobationists" and "Methodism." Third, he thought they all tottered on the very brink of hell. Whatever good he'd accomplished with the ridiculous wildflowers and the stirring hymn, he'd quickly undone with the ferociousness of his speech. Folks stood agape, some actually shaking their heads, but none taking a single step, despite the preacher's repeated pleas.

At long last, he gave up, offered a modest, humble prayer in an amazingly quiet voice, and declared them adjourned for dinner-on-the-ground. A chorus of long sighs followed the announcement, but the scuffling of shoe leather for those lucky enough to have it—and either wood or cardboard for those who didn't—swiftly obliterated all other sound as every person in the store headed for the door.

Betsy followed the Dunbars into a day no less dismal than it had been earlier. A cold westerly wind blew through the valley and banking dark clouds promised more rain. As she drew her shawl close, she pressed the preacher's Bible to her bosom—and remembered for the first time since he'd walked into service that she'd brought it. Betsy found the prospect of having to return it to him suddenly distasteful, since the action would most likely require conversation, and every time they talked she came away either angry or confused—or she said something offensive. At the least, he would probably ask what she'd thought of his sermon. The last thing she wanted to do was wound him, yet she couldn't be less than honest. With a heavy heart, she moved to the side of the porch, watching and waiting for the preacher to come out. Auntie Kee went with her.

"We didn't tote no food," the older woman whispered.

"It doesn't matter. We're going home," Betsy whispered back.

"The meetin' ain't over yet."

A series of snaps and creaks captured Betsy's attention, and she turned toward the clearing, where wagons loaded with families were beginning to roll out. "Might as well be. From the looks of it, the Rev may be preaching to an empty house this afternoon."

"Pore man!" Auntie Kee lamented. "What will we tell him?"

"The truth?"

"The truth would shame him fer sure, Miss Betsy." Auntie Kee planted her hands on her hips and frowned at the retreating wagons. "Bunch of infandels," she muttered, making Betsy smile.

"They're not infidels. They just don't like being told they are, most especially in a voice best reserved for wide open spaces."

"Is that what I did?"

At the sound of the preacher's voice close behind her, Betsy's joints froze up and her throat constricted. She managed to push one word through—a strained "Yes."

"Do you think they'll come back?" he asked.

"Not today." It hurt her to tell him, even more than she'd thought it would. "Here's your Bible," she said, holding it up, still unwilling to face him.

For the briefest moment, his fingers grazed hers. Her reaction was immediate and totally unprecedented—an electric charge that tingled all the way from her hand to her belly. This hadn't happened last night when she'd held his hand, so why had it now? Why was she suddenly so attracted to him, when almost everything she knew about him ran contrary to her ideals? Something told her to run from this man, to run as hard and fast as she could in the opposite direction and never look back. Thank goodness, she and Auntie Kee were going home.

"Would ye care to take dinner with us, preacher?"

Betsy could have swatted Auntie Kee for asking him. Thankful he couldn't see her reaction, she bit her lip and tensely awaited his reply. It wasn't long in coming.

"Thank you, ma'am. I'd be delighted."

Heavenly day! Now she was trapped for sure.

Uncle Begley stepped onto the porch and called to the preacher, thus delaying further discussion—but only, she was sure, for the time being. What would she say to him? How could she explain without hurting his feelings? So much time had passed since she'd concerned herself about anyone else's feelings that to do so now felt quite strange—not altogether bad, but definitely strange.

"Air ye coming?"

When had Auntie Kee left her side? Betsy wondered. She turned to see her with the Rev on the steps, both so radiant they looked like they'd swallowed sunshine. Before she could ask what she'd missed, Uncle Begley's wagon turned the corner. He pulled his mule to a halt in front of the store, and Auntie Kee and the preacher climbed in.

"I think I'll walk," Betsy said.

"Suit your ownself," Auntie Kee replied with a sniff, and the wagon pulled away. Betsy waited on the porch for a spell, stalling while she mentally formulated the best approach to take with the reverend. Rolling thunder interrupted her deliberations and gave her cause to regret her decision to lag behind. Perhaps if she hurried, she could beat the rain home—or at least catch up with Begley's wagon.

Despite her haste, she didn't manage either, though she almost made it to the front gate before the clouds released their torrent. With her hair plastered to her head, her dress stuck to her skin, and her teeth beginning to chatter, she sidestepped the broken plank in the porch floor and dashed into the front hall.

His first thought was that she resembled a drowned rat, but Steele quickly amended that observation. Rats looked skinnier when they were wet, not fatter. Not that she looked fat. Far from it. She looked round and alluring and positively feminine. He'd had no idea she possessed such delightful curves. The vision stirred something in him he'd thought long dead . . .

Her near-violent shiver jerked Steele out of the fantasy her wet clothes created. He snatched his coat off the hall tree and draped it around her shoulders, inadvertently brushing the peak of her breast with the back of one

MOUNTAIN MOONLIGHT

hand in the process. Molten fire shot through him, depriving him of breath and blinding him to everything except his sudden, intense need for intimate female companionship. He pulled her into his chest and held her tight. She turned her cheek into his chest and slid her hands around his rib cage to his back.

Steele gasped in awe and delight—awe, because she was the first woman who'd touched him in any way other than friendship or pity since the war; delight, because her slender body pressed so close to his felt absolutely wonderful. She was so tiny, so fragile, and yet the pressure of her breasts against his ribs and the delicate curve of her waist beneath his large hands were those of a woman, fully grown. He drank in her essence and wished he never had to let her go.

Suddenly, her spine went stiff and she wrenched herself from his embrace. She stood for a moment, glaring at him, her green eyes wild and accusing and a bit frightened, like those of a fox caught in a trap. Her breasts rose and fell as she took short, panting breaths, and twin spots of color flamed on her cheeks. Mumbling something about needing to change, she dashed up the stairs, leaving him in a state of utter confusion.

Betsy stepped out of her water-logged skirt, then peeled off her wet bodice and hurled it to the floor. Off came her petticoat, and then her chemise. These, too, she flung away from her, unmindful of where they landed. Hairpins flew across the room and a kicked shoe set the lamp prisms to jingling. She yanked a towel off the washstand and rubbed her hair with a vengeance, then tossed the towel aside with the same lack of concern. Moving to the dresser, she picked up her brush and began to work the knots out of her touseled red mane.

Whatever had come over her? How could she have allowed him to hold her so tightly? How could she have put her arms around him and pressed her breasts into his shirt? How could she have behaved so wantonly? How could she ever face him again? How could she ever face herself again?

The last question drew her attention to the reflection in the mirror, and she gaped in astonishment. Could the face in the beveled glass belong to her? When had her freckles faded and her complexion assumed a peachy glow? When had her cheeks filled out and her nose slimmed down? When had her eyebrows thinned into perky arches and her eyes become big, round orbs that dominated her face? When had she grown into the attractive young woman in the mirror?

This acknowledgment took her completely by surprise, but there was no doubt in her mind that her observation was accurate. All her life, she'd thought of herself as plain. As a girl, she'd coveted Mary Carter's blond curls and unblemished complexion, she'd envied Annie Bartlett for her blue eyes and oval face, and she'd cried herself to sleep many a night after one of the boys had teased her about her frizzy red hair or the sprinkle of freckles across her too-short nose. Rebecca Tyler had assured her only daughter that she'd grow into a stunning woman—"Pratt women are never pretty before age twenty," she'd said, referring to her own family. "Give it time."

Betsy did . . . and watched her legs grow too long and gangly for her diminutive stature, giving her the appearance and ill grace of a colt. While all the other girls were sprouting bosoms and round hips, Betsy was sprouting more freckles and new cowlicks. And when the young men in Peculiar Cove started courting the young women, they ignored Betsy.

Auntie Kee fussed at her for not socializing more, but the Tylers looked down their noses at barn raisings and husking bees. That left church, and since there was no such thing as organized religion in Peculiar Cove, the Episcopalian Tylers spurned services as well. So Betsy stayed at home, her too-short, freckled nose buried in a book.

Her father's extensive library had been her salvation, for there she found books that transported her to faraway places—to castles in Spain and thatched-roofed cottages in Ireland, to the turquoise waters of the Mediterranean and the snowy peaks of the Alps, to arid deserts and tropical islands. One day, she vowed, she'd see such places. More than anything else in the world, she wanted to separate herself from Peculiar Cove—not because she thought she was too good for the mountain community, but because she thought that the people there thought they were too good for her.

Betsy reckoned that observation might be a bit harsh, but she'd always known the Tylers were different. They were outsiders, transplants from another world, another way of life, and always would be. Why Papa had ever left Boston and come to the mountains in southeastern Tennessee remained a mystery. When anyone asked, he said he had his reasons, and that was that. His refusal to speak of his homeland and his relatives made Betsy wonder if Tyler was even Papa's real name.

But it wasn't a search for either roots or relatives that fueled her desire to leave Peculiar Cove. It was, rather, a search for a place where she belonged. She didn't know where that place was, but it was out there, somewhere, waiting for her to find it. So she plotted and planned and waited for the day she was old enough to set out on her own.

Money was no object. Papa had lots of it stashed in a metal box he kept hidden behind the decorative iron plate at the back of the fireplace in his room. No one was supposed to know it was there, but she'd accidentally found it one summer when she was cleaning out the fireplaces. There were jewels in the box, too—emerald rings and diamond necklaces, ruby brooches and pearl chokers, sapphire earbobs and topaz hatpins. She's always known her papa had money, but she'd never dreamed he had quite so much of it. All she had to do was convince him to part with enough to get her to Europe. He wouldn't want to see her go, but he'd never denied her a single request.

He denied that one—with a vehemence that astounded her for one so typically even-tempered. The truly astounding thing, however, was his refusal to explain, leaving Betsy to reach her own conclusions. It wasn't the cost and Papa had never been miserly, so it had to be her going away. Despite his objections, she'd continued to plot and plan and dream, all the while chiseling away at her papa. Somehow, someday, she'd persuade him.

In the meantime, she talked him into letting her learn to ride a horse, something he insisted proper young ladies shouldn't do, and she acquired as much information as she could about mountain roads and passes, relying mostly on Auntie Kee's limited knowledge. If she had to set out on her own, she would. But she was leaving Peculiar Cove. Somehow, someday, she was leaving.

And then one day, Papa just keeled over dead. Betsy was sixteen, almost seventeen, at the time. He'd been his usual self all day, but at the supper table in the middle of dessert, he'd gasped, clutched his chest, and collapsed. Afterwards, her mother, who'd never been a strong woman, took to her bed and her delicate health declined fast. Less than a year later, both parents were buried in the small cemetery under the big oak, alongside the three baby boys who'd been born between Betsy and Willie.

All her dreams died with her parents. First, she couldn't abandon Willie, who was five years younger, then she couldn't bring herself to abandon Auntie Kee, who'd lived with the Tylers since the forties. But she could send

Willy away. She could see that he escaped the peculiar people in Peculiar Cove . . .

Her mirrored image wavered and she brushed hot tears from her eyes. Yes, Willy had escaped. He hadn't wanted to go, but she'd pushed him . . . pushed him right into a grave somewhere near Shiloh.

And now, here she was, twenty-six years old and finally an attractive woman, one a handsome man had seen fit to hold in his arms, if only to give her warmth. And what had she done? Gone and ruined it, that was what. Not because she'd hugged him back, but because she could never allow herself to fall in love with a man. Not now. Not since she'd come back from the Confederate army camp.

But Betsy was very much afraid she'd fallen in love with the Rev. Steele Montgomery.

For the umpteenth time, Uncle Begley twisted around in his chair and peered into the dining room. "What d'ye reckon's keepin' Bets?"

The same question had been chasing itself around in Steele's head since Auntie Kee had set the food on the table—and that had been awhile back.

"I'll put the sweet taters and biscuits back in the oven," Auntie Kee said, rising stiffly from the sofa, "so they'll be warm enough to at least soften the butter." She snorted. "Course, the butter's settin' out, too. Hit's prob'ly melted by now. Then I'll see about Miss Betsy—if she ain't come down yet."

"Would you like for me to check on her?" Steele asked.

"I 'preciate the offer, Preacher, but I reckon ye're in worse shape than me. Perchin' on that stack o' crates sure has got my ole rheumatiz to mommickin' up, though."

"Ye come next Sabbath," Begley said, "and I'll tek keer

to save my rocker fer ye. They ain't no better settin' chair in all of Peculiar."

Begley's mention of the following Sunday prompted a question that had been eating at Steele since they'd left the store. But even with the perfect opportunity—and the perfect person to ask—he had trouble getting the words past his throat. After several attempts, he managed it in a halfway normal tone. "Do you suppose folks will come back to hear me preach?"

The old man rubbed his jaw and fixed his gaze on the lace curtains covering the window directly across the room from the wide, heavily padded, low-backed chair he'd chosen to park himself in. "Peculiar folks got long mem'ries," he observed. "Mighty long mem'ries. They got prickly consciences, too. I 'spect ye got through to their souls a speck too much today. Kindly got 'em running from theirselfs, if'n ye know what I mean. Course, it may be a few days 'fore any of us hears good again"—Begley chuckled—"but I reckon we'll git over it."

"It was bad, huh?"

Begley turned to Steele. "Not bad, really, just diffrent. If ye was to go back fur enough, ye'd find that Peculiar folks in gen'ral has got Presbyterian roots. And ye've got to 'member that we ain't had no preacher-man through these here parts in more years'n I kin count. These folks just ain't used to sech farry preachin', that's all."

"Does anyone ever preach?"

"Preach? Nope. Folks gives testimonies. Some ast to be thought of in prayer. Those that kin, read from the Bible or a prayer book. Ever'body sangs. But preach? Nope."

"So, do you think they'll come back next Sunday?"

"You gonna be here?"

"Probably not."

"Then how come ye to keer?"

"Because I will be back eventually. Besides, I don't want

Nine

Acutely aware of Betsy standing on the steps behind him, Steele adjusted the Indian blanket draped over Dusty's back for the dozenth time and checked to see once more that his rolled pack was securely tied in front of the mule's rump. Before, he hadn't minded riding into a community as a stranger and riding out a few days later knowing everyone within walking distance and beyond, then going on to another community to repeat the process. But the few days he'd spent in Peculiar Cove didn't compare to those he'd spent elsewhere, and all because of a crazy woman.

Of course, Betsy wasn't really crazy. Eccentric and reclusive, perhaps, but not crazy. Uncle Begley told Steele that he realized now what a terrible injustice he and all the other townsfolk had done her by spreading such awful tales, and he assured Steele that he'd do what he could to repair the damage. It was an admirable first step, but they both agreed it would take years to smooth over the mess, and even then a few spurs would remain.

"I think you owe her an apology, too," Steele added. He and Begley were sitting on the front porch Sunday afternoon, alone for a few minutes while Betsy and Auntie Kee made tea cakes and sassafras tea.

"That's fer sure and certain," Begley agreed. "Howsomever, it might be best jes' to hold off fer a spell. Ye know, give folks some time t' see they was wrong, give the wounds a chance to do a spot o' healing first. Course, if ye thank hit needs t' come now, I'll tell her today how sorry I am for ever'thang."

The last thing Steele wanted was for Betsy to be hurt any more than she already had been. "I think you're right," he said. "Verbal apologies without actions to back them up are empty."

"I'll make sure I show her how wrong I was t' judge her like I did. Most folks'll foller my lead. You'll see."

Steele did see. Accepting Betsy's and Auntie Kee's invitation to stay at the Tyler house for this and future visits to Peculiar Cove allowed him to see firsthand. Monday morning, Molly Dunbar and Imer Bailey came by, ostensibly to welcome Steele and apologize for the mass exodus after the sermon—"The weather was lookin' really bad," Imer explained, blushing when Steele promised not to speak so loudly next time. But while they were there, they said, they wanted to tell Betsy how glad they were that she'd come to service and how they were hoping to see more of her in the future. Steele left them in the parlor while he went looking for Betsy, who'd disappeared after breakfast.

Betsy's dreams-turned-nightmares left her shaken and confused. Somehow, she got through breakfast with Steele, whom she couldn't quite see in the morning light as the rutting hog she'd imagined him being in the darkness of her room. But he'd fought for the South, she reminded herself—fought with men like the Confederate captain and his soldiers, fought against Willy at Shiloh. For all she knew, Steele's bullet had killed Willy. How could she even consider him as anything more than an animal, let alone a man worthy of her love?

She really was as crazy as they said. She had to be. On the one hand, she couldn't abide being in the same room with Steele Montgomery, yet on the other, she wanted his company. When they were together, she never knew from one minute to the next how her heart was going to react. She might fall into his arms and relish the peace that settled over her—or his very touch might anger or frighten her beyond reason. In turns, she loved him, then she hated him. Never had she felt so torn, so bewildered, so crazy.

As was her wont, she sought refuge in physical labor, hoping that taxing her muscles would serve to alleviate at least a portion of her distress.

He found her furiously working cow manure into the soil of the kitchen garden, the only plot of ground near the house that wasn't overgrown with weeds and wildflowers. To his surprise, she'd donned a pair of men's trousers and a homespun shirt, both of which were too big for her in some ways and almost too small in others, emphasizing the differences in the male and female physique. For a moment, he stood on the back stoop and watched, fascinated with the way the trousers stretched across her hips and relishing an occasional glimpse of the shirt straining to hold her full breasts. He'd never stopped to consider how fetching a woman could be in men's clothes, but that's what Betsy was—fetching. Even with manure splattered on the trouser legs and her heavy brogans coated with mud.

She turned toward the house then and caught him staring at her. "No sermons, please," she called, leaning on the potato fork and wiping the back of a gloved hand over her brow, smearing it with what he hoped was mud rather than natural fertilizer.

Her request caught him by surprise. He'd fully expected reproach at his ogling. "I see nothing wrong with your attire," he assured her, stepping off the stoop and sticking to a narrow walkway lined with knee-high weeds that begged for snakes to hide in them, "so long as you restrict it to such activity as you are now engaging in."

"Where is it written that women must wear skirts?" Although a smile accompanied her question, he detected a bit of acidity in her tone.

"Well, it isn't exactly written anywhere, but there's much to be said for adhering to accepted standards of conduct."

"And who decides what standards are acceptable in female apparel? Not women, surely. No woman in her right mind would choose the constriction of a corset or the weight of six to eight petticoats."

Her frank language was making him uncomfortable. He ran a finger under his tight collar and realized it was the only part of his clothing that ever bound him at all. He tried to imagine how it would feel to wear a corset, but that required imagining he had a bosom, which he couldn't quite manage. Perhaps she had a point, but agreeing with her violated the precepts of the Church. While he was searching for a middle ground, she changed the subject.

"Was there something on your mind, Rev, or did you come out here just to gawk at me?"

So, she had noted his appreciation of her figure. He coughed, found he couldn't meet her gaze any longer, and looked down at her mud-caked shoes. "You have company."

Suspicion flashed in her green eyes. "Who?"

"Mrs. Dunbar and Miss Bailey."

A smile flittered across her face, but a frown quickly displaced it. She took her weight off the potato fork, and went back to tilling the soil, thus stirring up the odor of manure again. "I have work to do."

Steele couldn't see her flouncing into the fancy parlor, adorned as she was in mud and cow droppings, nor did he think it wise to invite the ladies out to the smelly garden. "Shall I tell them to call another time?"

"Do what you want, Rev."

Her brusque tone caught him off guard, but also made him stop to think about the situation from her perspective. Emotional bridges, as he well knew, weren't built in a day, nor could they be built from only one side. This had all begun when she shut herself off from the world. Reentering that world was going to take some time. At least she'd taken the first step by going to service yesterday, and now the townsfolk had started construction from their side. All he wanted her to do was give them a chance—and to give herself a chance as well. "Betsy, they're trying to make amends."

The fight went out of her, and when she spoke, her voice was soft and resigned. "I know that. Yes, please ask them to call again."

Her capitulation thrilled his soul. The victory might be tiny, but it was a step in the right direction. Guiding Betsy along the journey to full restoration of her soul became his challenge, his goal, governing everything he said and did that day and the next. As each layer of resistance peeled off, he yearned for more. He yearned to know the real Betsy Tyler, yearned to stay in Peculiar Cove for as long as it took to reach the core of her very essence.

But here it was Wednesday morning—time for him to leave, and he didn't know when he'd be back.

"You can't leave yet," Betsy said, her voice unnaturally throaty. "Your leg hasn't healed."

Please, don't make this harder, he silently pleaded. Aloud, he said, "Not completely, perhaps, but enough to allow me to ride, and it doesn't pain me much anymore. I'll take care of it properly. Honest I will."

"You didn't pull my tooth either."

He'd forgotten all about her sore tooth, which she hadn't mentioned since Sunday morning, but it shouldn't take long to get it out. "Come on, then," he said, moving away from Dusty, "and let's get it done." A long-buried memory sliced through him as he reached the steps, stopping him short. "Wait, let's talk about this first."

"Why?"

"I just remembered an instance where an army sawbones refused to pull a man's tooth. He said it might be abscessed, and if it was, pulling it would spread the infection and might kill the man."

Her eyes flew open wide and she licked her lips nervously. "Do you think mine might be abscessed?"

"I don't know. Are you willing to take that chance?"

"No."

"Does it still hurt?"

"Only a little now and then. Mostly when I first wake up. When I chew on one of the Hercules'-club balls, the ache goes away." She chewed on her lower lip for a bit, then took a deep breath. "I'm worried about it coming back, like it did before, and I'm almost out of medicine."

He needed to be on his way, but he didn't suppose a short trip to the woods would delay him much. Besides, since he didn't know when he would return, Betsy should know where to find the toothache tree.

"You got your walking shoes on?" he asked.

She didn't, nor was her best gown suitable for scrambling up rocks or wading through streams, but she wasn't about to tell him lest he decide he didn't have time to wait for her to change. Never had she thought she'd be grateful for a sore tooth, but hers had brought him to her in the first place, and now it was allowing them a few more minutes together.

This is crazy, a niggling voice warned. *You'll be alone with him in the woods. Anything could happen.*

She didn't listen. This morning, she wasn't afraid of him.

"Just let me tell Auntie Kee."

Never had Steele imagined he'd find himself grateful he'd lost his leg or injured his good one. Not only did the combination make for slow going, but it also provided a ready excuse for him to take Betsy's hand or use her as a crutch now and then. These things pleased him immensely. Each time he touched her, a frisson of delight shimmied through him. Amazingly, just being with her made him feel young and whole again.

He held her now, his arm around her shoulder, her body supporting a small portion of his weight as they climbed a steep embankment. He'd managed to get them thoroughly lost, but Betsy didn't seem to mind—and he sure as thunder didn't. He looked down at her sun-dappled hair, breathed in the sweet scent of jasmine that clung to her, and wished they could stay lost forever.

With his attention thus away from his footing, he stumbled on a loose rock and into Betsy. In reaction, she reached for a branch of a mountain laurel . . . and screeched at the top of her lungs. Steele's heart jumped into his throat.

"What's wrong? What happened?"

She jerked her hand back and crammed the heel of her thumb into her mouth, allowing him only a cursory glance of her palm. But it was enough to see several droplets of blood gathered there.

"Thorns?" he asked.

Her hand still in her mouth and tears puddling in her eyes, she bobbed her head in reply.

"Could be another Hercules'-club."

She removed her hand long enough to say accusingly, "You didn't tell me they had thorns."

"That's why it's called a Hercules'-club. They're sharp, aren't they?"

Nodding again, she moved out of his way to give him room to inspect the prickly limb hidden behind an umbrella of laurel leaves. "That's what it is, all right. Hold this up, will you?"

While she held the laurel branch, he fished out his pocketknife and used it to remove several large nodules from the trunk. "Can you see what I'm doing?"

"It's awfully dark under there," came her muffled reply.

"Then come under here with me so I can show you how to harvest these things. Be careful or you'll get stuck again."

Betsy shivered, whether at the prospect of getting stabbed again or being alone with the Rev in the darkness behind the laurel she didn't know.

Steele blinked in the darkness behind the thick-leaved branches of the laurel. It was much darker than he'd realized. Perhaps too dark for either of them to see well, now that she'd dropped the limb and stood beside him in the thick shade. The air seemed thicker there, too—thick with the fragrance of jasmine, thick with their breathing, thick with expectancy.

He forced himself back to the task at hand. "See how the bark has enlarged the older nodules? You simply break off the thorn, then slip the point of the knife under the nodule, and it comes right off." He demonstrated while he talked, not in the least sure she could see, if she was even watching. Keeping his hands and mind occupied had become crucial, however. "You peel off the bark and what you have left is a little ball of pith, like those I gave you before. The medicine's only good while they're green, but it takes them a couple of days to dry out. You can also skin off a strip of the inner bark from a limb and use it the same way."

"And what if I can't find this tree again?" Her voice was whispery hoarse, her mouth so close to his face that the breath of her words tickled his cheek, making his insides squishy and his loins ache. He couldn't seem to draw enough air into his lungs or stop his pulse from racing out of control.

"You'll find it," he murmured, folding his knife and putting both it and the balls of pith into his pocket, "or another one, now that you know what it looks like."

There was nothing else to tell her about the toothache tree, nothing left to do with his hands, nothing else to think about except the one thing he'd been pushing back: holding her close and kissing her until they were both senseless. *This is insane,* he thought as he found her chin, caught it between his thumb and forefinger, and gently tilted it upward.

I can't believe I want him to kiss me, she thought. *I really am crazy!*

His lips touched hers then, as soft as the flutter of a butterfly wing, a tender grazing that took her breath away and left her begging for more. She strained against him, slipping her arms around his torso and pressing her breasts into his chest. Moaning, he cupped her face in his palms, but instead of deepening the kiss, he raised his mouth to her forehead and nuzzled her hairline with his nose. She felt as though he'd allowed her the tiniest taste of the sweetest honey bees ever made, then snatched it away. What had she done wrong?

Steele fought for control. It would be so easy to take her, right there in the shady bower of the mountain laurel, but to do so would make him as low as the men who'd taken advantage of her during the war.

"We have to get back," he said, the words cutting his throat, making it raw.

"Yes," she breathed, trembling as she removed her arms and stepped out of the bower.

They walked back to the Tyler house in silence, finding their way with an ease that dumbfounded him, walking close but neither daring to touch the other. She scurried onto the porch and hovered near the door. He made a little pile of the Hercules'-club balls on the porch railing, then slipped Dusty's reins off the hitching post and mounted the mule. "I'll be back," he said. "I don't know when, but I will be back."

Although she nodded, her look bespoke skepticism. He hated to leave her this way, but he had no choice. He could make no further promises, could assure her of little, could offer her nothing but a crippled body and a scarred soul. She deserved much, much more.

Without looking back, he headed the mule east.

"You plant the seed," Bishop Marley had said, "then you go back a month or two later and discover that it sprouted while you were gone. You water it and cultivate it, and then you leave it alone again to grow some more." Such was the way of it with circuit-riding preachers and their far-flung congregations.

But planting a seed for the Church didn't compare with planting a seed in your heart, and that was surely what he'd done where Betsy Tyler was concerned.

Despite the distances between farms and communities, despite the rugged terrain and oftimes inclement weather, news traveled through the mountains like fire through a dry corn patch. No one knew how; no one really cared. Folks simply accepted the fact that the grapevine was both fast and extremely efficient.

The grapevine in the tiny settlement of Hudson's Mill was firmly rooted in Grandma Carter: mother of ten, grandmother of forty-three and counting, and great-grandmother, aunt, cousin, sister-in-law, mother-in-law, and grandmother-in-law to an additional hundred or two more. No one, including Grandma Carter herself, rightly knew the exact number. With relatives scattered from Knoxville to Chattanooga and from Asheville to Tullahoma, and with Hudson's Mill sitting almost dead center between these towns, Grandma's vines spread out for miles in all directions. Between letters and visits, she was privy to an abundance of knowledge. It was through her that Ty Williams had first heard the tales about Crazy Bets over in Peculiar Cove.

According to Grandma Carter's latest gossip, which had come to her from a second cousin once removed who'd heard it from a Knoxville relative whose father-in-law was a close friend of Bishop Marley, the Methodist Church was sending a circuit-riding preacher to Hudson's Mill. Ty Williams hoped it wasn't true, but he knew deep in his heart that it was. He knew this partly because the grapevine was generally accurate, but mostly because he was due a setback—way past due, actually. Things had been going too well for too long.

If he told anyone he considered the arrival of an ordained minister to be a setback, they'd laugh him all the way into the next hollow. But to Ty, having a preacher right there in Hudson's Mill could mean nothing else. He'd been putting Lydia off, using the want of a proper minister as an excuse to postpone their wedding. As soon as the minister arrived, Ty's justification would evaporate. With perfect hindsight, he wished he'd fabricated at least one more reason why he couldn't marry Lydia right now.

Another fabrication would just add more sticky threads to the vast web of deceit he'd already spun. Maybe it was time he tore down the web and told her the truth about who he really was and what he'd really done in the War Between the States. Eventually, he'd have to anyway. He'd known that all along. He just hadn't planned to tell her now. When he spilled the proverbial beans, he wanted to be long gone from Hudson's Mill, long gone from the

Smoky Mountains, long gone from Tennessee. He wanted to be way out West—on the prairie, in the Rockies, maybe even all the way to California before he told her. He wanted to be far, far away from everyone he'd ever known—*they* had ever known, he mentally corrected—so far away that they would never likely cross paths with any of those people again.

But Lydia would know. He'd hoped to protect her from whispered gossip and pointed fingers, but he couldn't continue to live a lie, not once he and Lydia were husband and wife. What would she do when he told her? Would she calmly accept it or fly into a rage? It wasn't her immediate reaction that was important, though, rather the long-term effects of being faced with the truth.

In his mind's eye, he could see the initial shock in her big hazel eyes. She'd try hard not to show it, but it would be there. When the shock wore off, hurt would set in. She'd want to know why he hadn't trusted her enough to tell her everything in the first place. Revulsion would follow, and then, perhaps, retreat. Even if she stayed with him, the truth would destroy their relationship. No, he couldn't tell her. Not now. Maybe not ever.

Ty missed a lick with the ax. It glanced off the piece of firewood, skinning off some bark, and knocked the log onto the ground before it landed safely on top of the notched stump. Such mistakes had cost many a man a foot—or worse. He closed his eyes and concentrated on breathing normally for a spell before using a hiked shoulder to wipe the sweat from his eyes and forehead. Splitting wood might be a mundane chore, but it required focus, and right now Ty didn't think he could focus on anything other than his predicament.

Determined to settle this in his mind before he fooled around and hurt himself, Ty laid the ax aside and plopped down under a big red oak nearby. Leaning against its massive trunk, he pulled his knees up, planted his feet on the ground, and rested his wrists on his kneecaps. He fixed his gaze on the big puffy clouds hovering over Hogback Ridge and worked at directing his attention toward finding a solution to his dilemma.

His mind rebelled at the onerous task, reminding him that he didn't have to worry about this turn of events before tomorrow, which was as early as he was likely to see Lydia again. She and her mother had left three days ago for Maggot Spring Gap to assist with the birth of Lydia's sister Rachel's second child. If the delivery was delayed or difficulties arose, they'd be even later getting back. That left him the entire evening and a good portion of the morning to make a decision. Perhaps he merely needed to rest a few minutes.

When a few minutes turned into half an hour and he was still thinking about it, Ty gave up and forced himself to thrash it all out. He could leave, he supposed, right now, tonight. He'd write Lydia a note, tell her he'd send for her when he got resettled. But what reason could he give? Try as he might, none came to mind.

It didn't matter. He didn't want to leave anyway, was sure he'd never be able to bring himself to walk out on Lydia and her mother. They leaned too heavily on him—ever since Lydia's father, Jude Hudson, died last summer. Lydia wasn't like Betsy, who didn't mind chopping wood and never blinked an eye when it came to killing a snake. Lydia needed a man to take care of her. If Ty weren't around, she'd most likely find someone else to fill his shoes, which she could do without any trouble a-tall. As pretty as she was—and sweet to boot—every eligible swain for miles around was liable to line up at her door the minute Grandma Carter got wind of his departure and set the grapevine in motion.

Of course, Lydia's taking another man wouldn't mean she didn't love him anymore. She was simply a woman who needed a man around the place, and for all her sweetness, she tended to be a mite impatient. No, he couldn't leave.

But if he stayed . . . and if the traveling preacher really did come to Hudson's Mill, then Lydia would be insisting on a wedding. Could he let her say "I do" without knowing exactly what she was getting in a husband?

A fly buzzed by his ear; Ty swatted at it with a cupped palm and caught it. He was good at catching flies that way. In fact, he was good at a lot of things. Imbued with a touch of pride, he sat up straighter and considered himself through Lydia's eyes.

Was what she was getting so very bad? He was a good man, he reasoned, a man who didn't mind hard work and who worked hard at making life's work a little easier. Lydia teased him about his farfetched ideas, but pride shone in her eyes when one of his inventions worked, and he never ever neglected his chores to work on a new invention. He seldom partook of liquor and then only a jigger or two, was slow to anger, not given to mercurial moods, and certainly not the least bit violent. Sure, he had his faults, but no man on Earth could love her more than he did. She could do far worse than he.

Ty broke off a piece of grass and chewed on it for a spell. Its sweet taste combined with the movements of his lips and tongue brought kissing Lydia to mind and soon led to other things he hadn't done with her yet but wanted to do. He had to have Lydia, no matter the cost. He'd lived in Hudson's Mill for almost a year, and so far no one had an inkling of the truth. Maybe they never would. Maybe he wouldn't ever have to tell her. If he tried real hard, maybe he could forget it all himself. He seldom thought of himself as Willy Tyler anymore, seldom recalled much of anything beyond the war. If he could just put those memories behind him, too, convince himself that none of it had ever happened, then he could live with the lies. Yes, that might work. It was certainly worth a try.

Smiling for the first time all day, he pushed himself away from the tree and went back to splitting firewood. When he finished, he'd fix himself a little supper, then spruce up the house. Tomorrow, he'd test the clothes washer he'd invented, and when Lydia came back, he'd present it to her as his wedding gift. She'd be surprised—not at his ingenuity, which she had grown accustomed to, but at the mention of a wedding. Then, he'd tell her to start planning their wedding because a preacher was coming to Hudson's Mill.

Ten

Thirty-two years of living in the mountains hadn't dulled Steele Montgomery's reverence for their beauty. On the contrary, his awe at their majesty increased with the changing of each season, but the coming of spring thrilled him most of all. Spring crept up the mountains about a hundred feet a day, transforming the almost barren slopes into wave upon wave of color as the dogwoods, rhododendrons, chestnuts, and other bushes and trees burst into bloom.

The spring of 1865 had worn an especially bright crown, for it marked not only the end of a long, hard winter, but the end of a long, hard war as well. Nestled snugly in all ends are beginnings, and Steele's heart had embraced the promise of a new beginning with the same exuberance for life as a wild crocus thrusting its head through a crusty cap of snow.

It had taken almost a month to get mustered out and another two weeks to get home. The snow had long been gone from White Oak Flats, judging from the blanket of green that spread out below him as far as the eye could see. Home. At last, he was home. His heart soared with the word, sprouting wings and flying straight to the Montgomery farm. As much as he wanted to break into a run, to re-meld his body with his heart, the absence of his lower left leg prevented such quick movement. Indeed, his entire body ached from days of traversing rugged terrain and compelled him to take a short rest.

Settling himself on a boulder, he shaded his eyes against the glare of the late afternoon sun and gazed at the peaceful valley dotted with houses and barns, crisscrossed with split-rail fences, and patched with brown, furrowed fields, green pastures, and clear springs that sparkled like gems. Here and there, small orchards created speckled squares, while Pigeon River meandered its way through the valley and disappeared in a stand of hardwoods hugging a slope on the other side. Somewhere up that slope, behind the trees, lay a fairly flat shelf just begging for someone to build a cabin on it. He'd been thinking he ought to be that someone.

For a while, of course, he'd stay at the farm, fatten up a bit on his mother's cooking, and whittle him a leg so he didn't have to use a crutch to get around. Then he'd lay in a supply of firewood and make all the necessary repairs around the place. With only women to tend to it for the past four years, the farm had probably run down some, maybe so much he'd have to stay through the winter, but come next spring, he was going to build that cabin.

What he was going to do with the rest of his life afterwards gaped uncertainly at the moment. He'd always thought he'd get married and raise a few children along with his corn, wheat, oats, and rye, but he wasn't at all sure now how well he could handle the demands of farming—nor could he imagine a woman wanting to shackle herself to a man crippled in both body and soul. Better to live alone, hunting and fishing when he felt like it, planting a little garden behind the cabin so he'd have some potatoes and beans, and filling the rest of his hours with reading and whittling and maybe even a little writing from time to time. It wouldn't be such a bad life, not if he had his family to visit on Sundays and the mountains to keep him company the rest of the time.

He'd decide all that later. Now, all he wanted to do was see his mother and his two sisters again, to sit at the supper table with the three of them and reminisce about old times over a plate of wild greens seasoned with a little sidemeat, a pone of cornbread soaked in pot liquor, and a tall glass of cool buttermilk. If the orchard had borne well last year, maybe Maw'd still have some dried peaches or apples on hand and would make fried pies for dessert.

His mouth watering and his stomach grumbling, Steele let his gaze roam back to the valley, where he searched for a glimpse of the Montgomery farm through the hilly woodlot that masked the view, even from this height, except in winter. But he couldn't see anything, not even a thin column of smoke from the cookstove. Oh well, a cold supper was better than none at all. Tomorrow he'd chop some wood and gather some wild greens; tonight, he'd enjoy the simple pleasure of being home. If he hurried, he could get there by nightfall.

Driven by a force far greater than physical strength, he stepped out of the woodlot while the gauzy haze of twilight still clung to the valley. He spied the house then, or rather what had been the house, for all that remained were the chimney and a pile of charred rubble. His heart lurched, stopping him cold, and he blinked at suddenly moist eyes, thinking surely the pale light was playing tricks on him. But no, there it all was, just as he'd originally seen it, as clear as though the sun rode high in the sky.

Where was Maw? Where were Sissy and Susan? Out of the corner of his eye, he saw three fresh mounds of earth, but he refused to turn his head and look at them, refused even to acknowledge that they were there. He broke into a hobbling run, moving faster than he'd ever imagined he could, calling "Maw!" at the top of his lungs. Around the pile of rubble he went, his eyes now pouring tears, his lips trembling as he continued to cry the names of his family. There were no other sounds in the twilight, not even that of a lone cricket chirping, not even the whisper of a breeze in the treetops. Only his voice, growing hoarser by the minute, and that of his heart thrumming in his ears, thrumming louder and louder, threatening to tear itself asunder.

And then, from somewhere deep in the woodlot, came the lonely cry of a whippoorwill, a sound as mournful as any Steele Montgomery had ever heard.

Without his realizing it, his steps had taken him to the three fresh mounds of earth. A final glimmer of light fell upon the three wooden crosses, illuminating three names: Mattie, Sissy, Susan. The crutch slipped from under his left arm and he collapsed upon the ground, deep sobs wrenching from his throat, his hands tearing at his hair.

The whippoorwill called to him again, then all was silent.

He awoke to a blazing sun and the nicker of a horse.

"Marauders," a familiar voice said. "I'm sorry you had to find out this way."

Steele looked up at the black-garbed figure of Parson John, founder and preacher of the Gloryroad Methodist Church in White Oak Flats, but he quickly dropped his gaze when the sunlight burned his stinging eyes. "When?" he rasped.

"Last week."

"Did you—" Steele couldn't finish the question.

"Bury them? Yes, they got a proper funeral."

Using his crutch for support, Steele rose to his feet. "Much obliged."

"I'm sorry, son," Parson John repeated.

"Save your pity"—Steele bit off each word—"and tell

me why. Why did God allow this to happen? They were good Christians. You know that."

"It's not for us to question. Isaiah says that good folks perish before their time because God is taking them away from evil days ahead, and he assured us that the godly shall rest in peace. Your mama and sisters are at peace, son."

Steele shook his head in denial. They weren't at peace, nor would they be until their deaths had been avenged.

"Don't lose your faith," the preacher advised. "Your soul is in tatters now, but it will mend. In time, you will understand. As Paul said, now you're seeing through a glass darkly, but in time, it will all be made clear to you."

Steele saw clearly now. With startling clarity, he knew exactly what he was going to do. He was going after the marauders. He was going to track them down and kill them, but first he'd make them suffer, just the way he figured they made his mother and sisters suffer.

"You're welcome to come home with me, stay with me and the missus for a spell. We've got your chickens and livestock, and I'm sure the men will be happy to help you rebuild here."

Steele was only half-listening. The trail was already cold, and he was too weak to track a wounded bear right now. He needed time to get his strength back, to whittle a leg and get used to wearing it. He needed time to find out everything he could about the men who'd done this and to formulate a plan. He wanted to catch them as completely off guard as they had caught his family. But the first time he showed up in a strange place and started asking questions, his intentions would become suspect. Unless . . .

As he gave Parson John's black broadcloth suit and wide-brimmed black hat closer scrutiny, a plan began to take shape. Preachers were never suspect. His conscience told him it was wrong to hide behind the cloth. He reminded his conscience that his soul had been ripped in two. What better way to regain his faith and find the men at the same time?

"I'd like to go home with you, Parson," he said. "I thank you kindly for the invitation and for all you did here."

That had been almost a year ago. He'd spent the intervening ten months recuperating from the war, studying at the seminary in Knoxville, and interning with Bishop Marley, all the time chafing at the delay in pursuing the marauders, yet certain he'd made the right decision. Somewhere along the way, he'd begun to realize there was a lot of good in what he was doing, and only occasionally did his conscience prick him concerning his motive. His major concern, however, was that someone else would kill the bastards before he got the chance.

"An eye for an eye," the Bible said. Steele interpreted that to mean a life for a life. The folks back in White Oak Flats had told him they thought the Scoggins brothers and some fellow named Williams might have been the ones who'd killed his mother and sisters. No one knew who these men were or where they'd come from, but a man they'd left for dead had lived long enough to name them. They were a bad lot, folks said, who preyed on those unable to protect or defend themselves.

Were there not stories of other families who'd suffered at the marauders' hands, he'd think that perhaps they were nothing more than a legend. Of late, those stories had dwindled. The last attack he'd heard about was some three months old. Perhaps some other avenger had already found them. Perhaps they were already dead. Steele supposed he could live with that, but he had to know if it were true. He had to keep searching, keep asking, until he knew for certain. Only then would he be whole again.

* * *

"To every thing," the Bible also said, "there is a season." So it was true with the heart and soul. Steele's soul was deeply imbedded in the snows of winter and had been hibernating there far too long, but his heart . . . well, his heart pumped with the blood of rejuvenation.

Something had happened to him in Peculiar Cove, something as invigorating and as full of promise as spring itself. As he rode Dusty along mountain trails alive with the delicate pink and white blossoms of dogwood, through narrow, rocky streams swollen with melting snow, across valleys green with new grass and bright with wildflowers, he marveled not only at the wonder of the Earth renewing itself, but at his own apparent spiritual renewal as well.

Perhaps, he reasoned, all he'd ever needed was another spring to revive his doldrums. *You know better,* his inner voice countered. He supposed he did. He'd been dreading spring. He'd lost his leg in the spring. The South lost the war in the spring. His mother and sisters were brutally murdered in the spring. The coming of spring, he'd thought, would serve as a cruel reminder of all those past wounds, reviving all the emotional pain, plunging him backward into winter instead of forward into summer. Had he not gone to Peculiar Cove, had he not met Betsy Tyler, he reckoned that was exactly what would have happened to him, too.

With his heart thus near to bursting with the miracle of resurrection, he discovered a joy in meditation, a joy in meeting people, a joy in performing the work of the Lord that he hadn't known existed. Suddenly, his head fairly sang with psalms and psalters instead of commandments and doctrine. Suddenly, the work he was doing for the Church took on new meaning, new purpose. Suddenly, he didn't mind so much taking the time to stop at homes along the way and conduct prayer meetings with the families, even if such visits did prolong his journey to Hudson's Mill. The important thing was to arrive there

MOUNTAIN MOONLIGHT 135

by service on Sunday, and he reckoned he'd manage that with time to spare.

"A preacher's really coming here? For true? When? Does this mean we kin finely be married?"

For a moment, Ty wallowed in Lydia's enthusiasm over his announcement. Pleasing her, he'd discovered, brought him tremendous gratification. Besides, he liked drawing out the suspense. When she started thumping on his shoulder, though, he knew she was quickly losing patience with him.

"Grandma Carter says it's true. She doesn't know exactly when, only that it's supposed to be soon."

Lydia's eyes opened even wider and she dramatically clutched her heart. Drama infused all her reactions, which oftimes complicated discerning how she honestly felt. This time, though, Ty knew she was truly excited.

"I'll git started right away on my dress," she babbled, "and I'll ask Esther to be my bridesmaid. Course, I druther have Rachel, but she prob'bly shouldn't be traveling so fur just yet. We kin have the weddin' in the parlor, or maybe over there in the meadow. It don't look like rain. What do ye thank?"

She wasn't going to like what he thought, but he'd made up his mind to say it anyway. He tempered the blow with a chuckle and a hug. "I think you need to calm down. Let's just talk to the preacher this time and have the wedding when he comes back."

She pushed away from him, her blue eyes awash with tears. "But we've already waited so long!"

Sighing, Ty pulled her back into his embrace. "Then another month or so shouldn't make much difference. Besides, if we wait, then Rachel can come." When she didn't agree with him, he added, "Wouldn't you like to have some time to plan the wedding? You just said you had to make your dress. You can't do that overnight."

"Well . . ." she hedged.

"I'm not going to run off and leave you, Lydia. Things will work out better this way. You'll see."

When he felt her hesitant nod against his chest, Ty backed away and took her hand. It was time to show her the clothes washer. "I made you a wedding present. Come, let me show you."

Seldom in a hurry and usually downright finicky about where he put his feet, Dusty meticulously picked his way along the rocky bank of Hudson's Creek. The mule's predilection to such behavior combined with the warmth of the afternoon sun and the sweet orchestration of warbling birds lulled Steele into a lethargic serenity that overrode his eagerness to reach Hudson's Mill. Indeed, he'd given in so completely to the mule's gentle swaying that he was almost asleep.

And then out of nowhere a piercing scream destroyed the peace, catching mule and rider unawares. Steele jerked awake and Dusty stumbled, and the next thing Steele knew, he was in the creek and Dusty had bolted.

"Come back, you no-account mule!" he hollered to no avail, leaving Steele with no choice but to extricate himself from the creek and either wait for the mule to return or walk until he caught up with the varmint. He chose to walk.

Luckily, he'd fallen between the larger rocks, thus averting any real physical harm, although he expected his arm and shoulder would be covered in little pebble-shaped bruises come tomorrow. He wobbled to his feet, collected his hat, which had lodged between two rocks, and counted himself blessed to have come through unscathed. Apparently, however, someone else hadn't fared so well, judging from the sound of the screams that had initiated his fall and persisted in short bursts. Now that he listened more closely, he realized that the screams weren't punctuated with pauses so much as gurgles.

Concerned that the screamer might be drowning, Steele moved as quickly as his gimp leg allowed toward the source of the yelling, which was upstream and not too far away. With his view fairly unobstructed, he was amazed that he couldn't see someone in the creek. As high-pitched as the shrieks were, however, they could be coming from a child, and a child caught behind or between some of the larger rocks might be difficult to see. He pushed himself harder, relief coming with each cry, near-panic arising as the cries grew both weaker and farther apart.

When he broke through a thick growth of willows and saw at last what was going on, Steele had to clamp a hand over his mouth to keep from laughing out loud. Someone had rigged a flue from the stream to a large wooden tub and set a small waterwheel to catch the flow. An assortment of garments turned on the wheel, and soapy water spilled over the sides of the tub and through holes in the bottom. The contraption smacked of ingenuity and might work quite efficiently were it not currently occupied by a woman who'd somehow fallen into the tub and whose repeated attempts to get herself out interfered with the mechanism. Each time her head bobbed up, she screeched for someone named Ty.

Assured now that her life was not in immediate danger, Steele slowed his pace, as much to enjoy the show as to rest his legs, which were beginning to ache. First, she jumped up, grabbed hold of the wheel, and tried to use it to pull herself up. Its constant downward spin, however, pushed her back in. Then, she turned and grasped the sides of the tub with both hands, but before she could wrangle her way out, the wheel caught her in the backside and pushed her in again. Resolutely, she jumped up and caught the wheel again. That time, it spit a garment into her face. She let go of the wheel, gurgled while she clawed the wet cloth from her face, hurled it to the ground, and grabbed the wheel again.

Steele couldn't recall ever seeing anyone more determined to win a losing battle in his life. Nor did he think he'd ever seen anyone look more absurd than this woman, who wore a cap of soap suds that slipped from side to side as she jumped and fell, but never completely slid off her head. A dollop of suds sat on the end of her nose, looking for all the world like a spoonful of whipped cream crowning a bowl of peach cobbler, while other dollops perched on her shoulders and the swell of her bosom.

"You can quit hollering, ma'am. I'll get you out!" Steele shouted over her screams. Before he could reach her, though, a young man dashed up from out of nowhere, thrust his arms around her rib cage, and had her out of the tub. She shivered violently, then straightened her back, let out a loud "Harrumph," and marched off toward a nearby house, still wearing the soap suds along with what was left of her pride.

"I'm done for now," the young man said, shaking his head in what appeared to be a mixture of confusion and chagrin. He was a pleasant-looking youngster, maybe twenty or twenty-one, tall and lanky with a shock of reddish brown hair, affable hazel eyes that crinkled at the corners, and feet way too big for his lean frame.

"Maybe not," Steele said, finally allowing himself to smile.

"Thanks for trying to rescue Lydia. I'm sorry you got wet. She didn't thrash you, did she?"

Steele laughed then, a full-bodied guffaw that rang through the hills. He liked this young man. He liked him a lot. "She never touched me, son. You got to her before I did."

"Then how—"

Steele started to tell him that the young woman was responsible for getting him wet, at least indirectly, but changed his mind and said simply, "I fell in the creek. My mule threw me." He moved closer to the tub and scrutinized its mechanism. It was an amazingly simple machine that seemed to be working quite well now that the woman wasn't gumming it up. "Did you create this . . . *contraption*? Pardon me, but I don't know what to call it."

"It's a machine for washing clothes. I call it a clothes washer."

Steele nodded his approval. "Makes sense to me. Does it work?"

The young man scratched his head. "I think so. Leastaways, it did for me."

"Well, I expect that once your wife learns to use this clothes washer properly, she'll be thanking you for inventing it."

"I hope you're right, sir, but Lydia's not my wife. Course, she will be, as soon as the preacher gets here and we can make arrangements." He eyed Steele more closely then, and a wide smile shortened his long face. "You wouldn't happen to be the preacher we've been expecting, would you?"

Steele thrust out his hand and introduced himself. "I'm a preacher," he added, "though perhaps not the one you were expecting."

"You are if you're circuit-riding for the Methodists."

"That would be me. And you are . . . ?"

"Ty," the young man said, pumping Steele's hand enthusiastically. "Ty Williams. Pleased to make your acquaintance."

Eleven

Williams!

The name slammed into Steele's brain with the force of a cannon discharge. Not this friendly young man with the laughing hazel eyes. No. He couldn't be either a rapist or a murderer. Steele didn't believe it was possible.

"I've been looking for a fellow named Williams." *Whoa!* It wouldn't do to show his hand. *Quick. Think of something.* "He ran off with my cousin Ella—Ella Scoggins." Steele did have a cousin named Ella, who was only twelve years old, but her last name was Murphy, not Scoggins. As long as he was stretching the truth, he figured it wouldn't hurt to cast the other name he had and see if Ty took the bait. "Her family hasn't heard from her since and they're awfully worried."

Ty shook his head. "I can't help you there."

"You got any relatives hereabouts?"

The light went out of the hazel eyes and Ty shifted his weight from one big foot to the other. "No, sir. Don't have a single relative left. Anywhere."

The "anywhere" seemed to be an afterthought, which bothered Steele as much as Ty's sudden nervousness. He was hiding something. If Steele were a gambling man, he'd make bet on it.

"You know anyone else named Williams from around here?"

"Not from around here, no, sir. But Williams is a fairly

common name. Could be a whole mess of 'em living across the ridge, and I'd never know it."

Steele didn't believe that either, not with a gristmill sitting less than a hundred yards from where they were standing. A gristmill drew folks for miles around. Nothing would be won by arguing the point, though, so he changed the subject. "When would you and Lydia be wanting to marry?"

"N-next t-time you come around. Wh-when do you r-reckon that will be?"

Ty's stuttering surprised Steele, who'd thought talking about the wedding would help the young man relax. It was natural, though, to be nervous about a wedding, especially for a man who'd never sowed his wild oats. If that were the case with this Ty Williams, then he definitely wasn't one of the men Steele was looking for.

"I can't say exactly," Steele replied. "About a month more than likely, maybe as long as five weeks. Sorry I can't be more accurate, but you see I only recently took this circuit, and I haven't finished making the rounds yet."

"T-that's close enough."

A moment of awkward silence followed as Steele waited for Ty to offer him a place to change clothes and rest for a bit. When no offer was forthcoming, he turned to collect his bag from Dusty's back, hoping Ty would take the hint, and remembered the mule had run off and hadn't returned. Without thinking, he muttered, "Dad-blame mule!"

Ty Williams burst into laughter. For the life of him, Steele couldn't see the hilarity in his situation. Everything he owned was on that dad-blame mule's back. *Dad-blame* . . . he—an ordained minister and emissary of the Methodist Church—had said *dad-blame!* Grateful the young man thought his blasphemous slip of the tongue was funny rather than appalling, Steele laughed himself.

"I reckon you'd like to get out of those wet clothes," Ty said between chuckles.

"I reckon I would, but I don't have any others right now."

Ty looked him up and down. "I'd lend you some of mine, but you're a mite bigger."

"I suppose the sun'll dry these pretty fast."

"Will your dad-blame mule come back?"

That got Steele to laughing again. "Eventually," he sputtered.

"What would you like to do until then? Are you hungry?"

"No, but I'd love a cup of coffee, if you have any."

Ty nodded. "The drummer came by last week."

"I need something to sober me up. It was all I could do to keep from laughing at your wife—I mean, Miss Lydia."

"That was pretty funny," Ty agreed. "Just be careful not to say anything about it in front of her. She can get riled up mighty easy."

They started walking toward the log house, which though small and unpretentious wore a cozy atmosphere with its deep porch and gingham-curtained windows. "Mrs. Hudson's got an apple pie cooling. I don't know about you, but I dearly love warm apple pie with my coffee."

Steele decided he might be hungry after all. "Mrs. Hudson?"

"Lydia's mother."

"And you help Lydia's father with the mill?"

"I did before he died. I run it by myself now."

"Must be dull this time of year."

Ty opened the front door and held it for Steele to enter ahead of him. "It is, but I don't mind. Gives me a chance to work on my inventions."

Unwittingly, Ty had opened another door. "Perhaps you could show me some more of them later," Steele suggested. "And if you have time, I'd appreciate your taking me around and introducing me to folks."

"It would pleasure me greatly, preacher," Ty said, his face beaming, "on both counts."

Something happened to Ty Williams's face when he smiled, something that struck a chord in Steele's memory, leaving him with an eerie sense of déjà vu. There was also something oddly familiar about Ty's speech patterns, which were a tad unusual for someone native to these mountains. Steele felt as though he'd met the young man before, yet he was certain he hadn't. Then, why . . . ?

Mrs. Hudson's greeting interrupted his musings, and her incessant chatter thwarted further deliberation on the subject for the time being. Steele tucked the feeling away, thinking to retrieve it later, when he was alone and without distractions.

Over the years, Betsy had grown so accustomed to being alone that she didn't quite know how to handle the sudden flurry of activity surrounding her. True, she'd never lived alone, but rather apart from a society that had always respected her privacy—until now. She never knew from one hour to the next, let alone one *day* to the next, who was going to knock on her door.

First, there were Molly and Imer, who'd come calling the day she'd been working in the garden and neither in the mood nor proper attire to receive visitors. The two sisters came back, though, on Wednesday morning shortly after the Rev left. Betsy had known both women since childhood, but she knew Molly better, she and Molly being of a similar age. Although she'd never spent much time in their company—or in anyone else's, for that matter—she'd heard all about Molly's marriage to James Dunbar some three years ago from Auntie Kee.

"Well, hit looks like Molly Bailey's spinsterin' days is

over," the older woman had said, "but that sister of her'n, Imer, is plain enough to stop a eight-day clock. I don't reckon they's any hope for her. Course, I ain't got room to tawlk. Look at me and you. We's both old maids our ownselfs."

Betsy had staunchly denied that they were any such thing. "We're single ladies—by choice. Maybe Imer is, too."

Whatever else Imer might or might not be, she was definitely a talker. She and Molly both. Their effortless chatter served to emphasize Betsy's social deficiencies, but before she knew it, she had relaxed and was chattering right back.

"Now that we have a preacher, we need a church," Molly said. "We cain't just keep meeting in the clearing or at Uncle Begley's store when hit's raining."

"That's right," Imer chimed in.

They weren't going to get an argument from Betsy. She didn't relish the prospect of perching on a stack of crates even one more Sunday, let alone for every service from now on out. A far more important consideration, though, was the good of the community. A church building could serve as a school during the week, and Peculiar Cove needed a school.

What would the Rev think when he returned to Peculiar Cove and discovered the townsfolk had built a church in his absence? He'd glow with pride, that's what. Making him happy appealed to Betsy far more than she ever would have believed possible. Yes, they needed a church.

"Surely the men can build one," Betsy said.

"Course, they kin," Molly agreed. "But ye know men. God must've give 'em all lazy natures, 'cause I don't know one with much gumption. Somebody has got to build a far under 'em to get 'em to move."

"First," Betsy pointed out, "we have to find a place to build it."

"We got that," Imer said, her mouth full of cake. She took a gulp of tea to wash it down. "Uncle Begley said he'd give us the land. Course, it's got to be cleared."

"Then somebody needs to decide how it ought to look and how big it needs to be," Molly added. "As we was comin' up yore walk, Imer and I was thanking about how nice hit'd be to build it out'n real lumber, like yore house. Reckon how much that'd cost?"

Before Betsy could answer, Imer said, "And we was talkin' about how nice hit'd be to have one o' them little pointy towers with a bell in it."

"Hold on a minute." Although Betsy was beginning to catch some of their enthusiasm, she was afraid they were getting a little ahead of themselves. "While I admire your ambition, maybe we need to proceed a little slower—you know, take time to thoroughly think this through."

A dimpled smile transformed Molly's round face from almost plain to downright pretty. Betsy was so busy contemplating the metamorphosis that it took her a minute to latch on to where Molly was leading her. "I'm so glad to hear you say that, Betsy. We—Imer and me—was hopin' you'd decide t' help us out, you havin' book-larnin' and all."

Help them out? When had she become involved in their plans?

"I spect you could draw up a pattryn," Imer said, "and even figure out how much lumber to get."

Their notions had Betsy's head spinning. Talk about a metamorphosis! Almost overnight, she'd gone from being the town crazy to one whose opinion and education were highly valued—at least by Molly and Imer. Whatever had happened to elevate her to such status? she wondered. All she'd done was let the preacher use one of her many spare bedrooms . . . and gone to church.

"Course, we don't even know how to get the lumber," Molly was saying. "But we figured ye'd know, yore papa having done got some to build this fine house with and all."

Betsy pulled herself back into the conversation, which someone had to temper with a little common sense. "Lumber is going to take money. Lots of money. You can't trade a pig and a couple of chickens for the materials to build a church. Then once it's finished, you'll need pews and a pulpit and a baptistry and prayerbooks—"

"And a organ." Imer eyed the elaborately carved pump organ sitting in the parlor.

You can't have Auntie Kee's organ, Betsy wanted to scream at them. Instead, she bit her tongue and tried another dose of logic. "And I don't know anything about construction. Papa built this house before I was born. You need to talk to Uncle Begley about lumber. He ought to know how to get it and what it will cost. I don't even know where the nearest sawmill is located."

"But ye kin draw us a pitcher to go by," Imer insisted.

Willy could. Willy could design a beautiful church and answer all their questions. He'd always been good at such things. But not Betsy. She shook her head. "I'm not the person you need to be talking to."

Molly reached from the settee where she was sitting to Betsy's chair and laid her hand on Betsy's arm. "Won't ye at least try?"

"I wouldn't know where to start." She racked her brain, trying to recall where she'd seen a church similar to the one Imer described, one with a bell tower and a steeple. "In one of Papa's books!" she blurted out, surprising Molly and Imer almost as much as she did herself. "I don't need to draw a picture," she explained. "Someone else already did. It may take me a while to find it, though."

Imer smiled, which made her look more pleasant but no less plain. "Hit's like ye said. No need to get in a hip and a hurry."

"That's right," Molly said. "We'll get the men started on clearing the lot while ye find us that pitcher and figure out how we're gonna pay fer the lumber."

Betsy was sure she hadn't agreed to raise money for the church, but apparently Molly and Imer thought she had. Didn't they understand what obstacles they were up against? Few people in the community had two coppers to rub together. They survived mostly on barter and trade and what food they could grow and livestock they could raise. The only real cash crop was sourmash whiskey, and there was no way Betsy was going to be party to raising money for a church with whiskey sales.

Or did Molly and Imer think she was so very wealthy she could just donate the money? Papa had left her what appeared to be a small fortune, but then she'd spent more than half of it buying Willy fancy clothes and paying for four years of school all at one time. The war shot prices sky high and they hadn't come down yet, might not ever for all she knew. She still had the jewelry, but she couldn't quite imagine Uncle Begley taking it for payment. What would he do with a bunch of fancy jewels? How could she explain all this to Molly and Imer—so poor themselves they could make what little money she had left last for a lifetime—without sounding selfish?

Before she could think of a way to weasel out, the two women thanked her for the tea and cake and took their leave. Perhaps that would be the end of it, but Betsy doubted it. There had to be a way out. A graceful way out.

While she was sitting in the parlor mulling over her predicament, Tom Dickerson showed up. "Uncle Begley sent me over," he explained. "Said ye had some rotten wood. From the looks of it, the whole porch floor needs t' come off. I kin fix it up fer ye real nice, if'n ye're interested."

She didn't know Tom well at all, but Uncle Begley

wouldn't have sent him had he not thought Tom would do a proper job. "I am. I've been meaning to find someone to take care of this, but I really didn't know who to ask."

"Well, I'm your man, if'n ye ain't in a hurry. I got a little farm, ye know, to take keer of, but hit don't take all my time." He glanced at the peeling paint on the clapboards, then looked down at his feet. "There's other things I kin do fer ye around here, too, ma'am. I kin make this place look brand new again, if'n ye're of a mind to fix hit up."

Betsy thought she might be of such a mind, but she cautioned herself to take her own advice and go slowly. "We'll start with the porch, Tom, then we'll see."

He grinned at her. "Yes, ma'am."

"How long do you think it will take to get the lumber?"

"Oh, 'bout a month, I reckon."

A few days ago, she wouldn't have thought of a month as long at all, but now it seemed like a year. A few days ago, she'd been unconcerned about how much she'd let her family home go to ruin, but that was before the Rev had come close to breaking his good leg on her front porch. She chewed her bottom lip. The house did need a coat of paint, even if it did take most of her reserves. "Go ahead and order the paint, too."

His grin broadened. "Yes, ma'am! I'll go terrectly to Uncle Begley's store and tek keer of hit. I kin get the house all scraped and ready while we're waitin'."

As he turned to leave, it occurred to Betsy that a conspiracy might well be afloat. First, Molly and Imer asked her about lumber, now Tom was ordering lumber for her porch, and all in the span of an hour. Surely Molly and Imer knew the habits and talents of everyone in the community better than she. Why hadn't they gone to Tom Dickerson about the lumber instead of her? Was he in on it, too?

She called to Tom, stopping him halfway down the steps.

"Did ye want sumpin' else?"

She did, but she needed some more information first. "Are you in a rush?"

"No, ma'am."

"You can quit calling me 'ma'am,' Tom. Betsy will do just fine."

"Yes, ma'am—I mean, yes, Miss Betsy."

"Are you any good at putting up buildings?"

"I ain't never done one all by my lonesome, but I've helped with many a one."

"And you like carpentry?"

"Oh, yes, ma'am! It's my fav'rite thing in the whole wide world, next to eatin', that is."

"Do you think you could supervise the building of a church?"

He scratched his jaw and allowed her question some thought before replying, giving her the impression that this was the first time he'd heard anything about the project Molly and Imer were so determined to launch.

"Yes'm, I thank I could. But I don't reckon I know 'xactly what it art to look like."

Neither did Molly and Imer. That was why they'd come to her. How convenient that she'd talked to them moments before Tom showed up. Too convenient. Someone had carefully laid this plan, and now too many of the important details had been dumped in her lap. Somehow, she had to find a way to show Molly and Imer and everyone else in Peculiar Cove that they couldn't afford to build a fine church, that they'd have to settle for one made of logs. They just weren't looking at this realistically. Presenting them with actual figures might sway them.

"If I show you a picture, can you determine how much lumber you'd need?"

"I reckon so."

"And you and Uncle Begley can then determine the cost of all the building materials, including paint and windows and such things?"

"I reckon so."

"If you'll come back this afternoon, I'll have the picture for you."

When Tom came back, he brought Uncle Begley with him. Auntie Kee invited them in for coffee, which they drank in the kitchen.

Betsy laid the book she'd found on the table and opened it to a sketch of a modest chapel with a single entrance. Her conscience pricked her just a mite for purposely omitting the sketches with two entrances: one for the women, another for the men, which was the custom for mountain folk. It was a custom for which she could see no valid purpose. Besides, building two entrances seemed a waste of both materials and manpower to her. She turned the book so Tom could get a better look at it, hoping neither he nor Begley questioned the single door.

"This building will seat a hundred people comfortably," she said, tapping the page, "and it has a small bell tower and a vestibule."

"What's a vestibule?" Tom asked.

"An entry room with doors on each end—one that comes in from the outside and another that goes into the sanctuary. I think we can live without a vestibule, and I know we can manage without a bell tower. A vestibule would be nice, though. We could put pegs on the wall on one side so people would have a place to hang their coats and hats. And we could wall off the other side to create a private space for the preacher to work or talk to folks when he's here. You know, sort of an office."

The more Betsy talked, the more excited about this

project she became. And to her relief, neither Tom nor Begley mentioned the need for separate entrances.

"Why don't you figure it all three ways, and then we'll decide." *The problem is how we're going to pay for it,* she mentally added—and then an idea struck her so hard she practically hollered. "The church!"

All three looked askance at her. "I forgot about the Methodists," she explained. "Maybe they can help us." She bit her lip. "Only, I wouldn't know who to write to or even where, but they must have a district office."

"Man name o' Bishop Marley, up in Knoxville," Begley said.

Betsy started to ask Begley how he knew, but Tom's fascination with the series of lined diagrams that accompanied the sketch snagged her attention.

"What's these fer?" he asked, tapping them with an index finger.

Betsy explained that they were drawings of the floor plan, roof design, and elevations. "This is a book on architecture." She closed it and pointed to the title: *The American Builder's Companion* by Asher Benjamin. "It was first published about forty years ago," she said, "and, according to my father's handwritten note in the front, it is widely used as an architectural style book covering the Colonial through the Greek Revival periods. There are seventy plates showing construction details, floor plans, and elevations. Would you like to have it?"

His eyes widened in obvious interest, but a look of abject embarrassment quickly replaced his enthusiasm. "Hit wouldn't do me no good, Miss Betsy."

"Sure it would! You just have to learn how to read the diagrams."

"That's just it," he mumbled, his voice so low Betsy had to strain to hear him. "I cain't read a-tall."

She frowned in confusion. "But you said you could determine how much lumber you'd need."

"Oh, I kin cipher with the best of 'em. Paw teached me ever'thang he knowed 'bout 'rithmetic."

"Why don't you take it anyway? It's just gathering dust in the library."

"I'm much obliged, Miss Betsy." With more reverence than Betsy had ever thought to give a book, he held the volume for a moment, then set it aside. "Don' want t' spill no cawfee on it," he said. "I ain't never owned no book before. 'Ceptin' the Bible, of course."

Begley cleared his throat rather loudly and abruptly changed the subject. "That's a mighty fine barn ye got, Bets."

"Thank you."

"Shame to let it go to waste."

Betsy wondered where he was headed, "I have no real need of horses or mules, but we do keep a cow."

"Any kind of ol' lean-to or shed'll do fer one measly animal," Begley observed.

"But I have a barn."

"Yes'm. A big barn. Does the roof leak?"

What a strange thing to ask! "A little bit. Just in one corner, though. Why?"

" 'Cause I been figurin' on where we could be holdin' sarvice, my store bein' too crowded, what'n'all."

Betsy couldn't believe what she was hearing. "And you want to use my barn? But it's full of old moldy hay and rats and Lord knows what other vermin. It wouldn't do at all."

Begley grinned. "Oh, we kin clean it up—and fix you a lean-to on the side fer your cow. I'll get a crew over here come mornin' soon. Hit'll work out just fine. Ye'll see."

Twelve

Auntie Kee gasped and her black eyes widened in horror. "Sarvice in a barn? Air ye addlepated?"

Begley grinned sheepishly. "I don' reckon I am. I been givin' this a passel o' figurin'."

"I like the idee myself," Tom said. "We could make some benches, rough 'uns o' course, jes' t' git us by. And I'll fix the roof."

"I still don' like it," Auntie Kee maintained.

Betsy wasn't sure she did, either. It just didn't seem appropriate, but she couldn't come up with a better idea. The suggestion also assuaged her conscience a bit. If she couldn't donate the money for the church, then at least she could offer the use of her barn.

Thinking about money reminded Betsy of the jewelry in the metal box. Now might be an opportune time to show a piece of it to Uncle Begley, but not in front of Tom and Auntie Kee. As far as she knew, no one in Peculiar Cove had any knowledge of the jewels except her, and the fewer people who knew, the better.

"Why don't you go on out to the barn and look at the roof," she said to Tom. "Maybe Auntie Kee will go with you."

The older woman frowned. "Tom kin find the barn by his ownself, Miss Betsy."

"But he can't show you how we can turn it into a church if you're in here, can he?" It was a terribly lame excuse, but it worked. Huffing, Auntie Kee rose and followed Tom outside.

The instant the door closed, Betsy told Uncle Begley to stay put and that she would be right back, then she dashed upstairs to her parents' bedchamber. In short order, she removed the box from behind the firescreen, selected the emerald ring, stowed the box again, and ran back downstairs, all the while planning her strategy. Foremost in her mind was the short time available to talk to Uncle Begley privately. Auntie Kee and Tom could return any minute.

"What in tarnation is goin' on?" he asked as she collapsed into her chair.

Betsy paused only long enough to catch her breath. "Can you keep a secret?"

It was a silly question, she supposed, for someone renowned for telling tales, but she had to ask. To her surprise, he said he could.

"Papa's money's almost gone."

"That's the secret?"

She nodded.

"We all knowed it was goin' t' run out sometime. I'm su'prised it lasted this long."

"But Mama had this ring. Can you use it to buy the paint and lumber Tom ordered for the house?"

Begley held the ring up to the window. The deep green stone sparkled in the sunlight. "If it's genuwine, it art to be enough. I'll have to send it to my banker-friend in Maryville."

"You can trust him?"

"I've sent him stones afore, mostly little'uns. Raw, o' course. They's all kinds o' stones in these hills—garnet, topaz, sapphire, even emerald. Folks find 'em now and then and trade 'em at the store fer yard goods and shoes and sech. I ain't never sent him one this big or already cut and polished, so I cain't say fur sure and certain."

He slipped the ring into his watch pocket and winked at her. "And don' you worry none. I ain't goin' t' tell. I already done you and Kee enough wrong t' last a lifetime."

When Betsy had time to reflect on the sudden change in Peculiar Cove, which wasn't often, she marveled at how the appearance of one stranger could cause such a furor of activity, especially among people as passive as mountain folk. Why, you could call most of them lazy to their faces and they wouldn't blink an eye. Such was the case no more. By the time she arose, washed, and ate breakfast, those same previously languid people were already gathering in her yard and barn and starting to work.

And work they did! With no apparent organization, they divided themselves into small groups to accomplish specific tasks. Tom and two other men repaired the leaking barn roof, while four youths eliminated the weeds and saplings in her yard. Some folks swept up the moldy hay, while others hauled it to an ever-growing pile some distance from the house. Everyone brought foodstuffs with them, and at least two of the women assisted Betsy and Auntie Kee with meal preparations for them all.

The truly amazing aspect of it all, however, was that this activity revolved around her—the town crazy, a woman no one had taken the least bit of interest in beyond deriding her character. She would have sworn they were frightened of her, terrified to come near her for fear some of her madness might rub off on them. But now, almost overnight, they treated her with respect and talked to her as though she were an old and trusted friend.

A part of her relished the change. It was only human nature to feel flattered. But it was also human nature, she reasoned, to view such peculiar and perplexing behavior from the townsfolk as suspect. People didn't just throw away ingrained notions without cause. Someone had pled her case well. Someone the townsfolk trusted implicitly. Someone who possessed personal knowledge of her sanity.

Auntie Kee? If so, why had she waited so long? The Rev? Folks liked him well enough, she supposed, and as a man of the cloth he commanded respect, but he didn't really know her that well. Besides, he'd had no opportunity to talk privately to anyone before Molly and Imer had come to visit Monday morning—except Uncle Begley.

Uncle Begley! Of course, he was the one. He saw more people on a regular basis than anyone else around. And due to his love for storytelling, he was more than likely largely responsible for spreading the tales about her in the first place. He'd made it clear when she gave him the ring that he felt guilty about it. What better way to assuage that guilt than to attempt to undo the harm he'd caused her?

In all fairness, Betsy conceded her own liability in fostering and nurturing the nasty rumors. She'd wanted people to stay away, and although she was beginning to enjoy the company and attention, she wasn't so sure the pendulum hadn't swung too far.

She supposed she could always fake lunacy again—and would if she had to. Knowing she had that option at her disposal offered little comfort, though, for a reversion could well damage the tenuous thread of trust and respect between her and the Rev. And it was his opinion, she realized, that meant more to her than any other.

She wondered how he'd view holding service in a barn. It was definitely unconventional, but she suspected he'd preached in surroundings no less odd. Besides, this was Peculiar Cove, where folks expected things to be a little off center. She wondered, too, how soon he'd be back. As each day passed and she grew more and more accustomed to her loss of solitude, she yearned more and more for his company above all others.

It was that yearning which occupied the tidbits of seclusion left to her. Although exhausted from the day's labors, she nevertheless lay awake for a while, sometimes for hours, recreating the thrill of his chaste kiss and pondering the awakening of her physical longing for intimate male companionship. This she found as baffling as the sudden changes in the people of Peculiar Cove, but unlike those changes, the kindling of desire frightened her almost as much as it excited.

What if the Rev was no different than the groping Rebel captain? She didn't want to believe they were the same, but they were both men and she had so little experience with men to fall back on. Her father and her brother had been men, too, she reasoned, and she couldn't imagine either of them ever treating a woman with anything less than the utmost respect. But they were her kinsmen. What did she really know about Steele Montgomery?

He was caring. After what must have been a long and exhausting day, he'd gone to the woods and looked until he found a Hercules'-club to ease her toothache. Someone like the Rebel captain would never have done that.

He was tolerant. He'd had every reason to blame her when he'd fallen on the porch and injured his leg. True, he'd slapped her when she bit him, but in the depths of her soul, she knew she would have reacted similarly, and he'd given her no other reason to believe he was a violent man.

He had other good qualities, too. He could laugh at himself. He was intelligent and well mannered. And he pretty much minded his own business.

As admirable as those qualities might be, their appeal paled in comparison to his vulnerabilities. Although Betsy couldn't delineate them, she knew Steele Montgomery fought his own host of demons. She embraced the kinship their mutual demons created between them, and yet feared that their struggles to overcome those demons would orchestrate the demise of that kinship in the end.

Revenge numbered among Steele Montgomery's resident demons. For the most part, it remained dormant, but every time Steele thought he was getting close to finding the three men who'd murdered his mother and sisters, his zeal tossed fuel to the demon and it flared in his soul. The fire then burned until temporary defeat extinguished it.

All the while that Ty Williams escorted Steele among the farms in the Hudson's Mill community, the fire burned in his soul. Perhaps somewhere, on one of these farms or in a small cabin or cave in the surrounding hills, dwelled the objects of his revenge. As usual, he counted on the trust his minister's garb begat to gain the information he so desperately sought. Now that he'd created the tale about his cousin Ella and the Williams boy she supposedly eloped with, he continued to use it. Folks appeared to be open and honest. No, they didn't know anyone named Scoggins, and Ty was the only Williams boy they'd ever known.

And did they ever love Ty Williams! If Steele was to believe everything he was told, there had never been another like Ty, who was trustworthy and honest and the most generous and helpful man who'd ever walked the earth. The young man was certainly talented, no doubt about that. Folks came one behind the other to gape at his clothes washer. Some even offered to pay him to construct the machine at their houses.

"Ain' it jes' the most bodacious contraption ye ever did see?" Grandma Carter asked Steele. They were standing in a semicircle of folks, watching Ty demonstrate how it worked. "When my niece Mary hears about it, she'll have to git one. That'd be my brother Dan's youngest. She lives over in Peculiar Cove. You been there, Preacher?"

"Just came from there."

"Ain' nothin' so odd 'bout Peculiar. I reckon I use to know why they called it that in the first place, but I've heared so many stories over the years, I've plumb disremembered which one's the truth."

"I don't think even Uncle Begley knows the truth anymore."

"Now that Begley, he's a tawlker." She launched into a monologue about Begley, during which Ty joined the onlookers. Between glad-handing and answering questions about the clothes washer, it took him awhile to get around to Steele and Grandma Carter, who were on the opposite side from where Ty had started. By that time, she'd returned to talking about Ty and his inventions.

"Did he show you how he piped water t' the house?"

"It's a simple procedure," Ty said, looking a bit sheepish. "You just find a spring on higher ground than the house and gravity takes care of the rest."

Steele suspected there was a bit more engineering involved than Ty let on. He knew there was a lot more to Ty Williams' identity and background than the young man wanted to admit. The first time he was alone with Grandma Carter, whom he'd learned knew more about everyone's business than common courtesy allowed, he worked the conversation around to Ty, a relatively easy feat.

"He must have made his mother proud," Steele said.

"I'm 'most sure he did," she replied, the twinkle in her eyes and her emphasis on the word *most* begging him to dig deeper.

He was happy to comply. "Why are you only *almost* sure? Didn't you know his mother?"

"Nope. Nobody around here did."

"Then his father must have been proud."

"I spec' ye're right."

"No one knew him either?"

She shook her head.

"An orphan, huh?" he guessed.

She lifted a bony shoulder. "Says his fam'ly's all dead."

"So he was old enough to remember his family when he was adopted."

The old woman hooted at that. "Adopted? Why would anybody want to adopt a growed man? Not that there ain't some what needs adoptin'. Take Romey Faircloth. Why, he must be gettin' nigh on to thirty year, but I ain't never seed a body need lovin' guidance more'n Romey. He'd be a good 'un for ye t' take under your wang, preacher."

As much as Grandma Carter seemed to enjoy telling tales on folks, she carefully guarded everything she said about Ty, as did everyone else Steele met. By the time folks gathered in the meadow by the mill for service on Sunday morning, Steele was convinced he'd run into another dead end. Yet, he refused to discount the feeling that Ty Williams was hiding something. Perhaps not rape or murder. Maybe not anything criminal at all. But Steele's instincts screamed that the boy feared exposure of something in his background.

It wasn't until the middle of Sunday service that Ty realized a circuit-riding preacher linked communities together. Once he got to thinking about it, his mind shut out everything else—the sermon, the meadow's sweet scent, the twitter of birds, the way the tall grass he was sitting in tickled his bare lower arms when the wind blew . . . everything.

Did the Reverend Montgomery's circuit include Peculiar Cove? Of course, it did. Peculiar was one of the largest settlements in this part of the Smokies. For all Ty knew, it might have even grown some in the six years he'd been gone. Maybe it had grown so much it had its own church with its own minister by now. And if it were a Methodist Church, then Steele would have no reason to go there. Ty didn't suppose it would hurt to ask. He'd have to be careful not to give anything away, just show a little more interest in Steele's travels and the growth of the Methodist Church. Should he learn that the preacher had, indeed, visited Peculiar Cove, Ty would tell him what he'd heard about Crazy Bets and hope Steele would say whether or not he'd met her.

No, he couldn't do that! Even mentioning her name could be dangerous. But he had to know. Somehow, he had to find out, not only to calm his anxiety, but because he needed to hear that his sister really wasn't crazy from someone who'd actually seen her. He could learn anything he wanted to know about Peculiar Cove from Grandma Carter if he just listened long enough, but he didn't want to believe what she was saying about Betsy.

He felt a pang of guilt, as he always did when he thought about Betsy. Ty didn't believe she'd lost her mind over him. He'd watched her cope with first Papa's and then Mama's death, and knew that she handled grief better than most people. If she really were crazy, something else had set her off, but if Grandma Carter knew what that something else was, she'd never said. His guilt stemmed from the lies he'd concocted when his survival depended on covering the truth, from allowing Betsy to continue to believe that he was dead, from not being there to help her if she needed him.

Because no one in Peculiar liked the government and most didn't care one way or the other about the war, he'd probably be safe going back. He could always say he'd been suffering from temporary memory loss, which was partially true, and that it had all suddenly come back to him. Or he could say the army had made a mistake. He'd heard about such things happening, about men returning home from the war to families who'd been notified of their deaths. To return to Peculiar Cove, however, put more than his life in jeopardy. He dared not risk allowing himself to return to Betsy's pampering ways and domineering control.

She'd done the best she could for him. He had to allow her that much. But what she considered best didn't come close to fitting Ty's notions about what he wanted to do with his life. He'd never even known who Willie Tyler was until he'd been in Maryville for a year, and then he'd only begun to scrape the surface when the war broke out. With foolish enthusiasm, he'd viewed military service as an adventure, never honestly expecting to see a single day of battle. God, had he been wrong!

A toe in his ribs jerked him out of memories best left buried. He looked up to see Lydia frowning down at him and realized he was the only person still sitting. He rose to his feet and joined in singing "Amazing Grace," plotting all the while to secure a spot near the preacher during dinner on the ground and praying he'd hear good news about Betsy.

One after another, folks moved forward to shake the preacher's hand and whisper in his ear. The congregation finished the last verse and started over again with the first. Soon, everyone had walked the aisle except Ty and Lydia. She tugged on his hand and he reluctantly accompanied her to the preacher's side.

"We'd like to declare our intent to marry up," she said, surprising Ty, who hadn't honestly stopped to consider the purpose behind they're going up together. He didn't know why she wanted to do this, since everyone knew already. There was simply no figuring out why womenfolk did some things.

"I'll be delighted to afford you two the opportunity,"

the preacher said. "Just stand right here till the hymn's over."

The public announcement entailed shaking hands with everybody there, even the smallest of children. By the time Ty and Lydia were free to serve their plates, every spot near the preacher was already taken, nor did Ty find another opportunity to talk to the reverend before the afternoon service. Immediately afterwards, Steele took his leave, explaining that he had an obligation to move on to other folks without further delay, while assuring them that he'd be back in four weeks or thereabouts.

With more than a little trepidation, Ty watched the preacher mount his pacing mule, which had come straggling back within an hour after bolting, just as Steele said he would. Ty wished he'd thought about Peculiar Cove and Betsy earlier, but there was nothing to do now but hope and pray that if the Reverend Montgomery ever met Betsy Tyler, he'd not make the connection between her and the young inventor in Hudson's Mill.

Assuming his calculations were fairly accurate, Steele didn't have to leave Hudson's Mill so early. His intention—and that of the Methodist Church—was to complete his circuit every four weeks. According to his map, Hudson's Mill lay slightly more than three-quarters around the lopsided circle, and he'd been on the circuit for only two and a half weeks. Therefore, he could have waited until tomorrow or even the next day to start out again. Were he even partially convinced that the men he sought lived near the area, he would have stayed and done some more visiting. As things turned out, he saw no reason to delay his departure. He might need the extra day or two somewhere else.

But that wasn't the only reason Steele was so eager to head out in the middle of the afternoon with no assurance he'd reach a farm or homestead before dark. Sleeping out in the open didn't bother him one whit, and the few miles he could make before nightfall put him that much closer to new territory—and to Peculiar Cove.

If anyone had told him a week ago that he could feel this way about a woman, any woman, he would have laughed himself hoarse. That he'd fallen for Betsy Tyler almost overnight magnified his amazement. Not that he expected anything permanent to come of it. This was nothing more than an infatuation, he assured himself, much like when he'd sparked eyes with Selma Thurlow back when their mouths were still too small for their teeth. It didn't matter where they were—school, church, community picnic, general store, even passing on the road—their gazes would lock and he'd get this weird queasiness in the pit of his stomach.

Then one warm June day when he was on his way to the creek, he saw her picking blackberries and decided he'd rather pick berries than catch fish. For a while, they simply laughed and talked and ate as many berries as they put in her basket. But when they both dropped berries into the basket at the same time and their hands touched, his body went to quivering and his blood went to pounding in his ears and he couldn't see anything but her berry-stained lips or think about anything except kissing her.

She must have had the same thing on her mind, because she tilted her chin, closed her eyes, and pursed her lips. Panic snatched at his insides. What if he didn't do it right? What if someone caught them? What if God struck him down for succumbing to temptation? But none of those things mattered. He had to know what kissing was all about. And he had to know right then.

Quickly, before he lost his courage, he lowered his head, pursed his own lips, and set them on hers, tasting the sweet blackberry juice that clung there. Nothing else happened. Maybe if he moved his lips a little bit. She moved hers, too. Still, nothing happened. Steele didn't know what he expected to happen, but whatever it was never occurred. While he was kissing her, the quivering subsided and his pulse gradually slowed to normal. He felt curiously dissatisfied. He broke the kiss, cleared his throat, and said he'd best go catch the fish his mother was expecting him to bring home for supper. Afterwards, he could stare at Selma Thurlow for what seemed like forever and not feel a thing other than disappointment.

As he grew into adulthood, he practiced kissing with other girls. Although he found such experiences pleasant, he always came away feeling dissatisfied. As a man, he discovered physical fulfillment in the sex act, but never had he been with a woman who made his heart sing.

Until Betsy Tyler.

Almost from the minute he'd laid eyes on her, even tied to a chair and screaming her head off, he'd felt that weird queasiness in the pit of his stomach. When her hand had touched his, his body had gone to quivering and his blood to pounding. It was like reliving his experience with Selma Thurlow all over again. The queasiness and quivers increased with every moment he was near her, until finally he couldn't stand it anymore. Since kissing Selma Thurlow had destroyed his infatuation with her, he assumed kissing Betsy would, too.

It hadn't. Nothing more than an innocent brushing of his lips on hers had set him afire. Steele didn't quite know what to think about that. He knew he had to kiss her again, and the sooner the better. Next time, he'd do it right. Maybe if he kissed her enough, he'd eventually get her out of his system.

And that was what he had to do. Finding the Scoggins brothers and their friend Williams required every ounce of his energy, every bit of his concentration. He couldn't afford to let a woman, any woman, interfere with that goal.

Maybe, when it was over and done with, and he could get on with his life, then . . . no, not even then. He was a fool to consider a future that included Betsy or any other woman. No woman wanted to shackle herself to a cripple.

Thirteen

Dusty's incessant braying awoke Steele the next morning. Only marginally aware of the golden light announcing the dawn, he sat up in his bedroll and rubbed his eyes, which were dry and a bit swollen. He'd lain awake for a long time, fighting the sweet but unrequited ache his memory of kissing Betsy provoked. When he finally slept, he tossed and turned so much on the hard, rocky ground he felt like he'd been beaten half to death by Ty's clothes washer.

Yawning, Steele stretched his arms over his head and pointed his right toe in an attempt to release a kink in that leg. He considered lying back down. Even if he couldn't sleep, he could at least rest his weary bones for a spell. After all, he wasn't in any real hurry to get anywhere. Another hour or two wouldn't make much difference.

But Dusty wouldn't quit braying. "Hush up, you sorry mule," he muttered, to no avail. What was wrong with the animal, anyway? He never, ever brayed unless he sensed danger—a snake or a mountain lion or . . .

Wide-awake now, Steele snatched up his Enfield rifle musket, which he kept loaded and by his side when he slept outdoors, and listened for the sound of a hiss or rattle from a snake or a scream from a panther. Instead, he heard nothing. Nothing at all. The close darkness was quiet. Too quiet.

He'd have to get up to investigate. Setting the rifle aside, he reached for his wooden leg and realized there wasn't enough light yet to see to put it on. Not that he really needed to see; he'd strapped the contraption on so many times he could in all probability manage it blindfolded. Rather, the absence of expected light prickled the skin at his nape and shot a dart of fear into his heart. He jerked his head around and stared at the golden light emanating from the valley below him and casting the ridge behind it in stark relief.

That wasn't the sun. It was fire.

And then he heard the scream—a long, low wailing that tore at his heartstrings and demanded immediate action. Quickly and methodically, he buckled the straps that held his artificial leg in place, pulled on his trousers, and rolled up his bedding. Within minutes, he was urging the recalcitrant mule down the mountainside and toward the golden haze. As long as the cries ripped through the night, he clung to the hope that he'd reach the farmstead in time to save the woman's life. He hadn't been there to save his mother and sisters. Perhaps God was granting him another chance. Steele prayed that it was so.

"He's a good boy," Steele assured the McGuires, a young couple in a long line of couples Steele had talked to about taking five-year-old Matthew Cain to raise. From the frowns on their faces, Steele held little hope that their reply would be any different from the others, but he had to try—for the boy's sake if not for his own.

"He might be," Reed McGuire said, "but we already have six mouths to feed and anothern on the way. I don' reckon we kin be a-takin' him."

"It's awful what happened to his maw," Cassandra McGuire said. As she watched young Matt playing tag with two of her children, her face softened. She laid a supplicating hand on her husband's arm, but she didn't say anything more.

Please, God! Steele prayed.

Reed patted her hand and his frown thawed a little. "Kin we sleep on it?"

"You certainly may. What if I leave him with you tonight, let you see how you all get along?"

The young man's frown returned, only this time it was a goodly shade darker than before. "Just fer tonight?"

Steele took Reed's hand and shook it firmly. "I'm a man of my word, Mr. McGuire. I won't depart Walnut Ridge without coming back by here and talking to you and Mrs. McGuire first."

"I'm beholden t' you," Cassandra said, her voice low and on the scratchy side. Steele wasn't sure if she was speaking to him or to her husband or perhaps to both. But that didn't matter. What mattered was what she and Reed said tomorrow.

"Let me tell him what we're going to do," Steele said. "You know, prepare him so he won't panic when he discovers I'm gone—even for the night," he hastily added. "He's still skittish about strangers, which is to be expected, considering what the tyke's been through. I'll be staying over at the Knapps' house, in case you need me."

He called to Matthew and walked him some distance from both the couple and their children. "Are you having fun?" he asked.

Matt nodded enthusiastically. "Kin we stay a spell longer? I'm winnin' the game."

Steele crouched down, ignoring the pain that position caused, and took the boy's hands. "How would you like to stay here for good?"

"I'll stay wherever ye stay, Preacher."

"I'm staying somewhere else tonight."

The boy's smile faded. "Then I want to go with ye."

"They don't have small children where I'm going."

"That's all right."

"No, it isn't." Steele took a deep breath and told himself to take it easy on the boy. "We've already talked about this, Matthew. You need a family—and I need to be alone. I can't be traveling with a little boy forever."

Tears welled in the boy's hazel eyes and his lower lip trembled. Steele fought the urge to hug him close. The less affection he showed, the easier it would be on both of them. He settled for squeezing Matt's hands a little tighter.

"We've talked about this before. Now dry your eyes and go play. I'll be back in the morning."

Sniffing, Matthew wiped the back of a grimy hand across his eyes. "Promise?"

"I promise."

Steele closeted himself in the tack room of the Knapps' barn, where he fasted for the remainder of the day and prayed as fervently as he'd ever prayed in his life. As was so often true, however, he felt as though no one listened, as though maybe there was no one out there to listen. But there had to be. He heard God's voice in his heart, directing him, telling him what to do. Not all the time, of course. Usually, it was when he least expected it. Maybe that was the problem. Maybe he was talking too much or listening too hard.

He lay down on the hard wooden bench, thinking to clear his mind of all thought and to empty his heart of all emotion, to make himself a vessel to receive God's purpose.

Within minutes, he was sound asleep. He didn't awake until the rooster announced the dawn.

* * *

"They really was a nice fam'ly," Matthew said. "I'm kindly sorry they didn' want me."

Steele snorted. He wished he could see the boy's face, but Matthew rode behind him on the mule. "Kindly sorry? I wish you'd realized that yesterday. From what I heard, you made every effort to ensure they didn't want you."

"I didn' do nothin' wrong, Preacher. Honest, I didn'. Hit was that biggest boy of theirn, Jacob. He didn' want me there. Tol' me so hisself."

Steele had heard similar stories from the boy before—numerous times. There was always another child who didn't want him in the family. "Maybe I've been going about this all wrong," he said, as much to himself as to Matt.

"How's that?"

"Thinking you need a ready-made family. You lived alone with your mother, right?"

The boy nodded against Steele's spine. "Ever since my paw went off to the war and didn' come back. He lef' 'fore I was borned, you 'member."

Steele recalled being told, but Matt said it as though Steele had actually been aware of the facts of the boy's life for a long time. Matt's attitude created an easiness between them, like they were old friends. It had been this way from the moment Steele arrived at the burning farmhouse to find the boy trying to shake some life into his mother's inert body.

"I never knowed him, ye know, but I loved him," the boy continued. "Maw said his name was Matthew, too. She called him Big Matt and I was Li'l Matt, but you kin still call me jes' Matt, seein' as how Big Matt's not comin' back. My maw ain't comin' back neither, is she?"

"No, Just Matt. She isn't coming back either."

"Jes' Matt! That's funny." The boy laughed thinly, as though he was trying very hard to be brave. Steele suspected little Matthew Cain carried a far heavier emotional burden than he let on.

They fell into a comfortable silence. Matt seemed to know when Steele didn't feel like talking and respected that wish. He also seemed to know that Steele's mother and sisters had suffered a fate similar to that of his own mother, even though Steele hadn't said a word to Matt about it.

Steele had, of course, grilled Matt for information about the marauders, but he'd couched his questions in natural curiosity. He'd also told the child to be prepared to answer similar questions for the law, assuming they ever found a U.S. marshal to talk to. If the boy was telling the truth—and Steele had no reason to believe he wasn't—Matt had seen little beyond the shadows of three men. At his mother's urging, he explained, he'd slipped out a back window seconds after the front door crashed in, then ran lickety-split to the woodlot and hidden in the trees until the men rode away. Steele suspected that if the marauders had known the boy existed, Matt wouldn't be alive today. He shuddered to think what these men were capable of doing.

Just a few weeks ago, he'd thought maybe the Scoggins brothers and Williams were dead. Now he knew they were not only alive, but back to their old way of life as well. For the first time since he'd left White Oak Flats, he wished someone else had hunted them down and killed them. It didn't matter to him anymore who performed the deed. He just hoped someone did . . . and soon.

He'd had Matt with him for almost three weeks. In that time, they'd become good friends, and Matt didn't understand why he couldn't stay with Steele forever. Riding around the countryside on a mule, depending on the goodness of strangers to feed and shelter them, was no life for a boy, Steele had explained. What he didn't tell Matt was that he couldn't put the boy's life in jeopardy, as he surely would if he found the marauders while Matt was in his care. Yet, Steele dreaded the day he had to give Matt up. That day was coming, though, and it needed to come soon.

"Where we goin'?" Matt asked out of the blue.

Steele smiled. "To a place called Peculiar Cove. Ever heard of it?"

"Nope. When we goin' t' get thair?"

"Sometime tomorrow. Probably about dinnertime."

"Ye ever been thair a-fore?"

"Yep."

"Ye got a girl thair?"

Steele reined Dusty to a halt, then reached around behind him and pulled Matt onto his lap. "Now, whatever made you ask a question like that?"

Matt fingered a button on Steele's shirt. "The way ye was a-grinnin' so big I could see it from behind."

Dare he tell Matt about Betsy? He didn't know himself exactly what she meant to him. Indeed, he'd not thought of her as his girl until just this moment, and he wasn't too sure thinking of her that way was a good idea. It could get to be real comfortable. He might even start acting like she was his girl, and that could only lead to heartache.

But he did like her. In fact, he liked her a lot. He didn't suppose looking forward to seeing her and enjoying her company when he was in Peculiar Cove could hurt anything, so long as he was careful to keep their relationship on a friendly plane.

He'd have to be careful around Matt, though. The boy's perception was far too accurate for his own good. And Steele wasn't at all sure he could trust Matt not to go around blabbering everything.

"Well, do ye?"

Steele had to tell him something—and fast, before the boy decided he was trying to hide the truth. "There's a lady there I want you to meet," he said. "In fact, we're going to stay at her house."

Matt dropped his hand and lifted his chin, but his expression was impassive. "What's her name?"

"Auntie Kee." Lord, where had that come from? Once he said it, though, Steele was glad he did. When Matt met the half-breed woman, he'd never believe Steele could be sweet on her.

"She yore auntie?"

"No relation at all. That's just what everyone calls her." He resettled Matt on the bedroll behind him and started Dusty to moving again. "You'll meet Uncle Begley, too. And before you ask, he's not my uncle or anyone else's, far as I can tell."

"I ain't su'prised they call that thair place Peculiar. Tell me 'bout Auntie Kee and Uncle . . . what'd ye call him?"

"Begley. It might take a spell," Steele said.

"I ain't goin' nowheres."

"I ain't goin' in that thair cold crick!" Matt screeched. "It's li'ble to make me sick!"

"Oh, yes, you are!" Steele struggled to hold onto the writhing, naked boy. "You're going in and you're going to stay in until you're clean as a whistle."

"Why cain't I take a bath after we get to Auntie Kee's?"

"Because you're not going to meet those people as filthy as you are, that's why. There's enough dirt behind your ears to plant a garden." Steele strode into the rushing water, sat down on one large rock, propped his wooden leg on another, and set Matt on still another. "If you run," Steele warned, holding the boy at his skinny waist, "I'll leave you right here to fend for yourself."

"Ye wouldn't do that."

Steele raised his eyebrows. "Do you really want to find out?"

The fight went out of the boy. "No."

Steele let go of Matt and removed a drawstring bag he'd hung around the boy's neck. From the bag he took two washrags and a bar of lye soap. For a while, they bathed without talking, then Matt said, "Ye're fibbin' to me 'bout Auntie Kee."

Laughter erupted from Steele's throat. "Why am I always surprised at the things you say?"

Matt shrugged.

"Why do you think I'm not telling you the truth?"

"She ain't yore gal."

There it was—that perception again! "I never said she was."

"Then who is yore gal?"

"I don't have one."

"Now ye're fibbin' agin."

"Wash your neck."

"I did."

"Wash it again. You left a necklace of little dirt balls in the crease."

While they were using Steele's blanket to dry off, Matt hit Steele with another question from nowhere. "Kin preachers jump the broom?"

Steele deliberately misunderstood. "Most preachers can. Of course, jumping anything's hard for me with this wooden leg."

"I'm not tawlkin' 'bout real jumpin'. I mean gettin' hitched up."

"Far as I know, only Catholic priests are forbidden to marry. Here." He handed Matt a clean set of clothes Cassandra McGuire had tearfully donated. Had the decision been hers to make, she would have taken Matt. "Put these on."

Matthew turned up his nose. "Them was Jacob's. I don' want 'em."

"You're the contrariest one child—" Steele bit off the

remainder of the tongue-lashing he wanted to give Matt. "Just put them on. You're not in a position to be choosy. I'll get you some new clothes at Uncle Begley's store once we get to Peculiar Cove."

The boy pulled Jacob McGuire's old shirt over his head and rolled up the sleeves, which were several inches too long, then stepped into a pair of patched and faded overalls. A large brown stain spattered the bib, and the button was missing on one of the straps, which hung down at the back.

"Ye never tol' me why they call that place Peculiar."

"Get Uncle Begley to tell you." As soon as the words left his mouth, Steele wished he could call them back. Maybe things had changed in Peculiar Cove since he'd left. Maybe no one was calling Betsy crazy anymore. And maybe that was wishful thinking to the extreme.

For the next hour, Steele fretted over what Matt might hear about Betsy, but as they neared the cove, he realized he was most probably worrying for nothing. Matt would draw his own conclusions. Once the boy met Betsy, he'd never believe she was crazy. What he ought to be concerned about was convincing Matt and Betsy—two people as stubborn as any Steele had ever met—that they needed each other.

A feeling of expectancy pervaded the April morn. The sun played hide-and-seek with scudding clouds, bees hovered over gently swaying red clover heads, and even the birds called to each other in hushed tones, as though Nature had raised her baton and was holding all in her domain at bay until such time as she chose to begin the concert.

It was Saturday, four weeks to the day since the Rev had first arrived in Peculiar Cove. Certain he would return today, Betsy arose well before dawn to prepare for his arrival. Auntie Kee had gasped in pleasant surprise to find Betsy in the kitchen rolling out pie crust at five o'clock that morning.

"Don't ask me how I know," she'd said. "I just do."

"The heart has its own mind," Auntie Kee said. "What ye want me to do?"

For several hours they'd worked side by side, preparing food for both that day and the next, then Betsy left Auntie Kee to finish up in the kitchen while she freshened bed linen, dusted furniture, and swept floors. When it warmed up a bit, she opened windows all over the house to allow the fresh but crisp breeze to circulate, adjusted lamp shades, straightened pictures, and otherwise occupied herself with trivial matters until she ran out of things to do in the house.

"Ye're wearin' yoreself plumb out!" Auntie Kee chided. "Why don' ye rest a spell while I make us some dinner?"

Betsy moved the apple pies, which had cooled sufficiently, from the window to the safe, then moved back to the window. "I'm too excited to rest."

"He might not even come t'day."

"Oh, he will. Don't you feel it?"

Auntie Kee chuckled. "Naw, I cain't say as I do."

Betsy watched a big, fat bumblebee light on the clover and dip its head into the red flower. She leaned over the windowsill and looked up at the sky. The clouds had all but disappeared, leaving the sun to reign alone. Suddenly, the birds burst into song. She thought her heart would burst with joy.

"He's here!" she declared, straightening up too soon and bumping her head on the window frame.

Frowning, Auntie Kee twisted her hands in her apron. "Law, Miss Betsy! Don' go tawlkin' crazy on me again. I don' hear a thang, and I know ye cain't see the front o' the house from thair."

Ignoring her, Betsy headed for the front door. "Are you coming with me or not?" she called over her shoulder.

"Not. I ain't no foo—" A creaking board swiftly followed by a sharp knock cut her off mid-word. "Ye go on," she called, a smile in her voice. "Don' keep the man waitin'."

Betsy didn't plan to. Not even for a second.

Fourteen

It was a big house. The biggest and bestest house Matt ever laid eyes on, and the first he'd seen that wasn't made out'n logs. It had a long porch on the front, real glass in the winders, and two doors—one reg'lar wood door, 'cept it was real fancy, and another one made out'n some kind o' wire stuff you could see plumb through. The purtiest lady he'd ever seen was standin' behind it.

He kept waiting for the lady to look down and see him, but her eyes was too full of the preacher to see anything else. The preacher was staring right back. So this was his girl, the one he tried to pretend he didn't have. Matt gulped down a snicker so fast his eyes watered. He reckoned it had to come out somewheres. Better his eyes than a couple other places he could think of.

While the lady and the preacher was filling their eyes with the sight of the other, Matt studied the gray-and-white lapped boards that covered the house. He didn't know what to call 'em, but he knew he liked 'em. They had what his maw called class. Only thing he'd change was to make 'em the same color all over. They looked kindly strange, all mottled the way they was.

Through the open winders he could see an older woman moving around in what appeared to be a room jes' fur eatin'. Imagine! A room jes' fur eatin'! She was a mite on the dumpy side, as Maw would say, with dark skin and almost white hair. Auntie Kee! The name fit her perfectly. Did the lady at the door live here, too, or was she just visitin'? Naw, she lived here. Elsewise, the preacher would a-been surprised when she opened the door.

Suddenly, Matt got an idea. He coughed loud enough to make her notice him.

"And who is this?" she asked. Her voice was as rich and sweet as sourwood honey. No wonder the preacher smiled when he thought about her.

"Matthew Cain, ma'am," he answered, puffing out his chest and making his voice sound as growed-up as he could manage. "Ye must be Auntie Kee."

She laughed at that, and then the preacher laughed, so Matt laughed, too. 'Fore long, they was all three laughin' hard enough to bust seams. Course, Matt didn't have to worry none about bustin' his out, as big as Jacob McGuire's clothes was on him. It was the first time he'd laughed, really laughed, since his maw died. This was definitely his day for firsts and bestests.

The real Auntie Kee came to the strange wire door then and pushed it open. She was smilin' big enough to make her black eyes twinkle like the first star after sunset. "Ain't ye goin' t' invite the preacher-man and his li'l friend in?" she said. "I spect they's as hunger-bit as painter-cats after a long winter."

Matt couldn't recall ever being quite that hungry, but the delicious smells comin' from the kitchen sure did make the juices in his mouth flow. With every passing minute, he was understandin' better why the preacher liked this place and these folks. Maybe they could just move into this big, purty house and live there forever.

While Uncle Begley was outfitting Matt with new clothes and filling his head with tall tales inside the store, Betsy and Steele sat outside on the porch and talked—

though not to each other. Betsy had thought to have a few minutes to themselves, alone, but the minute they sat down, Tom Dickerson walked up. Right behind him came Molly and Imer, then Mrs. Patridge and her daughter Charlotte. Everyone had to welcome the preacher back, of course, and seek his opinion on the design of the new church and whether or not it should have a bell tower. The conservative Patridges thought a bell tower frivolous, but Imer insisted they had to have one.

Betsy and Steele left the debate in progress to walk Matt back to the Tyler house. The boy voluntarily took Betsy's hand, which warmed her heart, and babbled about Uncle Begley and all the wondrous array of goods in the store. He was amazingly cheerful, she thought, for a child who'd so recently lost his mother.

"Ye must be very rich," he blurted out as they turned onto the flagged walkway.

Having been taught that it was rude to discuss money, Betsy didn't quite know what to say. He was just an innocent little boy, she reminded herself, who'd probably enjoyed few luxuries in his life. It was only natural for him to view her as wealthy, but that didn't make her feel any less awkward about it.

"Miss Betsy's father was a successful businessman back East," Steele said.

Where had he gotten that idea? Betsy wondered. She had no idea how her father had come by so much wealth, but she didn't want to contradict the Rev in front of the boy. She'd ask Steele about it later.

"Have ye been a orphan fer a long time?"

Betsy couldn't recall ever thinking of herself as an orphan, but she could see why the boy would think of her that way. "A few years now."

"Do ye miss yore maw?"

"Yes, I do. And my papa and my brother."

His eyes grew big. "Ye had a brother? What happened t' him?"

"He was killed in the war."

"So was my paw." Matt encircled her waistline with his arms and hugged her tight. "I'll look out fer ye, Miss Betsy."

"Thank you, Matt. That's very kind of you." The words seemed so inadequate. As she hugged him back, her throat swelled with emotion. This boy was very special. Very special, indeed.

During the short time he'd been on the circuit, Steele had held services in parlors, stores, front porches, and meadows, but this was the first time he'd preached in a barn. This was Peculiar Cove, though, where the out-of-the-ordinary could easily become quite commonplace.

From all appearances, the townsfolk had taken great pride in preparing the unused building as a place to worship. Using trees felled while clearing the spot for the new church, they made primitive benches and a pulpit with an attached high seat so that Steele had a place to sit and rest his leg. They'd even hung a lantern over the pulpit to provide light for him to read. But the most wonderful thing of all was Auntie Kee's pump organ, which she had agreed to have moved to the barn once she was convinced the leak in the roof had been successfully patched. With the exception of the faint smells of moldy hay and manure, the barn served surprisingly well as a sanctuary.

"I'm grateful—and I'm sure the Lord is, too—for all the thought and effort you put into this," he said, sweeping an arm to encompass all their labors. "Although it may be the wrong time of the year, this puts me in mind of our Savior's birth and reminds me, too, that all God requires for His worship are open hearts and penitent souls. With that thought in mind, I'd like to read today from the gospel of Luke . . ."

As Betsy listened to the melody of his voice—so resonant when he wasn't hollering—her heart filled with pride, partially in her own role in transforming the barn, but mostly in the transformation of the Rev. Steele Montgomery, for which she could take no credit. Something had happened to change him during the month of his absence, something more than a few lessons learned in the art of delivering sermons, something that softened his heart as well as his voice. Nonetheless, the hardness in him remained, a bitterness he had yet to resolve. This she recognized only because she, too, carried bitterness in her heart.

Was it the loss of his leg? Perhaps the horrors of the war in general? Did he feel, as she so often did, that God had deserted him in his time of need? If that were true, why had he become a preacher? Granted, ministers were only human, but one usually thought of them in terms of pureness and light. Although the Rev hid his dark side well, it was there for the discerning heart to see.

Betsy understood Steele's spending all of Saturday night in the barn. It was quiet there and he needed to prepare for Sunday service. But when he insisted on retiring to the barn after supper Sunday night, she took him to task.

"We have ample beds here, Rev," she reminded him.

"I know." He sighed and stared into the flickering candle flames. "It just doesn't seem proper for a single man to stay under the same roof with a single lady of similar age."

"That didn't bother you last month."

"Well, it's bothering me now."

"I don't know why it should. If anyone in town thought

it was improper, someone would have said something. Auntie Kee is here, and now there's Matt."

"Now, Miss Betsy," Auntie Kee said as she bustled back into the dining room from the kitchen to collect more dirty dishes, "ye're puttin' the preacher-man here under the gun. He's a growed man what kin make up his own mind."

"And he doesn't need you to fight his battles for him either, I'm sure!"

"Both of you, stop it!"

Steele's sharp tone startled Betsy. Little Matt, who had been unusually quiet during the meal, sniffled twice, then bolted out of his chair. His quick footsteps on the stairs resounded in the sudden quiet.

"See what ye two have gone and done?" Auntie Kee admonished. "Ye art to be ashamed o' yore ownselfs."

Rising, Betsy tossed her napkin on the table and stared at Steele with a mixture of anger and disbelief. She'd so looked forward to his return, thinking he liked spending time with her, knowing she enjoyed his company, yearning for another kiss. Some show of affection from him—even something as insignificant as holding her hand—would demonstrate that he did, indeed, like her, but he'd avoided being alone with her since he'd arrived. Had she completely misread the meaning behind his kiss? Had he found another woman in another town he liked better? Perhaps he'd had another woman all along.

Her own sniffles threatening to break through, Betsy hurried from the table and up the stairs to comfort Matt.

Why in all that was right and holy couldn't he at least talk to Betsy?

Steele paced the length of the aisle between the rough-hewn benches in the barn, occasionally finger-combing his hair off his face, sometimes stopping to straighten a bench, and seeing in his mind's eye Betsy sitting on the front row with Matt sitting next to her. A stranger would think they were mother and child, not because they bore a physical resemblance, but because the love between them jumped out and grabbed your heart. He'd seen the immediate bonding between the two of them when they met yesterday. In the ensuing hours, that bond had grown. And the more it grew, the greater the distance he felt between himself and both of them.

Was he jealous? Could that simple fact be the answer to his emotional quandary? But jealous of their relationship? That didn't make sense. He wanted Betsy and Matt to get along, wanted Matt to agree to stay with Betsy, wanted Betsy to ask him to stay with her. Maybe if they'd pushed him aside . . . but they hadn't, and there was no reason for him to believe they ever would.

Was he jealous because Matt and Betsy possessed the capacity to love when he didn't? That made more sense. A lot more sense. But it was also something he didn't know how to fix. He'd lost the ability to love the night he came home from the war. It had died, right there with his mother and sisters. Perhaps when he found the bastards who'd murdered them, when he'd tortured them until they begged for death, much as his mother and sisters must have begged . . . perhaps then, he could forgive himself for not being there when they needed him. Perhaps then, he could love again.

He sat on one of the benches, propped his aching left leg on another one, and held his head in his hands. His long hair fell forward, hiding the tears that streamed from his eyes. He saw only blind rage, felt only hatred in his heart, and knew himself for a fake. Most of the day, he'd sat in the pulpit, preaching loving-kindness to folks who lived for the most part by God's teachings, but who still looked to him for spiritual guidance. And then he'd frightened and confused Matt and hurt Betsy, hurt her deeply, judging from her quaking shoulders and misty eyes.

Tomorrow, he'd ask for her forgiveness, but how could he explain to her what he himself didn't understand?

They sat in rocking chairs on the front porch, watching Matt chase butterflies in the field across the road from the Tyler house.

"He's a delightful child," Betsy observed. "It's a wonder to me no one wanted him."

"I'm not certain that was the case," Steele said.

"What do you mean?"

"I think Matt didn't want them."

She was quiet for a moment, perhaps pondering his observation. "He must miss his mother terribly. You never did say what happened to her."

"She was . . ." Steele gulped down the lump in his throat. "Murdered."

"How awful! But Matt wasn't home. He didn't see—"

"He was hiding in the woods, but I think he saw more than he lets on."

For a while, they were silent, listening to the hum of bees and the swish of the breeze through the cedars in the yard and an occasional shout from Matt, trying not to hear the agonized voices in their heads. Betsy broke the silence.

"What will you do with him?"

Steele took a deep mental breath and held it. "I'd hoped to leave him with you."

Betsy gaped at him. "Me? Why?"

"He likes you. And you like him. You might even love each other, in time."

"I love him now." Her voice was whispery soft. "That's not enough."

"It seems enough to me."

"Well, it's not. He needs a real family, not two old maids. Sure, Auntie Kee and I can provide for all his physical needs. And we can love him. But it's not enough. He deserves more."

Steele wasn't ready to give up. "I don't know how he could ask for more than that."

"He could ask for the father he never had. He *deserves* the father he never had. And he deserves a mother who knows how to be a mother. I don't." Her voice was near to breaking, but you'd never know it from looking at her. She sat with her back stiff and her shoulders straight, her face wiped clean of emotion, her eyes stoic.

"I can't keep him with me, Betsy. You know that. A life on the trail is no life for a little boy. And how do you know you don't know how to be a mother, when you've never been one?"

"But I have," she said, rising and going to the door. "And I failed miserably."

Betsy's softly spoken declaration thrummed in his head and pricked like a sharp needle at his heart, making it bleed in little spurts. He had to get away—away from the Tyler house, away from Matt and Auntie Kee, who both seemed bent on talking his ears off, away from Betsy, who'd cloistered herself in her room and wouldn't come out. The day was too warm and the air too close for pacing in the barn, so Steele chose the cooler solitude of the woods. Without fully realizing where his feet were taking him, he didn't stop until he reached the outcropping of granite where he'd rested that first day he'd come to Peculiar Cove, the day he'd combed the woods for a toothache tree and heard the lonely call of a whippoorwill.

When had she given birth to a child? Who was its father? What had happened to the baby?

Uncle Begley had said no one honestly knew what transpired at the Rebel camp, but folks suspected she'd been raped. Steele realized he'd been shying away from facing that possibility. Her admission, however, forced him to confront it. Apparently, she had not only been raped, but had borne a child as a result. Was that why she'd shut herself off from society for so long? First because she was pregnant, and then because she had a baby to care for? It made sense, like pieces of a puzzle coming together, yet this explanation offered no clue as to what had become of the child.

I failed miserably, she'd said.

Did she mean that the child had died? Did she blame herself? How very sad for her! No wonder she'd become reclusive.

Only two people could answer his questions: Betsy and Auntie Kee. To approach either one risked incensing both of them, and thus losing the chance of leaving Matt at the Tyler house. If Betsy wouldn't assume responsibility for the boy, then perhaps Auntie Kee would. That way, Matt could remain at the Tyler house, and hopefully Betsy would come to realize she could be a good mother and that she wanted to be Matt's.

Steele hadn't asked anyone else in Peculiar Cove to take the boy, and now that he thought of it, he wasn't sure why—except he'd made up his mind that Betsy and Matt belonged together, that they needed each other. At the first opportunity, he'd talk to Auntie Kee, and if she refused, then he'd talk to everyone in Peculiar Cove if he had to. Surely someone there would take the boy. It wasn't the solution Steele wanted, but at least Matt could visit Betsy from time to time and see her on Sundays.

Whatever he did, it needed to be soon. Ty and Lydia were expecting him back in Hudson's Mill by the coming Saturday to conduct their wedding ceremony, and he dared not disappoint them.

Strange, how he'd looked forward to spending an extra

day or two in Peculiar Cove, and now that he was here, all he could think about was finding a home for Matt and leaving. He wanted to blame Betsy for his change of heart, but he couldn't. It wasn't her fault that she didn't need him anymore. She'd come out of her shell, just as he'd hoped she would, but the fact that she'd completed her rebirth without further guidance from him chafed. Nor was it her fault that she'd been raped and borne a child as a result, and it wasn't fair of him to think of her any differently because of it.

But he did. He couldn't look at her anymore and see purity and innocence, yet he knew down deep that she was innocent—not pure, perhaps, but innocent. She hadn't asked to be raped, had apparently fought it with everything she had. She hadn't asked to bear a child, but Steele was certain she loved it. He was also certain she hadn't been responsible for the child's death. Yet she blamed herself. He suspected that she blamed herself for all of it.

That he could understand. Hadn't he blamed himself for his mother's and sisters' deaths? If he'd been home, it wouldn't have happened. They'd still be alive today, and he'd be living in his cabin on the ridge above the farm. He wouldn't have ever traveled to Peculiar Cove, wouldn't have met Betsy, wouldn't have rescued Matt. But because it happened, he'd never live in that cabin, never be truly at peace, never be able to love Matt and Betsy as they deserved to be loved.

"Why, God?" he cried, unchecked tears streaming from his eyes. "Why do you let bad things happen to good people?"

His heart ached—for Betsy, for Matt, for himself . . . and for every other lost and lonely soul destined to live out their days on Earth asking but never knowing *why*.

Fifteen

"Tell me 'bout yore brother," Matt said.

Both Betsy's heart and her hand on the spoon missed a beat. She was stirring up a peppermint cake and thinking about how it had been Willy's favorite. Strange that she and Matt should be thinking about Willy at the same time. Too strange. It gave her the heebie-jeebies. With genuine effort, she kept her voice even. "What made you think about Willy?"

"I wasn't thankin' 'bout him. Ye was." His matter-of-fact tone unnerved her even more.

"Yes, I was." She shivered despite her best efforts not to. To compensate, she poured all her energy into beating the cake batter. "But how did you know that?"

" 'Cause ye was tawlkin' 'bout him. Kindly mumblin'-like 'bout how much he liked peppermint cake. I ain't never had no peppermint cake, but if'n yore brother liked it so good, then I spect I will too."

His explanation salved her uneasiness like butter on a burn. She chuckled. "For a moment there, I thought you could read my mind."

He screwed up his freckled nose. "What does that mean?"

"That you could hear what I was thinking." She poured the batter into three different-sized iron skillets. "I didn't realize I'd said anything out loud."

"Well, air ye gonna tell me 'bout Willy?" His voice bore a tinge of impatience.

She opened the oven, slid the skillets onto the rack, and closed the door before sitting across from Matt at the kitchen table. "I was your age when Willy was born," she began, looking down at her hands folded on the tabletop instead of into Matt's hazel eyes, which were entirely too much like Willy's. "I remember that day well. It was in the fall, a bitter cold day with the wind whipping through the cedars and the smell of snow in the air."

"But ye warn't outside."

"No, I was inside, where it was warm, but I always helped Papa bring in firewood and feed the livestock. That day was no different—except that Papa said I was getting a brother or sister that day. I said I hoped it was a sister, and he said he hoped it was a brother."

"He didn' like ye?"

The distress in his voice brought her head up, and she smiled, more for his benefit than her own. "Oh, he liked me just fine. But he already had a girl. This time, he wanted a boy."

Matt smiled wistfully. "Maw use t' say she wanted a girl. Course, my paw never comed home, then she . . ."

"I understand, Matt. Talking about those we loved who aren't with us anymore is hard."

He nodded but didn't comment.

"Anyway, Papa got his boy that day."

"What'd he look like?"

"At first, he was just a wiggling, crying, red-faced baby, but he grew up to look a lot like you, sandy hair, freckles, and all."

Matt smoothed down a sprig of hair that grew straight up from his forehead. "Did a cow lick him right here, too?"

She stifled what was surely to turn into a fit of giggles

if she so much as let a sputter of laughter escape. "No, Matt, a cow didn't lick his head anywhere."

"I ast Maw how come her to let a cow lick me."

"What did she say?"

"Said she never knowed when it happened."

"I don't think you can hold her accountable for your cowlicks."

"They's only the one to count, Miss Betsy," he patiently explained. "I ain't got anothern, leastways I don' thank I do. I reckon thair could be one back here"—he skimmed his palm down the back of his head—"where I cain't see."

His mention of counting got Betsy to thinking about his education. "Did your maw teach you to count?"

He puffed his chest out and grinned, exposing baby teeth his mouth had outgrown, but they looked healthy enough. His mother had taken good care of him. "Yes'm. I kin count to a gazillion," he boasted.

Betsy's eyebrows shot up before she could stop them. She hoped he thought her reaction was from amazement rather than disbelief. "A gazillion! I don't think I can count that high."

"I'll larn ye. See, first ye got t' count to a hunerd. Kin ye do that?"

She almost choked on suppressed laughter. "Yes, I can do that."

He shrugged his thin shoulders. "Then ye jes' keep on a-goin' till ye git to a gazillion."

"Do you know your alphabet, too?"

"My what?"

"Your letters."

"Oh. Some of 'em. We was workin' on that." He dropped his gaze to the green-checked cloth that covered the table. "Ye reckon ye could finish larnin' me ever'thang I need t' know, Miss Betsy?"

How could she refuse him? She'd meant every word

about not being a good mother, about Matt needing a father and a family to belong to. Somewhere there was a family who wanted him, the family he deserved. The question was how long it might take the Rev to find that family. Times were hard and food was often scarce. Clothes and shoes were in short supply. Folks had enough trouble just taking care of the children they already had.

In the meantime, Matt couldn't keep tagging along with the preacher. Steele was right about that. Maybe she could keep him with her and Auntie Kee for a while. But only for a while. She'd make that very clear to the Rev.

"I reckon I can try, Matt, but I have to warn you. I've never attempted teaching before. I may not be any good at it. And living here with me and Auntie Kee might not be easy, either. We're kind of set in our ways and not accustomed to having a child around." She took a deep breath and prayed she wasn't making a big mistake. "Do you want to try living here with us for a spell?"

His whole face glowed. "Oh, yes'm," he gushed. "I surely do. I promise not t' be no trouble to ye. Not to Auntie Kee neither. Ye won't even know I'm around. And I'll milk the cow fer ye and gather the aigs and sweep the porch and—"

She held up a restraining hand. "I don't expect slave labor from you, but I do expect obedience and good manners. You've given me no reason to believe you're lacking in either discipline, so we ought to get along just fine until the preacher finds you a family to live with."

The look of pure dejection that replaced his enthusiasm pulled at her heartstrings. But he'd change his mind. He'd discover soon enough what her failings were and he'd be ready then to move on. In the end, he'd take it all in stride, as children usually do. But she . . . she would be the one who would hurt, the one who wouldn't want to let go. Distance was her only defense, and keeping an emotional distance from this child was going to be close to impossible.

Betsy sat on the chaise in her room, holding the daguerreotype of Willy—the only picture of him she had—and crying softly. He'd been such a handsome young man, so intelligent, so energetic and full of promise. She'd done everything she could to curb his energy, to steer him in all the wrong directions. The fact that she hadn't meant to, that her intentions had been good, didn't matter now. All that mattered was that she'd made him miserable—and now he was dead.

She swiped at the tears and took a long, hard look at her brother's face. She'd almost forgotten how his sandy hair grew to a point on his forehead. She'd almost forgotten how his bottom teeth overlapped in the front. She'd almost forgotten how his hazel eyes sparkled with a hint of mischief, despite her efforts to mold him into a staid gentleman.

It had been years since she'd looked at the daguerreotype, which she'd packed away with all the Union flags and banners she'd made for his room. Remembering hurt too much.

Perhaps it was time to remember. Perhaps it was time to face the mistakes she'd made in the past. Perhaps God was granting her another chance.

Matt and Betsy were sitting on the front porch, she in one of the rocking chairs with a book on her lap and the boy at her feet. Steele spied them from the edge of the woods on the back side of the field across the road from the Tyler house. Secluded in the deep shade, he leaned against a tree and feasted his eyes upon the sight. Even from such a distance, he could see the camaraderie between them. For the briefest of moments, he forgot that only the most fragile of emotional ties bound the three of them together, and imagined that they were his family, eagerly awaiting his return.

And then reality came crashing in.

They weren't his family and never would be. He was crazy to even consider such a preposterous circumstance. Betsy was right. Matt deserved a father, a real father who'd be there to tuck him in at night, to teach him to ride a horse and hunt squirrels, to tend his cuts and calm his fears, not a man like Steele Montgomery, who didn't intend to stay anywhere for more than a few days at a time. He had to consider Betsy's needs, too. And then there was the matter of the loss of her virginity. No, better to forget how her very presence stirred his blood, how her touch sent his senses reeling.

He recalled his plan to kiss her again, to kiss her enough to make the ache go away. It might work. He'd never know until he tried.

"Hi, Preacher!" Matt hollered, practically jumping into Steele's arms.

Steele gave the boy a squeeze, his attention on Betsy's upturned face, her expression a paradoxical mixture of rapture and chagrin. He raised his eyebrows. She shrugged, which told him nothing, closed the book, and went into the house.

Matt wiggled out of his arms. "I git to stay here with Miss Betsy and Auntie Kee. Ain't that the most wondery thing ye ever heared?"

"Well, yes, I suppose it is," Steele agreed, more than a little amazed at the boy's announcement. "But are you sure? I mean, have you asked Miss Betsy?"

"She said so herself. She's goin' t' larn me to read and

write. And I git to keep my room and all them clothes she done buyed me."

Lord, please don't let the boy be dreaming this! It will kill him if it isn't true. "I need to talk to Miss Betsy—alone."

"Sure." Matt walked to the steps, then turned around, a look of concern on his face. "It's all right with ye, ain't it, Preacher? For me t' stay here, I mean. I know hit ain't no reg'lar fam'ly like ye said I was a-needin'. But ye said maybe ye was wrong. 'Member?"

"Yes, Matt. I remember. It's all right with me." More than all right, if what the boy said was true.

"I'm goin' t' pick Miss Betsy some flowers." Grinning from ear to ear, Matt dashed down the steps and ran to the field across the road.

Steele found Betsy in the kitchen, standing at the stove stirring something in a pan. Perspiration beaded on her brow and dampened the hair around her face. He'd never thought of her as domestic, but she looked perfectly at ease with her surroundings.

"I didn't know you cooked," he said.

She flinched, whether because he'd startled her or because she didn't want to talk to him he didn't know. "I do most of the baking. Auntie Kee does the rest."

Her voice was tight, which didn't bode well. A knot of misgiving curled in his stomach. What if Matt were wrong? Steele wasn't quite ready to find out. "Where *is* Auntie Kee?"

"Taking a nap."

"What are you making?"

"Icing for that cake." She inclined her head toward three layers of various sizes that were laid out on a large white cloth on the enamel-topped worktable.

"Smells good." It did. Very good. Almost like peppermint candy.

"I could use your muscle."

"How's that?"

"To crush that candy." She used her head again to indicate a small brown paper bag sitting near the cake layers. "Sorry. I can't stop beating this right now."

He picked up the bag. "I understand. How am I supposed to do this?"

"There's a wooden mallet in the right drawer of the worktable and a stack of flour sack towels on that shelf over there. Dump the candy on a towel and have at it. You'll have to sort of make a bag with the towel and hold it closed with one hand to keep the pieces from flying everywhere."

When he'd collected everything, he looked around for a place to work and chose a small butcher-block table. The noise his task created prevented further conversation for a few minutes. "How do I know when it's small enough?"

"Let me see." He opened the towel to expose red-and-white shards in sundry sizes, none of them large. "That's fine. You can leave them there. Thanks." She sounded pleased—and relaxed, which served to melt his qualms a bit.

He grinned. "You're welcome. Is there anything else I can do?"

"Not for this cake."

"Sounds like you have something else in mind, though," he said teasingly. Maybe she wanted him to kiss her again, too. Would she be so bold as to say so? Her response quickly deflated him—and caught him completely off guard.

"Who told you my father was a successful businessman back East?"

"Well, no one. I mean, Begley told me your parents had come here from . . . no, he said your father had graduated from Harvard. I assumed he was from the Boston area."

Betsy moved the pan from the stove to the worktable and beat the contents hard. Did she really need to, he wondered, or was it because she was angry with him?

"That looks like an awful lot of work," he observed, seating himself at the eating table.

"It is. You didn't finish answering my question."

"What part did I not answer?"

"The successful businessman part."

"I assumed that, too. Wasn't he?"

A cloud passed over her face. He wondered if she was about to cry. "I don't know," she said, her voice scratchy. "My father never talked about it. Nor Mama. All I know is that her maiden name was Pratt. Willy and I both asked about aunts and uncles and cousins and grandparents, but they refused to discuss it. I was hoping you knew something I don't."

How awful not to know anything about your family's background! Why, he could name everyone on both sides of his family for several generations back. He didn't know what to say to her, wished he'd never said anything to Matt—which was another open subject.

"Do you do this kind of thing all the time or only for special occasions?" *Please let this be a special occasion!*

"Auntie Kee and I don't eat sweets much. This is for Matt."

Finally, she'd opened the door. Steele took a deep breath and lunged through it. "Matt tells me he's going to live with you."

Frowning, she pulled the wooden spoon out of the pan, scrutinized the thick, glossy icing, and pronounced it done—all as though she hadn't heard him. He knew she had. Why did she have to be so contrary about this? He started to repeat himself, then decided to wait her out.

She removed a footed glass plate from a cupboard, set it on the worktable, and carefully moved the largest layer to the plate, then with precise, measured strokes, she began to apply the icing. Up the cake went while he waited, his patience growing thinner with each swipe of the flat knife she used to frost the layers. When she finished the third tier, she sprinkled the entire cake with the peppermint candy he'd crushed, then stood back and surveyed her creation.

"Do you think Matt will like it?" she asked.

"If it tastes half as good as it looks, he will. Are you planning to spoil him with such delicacies?"

"No." She pulled out a chair at the table and sat down. "I'm not planning for him to stay here that long."

Steele's heart plummeted. "But he said—" He couldn't finish the sentence.

"I told him he could stay here until you found him a proper home."

"And what if that doesn't happen?"

"It will," she said, her voice catching in her throat.

"Why are you fighting this so hard?"

Tears sprang to her eyes. "I'm not fighting anything! I told you. I tried being a mother. I wasn't any good at it."

"I don't know what happened, but I'm sure it wasn't your fault."

She jumped up so fast the chair toppled over. Ignoring it, she stalked to the window and stared outside, one hand clutching the curtain so tightly her knuckles turned white, the other hand a tight fist at her side. "You don't know anything about it."

He rose, picked up the overturned chair, and moved to stand behind her. For a long moment, he kneaded her shoulders. When some of the tension went out of her muscles, he whispered, "Why don't you tell me?"

Her sniffle was the first indication she'd been crying. Her shoulders trembled, then stiffened up again. "I was too protective, too overbearing, too domineering, too sure I was right and everyone else was wrong."

"Obviously, you learned from the experience." He turned her around so that she faced him, but when she refused to look at him, he gently lifted her chin. "If you perceive yourself as a failure, then surely you will be.

Think of this as your opportunity to employ what you've learned. Surely, you won't make the same mistakes again."

"I don't know that. I can't risk destroying another life."

Destroy? She did blame herself for her baby's death. "But Matt is five years old. The same circumstances can't apply."

Steele wanted to pull her against him, to drink in the jasmine fragrance that clung to her hair, to comfort her with more than words, maybe even to kiss her again. But her green eyes blazed with defiance and she was already stepping away from him.

"They most certainly can! I'll be Matt's friend. I'll even try to educate him. But I won't accept the role of his parent." She walked toward the dining room. "Now, if you will excuse me, I need to check on Matt. He can get into all kinds of trouble in that field—"

A shrill scream cut her off and she broke into a run. His heart in his throat, Steele followed as quickly as he could. Envisioning everything from snakebite to an attack by a rabid wolf, he barreled through the front door to find Betsy on her knees, cuddling Matt to her breast. The boy was sobbing loudly and nursing his right hand.

"What is it? What happened?"

"Bee sting."

Steele let out a long breath. "Thank goodness it's nothing serious."

"Bee stings can be very serious, but I don't think this one is." She stood up and took Matt's left hand. "Let's go put some soda on it. And you can see the peppermint cake."

Matt played his bee sting for all it was worth, monopolizing Betsy's time throughout the remainder of the afternoon and evening—and dashing any opportunity for Steele to be alone with Betsy again.

* * *

MOUNTAIN MOONLIGHT 201

Long after she extinguished the lamp, Betsy lay awake thinking about Matt and Steele and the course her life had taken. In all honesty, she didn't suppose she'd been on any course at all before. She'd merely laid at anchor in a dead sea with no meaning, no purpose, no direction to her life other than getting through each day as it came. Then a squall had blown up in the form of the Rev. Steele Montgomery, and although her ship was now sailing, she still didn't know where she was headed.

All courses should be plotted, with the final destination firmly in mind. But this wind blew her first one way and then another, leaving her hurt and confused one day, happy and contented the next. Somehow, in the midst of the storm, she'd completely lost control of her life.

And therein lay the answer: She had to regain control. None other could captain the ship but her. Winds weren't controllable, but sails were. She'd unfurled hers, then left them unmanned. How she'd let such a thing happen amazed her, but now that she'd figured it out, she knew what she had to do.

For one thing, someone had to organize the construction of the new church, from design to financing to building. The townspeople had thrust this project in her lap, and while she'd never actually said she would accept the responsibility, she hadn't refused, either. Now the project floundered for lack of a head. True, the men had cleared the lot, but no one seemed to know what the next step should be. She'd call a meeting for Saturday afternoon and they'd map it all out.

For another, Matt wasn't the only one around who needed schooling. Tom Dickerson had admitted he couldn't read, and she'd wager few other adults in Peculiar Cove could, either. She'd find out who could and she'd start a school—no, two schools: one for children, another for adults.

Finally, she had to come to grips with her feelings for the Rev. Steele Montgomery. If she truly loved him—and she thought she probably did, she had to put aside her fear of him. She had to separate him in her mind from the Confederate captain. She had to let him into her heart, completely let him in, or else she'd never know how to chart this particular course, which was by far the most important of all.

Sixteen

He was leaving again.

The sun had barely topped the mountains, but already he'd packed his things and secured them to the mule, wolfed down a generous breakfast, and hugged Matt goodbye. He was always in a hip and a hurry to leave.

If only they'd had a few more days together . . . if only they'd had some time alone, without Matt, without Auntie Kee and Uncle Begley, without obligations and interruptions . . . then perhaps they could have worked at strengthening the tenuous bond of their relationship.

You're just dreaming, Betsy chided herself. *Dreaming won't get you anything except more empty dreams.*

She stood on the flagstone walk, looking out at the nodding flowers in the field across the road and at the mountains beyond. The chestnuts were blooming, their blossoms so thick and white they made the mountains look like fluffy cumulus clouds. And like clouds and dreams, the blossoms wouldn't last.

Steele wanted to walk in those clouds. Oh, he'd be riding through them soon enough, but he wouldn't have Betsy by his side. He wanted to walk with Betsy in those clouds and kiss her again under one of the snowy chestnuts. He was determined to rid his system of the constant desire to kiss her until they were both senseless. If he didn't do it now, he'd have to wait another month. Another month of pure misery . . . of wondering what it would be like to really kiss her.

"Walk with me," he said.

She didn't move, didn't speak, didn't even blink an eyelid. She just stood staring at the clouds of chestnuts, mesmerized, almost trancelike.

"Walk with me up to the ridge. Walk with me among the chestnuts."

She nodded then, ever so slightly. He took her elbow and hollered at Matt. "We'll be back in a bit. Stay close to the house."

Betsy felt the scant pressure on her elbow propel her forward and she knew, at least peripherally, that she was walking with Steele. In her mind, she was sleepwalking. This was no more than an extension of her dream. In a few minutes, she'd wake up and he'd be gone. He was always in such a hurry to leave, and this time he hadn't even hugged her. She'd been so excited to see him when he arrived, had thought he was equally excited about seeing her. His excitement may have lasted all of three minutes. For a few moments as they stood looking at each other through the screen door, magic had sparked between them. Then Matt had spoken, breaking the spell, and they'd not been able to recapture it.

Now he was leaving again . . . without so much as touching her arm or holding her hand. She'd wanted him to kiss her again. She didn't want to wait another month to find out what his kiss, a real kiss, would do for that warm, funny feeling she kept in her stomach as long as he was near.

As she'd lain awake in the wee hours that morning, she'd decided if ever God intended for her to have a man, Steele Montgomery was the one. In all honesty, he wasn't so very special to look at, to anyone except her. If he were even remotely handsome, Imer Bailey and Charlotte Patridge would both be on him like two ducks fighting over a june bug. Everyone knew Imer and Charlotte, who had both long since passed marriageable age, chased every eligible bachelor around, but they hadn't so much as batted their eyelashes at the Rev. It was positively amazing that no one saw his physical beauty but her.

She knew now that the day she'd looked in the mirror and found herself attractive, she was looking at her face through his eyes. In truth, she was still plain-old-nothing-special Betsy Tyler, an old maid herself.

But there was far more that bound her and the Rev together than a general lack of eye-pleasing looks. They were two lost souls looking for home. And home was with each other. One day, maybe, he'd realize that . . .

"Betsy. Betsy!"

It was time to wake up. Time to stop dreaming and face reality.

But the dream refused to subside. They were standing on the crest of the ridge, the blossom-laden limbs of a huge chestnut tree forming a lacy white parasol over their heads, the sun peeking around the blooms, the birds twittering in sweet harmony. A soft breeze fluttered through the blossoms, caressing the petals, tossing the fragrance around, plucking a flower now and then. Some floated away, looking like creamy white butterflies too lazy to fly, content to let the breeze take them where it would. Others wafted downward, preferring the verdant sanctuary of the undergrowth.

One of the blossoms landed on Betsy's head. Laughing lightly, Steele plucked several more and sprinkled them onto her hair. He studied the little pile, then frowned and shook his head.

"What's wrong?" she whispered, afraid to speak any louder lest she wake herself up.

"The effect." His voice was hoarse, scratchy. "They're beautiful on *your* head."

"On *my* head? Oh!" She cupped a palm over her

mouth to stifle a sudden fit of giggles, then decided the giggles fit the dream and let them loose. Amidst her bout of hilarity, she pulled blooms off the tree herself and reached on tiptoe to place them on Steele's dark head, which made her laugh all the more. "I'll never forget the way you looked that day, standing in the door in your black suit and hat, so very much a man of the cloth and yet so tantalizingly male. In truth, the sight of you took my breath away."

She was no longer laughing. At some point, she'd become quite sober. Giving voice to her feelings planted the seed of desire in her belly again, and standing so close to him in this idyllic setting nurtured the burgeoning shoot. If he kissed her now, she would burst into a cloud of white blossoms, as full, as beautiful, as wondrous as the chestnut tree.

There were so many things he wanted to say to her, but suddenly he couldn't remember what any of them were. Her confession consumed him. He'd never felt so virile, so handsome before. Amazingly, this lovely woman thought him attractive and desirable. *The sight of you took my breath away.*

The breeze ruffled his hair, lifting the strand that covered his scar. She lifted her hand and laid a fingertip on his temple, then traced the saber scar to his jaw. The intense light in her pale green eyes held him in thrall, guiding his mouth to hers like a lodestar. Her lips trembled beneath his, hesitant in their sweetness, eager but unsure. Never had he felt quite so confidently male. *The sight of you took my breath away.*

He covered her mouth with his, and as he moved his lips upon hers, she responded in kind. He plucked, he nipped, he drowned in the heady fragrance of jasmine and chestnut blossoms. His head reeled, his body quaked.

Passion coiled in his belly and infused every fiber of his being. *The sight of you took my breath away.*

His hands, so large in comparison to her delicate features, held her head, then crept to her shoulders and down her back, pulling her closer. He wanted to meld his body with hers, to become one with both her spirit and her flesh. When his hardness pressed against her belly, she gasped, opening her mouth. He flicked his tongue across her top teeth, touched it to the tip of her tongue, skimmed it over her gums. She moaned and clutched him tighter.

Sanity penetrated then. He had no idea why. He knew only that if he didn't stop now, he wouldn't be able to. Slowly, tenderly, he took his mouth from hers and pressed her head into his chest. For a long moment, they stood clinging to each other under the chestnut tree, their hearts united.

"I don't want to go," he whispered against her hair.

"I don't want you to go, either. But you'll be back," she said. "And I'll be waiting."

"Weren't it jes' the most wondrous marryin'-up ye ever did see?" Grandma Carter said to Steele, raising her voice to be heard over the fiddle music. She was a small woman, as delicate-looking as the handkerchief she touched to her face, not at all what one would expect of a renowned and unashamed gossip. "Why, my eyes're shammily with tears."

"A beautiful ceremony," Steele agreed, his mind not on the details that made the wedding wondrous. Rather, as he watched Ty dance with Lydia, he couldn't quite shake the memory of the groom flinching when Steele said, "Do you, Ty Williams, take this woman . . ." It wasn't the vow itself that shook the young man; it was his name. If Steele were a gambling man, he'd make bet on it. He was now more certain than ever that Ty was hiding something, including his real identity.

Grandma Carter continued her commentary, apparently oblivious to her companion's lack of attention, perhaps because her huge hat and diminutive stature made it difficult for her to see his face. "That Lydia—she can really sew. That dress looks plumb store-boughten. And lookit that cake. Have you ever seed anythang so purty?"

Steele had only glanced at the refreshment table, which was actually some wide planks laid across two sawhorses covered with a white bedsheet and decorated with garlands of wildflowers, but Grandma Carter's question demanded he look more closely. Several corked crocks occupied one end—Mrs. Hudson had made a point of telling him they contained clover tea, not popskull—while bowls and platters holding such foods as pickled peaches, blueberry tea cakes, tiny fried apple pies, and gingerbread occupied the other. In the middle stood a three-tiered cake covered with fluffy white icing and sprinkled with crushed peppermint candy.

Before that week, he'd never seen or even heard of a peppermint cake—and here was another one. It must be a local confection.

Grandma Carter inadvertently divested him of that notion. "Never tasted mint cake afore myself, but if hit eats half as good as it looks, it won't last the evenin'."

"I wonder why they decided to serve peppermint cake." He made the statement innocently enough. Grandma's answer, however, walloped him good.

"Oh, it be Ty's fav'rite. Said his sister use to make it fer him all the time."

How d'you like this here mint cake, Preacher? Matt had said. *Miss Betsy said 'twas her brother's fav'rite. She used to make it fur him all the time. Ain't it good?*

Steele's mouth went dry. "His sister?"

"She raised him. He use t' live back East, ye know.

Some place name o' Boston, I thank he said. That's how come him t' tawlk so funny, I reckon."

Ty didn't talk funny. He merely sounded well educated. But there was something about his intonation that reminded Steele of Betsy's speech. And his smile . . . that familiar smile. It was Betsy's, too. Steele's pulse pounded in his ears so loud he had to strain to hear Grandma Carter.

"His maw and paw died when he warn't but a tyke," she was saying, "then the new mony fever took his sister. He come to the mount'uns with the Yankees and took to this part of the country like he was borned to it."

"Perhaps he was," Steele mumbled, his mind racing far ahead of his mouth. Although he had no proof, he knew in his heart that Ty was Betsy's brother. There were too many coincidences for it not to be true. Uncle Begley said Phineas Tyler had been educated at Harvard, and Cambridge was right outside of Boston. Ty was the right age. He had the same speech patterns, the same diction, the same smile as Betsy. Willy would be short for William. William Tyler—Ty Williams. Too many coincidences . . .

"Ye ain't listenin'," the elderly woman accused. "I done tol' ye he was raised off up there in Boston. I cain't blame him none myself fer not wantin' to go back, what with his whole fam'ly gone and all."

But his whole family wasn't gone, Steele wanted to scream. Ty's sister was alive and well. She'd been grieving for her dead brother all these years, and here he was, just three mountains, two flats, and a ridge away. How could Ty allow Betsy to believe he wasn't ever coming back? Didn't he know how much she loved him? Didn't he know she would keep his secret?

Maybe she did know. Maybe that was the reason she'd remained reclusive. Maybe Ty sneaked back into Peculiar Cove from time to time to see her and Auntie Kee. Steele wondered anew what Ty had done that was so awful he had to hide from it. Despite the young man's likable personality and probable relationship to Betsy, Steele couldn't deter the gnawing apprehension that Ty might somehow be connected with the marauders.

"He was some kind o' sad when he come here," Grandma Carter said, "but he's happy as a bear eatin' honey now. Jes' lookit that smile."

Steele nodded absently, glad the elderly woman was more open with him this time. Nevertheless, he wished she possessed personal knowledge of this man who called himself Ty Williams. All she seemed to know was what Ty wanted folks to believe was true. He couldn't just go up to Ty and accuse him of lying. And he couldn't just go back to Peculiar Cove and tell Betsy he'd found her brother. What if he was wrong? Getting her hopes up over nothing would be downright cruel. No, when he confronted Ty, he had to have something far more solid to stand on than a batch of coincidences.

When Betsy announced she was hosting a meeting on Saturday afternoon, she expected three or four people to come: Molly and Imer for sure, probably Tom, and possibly Uncle Begley. She begged Uncle Begley, telling him she needed another voice of reason.

"Don' look fer me," he told her. "Saturdee's my bestest day."

"It's also the day most people will be in town—other than Sunday," she reminded him, "and Sunday is inappropriate for a business meeting."

"I don' know why," he argued. "Hit's church binness."

"I've already set it up for Saturday. You can close the store. Just for an hour or so. If people can't come to the store, then maybe they'll come to the meeting. This is important, Uncle Begley."

He hedged. "I don' know. I'll have to thank on it."

MOUNTAIN MOONLIGHT

He scratched his chin and disappeared behind the metal boxes. "Maybe ye won't need me."

Uncle Begley was up to something. "Why not?" she asked suspiciously.

"Moss Gatlin brung the mail. If'n I recollect right, ye got a letter."

"You know full-well whether I got a letter or not," she said, laughing. "And you probably know who it's from, too."

He came out from around the counter holding a light brown envelope, his pale blue eyes twinkling. "That Bishop Marley feller." He handed her the letter, looking like a child waiting to blow out the candles on his birthday cake. "Well, ain't ye gonna open it?"

Her hands suddenly shaking, she ripped open the seal and took out a single sheet of paper, not calming completely until she'd skimmed through the letter.

"What does it say?"

"That they'll pay for the windows."

"Nothin' else?"

"That's it. But they're a major expense. I suppose we should be grateful." She returned the letter to the envelope. "I really do need you there, Uncle Begley."

"We'll see" was as close as she could get to a commitment from him.

That was on Thursday, the day after the Rev left town. From then on, she dreaded the meeting. Molly and Imer had made it clear they wanted milled lumber and a bell tower, and Tom had given her every reason to believe he was leaning toward the same, despite the cost.

As it happened, so many people turned out that she had to move the meeting from her parlor to the barn. Even Uncle Begley came.

"Cain't do no binness with ever'one over t' here," he grumbled when he got there, the twinkle in his pale blue eyes belying his annoyance.

"We're here to discuss plans for the church," Betsy said as soon as everyone was seated. "Who would like to begin?"

"I got it all drawed up." Tom stood and removed a neatly folded square of brown paper from his pocket. With his chest thrust out, he opened up his sketch and held it high for all to see. "It's got a bell tower like Miss Imer wanted and a vestibule like Miss Betsy wanted and great big ole winders."

"Who wanted those, Tom?" James Dunbar asked.

Tom looked a bit sheepish. "I did."

Snickers broke out in the small crowd.

"What you buildin' it out'n?" the conservative Mrs. Patridge asked.

"Milled lumber," Tom answered.

"That's all well and good fer rich folks," Mrs. Patridge said, "but how're we gonna pay fer big winders and boughten lumber? Why don' we jes' build a sturdy lawg church—"

"This is for the Lord," Mary Snider interrupted. "Second best ain't good enough."

"What do blatherskite wimmin know anyhow?" Jobe Gannett, who was not known for his tolerance, blurted out. "And how come this here church ain't gonna have two doors—one for the men, t'other for the wimmin? Ever'body knows that's the way they's suppose to be built."

A hush fell over the small crowd and all heads turned to him. He looked from one person to another, his gaze skimming over the women and lighting on the men, his expression clearly asking for a show of support.

Betsy bit the inside of her lip, waiting breathlessly for one of the other men to concur with him—or worse, for Jobe or someone else to question why the town crazy woman was conducting this meeting. Instead, folks glowered at him.

MOUNTAIN MOONLIGHT 213

Deciding the best course to be disregard, she centered her attention on Mary Snider and forced herself to speak calmly. "I won't argue, Mary, but no one has suggested a way to pay for milled lumber and a bell and all that glass. Times are hard. I think the Lord will understand. Besides, if we build a log church, we can make it as big as we want."

"She's got a point," Uncle Begley chimed in. "Me and Tom's been figurin' on lumber and paint, what'n'all, and it's gonna cost more'n most o' you folks see in a lifetime. Hit could take us years to raise that much money. We need that church now. Don't ye agree, Tom?"

The young carpenter offered a reluctant nod in reply.

"I say we put it to a vote!" Imer bellowed.

Not yet, Betsy thought, searching for a way to stall. Her way might not be the right way. It might not even be the best way. In her mind, it was the only way for the time being. Regardless, she hesitated to ask people to make a decision yet, but everyone was looking at her, waiting for her to say something. "Does anyone else want to discuss this further before we vote?"

"We're ready," James Dunbar said.

No one disagreed and no one offered additional comment. Attempting to keep her voice even, Betsy asked for a show of hands from everyone who wanted to build a log church. Uncle Begley's arm went up, then Mrs. Patridge's and Charlotte's.

Three people—out of thirty or more. How did they expect to . . .

Tom Dickerson's hand slid up, hesitantly at first, then he thrust it high. Another hand followed, then another and another, until soon everyone had their hands in the air except Molly and James Dunbar, Mary and Harold Snider, and Imer Bailey.

Betsy breathed a mental sigh. "Tom's going to need lots of help from all of us."

"I'll make the pews," Sam Bartlett said.

"And I'll make the roof boards," Witt Rogers offered. "Ever'body knows I make the best oak boards around."

As more people volunteered for various tasks, Molly, Imer, and Mary folded their arms under their bosoms and glared into space, while Mrs. Patridge, her daughter Charlotte, and Uncle Begley grinned like cats that had licked up the last bowl of milk before the cow went dry. Betsy was glad the discussion hadn't turned into a fight, but she didn't want people going away angry or gloating over a victory, either. Victory lay not in a choice of materials or design, but in achieving harmony as the townspeople worked together to create a comfortable place to worship. They had to all pull together on this project to make it work. At the risk of sounding like a preacher, she said as much at the end of the meeting.

Slowly, heads began to nod and frowns dissipated.

"We made our decision," Tom said. "It might not be what some folks wanted, but it were fer the best. Let's listen to Miss Betsy and put our diff'runces aside."

He made Betsy feel so good she decided to make her announcement about school instead of waiting another week or so, as she'd originally intended. "Starting Monday morning at nine, I'll be holding classes here in the barn for children who want to learn to read and write. I'll be glad to have help from any mothers who can afford the time."

After the meeting, folks stood around in knots, the men discussing crops and making plans for the church, the women exchanging recipes and news. Betsy didn't feel comfortable joining the women, most of whom she had nothing in common with, but she couldn't just go back in the house and leave people standing in her yard.

Opal Rogers, Witt's wife, rescued her. "I'm much obliged to ye fer startin' a school. My three younguns'll be here." She patted her rounded belly. "This un'll come too, when he gets old enough."

Soon, most of the women were crowded around her and Opal. Even Mary Snider joined them.

"I heared 'bout the most wondrous contraption," she said loud enough to claim everyone's attention. Mary did always have to be at the center of things, Betsy thought. Obviously, she hadn't changed.

"What was that?" Opal asked.

"A clothes warshing machine. Does all the work fer you. All by itself!"

A chorus of *no*'s and *you don' mean it*'s erupted.

"Honestly," Mary said. "Grandma Carter sent me word. Said there's this young feller in Hudson's Mill—I don't recollect his name—what's full of the most bodacious idees. He's fixin' to marry-up with Lydia Hudson and he made her this here clothes warsher fer a weddin' gift."

"How does it work?" one of the women asked.

"I don't rightly know. Hit's got a big ol' tub and a water wheel. Grandma says Lydia fell in it and almos' drowned."

"Sounds dang'rous to me," Charlotte Patridge commented.

"Well, I want me one. I done tol' Harold to plan on takin' me over there to see it. Said he would soon's he got the seeds in the ground."

Betsy was only half listening. *A young fellow with bodacious ideas*, Mary said. Willy had always been full of such nonsense. He'd told her over and over about his ideas for "machines" that ran on water power. He'd even thought of one to wash clothes. It seemed incredible that another young man had similar ideas, yet she knew that was the case. It had to be. Willy was dead. She had the black-banded letter to prove it.

Seventeen

Ty sat in a dark corner of the bedroom, mulling over the mess he'd made of his life. Since he'd turned tail and run during the Confederate counterattack at Belmont, he'd known he was a coward. He'd gone off in the woods and vomited his breakfast, then hid in the bushes and quaked while minie balls flew all around him. His cowardice sent him back to his regiment, though, for General Grant had made it clear that deserters faced certain death. Luckily, confusion reigned, so no one noted he'd been gone.

From that moment on, he knew he'd made a huge mistake volunteering to fight. If he'd only been smart and signed up for ninety days, as many of the Illinois boys had, he could have gone home a few days later and been done with it. But no, he had to be cocky and sign up for the duration of the war.

"It'll only last a month, two at the most," Edward Tolbert, one of his classmates at Maryville, had assured him. "Come on. We'll roust those Johnny Rebs in no time and be back in school before the semester's out. It'll be fun."

Yeah, it had been fun, he thought, gall rising in his throat as memories slammed into him. Ed died at Belmont, along with three other boys from Maryville. Ty would probably be dead, too, if he hadn't run. After that, he'd waited for his chance, waited for a time when he could desert and no one would know. All he had to do was bide his time and survive until such opportunity presented itself. Finally it had. At the Hornet's Nest at Shiloh.

Of course, that meant allowing Betsy to think he was dead, but it couldn't be helped. He'd convinced himself it didn't matter, that she'd rather he was alive this way than dead on a battlefield. After the war was over, he'd go home, say the notification of his death had been a mistake, and no one would ever be the wiser.

Somewhere along the way, though, he'd changed his mind. The coward in him, that yellow streak that was an acre wide, persuaded him that going back to Peculiar Cove would be his undoing. If the reporting of his death was all a mistake, she'd want to know, why hadn't he written to her after Shiloh? Where had he been? What had he been doing? She wouldn't leave things alone. She never did. Eventually, she'd find out, and she would hate him for his cowardice—just as he hated himself.

If he had any strength of character, he would have put a pistol to his head and made truth out of the lies a long time ago. Instead, he'd moved from one place to another, each time getting a bit closer to home, until he'd finally arrived in Hudson's Mill and knew he could go no farther without risking exposure. Even there, he was at risk. He'd thought to find out what he could about Betsy and Auntie Kee, then head out again, maybe west where no one cared about a man's background.

But then he'd met Lydia and fallen in love. He shouldn't have married her without telling her the truth.

"Air ye gonna set over there all night?" Lydia said, her melodious voice a balm to his wounded spirit. He looked at the bed, where she lay beneath the covers, the single candle casting a warm glow on her honey blond curls. "I promise not to bite."

She was so beautiful . . . and so trusting.

One day, he'd have to tell her. He couldn't go on living like this forever.

But not tonight. Not his wedding night. Tonight he would hold her close to his heart and savor her sweetness.

He rose from the chair and began to unfasten his shirt. "There's parts of you I might want to bite," he said.

Giggling, she opened her arms. And he went into them.

The meeting left Betsy feeling all warm and fuzzy inside, but within a few short hours, she was so angry at herself for her compulsive announcement that she forgot all about how well plans for the church were developing.

Whatever had made her think she could teach at all, let alone be ready to begin the educations of heaven only knew how many children by Monday morning? From all indications, she'd have at least twenty, since every parent at the meeting told her they'd be sending one or more of their children to her school. And if that weren't frightening enough, it appeared she'd be solely responsible, since not one mother offered to help her.

Added to that was her concern over a lack of materials. A foray through trunks and crates in the attic produced a complete set of McGuffey's Readers, all with her name neatly penned inside; the first three volumes of a second set, which had been Willy's—Betsy had no idea where the other four might be; and two slates. While she was digging in the attic, Auntie Kee went to Uncle Begley's store and bought all the chalk, paper, pencils, pens, and ink he had in stock, which didn't amount to enough to last a week.

Betsy sat at the kitchen table, surveying the meager supplies. "Did you give him my order?"

Auntie Kee nodded. "He said the blackboard and the books might take a spell, but he'll have the other stuff, pencils and paper and sech, in a couple o' weeks."

"How long is 'a spell'?"

"Least a month, maybe two."

"I don't know what I'm going to do."

Auntie Kee took a sip of her tea. "Ye should a-thought about that 'fore ye started this schoolin' stuff."

"Yes, I should have," Betsy agreed. "In the meantime, I'll just have to make the best of what I have."

"Ye could always explain how it is at sarvice termarr, put it off fer a month or two."

Betsy considered the older woman's suggestion. "No, I can't. These parents have put their trust in me. If I back out of this, even temporarily, it will look to them like I lost all confidence in the project."

"I reckon they'd understand, if'n ye put it to 'em right."

"I'm afraid to postpone it—afraid I *will* lose the little bit of confidence I have left. As you are so fond of saying, I've made my bed and now I have to lie in it."

Her "bed" grew during Sunday dinner-on-the-ground, when several more parents told her they would be sending their children to school, bringing the count to thirty-three.

"Ye're gonna have t' ast some of them mothers to help out," Auntie Kee told Betsy. "They ain't never gonna volunteer their ownselfs."

She was probably right, but Betsy resisted. She'd asked when she made the announcement. To ask individually now seemed tantamount to begging—or admitting defeat, neither of which appealed to her. Besides, the children might not all come. Or she might not need any assistance. There was no need to panic quite yet.

Her head full of ideas and her heart tainted with misgivings, Betsy slept fitfully that night, not truly resting until the wee hours and then sleeping soundly until Auntie Kee awakened her at seven.

"Rats and mice!" Betsy screeched, throwing the covers back and hitting the floor with a bound. "I can't believe how late it is!"

"Ye got time. Jes' calm yourself and get dressed," Auntie Kee said. "Brakefust'll be waitin' fer ye. 'Sides, hit's rainin'. Ye ain't likely to have more'n three or four show up."

It *was* raining—hard enough to sound like a percussion band. How had she not heard the staccato beats against the window panes, the occasional cymbal-clash of lightning, or the bass-drum rumble of thunder? Given such inclement weather, she wasn't likely to have anyone to teach this morning other than Matt.

To her surprise, twelve children braved the storm to attend the first day of school in Peculiar Cove. It was only to be a morning school, she told them, and the first order of business was introductions.

"You probably all know each other, but I don't know any of you except Matt. We'll start with you," she said, pointing to the largest and presumably the oldest child, a pimply-faced girl who was almost as tall as Betsy and definitely outweighed her. "Tell me your name, first and last, spell it if you can, and tell me how much you can read, if at all, so I'll know which reader to put you in."

Tears sprang to the girl's eyes and she shook her head in dismay.

"Don't be shy," Betsy said cajolingly. "We're all here to learn. Come on now. Tell me your name."

The girl sprang from the bench and darted outside into the pouring rain. Betsy ran after her, but by the time she got to the door of the barn, the girl had disappeared. She didn't know if she should follow her, since that would mean leaving the others—many of whom were only six or seven—unattended.

"She'll be all right, Miss Betsy," one of the older boys said. "I reckon ye jes' sceered her good. Rena don' tawlk much."

Betsy returned to the pulpit, which she was using as a lecturn. "Why not?"

The boy lifted a bony shoulder, "I reckon 'c-cause she t-tawlks sorta st-stuttery-like."

All the children except Matt and the boy giggled.

"It's not kind to laugh at the misfortunes of others," Betsy chided, thinking about how she used to laugh at Willy's stuttering when he was nervous. This was all her fault. She'd pushed a shy child with a speech impediment to be the first one to talk. As she'd feared, she had no business trying to work with children. She was already failing, as she'd thought she would. She ought to send all the children home before she offended someone else, but when she looked at them, she saw excitement and an eagerness to learn. They'd come in a thunderstorm. The least she could do was try to teach them.

If you perceive yourself as a failure, then surely you will be, Steele had said. She'd made a mistake, hopefully one that could be rectified. At the very least, she could learn from it and perhaps not make the same error in judgment again. If she kept a positive attitude, if she told herself she could do this, then perhaps she would succeed after all. She owed it to herself . . . and she owed it to these children.

"I'll tell you what," she said, "we'll start with me. Most of you know me as Crazy Bets." A few children snickered; most hung their heads. Matt frowned in obvious confusion. "How many of you think I'm crazy?"

She waited, holding her breath, for a hand to go up or someone to say something. No one did. Smiling inside, she said, "Some folks think I am. Of course, people thought Columbus was crazy when he said the world was round. Even after he proved it by sailing across the ocean, some folks didn't believe it. For hundreds and hundreds of years, people had perceived the world as flat, and they had trouble accepting that it could be otherwise."

"Who was Columbus?" a little girl with blond pigtails asked.

For the next hour, Betsy talked about whatever subjects came to mind. As she talked, she gradually lost her own shyness and feelings of ineptitude, but she still didn't know the names of most of the children, and she was uncertain about the best way to find out.

The door opened and Auntie Kee came in carrying a basket covered with a piece of oilcloth in one hand and a basket filled with tin cups in the other. Rena, who was carrying a small tin milk can, followed. Betsy couldn't have been more surprised—or pleased.

"Who wants warm blueberry muffins and milk?" Auntie Kee said.

As the children crowded around her, Rena set the milk can down and joined Betsy at the pulpit. "I-I'm s-sorry I r-runned away," she muttered, her head down, a bare toe rubbing the hard-packed dirt floor.

"And I'm sorry I embarrassed you," Betsy said. "Will you forgive me?"

The girl nodded without raising her head. "I d-don' know n-nothin' 'bout r-readin'."

"That's all right. I didn't either, once upon a time. We all have to learn. I'm glad you want to."

Rena looked up and almost smiled.

Betsy took the girl's hand. "We'd better go get our muffins before they're all gone."

As each day passed and the school roster grew, managing lessons and students all by herself in the dark, poorly ventilated barn became increasingly difficult.

"We need desks and books and more teachers," Betsy told Uncle Begley the following Saturday afternoon. "The children have to hold their materials on their laps and then strain their eyes to see."

"Have you spoke to Sam Bartlett?" he asked.

"No. Why should I?"

" 'Cause he's makin' the pews fer the church. You art to ast him kin he hinge the backs so they fold down. That way, they'd be desks durin' the week. Ye *air* plannin' on usin' the church oncet hit's built."

"Oh, yes! I'll talk to Sam," she said, pleased to find a solution to one of her problems. "But what am I going to do about needing help? The children get restless while they're waiting for me to get around to all of them. And when they're restless, they have a tendency to become rowdy."

"Have ye done bit off more'n ye kin chew?"

Betsy worried her bottom lip. "I don't know. Maybe I have. I've considered dividing them into two groups and having half of them come in the afternoon."

"Sounds good t' me. Why don' ye?"

"Because I'm selfish, I suppose. I like having my afternoons free."

He shrugged. "Then don' complain t' me."

"Why won't some of the mothers help me?" Her question came out sounding whiny. She started to apologize, then decided she had a right to complain. "I mean, it's their children. Why don't they care?"

"I spec' they do. I reckon some of 'em's got babies t' tend to. Some's got to help their men in the fields, now that their childurn ain't there to do it. And most of 'em cain't read nohow, so how could they help?"

"I see your point," Betsy said. "Maybe I've been looking to the wrong people."

He frowned. "What d'ye mean?"

"Maybe I ought to be asking some of the other old maids."

Begley laughed. "Now, Miss Bets, ye ain't a ol' maid. Not yet."

"Yes, I am. You and I both know it."

"Thangs're changin' fer ye, Bets. That's goin' t' change, too. Ye jes' wait and see if'n hit don't."

Although Betsy didn't argue with him, she wasn't at all sure he was right. Her doubts didn't keep her from dreaming, however—or from remembering how wonderfully full and yet decidedly empty the Rev's kiss had made her feel.

Kissing Betsy had *not* quenched Steele's thirst for her. On the contrary, it awakened something in him he hadn't even known existed. It was something truly magical, something that kept his nerves tingling and his heart singing with the wonder of it all. And it made him want her even more.

That want drove him to complete his business at each homestead and in each settlement with quick and efficient dispatch. He lingered over nothing—not a prayer, not a sermon, not a meal . . . nothing. Each minute he saved was another he could spend with Betsy. And oh, what he planned to do with her during those accumulated minutes!

As much as he wanted to explore the full physical sensations her touch, her kiss promised, he dared not even consider such activity outside the bonds of matrimony. More and more often as he rode the mountain trails alone, he found himself daydreaming about marriage to Betsy. As pleasant as those daydreams were, they weren't reality, nor were they likely to be anytime in the near future. Even if she could overlook his wooden leg, marriage meant commitment, and he'd already committed himself to finding the marauders.

Therein lay the crux of his problem, for the more he thought about it, the more certain he became that Ty Williams was part of the gang. If that was true, the fact that Ty was quite probably Betsy's brother wouldn't stop Steele from stringing him up. He'd always known that such an act would get him thrown out of the ministry, but he'd never dreamed it might destroy his chance at love.

To Betsy's surprise and delight, both Charlotte Patridge and Imer Bailey agreed to help her at school. Although neither were as well educated as Betsy, they knew enough of the rudiments to be of tremendous assistance. Each took a group to teach, and Charlotte, who'd stuttered herself as a child, worked privately with Rena Wakefield in the afternoons. Since teaching was new to all three of them, they met for a while each afternoon to share experiences and ideas.

Betsy spent most of the little time left to her with Matt. They roamed the fields and the woods, searching out bugs, identifying plants, listening to birds sing, and otherwise observing the wonders of nature. Several days a week, they sat on a felled tree in the cleared lot and watched the men work on the church. Matt, who had never seen a building under construction before, asked the men a gazillion "how come" questions: Why does a broadax have a curved handle? Why do the men score the logs before they hew them? Why do some men use a broadax to hew while others use a foot adze?

His interest in these subjects pleased her. In fact, the boy's curiosity seemed to know no bounds. Nor did his propensity for peppermint. With each passing day, he reminded her more and more of Willy. The more he reminded her of Willy, the more she loved him. And the more she loved him, the more she wanted to keep him. He needed her and she needed him, but she continued to worry about repeating the mistakes she'd made with Willy.

One evening when Betsy and Matt were sitting on the front porch, listening to the crickets and waiting for the lightning bugs to come out, the lonely cry of a whippoorwill drifted through the valley from some distant spot in the hills.

"How come whippoorwills sound that a-way?" Matt asked, his voice as low and melancholy as the bird's call.

Betsy ruffled his hair, then squeezed his shoulder, pulling him into the crook of her arm. "What way?"

"Ye know. So sad. Like they's lost and cain't find their way home."

"I don't know, Matt."

"I spec' if they'd look in the daylight, they might not be so lost."

"You may be right."

"Did I tell ye a whippoorwill cried the night my maw died?" He took a ragged breath and his thin shoulders trembled. She thought he was tuning up to cry, but he didn't.

"You don't have to be brave, Matt. It's all right to cry if you want to."

"Maw said boys ain't s'pose t' cry. Cryin' is fer girls."

"I think your maw was talking about crying over little things like cuts and scrapes."

He was quiet and perfectly still for a moment, but when the whippoorwill called again, much closer this time, he turned his face into Betsy's bosom. She encircled his small body with her arms, one hand cradling his head. At first, he merely pressed his face against her, his own arms around her rib cage, holding her tight. He was a man trapped inside a child, trying so hard to be stouthearted and yet wanting so desperately to be coddled.

"Cry, Matt," she whispered. "Tears are good for the soul."

He sniffed once, twice. A quiver rippled down his spine.

"It's all right, darling," she encouraged. "Let it out."

And he did. Deep, heart-wrenching sobs ripped from his throat and shook his child's body. He clutched her even tighter while his tears soaked through her bodice and chemise, dampening her breasts. Her own tears slipped down her cheeks and dripped onto the top of his head.

Now perched in the big oak in the side yard, the whippoorwill sang its sad, lonely song while the velvety darkness enveloped two lost, lonely souls who had found home in each other.

Eighteen

"Why did you never marry?" Betsy asked Auntie Kee late one afternoon.

It was the first time they'd been alone in several weeks, and although Betsy was enjoying Matt's company as well as the activity both teaching school and building the church had created, she missed her long, intimate talks with Auntie Kee. The subject of old-maidenhood had been preying on her mind for days, and with Matt gone to visit the building site with Uncle Begley, now seemed a good time to bring it up.

Auntie Kee swapped pinching biscuits for pinching her eyebrows together. "Everwhat made ye ast me that after all these years?"

"Spending so much time with Charlotte and Imer, I suppose."

Auntie Kee heaved a big sigh and went back to her biscuits. "I ain' never tol' ye how come me to be here in Peculiar Cove, have I?"

"No. And you don't have to tell me now, if you'd rather not."

"It don't hurt so much no more. Law, I disremember even when I thought about it last." She removed an iron skillet she'd been heating in the oven, plopped the biscuits into the hot grease, shoved the skillet back onto the rack, closed the oven door, then sat at the table with Betsy. "My maw was Cherokee," she began, "an' my paw was a white trapper. I never knowed my paw, jes' heared about him from Dancin' Water. That was my maw's name . . . Dancin' Water."

Her black eyes misted up with long-forgotten memories. "She was the sweetes' one woman, always happy and smilin', even when nobody in the village smiled back."

"Why didn't they like her?"

" 'Cause she willin'ly give herself to a white man, I reckon. It was sumpin she never talked about." Auntie Kee plucked at the checkered tablecloth, but her eyes seemed to be focused on something far, far away. "Anyways, Dancin' Water was a good maw. She told me tales about the Cherokee, teached me how to sew and build a cookfar. Without a man to hunt fer us, we never had much meat, but there was always lots of berries and wild greens in the sprang, fresh corn in the summer, and nuts all year long. We had us this little garden . . . But that don' have nothin' to do with yore question."

Betsy refilled their teacups and stirred honey into hers. It was so quiet the spoon clacking against the porcelain resounded in the room. As she stirred, she thought about how she'd spent so much energy over the years feeling sorry for herself without ever giving any real thought to the fact that others lost loved ones. Auntie Kee had always seemed such a tower of inner strength, but she, too, had grieved, perhaps still did. "You must have loved her very much."

"I did. But she ain't really gone, ye know. They never are—those we love, I mean. They's always there in our minds and hearts. Death cain't steal the mem'ries. Mem'ries is the only legacy we leave behind that's worth anythang."

"What happened to her?"

"She warn't never a strong woman. She tol' me oncet she'd had a bad fever as a child what left her weak. Course that never stopped her from workin'. She had to, if'n she wanted to survive." Auntie Kee took a ragged breath. "Anyways, the white man come along and said the Cherokee had to go—that would a-been back in thirty-eight. They wanted our land, ye see. Dancin' Water knew she'd never make sech a long trip, so we hid out in the mount'uns 'long with a passel o' others what didn' want to go."

Betsy had heard about The Removal from her father, about how so many Cherokees had died on the way to the reservation in the Indian Territory, but she'd never connected that event to Auntie Kee's life. Now, she marveled that she'd missed the link. "You must hate us all."

Auntie Kee's eyes widened. "Oh, no, child. They's good and they's bad in all races. I ain't never hated white folks jes' to be hatin' 'em. Like I tol' you, my paw was white."

"But he deserted your mother."

"What give ye that idee? He loved Dancin' Water. He never would a-left her if'n he'd had a choice. He died afore I was borned. He was shootin' at a deer and his gun backfarred." She stirred her tea and took several sips before continuing. "Like I was sayin', we hid out in the mount'uns, fount us a little cave fer shelter. We made out all right for a spell, then we had this real hard winter and Dancin' Water took sick. I did the bestest I could nursin' her, but it warn't enough. She was already too sickly, I s'pose."

Betsy wanted to say she was sorry, but the expression seemed so inadequate. Instead, she asked, "How old were you then?"

Auntie Kee frowned, thinking. " 'Bout yore age, I guess."

Betsy wondered what Dancing Water and hiding in the mountains to escape exile had to do with the fact that Auntie Kee never married. "What did you do after that?"

"I thought my own life had come to a end. Dancin' Water was the onliest person I ever really loved. I didn' thank thangs could get worser. But they did. After I give Dancin' Water a proper buryin'—"

"Hey, Auntie Kee!" Matt cried, dashing into the kitchen and throwing himself onto her lap. Betsy had been so engrossed in Auntie Kee's story, she hadn't heard him come in. Judging from the look on the older woman's face, she didn't think Auntie Kee had heard him, either. "They got one o' the walls up," Matt said, his voice full of enthusiasm. "I watched 'em fit the notches. Ye art to come see."

Auntie Kee hugged Matt against her flagging bosom. "I will, but not terday."

Uncle Begley ambled into the kitchen, raised his nose, and sniffed. "Ye got sumpin in the oven?"

"Law, my biscuits!" She snatched them out of the oven, waved at the smoke with a dishrag, and dumped the charred biscuits into a bucket. "I ain't so sure the chickens'll even eat 'em."

Betsy marveled at the way Auntie Kee's sunny voice wove gilded threads into the dark tapestry she'd been stitching. She'd obviously inherited Dancing Water's propensity for smiles and laughter in the face of adversity, a trait Betsy decided she must attempt to cultivate.

"Got a wagonload o' supplies in terday, Bets," Begley said.

"Anything for me?"

"Something was fer ye, I know. Let me see if'n I can recollect what it was." He scratched his chin and frowned, but she saw the twinkle in his blue eyes.

"Don't tease me, Uncle Begley. Did you get the blackboard?"

"So that's what that big ol' thang was!"

"And the books?"

"Got those, too. And the slates and pencils and paper. And some other stuff, I thank. Tom's unloadin' it all."

Eager to see it all, she started for the door, then turned

back to Uncle Begley. "Was it enough . . . I mean, do I owe you anything else?"

He winked at her conspiratorially. "More'n enough. We'll settle up later."

She was unpacking the crates with the glee of a child on Christmas morn when Tom walked in shouldering a load of milled lumber. "I kin fix yore porch now, Miss Betsy. And paint yore house, too. Course, I'd like to wait till we finish the church."

"That will be fine," Betsy said absently as she set a box of pencils on a bench and reached inside the crate for another item. "When will you finish the church, do you think?"

Tom stacked the boards against a wall. "I wish I could say this week. It'd be wondrous t' have it all ready when the preacher comes, but I spect hit'll be middle o' next week or so."

His mention of Steele got her attention. "Heavens above! It is almost time for the Rev to be back, isn't it?"

Where had the time gone? To school and Matt, both fulfilling and yet not fully satisfying.

Betsy asked Tom to stay for supper. Uncle Begley stayed, too—he ate with them almost every night now—then they all sat out on the porch and rocked in relative quiet while the mist-covered mountains grew a darker and darker purple. When Betsy caught Matt nodding off, she ushered him upstairs for his daily washing. By the time she tucked him in, Begley and Tom were gone and Auntie Kee was in bed, leaving Betsy to wonder what the half-breed woman had meant about things getting worse.

"Ye better look out when thangs are gittin' better," Andy Manous told Steele, " 'cause that's when they's about to git worse agin."

The two of them stood beside a fresh grave on a rise

overlooking the Manous farm, which lay almost halfway between Walnut Ridge and Peculiar Cove. They'd just finished burying Andy's wife of almost thirty years. Steele wished he could offer more comfort, wished there was something else to say besides "I'm sorry" or "She's with the Lord now." He wanted to say "Damn the bastards who did this" so much that he came close to ripping his clerical collar off and denouncing the ministry just so he could. Such venting of his spleen, however, would provide only temporary relief. A calm demeanor and sympathetic tone would serve his purposes much better.

"Arie was a good wife," Andy was saying. "Course, like mos' wimmin, she had her bouts o' sheer contrariness, but she could be the sweetes' thing ye ever come acrost. She worked right beside me, helpin' me clear the land and plow the fields and plant the crops, and through it all she kep' her wimmin's work done. 'Twould a-been easier, o' course, if'n we'd had more'n one youngun to help out. Lord knows, she tried t' brang 'em, but it warn't meant to be. It's a cryin' shame she lived through seven stillborns, lost our only son in the war, and then have to end up like this."

"Yes, it is," Steele agreed.

"They had her in the house. I don' know what they was a-doin' with her, but 'bout the time I topped that ridge over yander"—he waggled a finger at a distant tree-covered crest—"she come runnin' out, screamin' and tearin' at her hair. It come loose and was flowin' out behind her like it did when we was jes' young folks. I stood there starin' at it, 'memberin' how it use to be sech a purty brown, all rich and glossy like the meat inside a black walnut." His voice caught in his throat and he harrumped loudly before going on with his story.

"Then them cads come tearin' out behind her. It were three of 'em, young fellers from the look of it. They was waving thair hats and totin' thair guns—two of 'em had pistols and the other'un had a ol' blunderbuss—and hollerin' at her. I couldn't hear 'xactly what they was sayin' with me bein' up thair on the ridge and the wind a-blowin' the words around, but they was tellin' my Arie to run. They let her git almos' to the tree line 'fore they opened far."

Tears streamed down the farmer's weathered face. Emotionally torn himself, Steele looped an arm around the man's shoulders and waited patiently for him to finish his story. Talking it out would be good for Andy, but hearing an eye-witness account of what had most likely happened to his own family was difficult for Steele. After several long minutes, Andy took a ragged breath and picked back up where he'd left off.

"That's when I went to hollerin' myself. It was strange, the way I jes' watched and couldn't do nothin'. I ain' never felt so helpless. I had my musket with me—I'd been out huntin' rabbits, but I was too fur away to do anythang 'cept sceer 'em off. Maybe if I'd fared off a warnin', they'd a-hightailed it afore they kilt my Arie."

"It probably wouldn't have made a difference," Steele said. "They would have known you were out of range. At least you kept them from setting fire to the house. This is the first time, as far as I've heard, that they didn't burn the house."

"What good's this place gonna do me now?" Andy's voice was hoarse, ragged, and bitter. "Like I said, we finely got the land all worked, got the place all fixed up like we liked it, and was lookin' to spend some time jes' settin' on the porch and enjoyin' the view. With Arie gone, my heart ain't in this place no more."

"You can't give up. You have to **go** on. Otherwise, they win."

Later, when they were sharing a supper of cornbread and milk, Steele asked Andy if he had any idea who the marauders were.

"I didn' reco'nize 'em, if that's what ye mean. Course, my eyesight's not so good no more. But one of 'em drapped a letter."

Steele's heart skipped a beat. He cautioned himself about getting his hopes up, then did it anyway. This was the first real clue he'd had in a long time, and he deserved to savor it, even if it didn't turn out to be helpful. "Do you still have it?"

Andy rose to his feet. "I put it on the mantelshelf in t'other room. Let me git it."

It was all Steele could do to sit still while the older man retrieved the letter. One negative possibility after another raced through his brain. What if it had slipped off the shelf and fallen into the fire? At this altitude, the nights were still plenty chilly enough for a fire. What if the man who dropped it had come back to get it while Andy was working in the barn or otherwise out of sight? What if the letter contained no last names, no mention of place, nothing that would provide any assistance in identifying and locating the marauders?

"Here 'tis," Andy said, waving it at Steele. "Let me git the lamp so's ye kin see to read. Me, I never larned. Ye bein' a preacher and all, though, ye art to be able t' make it out jes' fine."

Just give it to me! Steele wanted to scream. His heart was thudding now, his pulse racing, his ears thrumming. Andy seemed to be moving so slowly, but Steele dared not let his anxiety show.

Just about the time Steele thought he would explode, the farmer set the lamp on the table and handed him the letter. It was a single sheet, yellowed and torn, the fold lines brown and smudged with dirty fingerprints, as though it had been opened and read numerous times. The paper was of good quality, better than most folks could afford, the kind that came with matching envelopes in a fancy stationery box.

"There was no envelope?"

"Naw. Jes' that one page. What do hit say?"

The milk curdled in his stomach and threatened to come back up. *Please, God,* Steele prayed, *let it say something useful, something specific. You can't have let me come this close just to snatch hope away again.* He closed his eyes, took several deep breaths, and unfolded the sheet.

"My dearest Willy," he read aloud, then stopped abruptly. The small, meticulously neat writing blurred and Steele blinked to clear the sudden gathering of moisture in his eyes. There were hundreds, thousands of men named Willy, he told himself. It could be any one of them. It was only a coincidence. It was *all* coincidence. Betsy's brother was dead. Killed at Shiloh. The man who called himself Ty Williams might be an impostor. He might even be one of the marauders. But he wasn't Betsy's brother.

As the handwriting gradually came back into focus, Steele's gaze moved to the bottom of the letter. For an instant, he died. He plunged into the depths of hell and knew, really knew, for the first time in his life what it meant to suffer. He'd only thought he suffered before. But nothing—not the horrors of war, not losing his leg, not coming home to find his mother and sisters in their graves—nothing had ever affected him as deeply as the neatly penned name at the bottom of the letter.

It was signed: "Your loving sister, Betsy."

"Air ye all right, Preacher?"

Andy Manous hovered over him, fanning his face with the letter. Steele tried to speak, but nothing would come out.

"Ye look like ye seen a ghostie. They must be sumpin powerful bad in that thair letter."

"No." With the back of his forearm, he wiped the sweat

from his brow into his hairline. "No. It's just a letter from a woman to her . . . husband." He almost said "brother," but changed his mind. Betsy's only guilt could be in harboring a criminal. Even if that were true, he doubted she had any idea what her brother was doing. Folks might not see it that way, though. If they'd believed her to be demon-possessed, they'd believe anything. He had to keep her identity a secret, at least for the time being. His immediate concern, though, was in creating an explanation of his reaction that would satisfy Andy Manous.

"I think it was the milk." Yes that might appease Andy. "It soured on my stomach. Could I have some water?"

The farmer brought him a gourd dipper filled almost to the brim with cool, fresh spring water. Steele drank all of it and asked for more along with a damp rag to wipe his face. While Andy was thus occupied, Steele glanced over the letter, which he noted was dated January 11, 1862. The contents were innocuous enough, a simple accounting of a week's activities and an appeal to Willy to write back. She hadn't mentioned Peculiar Cove by name. When he'd emptied the dipper again, he read Betsy's letter to Andy, changing Auntie Kee to Aunt Kate and Betsy to Beth, hoping to avert any possible ties to the Tyler family. Someone else could come along, however, and discover the truth.

"What were you planning to do with this letter?" he asked when he'd finished.

"Thair ain't no law 'round here t' give it to. I figured on takin' it to Walnut Ridge next time I go and asting some folks thair what I art to do with it. But seein' as how ye're here and ye're a larned man, I'll jes' ast ye."

"I don't reckon there's much you can do with it, other than send it to a U.S. marshal." This was exactly what Steele feared would happen to the letter if Andy took it to Walnut Ridge, and that would never do. Even without an address or last names, too many people could easily identify Willy, Betsy, and Auntie Kee, should all their names appear together, as they did in Betsy's letter. He was no less determined now than before to vindicate his family, but he didn't want Betsy and Auntie Kee dragged into this. He had to persuade Andy to give him custody of the letter. "I'm on my way to Peculiar Cove. I can take it with me, if you'd like."

Andy nodded without hesitation. "I'd 'preciate that, Preacher. Maybe ye could write the marshal a note fer me, tellin' what happened to my Arie and all."

"I'll be glad to do everything I can to see these men brought to justice."

It wasn't a lie, Steele argued with his conscience. He *would* see the marauders brought to justice. All right, so he'd intentionally misled Andy Manous, but only to protect Betsy and Auntie Kee.

Although Steele hadn't begun his circuit in Peculiar Cove, it had become his reference point. From the moment he left, he started counting the days until he'd be back. Twice now he'd completed the circle in four weeks, but this time he'd tarried fewer hours along the way, enough all together to gain three extra days to spend with Betsy and Matt. The day and night he'd stayed with Andy Manous shaved off one of those days, and the recent events at the Manous farm made him take a closer look at how he spent the remaining two.

Given his druthers, he'd go straight to Hudson's Mill and nab Ty Williams, but unless the Scoggins brothers were there, he'd play hell catching them later. No, he'd wait until he could get all three at one time.

He considered, seriously considered, forgetting all about his ministry and taking off after them. The only thing that stopped him was not knowing where to look. They could be anywhere in these mountains, so well hidden he could spend the rest of his life searching and never find them. A mountain man knew how to cover his tracks, knew how to camouflage a cave to fool even the most discerning and experienced eye, knew how to cook without visible fire or smoke, knew how to hunt without firing a gun. And while he was looking, they'd be somewhere else, murdering someone else.

A far more logical plan was to go to Hudson's Mill, hide out in the woods, and watch the Hudson house and gristmill to see who came and went. Eventually, Ty would slip off or the Scoggins brothers would show up, and he'd be waiting. The problem with this plan was that weeks, maybe even months, could pass before he got such an opportunity, and in the meantime he'd have to have a ready water source and ample food at hand. He supposed it was crazy, too, to think he could stand watch twenty-four hours a day for an indefinite period of time.

But now that he had Betsy's letter, he couldn't just not do anything. Although the letter obliterated any doubt about Ty's real identity and his involvement with the marauders, it didn't satisfy Steele's curiosity about whether or not Betsy knew Willy was alive and well—and living a lie. If she did know, if Willy did slip into the cove from time to time, then maybe the best place to start was at the Tyler house.

He'd spend his two extra days in Peculiar Cove as planned, he decided, though not with Betsy and Matt. Instead, he'd watch the Tyler house from the woods across the road. And if he were lucky, Willy would choose this time to sneak home to see Betsy. Maybe, he was already there . . .

Nineteen

"I wish you'd quit moping over that gal-woman," Zero Scoggins told his younger brother Hobe. "She ain't even purty."

"Course, she is," Hobe countered, holding a small daguerreotype closer to the campfire.

"Watch out! Ye'll burn it," Lam Williams said.

Hobe snatched his hand back, then shot Lam a look as pizen-mean as any he'd ever displayed. "Copper don't burn. I don't like ye joshin' me, Lam, and ye know it."

"And ye got my knees a-quakin'." Nothing in either Lam's voice or demeanor indicated a smidgen of fear. "So what ye gonna do about it?"

Hobe lunged at Lam, who leaned hard to the right. Hobe sprawled belly down on the hard ground and got up swinging his fists and cussing. "Ye sorry, no-'count, two-toed varmint! I'm gonna git ye fer that."

Thinking on stopping the fight, Zero made a step or two forward, then changed his mind. Hobe and Lam had been spoiling for a fracas, and he figured he might as well let 'em go at it and get it outten their systems once and for all. Hauling off and hitting a man you'd been itching to whup was a lot like sidling up and kissing a girl you'd been longing to spark. It satisfied your craving so's you could put your mind to other things, leastaways for a spell.

He'd been thinking it was getting near time to let Hobe

kiss the gal-woman in the picture. Course, that'd be the end of her, which was one reason he'd put it off so long. Another was that they hadn't hit no other places quite so close to a town, 'cept maybe that Montgomery farm up near White Oak Flats. They'd been near enough to the gal-woman's house to spit on it, pert near anyways, it being right at the aidge of Peculiar Cove. Hobe didn't know that, and he'd be right angry when he found out, but he'd get over it. Just like he'd get over killing her.

It was a shame they had to kill one of their own kind. Snuffing out someone whose brother had fought and died for the Union went against Zero's scruples, but it couldn't be helped. The gal-woman might not be so handsome to look at, but neither was Hobe. Fact of it was, Hobe was downright ugly, had been since the Johnnies set fire to that train and Hobe burned his face half-off. Women took one look at Hobe and either ran the other way or fainted dead out. The poor boy had no choice but to force hisself on a woman if'n he wanted her. And with a face so easily recognized, they didn't dare leave no witnesses behind.

While Hobe and Lam rolled around on the ground, Zero sat back down near the fire and picked up the daguerreotype his brother had dropped. For the life of him, he couldn't understand why Hobe thought the woman was pretty. Her eyes were too pale, her nose was too narrow, and she had this real high-toned look about her, like she had more book-larnin' than sense. Zero hoped she had more money than either. Pickin's were getting slimmer all the time, and he was getting ready to move on.

He'd been thinking on Chattanooga. They hadn't hit that area yet, and it was bound to be full of Confederate sympathizers. Some jangling money would be nice when they got there. He was goin' to eat hisself a big ol' supper in a respectable place, buy him a decent pair of boots, and he might even find him one of them fancy parlor houses to pass the night in.

But first, they had to make a stop by the Tyler place over in the cove and take care of the little gal-woman, before Hobe made a mistake while he was thinking about her instead of what he was doing. The kid could end up in a bury hole that way.

"That's enough, boys," Zero called. When they didn't respond, he added, "I mean it now. Quit yore tusslin'. Git on back over here and bank this far 'fore it gets dark. We got some tawlkin' to do."

Zero was used to giving orders. Hobe and Lam were used to following them. The two broke off their scrapping and did as they were told.

Since Ty had lived at the mill for the better part of a year before the wedding, the pattern of his life altered little with marriage. He rose early, worked all day, and took long walks with Lydia in the woods and by the creek between supper and twilight. This was their special time, their one hour of the day to put the stress of life's labors aside and enjoy the beauty and wonder of nature. At times, few words passed between them during the entire walk, and when they did converse, the subject was never serious. This was their unspoken rule and they'd never broken it—until now.

They were sitting on rocks in the creek below the mill race, the cold, crystal-clear water rushing over their bare feet, their hands clasped between them. Ty had pretty much made up his mind to tell Lydia all about his deceit, but he never could seem to find an appropriate time. They were both so busy during the day, and he never knew who might show up at the mill. This was a conversation that could not be overheard and wouldn't bear interruption. At night, when they came back from their walk, they sat in the parlor with Mrs. Hudson for a spell before going to bed. And when they retired to their room, Ty thought of nothing beyond making love to Lydia.

That left their peaceful time between supper and twilight. Ty feared that once he'd told Lydia his story, they might never pass another such carefree hour together. But it had to be done. He'd postponed it far too long already. But where should he begin?

"What's troublin' ye, honey?" Lydia asked, taking him completely by surprise.

"Why do you ask?"

" 'Cause something is, and don't tell me it ain't. Hit's been a-gnawin' at ye since ye come here, maybe before. I use to think it had sumpin t' do with me. I know now it don't."

He squeezed her hand lightly. "How do you know that?"

"If'n there was anythang wrong with me, ye couldn't make love to me the way ye do. It's sumpin else, ain't it?"

Nodding, he looked off at the mill upstream, watched the water spill over the big wheel, and let his soul absorb the rhythm of the splashes. He couldn't look at Lydia. If he did, if he saw the initial shock in her clear blue eyes, he'd never be able to forget it.

"Ye don't have to tell me if'n ye don't want to."

"Yes, I do. I have to do it for me. I can't live with the lies anymore. I can't look at myself in the shaving glass without thinking about it. If I don't tell you, I'll go stark raving mad, like my sister did."

"I thought yore sister—"

"Died with pneumonia. That was one of the lies. My sister has never been sick a day in her life, so far as I know. She lives in Peculiar Cove." He heard Lydia's sharp intake of breath and wondered how he was ever going to make it all the way through his tale.

"Not Crazy Bets?" Her voice rang with sympathy, not the disdain he'd expected. "But her name's Tyler . . . oh."

"And my name isn't Ty Williams, it's Willy Tyler. I changed it—after Shiloh."

"What happened at Shiloh?" It was almost a whisper.

A shiver traced its way slowly down his spine, raising turkey bumps on the back of his neck. "For all practical purposes, Willy Tyler died there. I shouldn't have ever joined up. I had no business thinking I could be a soldier. I didn't even care about the war, didn't understand why we were fighting."

"Then why *did* ye join up?"

He laughed, a self-contemptuous snort. "The boys at school said it would be fun. We all thought it would be a grand adventure. We'd fire a few volleys in the air and the Johnnies would tuck tail and run, then we'd all be home in time for supper. We were so young. So very stupid."

She rubbed the pad of her thumb over his knuckle. "Ye had no way o' knowin' any better."

"No, I don't suppose we did. We were just foolish schoolboys. I'm probably the only one of our group who survived the war."

"It's all right if ye kilt a man. Hit was war."

Was that what she thought was troubling him? That he'd killed a man? "You don't understand."

"Ye lived. That's all that matters t' me. I don't care what ye had to do. I only care that ye lived through it."

The setting sun turned the deeper parts of the creek into dark red pools, reminding him of the bloody pond at Shiloh. "I lived through it because I wasn't there. Not after Shiloh."

"Was ye captured?"

He took a long, ragged breath and closed his eyes against the pain of remembrance. He couldn't tell her he'd deserted. Not yet. "Shiloh was awful, horrible beyond words, beyond belief. The Rebs attacked right after dawn that Sunday morning, catching us completely by surprise. They busted into our camp, firing into the tents. Hundreds of men were mercilessly killed, sleeping in their tents or running down company streets. Those of us who survived ran for our lives. We must have run two miles before someone got us organized. Green recruits who'd never spent a day in battle kept running. Some, like me, who had seen battle, kept running. We were rounded up at gunpoint and forced back into line."

She slipped her arm around his waist. "Hit must've been fearful."

"The Johnnies hit us from all sides at once. The noise was constant, a never-ending terrible roar. I fell in with Benjamin Prentiss's men. Must have been four or five thousand of us shooting back—and getting shot at. One man after another fell. I kept thinking the next one was going to be me. Then it hit me. Right on the forehead."

"What hit ye?"

"A shell. I guess it was a dud because it didn't explode. I fell, whether from the force of the impact or the surety that I was dead, I don't know. It sort of skimmed up my head, taking the hide with it. I remember the blood trickled into my eyes and I lay there wondering how I could feel it if I was dead. Then I heard someone shout that General Grant had ordered Prentiss to hold out as long as possible, and I knew by some miracle I was alive—and that by hook or by crook that would be the end of the war for me."

"What did ye do?"

"Just lay real still with my eyes closed, praying a stray bullet didn't get me. Ten, maybe twelve times the Rebs tried to overrun us. Finally, late that afternoon, they did, and Prentiss surrendered."

"And that's when they captured ye."

"No. The Federals scattered. We all feared capture

worse than death. The Rebs took out after the blue-coats and I was left alone with the dead and wounded. There was a man lying close to me who was about my size. A shell had exploded in his face and it was . . . unrecognizable. I switched caps and knapsacks with him, then crawled on my belly out of there. It was near dark by that time and things were quieting down. I moved away from the noise toward the river, but away from Pittsburg Landing. We had more men arriving in gunboats, so there was a lot of activity at the landing. I laid out by the river until late that night, listening for pickets, but it was all quiet where I was. Nothing but bullfrogs and crickets making noise—and scads of mosquitoes. I was afraid to slap them. The rascals made raw meat out of my face and neck and hands—until it started raining. It rained all night."

"But ye got away."

"Yes, somehow—by the grace of God, I suppose—I got away."

"I'm glad."

He looked at her then and saw even in the thin light the love shining through her eyes, saw her genuine happiness, and knew he need not fear condemnation from that camp. Yet, he wondered if she truly understood the magnitude of his deed.

"But I deserted. I broke my promise to serve the Union until the end of the war."

She leaned into him, laying her head on his shoulder. "I don't care what ye did back there at Shiloh. Just so long as ye don't break yore vows to me."

He put his arms around her and held her close. "Never fear, my darling. I won't ever leave you."

Late that night, when they lay sated in each other's arms, Lydia whispered close to his ear, "Does yore sister know?"

"No."

"Ye have t' tell her."

"I know, but I don't want to. I don't know if I should see her again."

"How come?"

He sighed. "It's hard to explain. You'd have to know Betsy. Her will was always a lot stronger than mine. I always wanted to be an engineer, but even though she knew I don't like animals, she thought I should be a professor of zoology. She never would let me be myself. I worry about falling under her influence again."

"Seems to me ye've got a purty strong head yourself now. Ye shouldn't put it off. Somebody from Peculiar Cove's li'ble to come here and reco'nize ye. Hit's bound t' happen."

"I'm surprised it hasn't already. I thought about leaving, about taking you out West and starting over."

She was quiet for a moment, considering the possibility, he supposed. "If'n that's what ye want t' do, I'll go with ye. I'll go with ye anywheres ye say. But then ye'll always be a-lookin' over yore shoulder, wonderin' who's gonna come along that knew ye from the war or school or some'eres else."

He'd thought of that, too, but what other options remained open? "What do you think we ought to do?"

She heaved a sigh and snuggled closer. "Men ain't suppose to ast their wimminfolk what they thank."

Although he couldn't see her face, he could hear the smile in her voice. "Well, I'm asking."

"I thank ye should go see Betsy. I thank ye should go tamarr, 'fore she has a chance to find out some other way."

The prospect of seeing Betsy again both thrilled and frightened him. "But what will I tell her?"

"The truth of it, like ye done tol' me."

"And what if she doesn't forgive me?"

"Hit's a chance ye have t' take.

"Maybe you're right," he said, not quite believing it.

"And what do I say when other people ask where I've been all this time and why I changed my name? If I tell everyone the truth, it could mean my life."

"How come?"

"Deserting is punishable by death."

She shivered and hugged him tighter. "I don't like fibbin', but I druther ye fibbed than . . . t'other."

"Then I suppose we need to create a story, one we tell to everyone, including Betsy. It has to be logical and credible—and simple. I have an idea, but it will require your going to Peculiar Cove with me."

Lydia giggled. "I've always wanted t' meet Crazy Bets. What're we goin' t' say?"

"I'll tell you on the way."

And please, Lord, Ty prayed, *don't let Betsy really be crazy.*

As Ty and Betsy traveled to Peculiar Cove from the east, Steele approached from the west.

Late that afternoon, Steele coaxed Dusty off the wagon road and followed the branch until he reached the wooded area that had become his sanctuary. Evening shadows mottled the creek and stretched deep into the trees, reminding him that it had been just about this hour of the day when he'd first found this spot. He made camp in a small clearing within the woods, put Dusty's feed bag on his head, and dug some dried venison and soda crackers out of his knapsack.

While Steele was eating a cold supper, Ty and Lydia were building a cookfire under a rocky overhang on a slope a few miles east of town. Although they could have easily made it to the cove by nightfall, this was not in their scheme. As they'd bounced along in the jolt wagon, they'd laid out their plan, taken it apart, and put it back together again so many times they'd both lost count.

"I think we can make it work," Ty said, as much to

convince himself as Lydia. She must have detected his lack of confidence, because she stopped unpacking the food basket to lay a hand on his arm and give it a reassuring squeeze.

"I *know* we can."

"If only I could be as certain as you are . . ."

She handed him a hard-boiled egg, then took one herself and began to peel it. "Ye must believe hit'll work, Ty, or it won't. Thank about how ye kept all of us fooled fer nigh on to a year. And ye could a-kept right on a-foolin' us if'n ye'd had a mind to."

He chewed thoughtfully for a moment. "But that was different."

"No, it weren't. Ye made up a tale before and stuck by it. Ye can do it again. And this time, ye got me t' help ye."

His heart filled with love. "You're the best thing that ever happened to me, Lydia. I don't know what I ever did to deserve so much happiness."

She smiled so wide her eyes crinkled up. "I don't know what I'd do without ye. Ye come through the war. Ye kin come through this. Ye have t' believe, Ty. Please tell me ye believe."

"I do," he said. And at that moment, he did.

"Something's in the air," Betsy said.

"Gnats," Auntie Kee replied, waving her hand in front of her face. "I ain't never seed so many in all my borned days. Wonder what brung 'em."

"What I'm talking about isn't tangible."

"What's that mean?"

"It's ethereal."

"Oh, the stars." Auntie Kee scooted her rocking chair closer to the railing and looked up at the sky. "They ain't out yet. May not be none with all them clouds to hide 'em. I spect them clouds is what brung all these bothersome gnats. The air's heavy with rain. That what ye mean?"

Given other circumstances, Betsy would have been laughing hard enough to get a stitch in her side, but she wasn't even smiling. "This is serious. I'm excited and scared at the same time."

The screen door banged. "What ye a-sceered of, Miss Betsy?" Matt asked, his hands full of oatmeal cookies. He gave one to Auntie Kee, offered one to Betsy, then shrugged his shoulders when she ignored him and plopped himself down in a chair.

"I don't know," she said, fully aware of everything going on around her and yet feeling strangely apart from it all.

"Hit's gittin' 'bout time fer the preacher-man t' be here." Auntie Kee laughed. "Ye reckon that's what's got yore blood all stirred up?"

"That may be part of it," Betsy allowed, "but it's more than that. I can't explain it. I just have the most peculiar feeling that tomorrow my life is going to change. *Our* lives are going to change."

"There ye go tawlkin' crazy again." Auntie Kee rose from her chair and limped to the door. "This ol' heavy air's got ye tetched in the head same as hit's got my rheumatiz cuttin' shines with my knees. Ye can set out here fightin' gnats if'n ye want to, but I'm goin' in the house."

Twenty

In warm weather, Uncle Begley left the door open and depended on howdies rather than the bell to announce his customers. Usually, he was sitting on the porch or in his rocking chair by the stove anyway, but sometimes he was in the back room, where he stored what little extra stock he kept.

On the morning of May third, a Thursday, Begley couldn't decide whether the unseasonably heavy, motionless air served to freshen or stifle the interior of the store.

"Hit's goin' to be a hot'un," he mumbled as he opened the door and set the wedge for the fourth or fifth time. The rain, if it ever came, should cool things off a bit. He ambled out into the road and gave the dreary skies a long, hard stare. The clouds were just hanging there, full and gray, but a long way from ready to release their wet burden. Unless something happened to stir them up soon, the rain would be a spell yet.

He wiped the nape of his neck with his handkerchief and was turning to go back inside when he saw the jolt wagon coming down the road. He couldn't recall ever laying eyes on the pretty young woman before, but the man holding the reins looked vaguely familiar. Begley narrowed his eyes against the haze, trying to get a better look. For all the world, the driver looked like Willy Tyler. But that wasn't possible. Willy Tyler was dead. Buried at Shiloh.

The young man turned the mule off the road and pulled the wagon up beside the store, temporarily blocking Begley's view of the couple while exposing the wagon's cargo—a large wooden tub with a small waterwheel attached to it. Why in tarnation would anyone want to bolt a waterwheel to a warshtub? It'd make a dandy head ranser, he supposed, but the wheel took up so much space that a body would have a dickens of a time tryin' to bathe in that tub. Maybe it wasn't meant for warshing bodies. He seemed to recall hearing Mary Snider rave about some fellow over in Hudson's Mill who'd invented a contraption for warshing clothes. Could this be it?

The couple came around the corner of the porch then. They were holding hands and eyeing each other like there was no one else in the world besides them. For an instant, Begley's vision wavered and the couple became him and Kee when they were both young. He should have married her then. He *would* have married her then—if she'd agreed.

"How do you do?" the young man said, jerking Begley back to the present. "Are you the storekeeper?"

The young man's resemblance to Willy was remarkable: the hazel eyes, sparkling with a hint of mischief . . . the way his sandy blond hair grew to a point on his forehead . . . the smile, so like Betsy's . . . even the way his bottom teeth overlapped in the front. His face was harder than Willy's had been the last time Begley saw him. The cheekbones were more prominent; tiny lines permanently crinkled the corners of his mouth; a wide, ugly scar ran up the middle of his forehead—but it could have been Willy's face six years later.

"That'd be me," Begley said, deciding to play along with the young man. Maybe he just looked a lot like Willy. That had to be it. "Folks around here call me Uncle Begley."

Not a single trace of recognition flickered across the

young man's face. Instead, his smile grew a mite and he stuck out his hand for Begley to shake. "Pleased to meet you, Uncle Begley. This is my wife, Lydia, and I'm Ty. Ty Williams."

And the voice! How had he missed the voice? It was Willy's, sure and certain. But, how? Could it be possible? "You from around these parts?"

"Hudson's Mill."

"And what brangs ye to Peculiar Cove?"

The man calling himself Ty Williams waved a hand at the contraption in the back of the jolt wagon. "My invention. With proper water flow, it washes clothes all by itself. Lydia and I are just starting out—we've only been married a few weeks, and we need furniture and linens and other household goods. We're hoping to find some folks who'd like to buy one of my machines—or maybe trade for it."

Begley scratched his jaw. This was too much to absorb all at one time, but not so much that he couldn't see the futility of such a contraption in flat country. "This is a cove," he said. "Onliest one I reckon could use yore invention would be Betsy Tyler."

Again, not a flinch. "How's that?"

"She's got the onliest piece o' land what backs up to the branch where it comes down the mount'un."

"Then I suppose we'll go see Mrs. Tyler."

"Hit's *Miss* Tyler."

Ty dipped his chin. "Would you be so kind as to direct us to her house?"

Weary of fighting sleep, Betsy rose at first light, bathed the sheen of perspiration from her body, and went downstairs with the intention of baking a cake or pie. The very notion of building a fire in the stove—and thus further heating up the already sweltering kitchen—stopped her, though. She couldn't recall a single time when the weather had been so muggy this early in the year.

Maybe the promise of rain and the sudden congestion of pesky gnats were all the thick, heavy air carried. As she'd tossed and turned, Betsy had worked very hard at trying to convince herself Auntie Kee was right, but she still didn't think so. There was something else, something she couldn't quite grab hold of, something that had nothing to do with the Rev's pending arrival. In fact, she had the strangest feeling he was already in the cove, or at least nearby. His being in the cove without her knowledge didn't make a lick of sense, but it didn't trouble her. If something had happened to him, she'd know it in her heart.

Continuing to ponder the reason behind this curious feeling didn't make a lick of sense, either. Whatever was going to happen would happen. She just hoped it happened soon.

Determined to put it behind her, she took the bucket and headed for Peculiar Branch.

Peculiar Branch tumbled down the mountain that hugged the rear of the Tyler property, then took a winding course westward for a bit before ambling off down a hill to the south. Years ago, some of the local men had constructed a crude but sturdy bridge across the stream where it crossed the wagon road. This was where Steele had left the road to follow the branch. From the bridge, the creek twisted and turned some more, eventually taking an eastern trek through the fairly level valley.

Although its initial loop formed a natural boundary on three sides of the Tyler property, clumps of trees and masses of dense brush masked the view of the house from all but a few locations. These were both narrow in scope and some distance from the house, thus enabling Steele to sneak along the banks of the branch in broad daylight with only minimal risk of detection, while allowing him far greater range of surveillance than the single secluded spot where he'd chosen to set up camp. He couldn't watch the house from every angle, but he could, perhaps, discover a trail of disturbed undergrowth somewhere along the outskirts of Betsy's acreage.

If he wanted to slip in and out of the cove, he surely wouldn't come down the road. Instead, he'd worm his way through the woods and come in on the blind side. He was counting on her brother doing just that. Besides, Steele had to move around, to work some of the stiffness out of his joints. He made it all the way to the spot where the branch came off the mountain, though, without finding even one sign of someone's having recently passed by. Tired and frustrated, he sat at the base of a good-sized black oak, leaned against the trunk, and was nodding off to sleep when a chorus of shouting children snatched him awake.

What in tarnation! Children at Betsy's house?

Matt. They were there to play with Matt. But why so many of them?

He inched forward through the trees, careful to move quietly, stealthily, yet eager to see what had brought so many children so early in the morning.

Even over the rattle of the jolt wagon Ty heard the shouts and laughter of children at play long before they reached the big frame house on the outskirts of town.

"I thought ye said yore sister wasn't married-up," Lydia said.

"She isn't. She wasn't. She couldn't have that many children even if she was. Not in such a short time."

Lydia laid a hand on his knee. "Ye sound a mite narviss."

"I am. I'm not worried about saying the wrong thing. After all, I got through the part with Uncle Begley okay . . . but—"

"Hit's seeing Betsy again, hain't it?"

He nodded.

"She'll reco'nize ye. Even if Uncle Begley didn't."

"It's not that. What if she doesn't love me anymore? What if she doesn't want me back in her life?"

"Did she love ye before?"

"I think she did. In her own way."

"Then she'll love ye now. In her own way."

Ty hoped that "way" would be different. He hoped the years had changed her, mellowed her, chipped off some of her reserve, slashed away at her need to control others' lives—his life. The important thing, he supposed, was that he was different—stronger, more confident in himself and his abilities. And now he had Lydia to love, to focus his attention on.

They rounded a curve and the house came into view. Even in the gloom, the entire front and half of the east-facing wall sparkled with fresh paint, which a man on a ladder was applying. To Ty's surprise, the yard wore a well-tended air, and four rocking chairs sat in a conversational grouping on the front porch. Betsy and Auntie Kee had never been porch gossips, nor had there ever been more than a chair or two on the porch. Ty had spent many a solitary evening there, looking out at the distant peaks and reflecting on life in general. From the looks of it, the porch had become a gathering place, and for more people than Betsy and Auntie Kee. Was it possible? Had Betsy found herself a husband, maybe a widower with children?

All those children in front of the barn had to come from somewhere . . .

All those children! There must be thirty or more, big ones and little ones, girls and boys, some running around the yard in front of the barn, some standing or sitting in small groups. A woman who looked vaguely familiar stepped out the door of the barn and rang a hand bell. Quickly, the children gathered up books and syrup buckets and filed inside.

Books and syrup buckets? Children in the barn? What was going on?

"School? Air they havin' school in the barn?" Lydia asked, echoing Ty's own questions.

"That's what it looks like to me." He guided the mule into the side yard and pulled back on the reins.

"Was that yore sister?" Lydia whispered.

He lowered his voice, too. "Nope. I'm not exactly sure who that woman is, but I think she's from around here."

"What air ye a-goin' to do?" For the first time since they'd left Hudson's Mill, Lydia sounded anxious.

Ty set the brake and climbed down, then helped Lydia alight. "Knock on the back door, I suppose, and hope either Betsy or Auntie Kee answers. They must still live here. Uncle Begley sent us here, remember?"

And Uncle Begley had corrected him when he'd said, "Mrs. Tyler." Ty had been so anxious and confused he'd forgotten. He wondered when she'd started holding school in the barn. He couldn't quite imagine Betsy teaching school. Of course, she might not even be involved. Perhaps she'd only donated the use of the barn.

" 'Lo there, young feller," the man on the ladder called.

As Ty watched him climb down, he searched his brain trying to recall the man's name. John, maybe? No, Tom. That's who he was. Tom Dickerson. He hadn't changed much at all.

"Ye 'pear right familiar. Do I know ye from somewheres?"

"I don't think so." The lie stuck in Ty's craw. Reminding himself of the importance of his performance, he stuck out a hand. "Ty Williams from Hudson's Mill. And this is my wife, Lydia."

"Howdy do." Tom tipped his slouch hat at Lydia, pumped Ty's hand, and introduced himself, adding, "Ye sure do look like somebody I use to know."

Ty smiled, holding his breath and waiting for Tom to say more. He didn't suppose it mattered much now if Tom realized who he was, but he'd planned for it to be Betsy and he really wanted everything to go according to plan.

"Ye here to see Miss Betsy?" Tom asked, his eyes twinkling mischievously. So, he did know! At least, Ty thought he did.

Praying Tom wouldn't give him away, Ty inclined his head toward the jolt wagon. "The man at the store told me she might be interested in buying one of my clothes washing machines."

"That'd be Uncle Begley. She's in there"—Tom jerked his head toward the barn—"holdin' school. But she's got Miss Charlotte and Miss Imer to help her. I reckon she could break a-loose fer a spell. I'll git her fer ye."

Tom sauntered off toward the barn. Lydia took Ty's hand in hers and squeezed it gently. "Have faith. Hit'll all work out."

"I hope so."

"Well, I'll be a treed coon!" Steele muttered to himself. He'd barely gotten over his amazement that Betsy had not only started a school in the cove but was also holding it in her barn, when Ty and Lydia drove up. So much for his theory about sneaking in instead of coming down the road.

His position in the brush was too far away to allow him to hear what was being said, but he gathered from the way Tom merely talked to Ty that the carpenter either didn't recognize him as Willy or already knew he was alive. Of course, Steele couldn't completely discount the possibility that he was wrong about the whole thing, that there was no reason for Tom to recognize Ty Williams one way or the other. He reckoned Betsy's reaction would be the telling factor.

He eased forward as much as he dared, leaving only the barest covering of laurel leaves between him and the clearing, every muscle and nerve as tight as a new fiddle string as he waited for Betsy to join her brother in the yard.

Because Tom stored his tools and materials in the barn, Betsy didn't give his sudden appearance a second thought until he motioned to her to join him at the door.

"Ye better come see."

Her heart leapt into her throat and her knees went to shaking. "See what?"

"There's a young feller out thair, wants to sell ye sumpin."

"Whew!" she breathed, laying her open palm on her palpitating heart. "For a moment there—" The expression on Tom's face arrested her tongue. His eyes glinted with mischief, or something closely akin to it, but his jaw was clamped tightly shut, whether out of repressed humor or concern she couldn't tell. "What is it, Tom?"

"I don' know. I mean, I ain't sure. Ye better come see fer yourself."

Was the appearance of this stranger the reason behind the peculiar sense of expectancy that had been troubling her? she wondered as she followed Tom into the hazy light. But how could that be? He was just a young fellow, Tom said, who wanted to sell her something.

With Tom walking in front of her, she couldn't see much besides his back, but she caught a glimpse of a young couple standing beside a wagon. Her curiosity getting the best of her, she hastened her steps, catching up with Tom and moving to his side.

They were almost upon the couple, no more than ten or fifteen paces away. The young woman looked up and smiled at Betsy, but the young man, who was lifting a large wooden washtub out of the wagon, didn't turn around. There was something oddly familiar about him, something that snatched at her heartstrings and wouldn't let go. It wasn't just the height or build or hair color. In fact, her Willy had been shorter and leaner the last time she saw him, and his hair had been a shade lighter. It was the grace of his movements, the slenderness of his hands, the curve of his jaw. If she didn't know better, she'd swear it was Willy.

But the name didn't fit this young man. Her Willy didn't have this man's strength, either of character or body. An aura of confidence and a powerful sense of purpose clung to this man—traits Willy had never possessed.

The young man set the washtub on the ground and straightened up. That was when she saw his eyes. The sparkle in their hazel depths sucked the breath right out of her, making her head spin and her knees weak. She grabbed Tom's arm for support and forced air into her lungs. They were Willy's eyes. How did this man get Willy's eyes?

"This is Ty Williams and his wife, Lydia, from over in Hudson's Mill," Tom said. "And that there contraption is a clothes warshin' machine."

Betsy gave the washtub a cursory glance. "How does it work?" Her voice sounded croaky and she cleared her throat.

Ty Williams smiled, showing her his overlapping bottom teeth, which were exactly like Willy's. "You set it up near a stream and run a mill race to it so the water turns this wheel . . ."

And he had Willy's voice.

Betsy gasped for air, her splayed hand pushing on her chest while her head spun out of control and her vision shimmered with a myriad of glittering dots.

"Catch her. She's going to fall," Willy said, sounding to her like he was down in a well. And then she was tumbling into the well, into a narrow black shaft from which there was no return.

From his hiding place behind the laurel branch, Steele watched Betsy crumple to the ground. Without thinking, he rushed forward to help her, but caught himself on the third stride. Fortunately, all attention was focused on Betsy, which allowed him opportunity to return to the brush before anyone saw him. At least, he hoped no one saw him. He'd never be able to explain to anyone's satisfaction why he was skulking in the woods, and though he was concerned for Betsy, she had Tom and Lydia and Ty to take care of her.

Steele was sure she'd only fainted and would come to soon. Nevertheless, he wasn't leaving until she did. He had to know she was all right. Lydia rushed to the house and opened the back door while Tom scooped Betsy into his arms and carried her inside, thus preventing Steele from seeing anything else. He wondered if Auntie Kee would faint, too, when she saw Ty, who'd followed Tom and Lydia into the house. Steele couldn't call him Willy—not only because he'd met him as Ty, but also because the name didn't fit. Willy implied weakness, even silliness.

He wiggled into a fairly comfortable position, his eyes trained on the open doorway, but his thoughts scurrying hither and yon. He brought them into focus as best he could. Obviously, Betsy hadn't known until this morning that her brother was alive, but Ty's method of letting her discover that had Steele completely baffled. It simply didn't make sense for anyone as intelligent as Ty Williams to choose to show up in the middle of the day, when everyone in town could see him—not if he honestly had something to hide. Nor did it make sense for Ty to stand there talking to his sister as though she were a stranger. And what did Ty's clothes washing machine have to do with anything?

Steele intended to find out, to obtain answers to all his questions, but now didn't appear to be the best time to barge into Betsy's house. She needed a little space—he wasn't willing to allow her much, though—to collect herself. Besides, he had to circle back around to his camp, pack his gear, and get Dusty.

Ty and Lydia had come from the east, which meant they had to travel straight through town to get to Betsy's house. Perhaps Uncle Begley had seen them. Steele decided to talk to him first.

Twenty-one

Steele found Begley sitting on the store porch, glaring at the gray sky.

"Ye're back early," Begley said without rising—and without enthusiasm. "Ye been to Betsy's yet?"

"Rode right by. She's got company."

Begley snorted. "I know. I sent 'em."

Steele took a chair and rocked in silence for a minute, giving Begley time to elaborate. He didn't, surprising Steele and leaving him no choice but to ask a question to get Begley started. "You know the folks at her house?"

"Met 'em this mornin'. Man and his wife from Hudson's Mill. Young folks."

The storekeeper was certainly no fountain of knowledge today, but Steele wasn't ready to give up. He suspected Begley knew far more than he let on. "Hudson's Mill is on my circuit. In fact, I officiated at a wedding there just last month. A charming young couple—Ty and Lydia Williams."

Begley's bushy eyebrows shot up and he jerked his head around. "That's who's here. What d'ye know about 'em?"

Apparently more than you do, Steele thought, his heart sinking. Could he have been wrong about Ty all along? Then why would Betsy faint when she saw him? Maybe it was just the heat, and not seeing Ty at all. Another coincidence to add to the growing pile? Not likely.

"Not much," Steele said. "Ty runs the mill and dabbles

with his inventions. He's got water running to their house, and he created a water-powered machine that washes clothes."

"Does hit work?"

"Sure does." Steele told him about Lydia falling into the tub and not being able to get out. Begley laughed so hard tears ran from his eyes.

"So ye met this Williams feller's family," Begley said when he'd sobered enough to talk again.

Steele was beginning to catch on to the older man's scheme. Begley had his own suspicions and was wondering how well-founded they were. But Steele wasn't going to give too much away. The more questions he made Begley ask, the better he could judge how much the storekeeper really knew. "Nope."

"They weren't thair?"

"Nope."

"But he's got fam'ly some'eres."

"Grandma Carter says he's an orphan."

Begley frowned. "Did she know his folks?"

"Nope. She said he was from Boston."

"Where's that?"

"A good ways north of here."

"How long's he been in Hudson's Mill?"

"Since the war. How come you're so all-fired interested in Ty Williams?"

"Jes' curious. Don' get too many folks in here what's not from the mount'uns. Last I knowed of was the Tylers, and that was nigh on to forty year ago. It was sech a peculiar thang to have high-toned folks like them settle in the mount'uns, I spect that's why folks started callin' this place Peculiar Cove in the first place." He leaned forward and spat his tobacco juice over the railing. It splattered on Dusty's hip, and the mule went to kicking. Begley and Steele laughed, which eased the tension a mite. "Ye reckon folks'll start callin' hit Peculiar Mill now that this Ty Williams feller has come there?"

"Who knows? They might."

"Don't ye think it's kindly odd his name bein' Ty Williams and Betsy's brother's name bein' William Tyler?"

Steele shrugged, trying to appear nonchalant when his heart was racing out of control. Finally, they were getting somewhere . . . he hoped. "Probably just coincidence. They're not unusual names. Of course, if there were more coincidences—say they looked a lot alike, then I'd agree there might be something to it."

"They look too much alike." Begley's voice was low but even. "They got the same eyes, the same crooked teeth, the same ever'thang. If'n ye ast me, they air the same."

"Are you saying Willy Tyler is alive? How could that be?"

"Ye tell me. Ye was in the war. Didn' they ever make a mistake 'bout who dead men really was?"

"I'm sure they did."

"The question is how come this young feller don' know who he is."

"Maybe he does."

Begley shook his head. "I tawlked t' him. That man really believes he's Ty Williams. I been settin' here for the past hour tryin' to figure it all out, and I cain't make heads nor tails of hit."

"What do you think we ought to do?"

"I been figurin' on that, too. I reckon we art to jes' go over to Bets's house and ast him. Course, that'd be puttin' our noses in where they don' belong, but that ain't never stopped me afore. 'Sides, we got Bets and Kee to thank about. They must've both fainted dead away when they seed him."

* * *

Betsy couldn't remember ever swooning before in her life—not when she'd received the black-banded letter, not when she'd shot the Johnny Reb at her door, not even when the Confederate captain had ordered her to take off her chemise. Perhaps she wouldn't have fainted today if she'd slept well last night and eaten a proper breakfast this morning—or if she'd had some warning, some time to prepare herself. She'd halfway been expecting those other catastrophic events—had known that Willy could die, that she might have to defend herself and Auntie Kee, that the Rebels were up to no good when they hauled her back to their camp. But this . . . Willy coming back from the grave . . . this was beyond belief.

"It's incredible," she murmured, sitting up on the settee but continuing to hold the damp cloth against her forehead. She wasn't sure how she'd gotten inside or who had brought the cool, wet cloth and washed her face. None of that mattered. All that mattered was that Willy was alive and well and sitting in her parlor.

As he sat staring at his own picture, she filled her soul with the sight of him. He'd grown a bit in six years, but it was his demeanor that had truly changed. Gone was the innocence. Gone was the insecurity. Gone was the awkwardness of youth. In their places shone love and courage and self-reliance. There was a hardness there, too—the badge of war, she supposed. The only blemish, so far as she could see, was the deception.

Auntie Kee and Tom hovered near the door, watching and listening. Now that her head was clear, Betsy knew she had to talk to Willy alone. She asked Auntie Kee to take her place at school. Tom said he needed to get back to work. Betsy waited until she heard the back door close before she said anything else.

"Why?" she asked. The question echoed in the room, as plaintive and full of woe as the lonely call of the whippoorwill.

He set the daguerreotype aside and looked at her with bewildered eyes. "Why did I come here today?"

"No. Why didn't you write? Why didn't you come back here after the war? Why did you let me think you were dead?" There was anger in her voice, anger and accusation.

"Because I didn't know who I was. I still wouldn't know . . . if Lydia and I hadn't decided to try to peddle my clothes washing machine." He told her then about being struck at Shiloh with a shell that didn't explode, evidenced by the jagged scar on his forehead. He told her how he'd awakened to find the Hornet's Nest deserted by everyone except the dead, how he'd run in terror and confusion, not knowing who he was but certain that if he didn't get away, the Johnnies would seize him as a prisoner of war and he'd die in one of their hellholes. A few days later, he said, he wandered into a Union camp. Two men there thought they recognized him, but they couldn't agree on his name. One said it was Tyler and the other argued it was William. He decided he'd take both names and started calling himself Ty Williams.

"And I've been lost ever since," he concluded. The young woman he'd married touched his arm then, and he turned loving eyes to her. "Well, almost. When I met Lydia, I knew I'd found my home. I never expected to find my family—ever."

Betsy wanted to believe him. With all her being, she wanted to believe that he hadn't known all this time who he was . . . who she was. She didn't know why she doubted him. Everything he said made sense. Too much sense—almost as though he'd carefully rehearsed every line, every explanation. He seemed so unaffected by it all.

But he was here. He was alive. And for that she was grateful. He was probably as stunned as she, and his absence of memories would contribute to a lack of emotion.

Now that she thought of it, she was certain that explained his attitude. It was silly of her to expect him to cry or fall into her arms when he must see her as a total stranger.

"How long can you stay?"

"Two or three days, I suppose." He looked at Lydia and she agreed.

"Good. That will give us some time to get to know each other again." She rose from the settee, prompting him to rise as well. For an instant, she resisted the urge to hug him, then decided to do it anyway. "This may feel strange to you," she said, holding him close, "but I didn't think I'd ever have the chance to do this again."

"Actually, it feels very right," he said, his voice husky. Maybe he was beginning to remember things already. In time, she hoped, all his memories of his life before the war would return.

She broke away and took his hand. "Now, why don't you come show me how this clothes washing machine of yours works. You used to plague me with your ideas about such gadgets."

"I'll bet I used to plague you about a lot of things," he quipped.

"You did, and I'm liable to tell you about every one of them."

The jolt wagon was still there but the clothes washing machine was gone.

"They're down at the branch," Tom called from his ladder. "Took that contraption with 'em."

Steele and Begley took off down the trail. "Ye reckon he ain't Willy after all?" Begley asked.

"I don't know." Actually, there was no doubt in Steele's mind as to Ty's true identity, but he wasn't quite willing to let go of his misgivings concerning the young man's role as a marauder. No matter how much Steele wanted to find the three men who'd murdered his mother and sisters, he couldn't bring himself to accuse an innocent man. He hoped the explanation he and Begley sought would exonerate Ty, not only because he was Betsy's brother, but also because Steele honestly liked the young man.

When they reached the clearing where Peculiar Branch came off the mountain and turned west, they found Ty rigging up a flue while Betsy and Lydia watched. Begley called hallo and they all three turned around. In short order, they exchanged greetings, Betsy introduced Ty as her brother Willy, and Lydia explained how they knew the preacher.

"Isn't it wonderful?" Betsy asked, her eyes shimmering with unshed tears.

"It's like Lazarus returning from the grave," Steele said, ripping his gaze from her glowing face to observe Ty's reaction, but the young man had resumed his work, "Of course, Lazarus's sisters were there to see him rise from the dead. Apparently, you weren't."

"Yes, I was. Sort of."

She recounted Ty's story for Steele and Uncle Begley. Steele supposed it was all possible; it didn't explain, though, why Ty had acted as though he had something to hide. Had he imagined it all? Steele wondered. Ty had definitely flinched during the wedding ceremony, but his uncertainty of his real name could account for that. Still, something didn't fit . . .

"And all this time he's been living within a day's ride of his family home," Lydia said.

"Did he ever tell you why he chose to settle so close to here?" Steele asked, pitching his voice low enough, he hoped, to prevent Ty from hearing over the noisy creek.

"He was jes' wanderin' after the war," Lydia explained. "He come to the mill one day an' Papa give him a job."

"Grandma Carter told me at the wedding that Ty told

everyone he was from Boston and that his sister died with pneumonia. Why do you think he'd make up such a tale?"

"Would you go 'round tellin' folks you didn' know who you was or where you come from?"

"No, I don't suppose I would," Steele said, realizing Ty's hesitations and other suspicious actions more than likely stemmed from his inability to remember his past. And from what Steele understood, Ty still didn't remember. Steele had heard about people losing part or all of their memories due to shock or head injury, but he'd never met an amnesiac before. "It must have been tough for him—not knowing, I mean."

"It must still be tough," Betsy said. "He doesn't know who I am. Not really. He's having to take my word for everything."

"Okay. It's all hooked up," Ty hollered. "If you'll bring me some soap and dirty clothes, Betsy, I'll show you how it works."

"I'll walk you back," Steele said, taking her elbow. Something continued to niggle at him, something he couldn't quite put a mental finger on. Somewhere in the back of his mind remained at least one unanswered question. He gave Betsy only half of his attention as she talked about Matt, the school, the progress on the church.

"With the men having to plant their crops," Betsy said, "the work's been slow. Tom says they should finish next week."

"I can help," Steele said.

Betsy laughed. "In your suit?"

"No. I hope Begley has overalls to fit me. I want to hold services there Sunday, even if the building isn't quite finished yet."

They were close enough to the house to hear the children laughing and talking as they left school. Steele stopped walking and pulled Betsy into his arms. He hadn't planned to kiss her yet. Since he'd visited the Manous farm, he hadn't thought much about kissing her at all—indeed, he'd feared he might never kiss her again. But being near her like this, being alone with her in the woods blocked everything else from his mind.

She met his lips with equal fervor, and he marveled at the depth of her passion—and of his when he was with her. He could lose himself forever in the sweet scent of jasmine that clung to her, in the tingles her touch elicited, in the warmth of—

"Air ye gonna be my daddy?"

Betsy's spine stiffened beneath his hands, and she tore herself from his embrace. Even in the dim light, Steele could see the flame of embarrassment on her cheeks. He looked down to see Matt grinning up at him. In the absence of speech—he figured he'd be in trouble with Betsy no matter how he answered Matt's question—Steele scooped the little boy into his arms and jostled him a bit before setting him down.

"I missed you," Matt said.

"I missed you, too. Have Betsy and Auntie Kee been taking good care of you?"

"The bestest! I been larnin' t' read an' Miss Betsy fount me some toys what use t' be her brother's an' I got a new bestest friend name o' Zach an'—"

Steele laughed. "Hold on there, Little Matt. We have lots of time to catch up. After dinner, let's you and me go over to the new church and work awhile, and maybe later we can go fishing—if it doesn't rain. I've got me a hankering for some trout."

"Really? Kin we really?"

"If it's all right with Betsy."

Composed again, she readily gave her approval, adding, "I have my own catching up to do."

* * *

Catching up on the last six years proved much easier than Betsy expected. Little had happened to her beyond the event with the Rebel soldiers, which she didn't care to discuss. Willy, who insisted he wanted to be called Ty, seemed equally reluctant to talk about the war. That left courting, a subject too personal to air, even with one's sibling. Betsy couldn't even be sure Steele was courting her.

Apparently, Matt thought he was. The boy's question—*Air you goin' t' be my daddy?*—kept running through her mind, usually chasing memories of Steele's kisses. She didn't know what to think about the way the Rev had adroitly sidestepped the issue when Matt brought it up, but she didn't dare approach the subject with Steele herself. Could he be considering marriage? Did she mean anything more to him than a few stolen moments of passionate kissing? Was it possible that he loved her the way she loved him?

They were both so busy—Steele helping to ready the new church for services, Betsy visiting with Ty and Lydia every spare moment—that they didn't see much of each other for the next few days, and then only in the company of others.

The rain held off until Saturday night and was over by Sunday morning, leaving the valley fresh and much cooler. Betsy talked Lydia and Ty into staying through Sunday so that they could all attend services together in the new church. The extra day also allowed Ty time to demonstrate his clothes washing machine to more people. By the time Sunday morning rolled around, virtually everyone in Peculiar Cove had seen it in operation—and every family wanted one of the washers. The problem, however, was the lack of running water higher than the machine. Ty promised to work on a solution, but he didn't offer much hope.

Outside of talking to him about his inventions, however, folks in Peculiar Cove didn't seem too eager to converse with Ty. At first, Betsy thought they were more than likely so stunned by his sudden reappearance that they didn't know what to say, but their reserve didn't wear off. In time, she supposed, they'd come around. Even she experienced some difficulty in maintaining warmth when Ty himself retained a certain aloofness.

Lydia, on the other hand, was both charming and lovable. Betsy told her repeatedly how proud she was to have her for a sister-in-law and how happy she was that Ty had married her. "I can see that you make him very happy," Betsy told her. "I only wish we lived closer so that we could visit more often."

"Me, too," Lydia said. "But Hudson's Mill's not so terrible far."

Betsy hated to see Ty and Lydia go, but she knew they had their own lives to lead, as did she. She supposed the best she could do was make sure they had everything they needed to set up housekeeping. At her insistence, Ty and Lydia selected various pieces of furniture from the Tyler house, and Betsy and Auntie Kee filled two large baskets with blankets, coverlets, and bed linens. Betsy also gave Ty the strand of pearls from the metal box to give to Lydia. He gaped at the necklace, his hazel eyes wide with surprise.

"Mama never wore these," he said. "Where did you get them?"

"I found them after she died," Betsy said, unwilling for reasons she couldn't identify to divulge the full truth.

Monday morning arrived all too soon. Betsy rose well before dawn to help Auntie Kee prepare a picnic lunch for the couple as well as breakfast for them all.

"Ye was right about the air," Auntie Kee said, her hands in biscuit dough and a grin on her face, "only I don' know why ye was afeared. Havin' Willy back's about the bestest thing what's happened 'round here in years."

"It is wonderful, isn't it?" It *was* wonderful, but she had to force her enthusiasm. She'd forgotten all about that part of her premonition. She wished Auntie Kee had never mentioned it. Now that she had, an unaccountable dread crept back into Betsy and refused to go away.

Twenty-two

"If'n ye'll brang me your blanket," Auntie Kee said to Steele as she poured him a fresh cup of coffee, "I'll add it to the warsh. Anything else ye got dirty, too."

Although the half-breed woman always included his soiled garments and blanket in the Monday wash when he was in Peculiar Cove, he couldn't resist teasing her this time. "You've been washing clothes since Thursday. There can't be another dirty garment in this house. You looking for an excuse to use the clothes washer?"

"Ye know better," she fired back, but a sheepish grin softened her rejoinder. " 'Tis a fine machine," she allowed. "Ye got t' give the boy credit."

"Yes, it is," Steele agreed, rising from the table and heading toward the dining room. "Don't pour out that coffee. I'll finish it when I get back."

Since Ty and Lydia were staying at Betsy's, Steele had decided to sleep in the house this trip. Now that the couple had gone home, he probably needed to spend the remaining night or two of his visit to the cove somewhere else. The office at the new church would suffice, he supposed. It certainly wouldn't be as comfortable as his room at Betsy's house, but at least it would keep him dry—and out of trouble. Sleeping under the same roof with her, he'd discovered, provided more temptation than he wanted to deal with.

In his room, he picked up his bedroll, which contained

his skillet and coffeepot, and tossed it onto the bed, then untied the rope that held it together and unwound the blanket. That was when he saw the letter Andy Manous had given him. Steele stood staring at it, chastising himself for not opening his bedroll sooner, for not remembering. How had he forgotten the letter? How *could* he have forgotten it? And now Ty was gone. He and Lydia had left an hour or so ago.

Angry at himself and uncertain of the best course to follow now, Steele sat down on the bed to assess the situation. There were a number of options open, he supposed. He could make up some excuse about needing to leave early and try to catch up with Ty, which shouldn't be too difficult if he left immediately. Or, he could wait until he got to Hudson's Mill and confront Ty with the letter then. The young man obviously didn't think he had anything to fear, which greatly reduced the chances of his running off. But what would he say to Ty when he did confront him? *I have this letter here that Betsy wrote to you. Can you explain to me how it ended up at Andy Manous's house?* Ty would probably appear shocked and deny being anywhere near Andy's house last week.

Now that Steele thought of it, Ty couldn't have been there. Andy lived almost a day's ride on the east side of Peculiar Cove, while Hudson's Mill lay a good day's ride on the west side. No one could be in two places at once. Of course, Ty could have planned to meet Lydia on the east side of the cove. Andy's wife had been killed late Monday afternoon, which meant Ty could not have been in Hudson's Mill past Sunday morning. Steele bet a couple dozen witnesses would swear that Ty had been in services on Sunday, and some of them would say they'd seen him on Monday, too. Unless he had wings, Ty Williams couldn't possibly be involved with the marauders.

If that were true—and it certainly appeared to be—

then who'd had Betsy's letter? And why would he still be carrying it around after all these years?

The letter was the key to finding the three outlaws, but no matter what angle of approach Steele used, he couldn't find the door.

All day long as he worked on the church, he pondered the situation, and by the time the men called it a day, he knew he had to talk to Betsy. She was the only person who might be able to help him, though for the life of him he couldn't imagine how. Regardless, he had to tell her about the letter. She had to know that one of the marauders had been holding on to it for heaven only knew how long before he lost it at Andy Manous's house.

Late that afternoon, Steele asked Betsy to walk with him up to the new church.

"She jes' seed it yestiddy," Auntie Kee teased, her dark eyes twinkling and her wide grin showing the gap in her top teeth.

"But we got the windows in today," he said. "It doesn't look like the same building with the windows in."

Betsy wasn't about to allow an opportunity to be alone with the preacher pass her by. She took her shawl off the hall tree and threw it around her shoulders. "And I want to see them."

"Supper'll be another hour or two," Auntie Kee called as they were walking out the door, laughter in her voice. "Take your time."

Steele closed the door and took her elbow. "You must have been thrilled to find out your brother is alive after thinking he was dead for four years."

"I still can't quite believe it," she said, hoping he wanted to talk about their relationship. But it was early yet and only natural for him to mention Willy—or rather,

Ty. Getting used to calling him by a different name was not going to be easy.

They turned onto the road toward town. A fresh but cool breeze played havoc with Steele's long hair and whipped Betsy's skirts around. She pulled her shawl down over her arms and tied the ends securely under her bosom.

"What amazes me the most is that he didn't know who he was all this time."

Betsy shivered, whether from the wind or the cold edge in Steele's voice she couldn't be sure. "He lost his memory. How could he know?"

"Did you ever write to him?"

"Of course, I did! Every week from the time he started to school in Maryville until I got the . . . letter."

"And you know he got your letters after he joined the army?"

"He wrote me back, if that's what you mean." A shudder besieged her shoulders then and she knew something was wrong. She hadn't completely put aside her feeling that something in Ty's story stunk like a day-old fish. Steele must also think so, or he wouldn't be pursuing the subject with so much determination. "What are you getting at?"

"I didn't know a soldier who threw letters away, Betsy. They were our only link to home."

"But Willy—I mean Ty—fought for the Union."

He slipped his arm around her shoulders and pulled her into against his side. "Home and family don't take sides, Betsy. The blue-coats missed their loved ones as much as we did."

Betsy didn't want to believe her brother would have knowingly let her think he was dead, even after the war was over. "Maybe he didn't have a place to keep them."

"He had a knapsack. Everyone carried a knapsack, regardless of the color of their uniform."

"Maybe he lost his."

"His cap, too?"

She frowned in confusion. "What does his cap have to do with anything?"

"It would have had his name inside. At the very least, his initials. Perhaps other information, too, like his company and regiment. Knapsacks did get separated from bodies during battle. There had to be a way to identify the dead."

"And caps didn't come off sometimes?"

He nodded. "Sometimes. But the chances of your brother not having either his knapsack or his cap are slim to none. If you woke up and couldn't remember your name, wouldn't you start looking for something with it on it?"

"He said he was in a daze," Betsy argued, more with herself than with Steele's logic. "He said he was in a place they later called the Hornet's Nest, and he was afraid the Johnny Rebs would capture him if he didn't run."

"So, he remembered the battle and he realized the danger he was in, but he couldn't remember anything else?"

"He was frightened."

They'd arrived at the church, but Betsy couldn't appreciate the addition of the window glass for the tears swimming in her eyes. Steele led her up the steps and into the shadowy interior. They sat in one of Sam Bartlett's new pews—he'd completed only three so far, but assured everyone he'd eventually replace all the rough-hewn benches with the hinged-back pews. Betsy hoped he made at least two more this week. She'd awarded the students a week's break while the men completed the finishing work at the church, and she'd been concerned about the battle she was in for next week over who got to sit in the pews. Now, however, that seemed such a minor problem.

"There's another thing." He took her hands in his, but he didn't look at her.

She pulled herself back into the disturbing conversation. "What's that?"

"It's not very likely that no one would have known him later. The war lasted three years after Shiloh. In all that time, he would have encountered someone who knew him before."

"Maybe, maybe not."

"Then there's the letter you got saying Willy was dead."

Betsy's heart sank to the pit of her stomach. The Rev's case against her brother gained strength with every contention. "What about it?"

"Someone was convinced he was dead. Not missing. Not captured. Dead. That means either his cap or his knapsack or both were on a dead man's body—a man whose face was no longer recognizable. Somewhere, there's a family still wondering what happened to that man."

The more he talked, the more convinced she became that he was right, that her brother who insisted on being called by a different name was guilty of a cruel deception. "Why?" she breathed, her voice whispery soft, yet the question rang in her ears. "Why would he do such a thing?"

"The way I see it, there's only one reason. He deserted after Shiloh and he doesn't want to get caught."

"Then why wouldn't he tell me? I would understand."

"Shame. Fear. Did Lydia seem surprised that you recognized him?"

"I—" She tried to swallow the lump in her throat, but it wouldn't go away. "I don't know. I fainted."

"What about when he told you what had happened? Did she seem surprised to learn that he'd made up the other story about who he was?"

Betsy closed her eyes and dragged up the memory of

the three of them sitting in her parlor talking about the war. "No."

"The only way she could have had prior knowledge was if he'd already told her the truth, which means he knew it before he came to Peculiar Cove."

She didn't want to believe that. She fought against believing it with every ounce of mental energy she could muster. "It doesn't matter. He's alive and he's safe. If he has to be Ty Williams with no memory for the rest of his life in order to remain safe, it's all right with me." She had an extremely distressing thought. "Please promise me you won't tell anyone else what you just told me."

"I won't."

"You haven't told anyone else already, have you?"

"No," he said without hesitation.

"And I don't ever want us to discuss this again. I want to pretend that we never had this conversation."

Steele squeezed her hands and looked her in the eye for the first time since they'd sat down. The sadness in his dark brown eyes said he had something else to tell her. Tensely she waited for the other shoe to fall.

"I found something that you need to see."

He let go of her hand to reach inside his black broadcloth suit coat and pull out a folded piece of paper that, though torn and discolored, closely resembled stationery she'd once used. Carefully, he opened it out. Even in the dim light, even through her tears, she recognized the handwriting as her own.

"Where—" She choked up and couldn't finish the question.

"At a farm west of here." As she listened to the story he told, her heart ached for the elderly farmer, but along with the pain came fear, the kind that terrorizes. One of the marauders knew about her and Auntie Kee. Although there was no envelope, the very real possibility that the outlaw knew they lived in Peculiar Cove certainly existed.

"At first I thought your brother had dropped this letter," Steele said. She could see the anguish his confession caused him. "I didn't want to believe it, but I didn't know what to believe—"

"I understand."

"—But now I know he didn't. He may be guilty of deceiving you to save his own hide, but he isn't a murderer."

She ventured her own speculation. "He left his knapsack in the Hornet's Nest, and someone took it. Or maybe the man took only this letter out. Maybe he never had anything else. Maybe he doesn't know who I am or where I live."

"Those are comforting thoughts, but I suspect you were right about the man taking the entire knapsack. I take it you never got the knapsack back."

"No. Should I have?"

"The army should have sent it to you."

"I wish you'd shown me this letter before Willy left. Then I could have asked him what he kept in his knapsack."

He sighed. "I wish I had, too. In all the confusion, I forgot about it until I undid my bedroll this morning. By that time, your brother was already gone. But if you had known about it, if you'd confronted Ty with the truth . . ."

"You're right. I have to go along with his lies, whether I want to or not."

It was so much to absorb all at one time—too much to think about. Suddenly, she was glad Willy insisted on keeping his new name, which should keep him safe from the marauders. But now that everyone in Peculiar Cove knew who he really was, knew that he was living in Hudson's Mill, word would get around, at least in the mountains, and then even the new name wouldn't protect him.

"I have to warn him," she said.

"Why? He isn't in danger."

"He might be."

MOUNTAIN MOONLIGHT

"I don't think so. Whoever the marauders are, they aren't from around here. No one knows much about them at all."

"But they could hear gossip. People will talk about Willy for a while."

He pulled her into his chest and set his chin on her hair. "You can't worry about him, Betsy. You have to worry about yourself—and Matt and Auntie Kee."

"Oh my!" she said, gasping. "These are the same men who killed Matt's mother."

He rubbed her head with his chin, acknowledging her statement.

"But you said they only prey on families of Confederate soldiers. Willy fought for the Union. They won't come after me."

"I wouldn't be so sure if I were you. People don't keep letters from strangers for years. The man who had yours may be looking for you. He may have formed a sort of fixation for you in his mind—an obsession of sorts. I've seen it happen to men in the field."

He paused, allowing Betsy time to absorb it all. If he was trying to frighten her, he'd certainly succeeded. The idea that some strange man had not only read all her letters to Willy—to her brother, for heaven's sake!—but might also have turned her into some kind of perverted fantasy gave her the heebie-jeebies.

"These men are dangerous," he continued. "I'm not willing to take any chances with your life."

Although she understood the danger she might be in, his words, which sounded almost like a commitment, brought a tremulous smile to Betsy's lips. "What are you going to do? What should I do?"

"First thing tomorrow morning, I'm going to teach you how to use those pistols of yours."

"I know how to use them!" she protested, jerking her head off his chest and glaring at him.

He laughed. "No, you don't. You're a menace with those pistols, especially to yourself and innocent bystanders."

"I suppose I have behaved rather irresponsibly with them," she admitted, "and I wish I hadn't shot that Rebel soldier, but I didn't know what else to do."

"That was war, Betsy. This is, too. You have to be prepared to kill again if your life is threatened."

She squeezed her eyes tight, trying to block out the memories. But they wouldn't go away. If anything, her effort intensified the images, the colors, the sounds. The private's face hovered over her, his leering lips exposing brown-edged teeth, his eyes hot, his breath rancid. His hand scalded her shoulder as he pushed her back into the front hall. His taunt echoed in her head: "You ain't gonna pull that trigger. You ain't got the guts." She gripped the pearl handle tighter, trying to stop her hand from shaking, and dug her heels in. But he kept coming. A dozen other gray-coats swarmed behind him.

The images sped up, flashing like tongues of fire leaping into a midnight sky, blinding her with their intensity. The deafening explosion . . . the gaping hole in a tattered gray jacket . . . the scarlet spread of blood into the dirty fabric . . . the hot eyes cooling with surprise and then comprehension . . . the man falling backwards into the crowd . . . his now cold eyes fixed and staring . . . his mouth agape in a permanent, soundless scream . . .

The scream rang and rang in her ears, and her cheek stung where someone had slapped her. Her teeth rattled in her head and she bit her tongue. A man called her name—"Betsy! Betsy! Stop it!"

Terror gripping her, she cracked her eyelids a mite, and then a mite more. What was she doing in a church? Who was the man sitting beside her? Why was he shaking her? How did he know her name?

Slowly, inexorably, reality returned. And with it came a flood of tears and deep, hiccuping sobs. The Rev tucked her head into the pillow of his shoulder and looped his arms around her back. For a long time, she clung to him and him to her, the black broadcloth of his suit coat absorbing her tears, her hair collecting his.

Outside, a whippoorwill sailed across a dusky sky and alit on the highmost branch of a massive red oak. For a moment it sat perfectly still, its head cocked to one side as though it was listening to the wind soughing through the pines. It opened its beak, then closed it, and turned its head to the other side. Perhaps it heard only the wind; perhaps in its breast it heard the outpouring of hearts within the new log building.

Its own outpouring of melancholy caught on the wind and wafted down to earth, the notes as somber and yet as soft as the night. "Whip-poor-will, whip-poor-will," it sang. "Lost and lonely," the soughing wind replied. "Can't find your way home. Follow me. Follow me."

With a flutter of wings, the bird sprang from the limb and flew off into the quickening darkness.

Twenty-three

Betsy disentangled herself from Steele's embrace and brushed the residue of tears off her face. "I'm sorry. I didn't mean to go berserk on you."

Only the palest light filtered through the windows, but it was enough to show her the loving concern in his dark eyes. "That's all right." His voice was husky with emotion. "We all get a little crazy sometimes. From what Uncle Begley tells me, you have more reason than most."

"Uncle Begley doesn't know what happened to me. No one does."

Steele flinched at the bitterness in her voice. "Do you want to talk about it?"

"No," she said with finality.

Perhaps someday she'd tell him, she thought. But not now. Not when the memories she'd just dredged up left her feeling like someone had taken a mallet to her emotions, pulverizing them much as Steele had crushed the peppermint for Matt's cake. If she allowed her other demons voice, she was liable to end up stark raving mad, and folks would be calling her Crazy Bets again—with good reason this time.

Perhaps someday she'd tell him, he thought. Until then, the events of that night at the Rebel camp hung between them, separating them from each other like a heavy drape blocking the sunlight. Only Betsy could open that curtain and let the cleansing light into her soul. Only then could she forgive herself.

But who was he to sit in judgment? He had his own confession to make, his own sins to assuage, his own cloud to expel.

He rose from the pew, pulling Betsy up with him. "It's almost dark. Auntie Kee will be wondering where we are."

They walked home in silence, twilight enveloping them in its silken cloak. When they got to the gate, Betsy brushed by him and he realized she was trembling.

"What's wrong? Are you cold?"

She stopped on the flagstone path and turned to face him. "No, I'm frightened."

Guilt ripped through him. "It's all my fault. I shouldn't have said anything. I'm probably wrong about the whole business with the letter."

"This has nothing to do with the letter, except that now I understand why I've been feeling like something awful was about to happen."

"What do you mean?"

"I can't explain it. It's just a feeling. The night before Willy came home, I got this strange sense of excitement and foreboding at the same time."

He pulled her against him and basked in the fragrance of jasmine. What if he never got to hold her again? What would he do if something happened to her, if he came back to Peculiar Cove to find her dead and buried? Steele didn't think he could live through another such occurrence. God had taken his mother and sisters. God had taken Little Matt's mother. Surely He wouldn't take Betsy away from both of them.

But He hadn't intervened before, and there was no assurance that He would this time. Steele wanted to scream at his Maker. He wanted to shake his fist at the heavens and denounce the bit of faith he clung to. Instead, he held Betsy tighter and silently vowed to wipe the sons-of-bitches off the face of the Earth before they had an opportunity to kill again.

"I'm not going anywhere right now," he assured her, wishing he didn't have to go at all ever again. If not for his commitment to the Methodist Church, he wouldn't go at all. "I'll watch out for you and protect you."

"Promise?"

"I promise."

"Watch out!" Steele hollered, but it was too late. As he hurtled to the ground, the bullet whizzed by his ear and lodged in the tree trunk he'd been leaning against. He picked himself up and glared at Auntie Kee. "The target's way over there!"

The half-breed woman ignored his pointing finger. "I cain't hit a thang with this here pistol. I need me a blunderbuss."

He laughed despite himself. "A blunderbuss? What you need is a shotgun."

She squinted at him, more in suspicion than an effort to see, he suspected. "What's that?"

He couldn't believe she didn't know. Shotguns had been around since before he could remember. "A shoulder gun, sort of like a blunderbuss, but it uses shells. The shells are full of little shot that spread out. Great for short range. If you can hold it steady, you can't miss with a shotgun."

She grinned. "Oh! A scatter-rifle."

"I guess you could call it that."

"We ain't got one."

"I'll bet I can get you one."

"Well, you kin have this pistol back. I ain't got no use fer it." She held the grip distastefully between her thumb and forefinger, barrel pointing down. Quickly, before she could fire off another wayward shot, he took it from her. And he'd called Betsy a menace!

Thankfully, his lessons with Betsy proceeded far smoother. She was a natural with a pistol, so long as she was relaxed. And therein lay the problem. He knew of no way to teach her to remain calm in the midst of danger. For him, it was instinctive. He could only hope that if the time came, she wouldn't "go berserk," as she put it.

"Keeping a clear focus is the key," he told her. "You take a bead on a target and you pull the trigger. You don't sweat. You don't scream. You don't panic. When it's all over, you can shiver and shake and cry all you want."

Her eyes bugged and her mouth went slack. When she found her tongue, she spat the words at him. "That's about the most arrogant thing I've ever heard anyone say!"

His own eyes bugged. "Arrogant? How so?"

"Maybe arrogant isn't the word, but I don't think there is one to describe that kind of remark."

Truly confused, he continued to frown at her. "I honestly don't know what I said that was so awful."

"Only a man," she ranted. "Only a man would characterize women that way."

"What way?"

" 'When it's all over, you can shiver and shake and cry all you want,' " she mimicked. She seemed ready to cry herself.

Steele threw up his hands in disgust. "Do you think *men* never shiver and shake and cry? I've seen grown men, *big* men, shiver and shake after they killed a man. I've even seen 'em cry."

She bit her lip then and lowered her eyes. "I'm sorry. I thought you were referring to the way I acted yesterday, when we were talking in the church."

Actually, he supposed that was exactly what he *was* referring to, but if he told her that, he'd just set her off again.

"How many men have you killed?" she asked, rescuing him from one unpleasant situation and thrusting him into another.

"During the war?"

"Did you kill someone before or since the war?"

"No." *Just planned to.* "I don't know how many I might have killed during the war. Hundreds, maybe. Most of them men just like me—hard-working, upright citizens. Men with families and friends back home. It sickens me to think of it."

She put the pistols back in the case and sat down on a fallen log. "It seems strange to me that a preacher would take up arms, even during war."

He'd started toward her, intending to sit down, too, but her comment stopped him. He stood with his side to her, his gaze fixed on a distant smoky peak, his mind wandering back to the evening he returned home. "I wasn't a preacher then."

"What were you?"

"A farmer."

"Why didn't you go back to being a farmer?"

"Because . . . because I didn't." He knew that was an unsatisfactory explanation, but he was as reluctant to reveal his personal demons to Betsy as she was to reveal hers to him. Perhaps she understood, for she didn't pursue the matter. Instead, she launched out on another subject he'd just as soon not discuss.

"You've never mentioned your family before. Where are they?"

He couldn't bring himself to say they were dead. "White Oak Flats." They were there . . . in spirit.

"Do you ever visit them?"

"Not recently."

"You don't have a, uh, a wife, do you?"

He sat down beside her on the log and took her hands in his. Hers were so small, with little calluses on the pads—from hoeing the garden, he supposed. His were so large, so rough, in comparison. "No, Betsy, I don't have a wife. I've never had a wife."

She plucked at the fabric of her skirt, and he noted—not for the first time that day—how pretty she looked in her crisp white bodice and pink-and-blue plaid skirt. "You ever had a sweetheart?"

He scratched his chin. "Let me see . . . There was Selma Thurlow and—"

"Selma Thurlow!" Betsy hooted. "What a name."

He grinned at her, enjoying her laughter, glad the conversation had taken a lighter bent.

"You made it up."

"No, I didn't." He raised his right hand, palm out. "Honest Injun."

"What'd she look like?"

"She was oh, so tall"—he measured with his hand—"with buck teeth and freckles. Real buxomy for thirteen, if I recollect right."

"Thirteen! You were robbing the cradle, weren't you?"

"Not when I was only fourteen myself."

A wistful light filled her green eyes. "So Selma Thurlow was your first love."

He dipped his chin, moving his head closer to hers. "The first girl I ever kissed," he whispered, his lips almost touching hers. "Only she didn't do to me what you do to me."

Betsy shivered in delight. "And what do I do to you?"

"I'll show you."

His mouth captured hers, his tongue searing her lips, demanding that they open to him. Gasping, she melted against him, her arms encircling his neck, pulling his head even closer. She could enjoy this, could revel in the rush of warmth to her belly, could allow her own passion to pour forth, for the Rev was the only man who'd ever kissed her on the mouth. This was something unique and special between them, something for which she had no precedent.

But when his hands skimmed down her shoulders and closed over her breasts, anger and fear flared within her, suffocating the passion. She twisted away, freeing herself of his clutching hands, then taking to her feet and running like a frightened rabbit.

He came after her, following her all the way to the house. She could hear his footfalls, one solid, the other faltering—*thump, ker-thump, thump, ker-thump*—in syncopated counterpoint to the inexorable pounding of her heart. She burst through the back door, tore through the kitchen, barely noting Auntie Kee's startled gasp. She didn't stop running until she'd reached the sanctuary of her room. She turned the key in the lock, then pulled it out and took it with her to the bed, where she collapsed in a sobbing heap of misery and confusion.

Auntie Kee looked up from the batter she was stirring to pin Steele with an accusative glare. "What's ailin' her?"

Closing the door behind him, Steele shook his head. "I don't know."

"D'ye kiss her agin?" Matt asked, his wide grin exposing berry-stained teeth and a blue-black tongue.

Steele ruffled the boy's hair and stole a glance at Auntie Kee, who was grinning herself now. "What're you eating there, Matt?"

"Tea cakes and elderberry jam." He licked his lips, smearing jam all around his mouth. "Well, did ye?"

"I think maybe that's my business—and Miss Betsy's."

"She liked it last time." He took another bite of jam-covered tea cake and chewed it thoughtfully, his thin, pale eyebrows drawn together. "Ye must a-done sumpin wrong, like that man did when he kissed my maw."

Matt was holding a tea cake poised in front of his open mouth. Suddenly, he clamped his mouth shut tight and dropped the tea cake. The light went out of his hazel eyes and he swallowed convulsively.

"Are you okay, Matt?" Steele asked.

The boy nodded.

Steele sat down across from Matt, then reached across the table and laid a comforting hand on the boy's forearm. "What man kissed your maw?"

"The one with half a face."

"Was it that night. . . ."

Again, he nodded.

"I thought you were hiding in the woods. I thought you said you didn't see anything."

"I slipped back. After they was in the house. I wanted t' help Maw, but I was too afeared of the one with half a face."

"What do you mean—half a face?"

Matt laid a hand over one side of his own face. "He had skin there. That was all. Hit were real thick and rough-lookin'."

Steele tried to conjure a mental picture. "Like maybe he'd been burned?"

"I don' know. I ain't never seed nobody like that afore." His thin shoulders trembled. Steele went around to Matt's side of the table, sat in a chair next to him, and pulled the little boy onto his lap. Matt slid his arms around Steele's rib cage and laid his head on the preacher's chest.

"It's all right, son. You're safe here." When Matt quit shaking, Steele asked, "Did you see the other two men that night?"

"Naw. They was in t'other room."

"Where were you?"

"Standin' on the porch, lookin' in the winder. It were dark outside, so the man couldn' see me. He warn't lookin' nohow."

Steele looked at Auntie Kee, who was standing stock-still, her black eyes awash with tears. "What did you do then, Matt?" he asked.

"It sceered me sumpin fierce to look at him. I runned back to the woods."

"Would you know this man if you saw him again?"

"I reckon anybody would."

"And you didn't hear their names?"

"Naw." Matt sniffed, and Steele realized the boy was crying. For a long time, he held Matt close, all the while maintaining eye contact with Auntie Kee, who was visibly shaken by the boy's story.

"Ye get me that scatter-rifle," she said. "Terday, if'n ye kin."

Steele got the shotgun from Uncle Begley, along with a good-sized box of shells. It was Begley's own gun, but he had others, he said, and would be right proud to give it to Kee. "And don' ye worry none. I'll tell ever'body I see 'bout that there man with half his face burnt off."

"I have another favor to ask," Steele said. "I don't want to leave Betsy and Auntie Kee and Matt alone, but I need to get back on my circuit. Do you think you could sleep there, at least until the danger's past?"

Begley grinned. "Shoot, that hain't no favor. That'd be a pleasurement."

"You might have to stay until I get back."

"Don' matter a whit. I'd marry Kee and move in there, if'n she'd let me."

So, there *was* something there stronger than friendship. "Have you asked her?"

"Oncet. A long time ago."

Steele gave Begley the space to elaborate. When he didn't, Steele prodded him a bit. "Maybe you should ask her again."

"I been a-figurin' on it. When ye thankin' on leavin'?"

"Normally, I'd go tomorrow, but I can wait until Friday and still make it to Hudson's Mill by Saturday evening. I could wait until Saturday morning if I didn't stop anywhere, but someone needs to pass the word, and folks expect me to read a bit from the Bible and pray with them. Most don't live right on the road, you know, which means extra time to make all the little side trips. Really slows you down."

"I kin see it would. Don' ye worry none 'bout Kee and Bets. I'll take good keer of 'em."

Steele hoped he wasn't sounding Begley's deathknell. "Take good care of yourself, too."

"How long ye reckon the preacher-man's gonna stay?" Hobe asked Zero for the umpteenth time.

Zero wished he'd never said a word to his brother about who "Betsy" was or where she lived or when Hobe would finally get to meet her. He wouldn't have—if he'd bothered to do a little observation before he'd told Hobe and Lam they were going to visit Betsy. Now, here they were, holed up in the mountains surrounding the cove, watching the house and waiting for the preacher to leave.

In his zeal to get this over with and move on to the Knoxville area, Zero forgot all about the preacher-man making his rounds, and he'd had no idea the reverend stayed at the Tyler house when he was in Peculiar Cove. Truth was, they'd paid the new circuit-rider little mind, other than staying out of his way. Zero had bumped into him once, over in Walnut Ridge, and seen the nasty scar near his hairline. The scar, combined with the crooked nose and the man's other craggy features, gave him a mean look, too mean for a preacher-man. He'd decided right then and there that he never wanted to tangle with the minister, and he hadn't changed his mind.

"I don't know how long, Hobe," Zero answered for the umpteenth time. "I guess until he gits ready to move on."

"And if'n he don't?"

"He will. He's a circuit-ridin' preacher. It's his job to move around."

"Reckon why he stays with my Betsy? What if'n he's done up and married her?"

Zero had taken just about all of Hobe's whining he intended to take. "What if he has?" he lashed out, curling his fingers into a fist to keep from slapping Hobe. "Hit don' make no nevermind."

"Yeah, hit does," Hobe muttered, his one eye downcast. Even after all these years, Zero hadn't grown accustomed to watching half of Hobe's face work while the other half just sat there, doing nothing. Damn Johnnies! If they hadn't a-blown up the train, Hobe would still be whole—and right. Something had happened to his mind, though. It was like the fire had burnt it, too. He didn't never use to be such a crybaby.

"I want my Betsy."

"Ye'll have her," Zero promised. "Ye will. Tamarr's Friday. If he's plannin' on preachin' some'eres else Sunday, he'll be a-leavin' tamarr. We'll give him till tamarr evening. If'n he's still here, we'll jest have to kill him."

Zero caught himself before he added "too."

Twenty-four

The more Steele thought about the danger to Betsy, the more it frightened him. The more it frightened him, the more he insisted she not leave the house unless he was with her. He could tell she didn't like it, but it was for her own good. He hoped she'd see it that way. She didn't.

"And what do I do when you're gone?" she railed at him following dinner on Thursday. Although they were in the parlor with the double doors closed, he figured Auntie Kee and Matt could hear her all the way in the kitchen. "I made myself a prisoner of this house for too long. I won't go back to it."

He told her about arranging for Begley to stay at her house. "He can walk you to school in the morning, and Tom assures me he'll see you safely home at noon. Just tell Begley what you need from the store, and he'll bring it to you that evening. Should you absolutely have to go anywhere else, tell Tom. He'll escort you."

"Escort?" Her wide-open eyes shot green sparks. "I don't need Tom and Begley playing nursemaid to me."

"Why are you being so contrary about this?"

"I'm not being contrary!"

"Yes, you are. Just listen to yourself."

She clamped her mouth shut and whirled away from him, her eyes emerald hard and her jaw obstinately set. He expected her to sashay out of the parlor and mount the stairs in heavy-footed outrage. Instead, she stood a few feet away, her spine rigid, her bearing regal yet coerced, much as Mary, Queen of Scots, must have held herself on her way to the chopping block.

Steele started to go to her, then changed his mind. This was something she needed to work through herself, without further interference from him. Besides, he wasn't about to apologize when he'd done nothing wrong. He'd promised to protect her, and by golly, that was what he was doing—the best way he knew how. If she couldn't see it that way, then she wasn't half the person he thought she was.

Betsy took a ragged breath in an attempt to stave off a sniffle, which would certainly prove her poise was a sham. Just a few months ago, she'd thought to live the remainder of her life a virtual prisoner of fear. Trying to be a part of the community was what had gotten her in trouble in the first place. If she'd never invited people to see Willy's room, no one would have known and the Rebels would never have heard about it. Maybe turning his room into a shrine was a crazy thing to do, but she'd been quite sincere about her tribute and she'd not expected people to make fun of her efforts. Because they did, a man was dead, and she'd been victimized by a sadistic Confederate captain.

For four years, they'd laughed and talked about it in Uncle Begley's store and on the streets. She didn't have to hear it to know they had. From time to time, some child would throw an acorn at her windows or run up and knock on her door, usually on a dare from other more cowardly children who stood in the road and waited for her to peek at them from one of the front rooms. As soon as she showed her face, they'd hurl their taunts, calling her Crazy Bets and Twitterwitted Tyler and other such unsavory appellations. Once, she'd walked out onto the porch, and they'd scattered like leaves in a windstorm.

For four years, she'd endured in her own private world, Auntie Kee her only contact with the townspeople. And then, this wonderful man who stood mere feet behind her had come into her life. By accepting him—a stranger—as a friend, she'd opened the door to a world she'd never thought to be a part of, even before the war. These last few months had been so blissful, her life so full of promise. Willy had come back from the dead and, symbolically, so had she. She liked her new friends, her newfound freedom, her independence. Most of all, she liked living without fear.

But it wasn't so much fear's returning that had her upset. It was Steele's going off and leaving her. He'd promised to stay and protect her. Perhaps it was selfish of her to want him to forget his ministry for a few days or weeks or months or however long it took, but she did not want to face what she feared was coming without him.

As Steele waited for her to say something, he pondered the fact that Betsy had accepted his escort, his protection, without objection. Was it possible she was upset because he was leaving? Didn't she understand he had duties and obligations?

Duties and obligations! The words rang in his head, telling him he might ought to take his own advice and listen to himself. He'd made those duties and obligations more important to him than Betsy, just as he'd made his duty to the South more important than the welfare of his mother and his sisters. Had the guilt he'd been carrying around in his heart for a year taught him nothing?

A few months ago, his first priority had been to find the marauders. And now that he had his chance, not only to catch them but to prevent them from harming Betsy, and perhaps Matt and Auntie Kee as well—three people he'd grown to love—what was he doing? Putting his work for the Methodist Church ahead of everything else.

He hadn't prayed about this. He hadn't even thought it through. He'd just made up his mind. He felt like the biggest heel. And now that he was finally listening, he heard that voice again, the one he'd stopped hearing somewhere along the way. *She needs you, and you need her.*

He closed the distance between them, placed his hands on Betsy's shoulders, and tenderly turned her to face him. "Can you forgive me?"

She looked at him with wide-eyed bewilderment. "Most likely. Of course, it might help if I knew what you'd done."

"Just got a little confused there for a while about what was truly important to me. Do you think you could tolerate me for another week or two?"

Her sweet lips curved winsomely. "I think I probably could, so long as you don't make me stay cooped up in this house all the time."

He took her elbow. "How'd you like to go for a walk with me?"

When they stopped by the kitchen to tell Auntie Kee what they were doing, Matt put up a fuss to go with them. To pacify him, Steele promised to take him fishing later that afternoon.

As soon as they stepped outside, where it was only a tiny bit cooler, Betsy shivered.

"Do you need your shawl?"

She shook her head. "This chill's coming from the inside out."

"What's wrong?"

"I don't know. I feel . . . weird again, like I did last week, but this is different."

His arms broke out in turkey bumps, but he didn't want to frighten her, so he made light of her uncanny perception. "You don't have any other long-lost relatives, do you?"

"No. I feel like we're being watched. Is that possible?"

"Very." His gaze raked the balds and laurel slicks on the slopes and ridges nearest them. There was nothing there, no movement at all, not even a deer. If the marauders really were watching, though, they wouldn't be out in the open. They would have found a dense patch of woods and undergrowth with a clear view of the house. He was leading her across the back of her property, toward the very spot where he'd hidden to watch her reaction to seeing her brother again. He knew firsthand what a good hiding place it was, and the last thing he wanted to do was walk into an ambush. Therefore, he gently steered her away from the woods.

"Let's stay in the open," he whispered to her, "at least for the time being."

"Do you feel it, too?"

"Exercising caution seems reasonable." They crossed the road and plunged into the field where Matt so often picked wildflowers and chased butterflies. As they skirted a patch of blue dwarf irises, Steele reached down and snapped one off just below the bloom.

"Oops!" he said, laughing. "I didn't get much stem." He stuck the blossom in the buttonhole of his lapel, then picked another one, reaching lower this time and handing it to Betsy. She twirled it in her hand and sniffed its delicate fragrance. They were walking through masses of chickweed, creeping phlox, and lousewort.

"Watch out," Steele teased, "or you'll get lice."

Betsy laughed nervously, silently blessing him for his efforts at relieving the tension. "You know that's an old wives' tale. Besides, it only applies to cattle."

"A lot of these mountain folk believe it."

"I don't suppose such notions truly matter, but I am concerned about the general lack of education among these people. I've been thinking about starting a separate school for adults."

"I don't know if that's wise."

"How so?"

They'd come to a small group of gray boulders. Steele

settled Betsy on the flattest and chose the next best one for himself.

"Because you don't want to point out their weaknesses," he said. "If one of them asks you, that's different."

She nodded, looking crestfallen.

"Your heart's in the right place, Betsy," he said, hoping to ease her disappointment, "and many of the adults have told me they think you're doing a great service for their children with the school you opened. Their only cause of distress is in not being able to reimburse you the money you've spent on books and supplies. I expect, come autumn, you'll find your pantry overflowing with strings of leatherbritches beans and jars of berries. You'll have to take whatever they give you graciously and let them think you used it all, even if you didn't."

"Do you honestly believe I'm that callous?" she asked softly. "I know how proud mountain people are."

He dipped his chin. "Sometimes I forget the truly important things, so I have a tendency to believe others do, too."

She smiled at that. "I haven't noticed your making too many false steps."

"My heart is far from pure, Betsy." *Tell her,* the voice urged. *Tell her everything.*

By the time he'd finished pouring out his heart, Betsy had forgotten all about feeling they were being watched. She knew only that she loved him, that he needed her as much as she needed him. They were like two whippoorwills, lost and lonely and looking for home, and they'd found it in each other as surely as she and Matt had.

She left her seat on the boulder and went to him, falling to her knees amidst a patch of pink phlox and opening her arms. He joined her on the ground. For a long time, they sat on their knees, holding each other, comfort and love flowing from each to the other.

"I had no idea," she said after a spell. "Why didn't you tell me?"

"I don't know. Because I was ashamed, I suppose, to be using God's work as a ruse to find the marauders."

"But you never let it interfere with your ministry."

"Not outwardly, but it's what's in a man's heart that matters. Mine was consumed with blood lust—until I met you. Since then, I've been consumed with something no less sinful."

His confession thrilled her and troubled her at the same time. Lust alone couldn't provide a solid foundation for a forever-after kind of relationship, but combined with love . . . and he did love her. Didn't he?

"Are you trying to tell me you love me?" she asked, taking her head off his shoulder and removing his broad-brimmed hat so she could see his expression.

A hint of a smile lit his dark eyes, but it enhanced rather than detracted from the earnestness written all over his face. "I think maybe I am."

Steele couldn't believe he'd given voice to his innermost feelings. The admission simultaneously excited and scared him. He felt as though he'd opened his chest, exposing his heart, and invited her to rip it out. He held his breath, searching her face, hoping beyond hope that it was love returned he read in the soft, misty green of her eyes, and not pity. He could take repugnance from her easier than he could pity.

"I love you, too."

The words flowed into his heart like warm honey from a pitcher, smooth and natural and oh, so sweet. He clutched her to him again, burying his face in her jasmine-scented hair, wonder filling his entire being. How any woman this beautiful could love a man with a wooden leg and a cold soul amazed him.

But his soul wasn't cold anymore.

"My soul isn't cold anymore," he said, eliciting a squeeze from Betsy and a deep-throated chuckle.

"Neither is mine."

"Yours wasn't ever cold."

"Yes, it was. It was dead, but you brought it back to life. You and Matt."

He'd momentarily forgotten about Matt. "Have you changed your mind about him then?"

"I want to be his mother, if that's what you mean."

And he wanted to be his father. But that required a wedding. Steele allowed that notion a moment's thought, then plunged ahead. "What do we do now?"

When she removed her head from his shoulder again and searched his face, Steele guessed what was coming. But it wouldn't be fair to make her ask him. It was his turn to be bold.

"We could fall into the grass and wildflowers and I could make passionate love to you," he said teasingly, "or . . ."

Light danced in her eyes. "Or what?"

"Or we could wait until we're married. The passionate love part comes either way. Take your pick."

"When?"

Although her question caught him off guard, he quickly recovered. "How about Saturday?"

Her eyebrows arched, crinkling her forehead. "This coming Saturday? As in day after tomorrow?"

"Can you be ready that soon?"

Smiling, she kissed him on the nose. "I can be ready tonight."

"You shouldn't have done that," he growled, capturing her mouth with his. This time when he touched her breasts, she flinched, but she didn't pull away. He deepened the kiss, his hands taking liberties they hadn't dared before. His mouth absorbed her moan, and he reveled in the sweetness of her. Despite the heat of her response, she held back. In time, he hoped, she'd learn to trust him. He was willing to wait.

"Shi-it," Hobe said, his one eye riveted on the couple in the field—*his* Betsy and the preacher-man. "I'm goin' to kill him!"

"If'n he don' kill ye first," Zero warned. "That's one mean sum-bitch."

Hobe didn't question Zero's judgment very often, but this was one time his brother wasn't making any sense a-tall. "How ye reckon that? He's a preacher-man."

"Don' make no nevermind. I seen him—up close."

"When?"

"Back yonder a spell."

"Ye seen him do anythang?"

"No."

"Then how come ye to know he's mean?"

"Same way I know when a dawg's plannin' on bitin' and when it's bluffin'. Sometimes, ye can see right into a man's soul. That man's soul is as cold as steel. If he ever comes after ye, he ain't bluffin'."

Hobe didn't believe him. "Ye ain't a-goin' soft on me, is you, Zero?"

"Course not. I jest got me a bad feelin' about this one, that's all."

Zero *was* going soft on him. It didn't make no nevermind. Hobe could take care of the preacher-man. Zero might have the smarts, but Hobe had more strength. "When do ye reckon we can go in?"

"I told ye. Tamarr evenin'."

* * *

Steele left the meadow feeling more at peace than he had in years. Within an hour, however, he wasn't so certain about the wedding anymore. At least, not about rushing it the way they were. He'd had no idea how much stock women put in ceremony.

All the talking and planning started the minute they told Auntie Kee. She went to untying her apron and rushing Matt to finish his milk and cookies. "We've got to git to the store," she told him. "I reckon I'm goin' t' need ever' bit of the sugar and flour Begley's got stocked, and then there's—"

Matt turned his attention to Steele. "Does this mean ye're goin' to be my paw?"

Steele ruffled Matt's hair with one hand and snitched one of his cookies with the other. "I reckon that's what it means."

The boy jumped out of his chair and wrapped his arms around Steele's thighs. "I love ye," he said.

"We all love him, child." Auntie Kee moved Matt's saucer and tin cup from the table to the dishpan. "That's how come he's marryin' up with us."

Steele was well on his way to a hearty guffaw when Betsy stuck her elbow in his ribs. He covered it with a fake choke and made a big to-do out of clearing his throat. When he recovered, he told Matt and Auntie Kee that he loved them, too. "I've never been so humbled," he said, "by so much love."

"You can be humbled later," Auntie Kee said, heading out the door. "We got work to do. Come on."

Shrugging and smiling, Betsy followed the half-breed woman. Mimicking her, Matt shrugged and smiled, too. "I reckon we better do like she says."

"I reckon we better," Steele agreed, taking Matt's hand. "You know this means I can't take you fishing today."

"That's all right. We'll go tamarr."

While Begley and Steele loaded the jolt wagon, they talked about what Steele would do once he was married to Betsy.

"I've been thinking about that," Steele told him. "Do you think Peculiar Cove might be ready for a full-time minister?"

"I think that's as bodacious a idee as I've ever heared."

"I'll write to Bishop Marley tonight."

Begley set a fifty-pound sack of flour in the wagon bed. "I reckon this means ye won't be a-needin' me to stay at the house."

Steele added a large bag of sugar. "I hadn't thought about it, but maybe you should. Maybe I need to move to the church for the next couple of days."

"How come?"

"Folks are liable to talk."

Laughing, Begley threw an arm around Steele's midsection. He was too short to reach higher. "Folks've been a-knowin' this was comin'. We jes' didn' know when."

"So they've been talking already." He didn't care for himself, but for Betsy.

"Only about when ye and Bets was goin' to jump the broom, ye bein' a preacher-man what'n'all."

"I'm still a man," Steele reminded him.

Begley stopped at the door and gave Steele a long, hard look. He seemed to be waiting for Steele to say something, but for the life of him, Steele couldn't imagine what it was. When the storekeeper finally enlightened him, Steele felt like seven kinds of fool for not thinking of it himself.

"Ye bein' the preacher-man and there ain't bein' t'other around, I reckon ye'll be a-needin' somebody to read the vows."

"I was getting to that," Steele said, reluctant to tell Begley he'd forgotten about his being a justice of the peace. In truth, he and Betsy hadn't even discussed the subject, but he couldn't imagine her wanting anyone else to perform the ceremony. "You will do it for us, won't you?"

Begley grinned. "It'd be a pleasurement."

"Now, if I can just make it through all the shopping and cooking and sewing and decorating . . ."

"If'n I was ye," Begley said in a conspiratorial tone, "I'd find me sumpin else to do for the next couple o' days."

"That's not a bad idea," Steele said. "I've been promising Matt I'd take him fishing, and I can always find something to do at the church."

"Jes' don' do too much." Begley chuckled. "Ye want t' be good and rested up come Saturdee night."

Twenty-five

"P-preacher-man! C-come quick!"

A pimple-faced girl burst through the woods, then stopped short at the edge of the creek and took several panting breaths. She'd been with her mother in Begley's store the day Steele had arrived in Peculiar Cove, but he couldn't recall her name, wasn't even sure he'd ever heard it.

"What's the matter, Rena?" Matt asked, setting his fishing pole aside and rising to go to her. "Ye look plumb tuckered out."

"I am." She swiped a hand across her damp forehead and turned pleading eyes to Steele. "Hit's my g-grammaw. She done took real s-sick and she's astin' t-t' see ye."

Steele picked himself up off the slick-surfaced rock he'd been using as a stool and gathered up the poles and bait. "Where does your grandmother live?"

"Not t-too fur. I'll take ye."

He started to follow her, but Matt lagged behind. "Come on, boy. We'll fish some more tomorrow."

"Aw, cain't I stay a spell longer? I was gettin' a nibble."

Steele shook his head. "Tomorrow. I promise."

He left Matt with Auntie Kee, who was busy stirring up cake batter. Baked layers already occupied every available surface in the kitchen. "How many cakes are you going to bake?" he teased her.

"Jes' one," she shot back. "A big 'un."

"I'll stop by Begley's on the way and tell him you're expecting him for supper."

"But I ain't cooked nothin'!" she protested.

"Yes, you have." He waved an arm at the many cake layers.

"Now, Preacher, ye know that cake's fer the weddin'. Ye jes' like joshin' me."

His smile faded. "I don't know when I'll be back." While Matt was busy getting Rena a cookie, Steele sidled up to Auntie Kee. "You got the shotgun handy?" he whispered.

She pointed at the pantry with her spoon.

"Loaded?"

"Both barrels."

"Good." Louder, he asked, "Where's Betsy?"

"Upstairs, a-sewin' on her gown."

"Tell her I'll see her later tonight."

"An' you tell Miz Wakefield I hope her maw gets along all right."

As it turned out, Rena's grandmother lived clear on the other side of the cove from Betsy. If he'd realized how far, he would have brought Dusty. The farther he got from Betsy's house, the greater he felt a sense of impending danger.

"It's jes' a li'l p-piece now," Rena said, turning onto a narrow track barely wide enough for a small cart with the woods growing right up to the edges.

They'd made most of the trip without conversation, partly because Rena seemed reluctant to talk, which was natural, he supposed, the way she stuttered—but mostly because his thoughts were focused on the eerie feeling he had. What if he were off on a wild-goose chase? What if someone just wanted him away from the Tyler house for a while?

"What's wrong with your grandmother?" he asked, his voice rife with suspicion.

Rena didn't seem to notice. "The w-wastin'-away sickness. A b-blackb-bird flew in the winder this m-mornin'. Maw s-said that were a sure s-sign the end be near."

Whatever misgivings he'd had on the trail quickly dwindled when he entered the tiny log cabin and spied the frail, withered-up old woman lying in the bed and heard the harshness of her irregular breathing. When he took her nearer hand in his, her eyelids fluttered open and she licked dry, cracked lips.

"Much obliged," she murmured in a voice as raspy as a dull razor. He couldn't recall ever seeing her before, probably because she was too sick to come to church, and somehow he'd missed finding her cabin when he'd been out visiting. He felt a pang of guilt for neglecting her, but at least he could be here with her at the end.

"She wants ye should read that psalm 'bout the shepherd," Mrs. Wakefield said, vacating a chair beside the bed and collecting a worn Bible from the mantelpiece. Steele didn't need it, but he sat down and opened it anyway.

" 'The Lord is my shepherd, I shall not want . . .' "

"Paw promised I could ketch me a fish fer my supper," Matt whined.

Auntie Kee slammed the oven door, then got hold of her anger, which was really more exasperation than anything else. "He ain't your paw yet."

Matt ignored the correction. "Ye kin take me fishin'."

"No, I cain't." She wiped her hands on her apron and laid an open palm on several of the cooling layers, more to convince the boy she was busy than to check their progress. Since she wasn't going to ice them until morning, it didn't matter how long it took them to cool.

"Yeah, ye kin," Matt argued, an impish grin on his face. "Ye ain't even made the icin' yet."

"Ye spend too much time in the kitchen," Auntie Kee said, laughing. "I s'pose Miss Betsy kin take them out'n the oven. Let me tell her. And law, I forgot all about those men comin' to move the organ to the church. Course, they won't need me noways." When she got to the door, she pointed to a chair. "You set right there—an' stay out'n the cookies. You've et enough."

Betsy brought the sleeve she was making downstairs and sat in the dining room to sew. The kitchen was entirely too hot and messy, but the dining room was close enough for her to keep watch on the cake. Judging from the smell, it was done, but a few tiny moist crumbs clung to the straw she tested it with. She returned to the dining room, knowing she had time to make only another ten or twelve stitches before she had to check it again. If she wanted to finish her wedding gown before tomorrow evening, however, she had to make use of every available minute.

As she plied her needle, her head swam with visions of her walking down the aisle on Ty's arm, of Matt in front of her carrying her mother's ring on a satin pillow, of Steele standing straight and tall at the altar, of Auntie Kee playing the organ, and Uncle Begley holding a prayer book. In her daydream, she glanced toward the benches and pews—and saw that they were nearly empty. In her moment of panic, she put a stitch in crooked and had to rip it out.

What if people didn't come? Oh, she could count on Tom and maybe the Patridges, probably Molly and Imer. But she suspected lots of folks still thought she was crazy. Why had she ever thought she'd be accepted? She'd just been deluding herself. All they'd wanted was money from her to build the church, and since she hadn't been able to supply it . . .

Stitch number three, she mentally counted, directing her thoughts elsewhere.

Tom had lit out for Hudson's Mill yesterday afternoon and would be bringing Ty and Lydia back for the wedding. Betsy prayed they arrived in time.

She didn't know what she'd been thinking when she told Steele she could be ready for a wedding in two days. In truth, she hadn't been thinking about anything except becoming his wife. She refused to allow the rush to prepare for the wedding to mar her excitement over her future.

Stitch number five.

And it was the future that was important, she reminded herself, not the wedding. If she didn't finish the gown, she'd wear an old one. She and Steele would be genuinely married, regardless of how they were dressed.

Married! The word resounded in her head, bringing a moment of panic and the hot blush of humiliation to her cheeks. He would want to take further liberties with her. He would want to touch her all over, to put his hands on parts of her even she didn't touch except in bathing. The very prospect terrified her, and she wondered for the first time since she'd agreed to this marriage if perhaps she wasn't making a grave mistake.

At stitch number eight, the back door creaked open. Thank goodness, Auntie Kee and Matt were home! The house was entirely too quiet.

"Did you catch any fish?" she called, her voice catching in her throat on the word *fish.* That was not Auntie Kee and Matt coming into the kitchen. Nor was it the Rev or Uncle Begley, and it was too early for Tom to return from Hudson's Mill with Ty and Lydia. These were footfalls she didn't recognize, and they belonged to more than one person. Men, she'd say, from the gaits, big men trying to walk softly. She ought to go see, but a violent shiver paralyzed her limbs and her heart pounded against the wall of her chest.

Surely they were just the men coming to move the organ, which Auntie Kee had insisted stay in the barn until the windows were installed at the church. But if that were the case, what were they doing in the house, and why hadn't they called out and identified themselves? Why had she chosen to sit with her back to the kitchen? Why hadn't she brought the pistols with her?

She was being silly, she told herself. It was broad daylight, late afternoon but still a ways from dark. Surely the bad men Steele had told her about wouldn't risk an attack—

"Here she be." It was a friendly voice, a mountaineer's voice. Not one she recognized, but then she didn't know many of the local folks by voice. Just one of the men come to move the organ after all. Probably just wanted to let her know they were here so she wouldn't be concerned.

Breathing a heartfelt sigh of relief, she laid her sewing on the table and turned in her chair. The sight that met her gaze riveted her to the walnut seat and glued her eyes open. Never had she seen any man so huge, any human more pitifully ugly. Even if his face were whole and not half burned off, this man would still be hideous.

The man with half a face! The one Matt had watched through the window. Bile rose in Betsy's throat and her bones turned to jelly. *Don't just sit there. Do something!* her mind screamed, but she couldn't seem to get anything to work except her fingers, which curled into fists, each grasping fabric. Her right hand balled up a hunk of her skirt, while her left hand closed around the silk sleeve on the table. The needle punctured the pad of her middle finger, and she gasped—both in pain and surprise. It wasn't much of a weapon, but it was all she had.

"I fount her," the monster called out. Nothing moved

but his jaw. He just stood there in the doorway, his massive body filling the space, his single eye staring at her, the limp side of his mouth drooling spittle.

"I'm proud fer ye," a man said. "Move."

The big man stepped aside. Two men pushed past him and stalked toward the front hall. A gaunt-faced youth carrying huge chunks of cake in his hands followed the older of the three, a man who bore a strong resemblance to the monster, but lacked his size.

The monster moved closer to her. The stench that clung to him nauseated her. *You can't think about such things,* she told herself. *Concentrate on survival.*

Focusing all her attention on the big, ugly man, she worked at removing the needle from the length of silk, a difficult task to accomplish blindly with only her left hand and complicated by the slick surface of the fabric. She feared that the monster would notice, but if he did, he gave no sign. Perhaps he saw what she was doing and wasn't concerned with the minuscule torment a little needle could accomplish. She herself didn't know what she could do with one little needle against three burly men, but it was all she had.

The spittle poured from his mouth now, and his one eye—such a pale blue it was almost white—leered at her. Mere inches from her chair, he dropped to his knees, which put his head on a level with hers. She'd seen that look before, seen pure animal lust and knew where it led. The Confederate captain's face loomed before her. Shuddering inwardly, she forced the image away, compelling herself to maintain control. She couldn't let the monster see her flinch, couldn't let him know how much she feared him. Looking at him with a steady gaze took every ounce of self-discipline she possessed.

A part of her heard the banging and clattering from upstairs and acknowledged that the other two men were making a royal mess. Let them. She didn't care what they did, so long as they remained upstairs.

The monster reached into his britches pocket and pulled out something, then stared at it, his meaty hand hiding the object of his attention from her view.

"Ye're even purtier'n I spected," he said, his one eye directed on his palm, his tongue rolling around his lips, to collect the spittle, she supposed. "I been a-wonderin' what color yore hair'd be. It's sech a nice shade o' red, like I figured it'd be. But yore eyes . . . I never figured them fer green."

He was talking like he'd seen her picture somewhere, which made no sense—unless . . .

He held his palm up and turned it around, and she gasped involuntarily when she saw her own picture, the small daguerreotype she'd given to Willy when he went off to school.

"Where did you get that?" Each word came out separately, distinctly, forced from her throat.

"I fount it," he said. "A whole passel o' letters, too."

She recalled what Steele said about the man who'd taken Willy's knapsack possibly forming an obsession for her, and she knew that was exactly what had happened.

"I been a-dreamin' 'bout ye. Dreamin' o' kissin' ye. I kissed them other wimmin, too, but they warn't ye." He rocked as he spoke, each forward movement bringing his face closer and closer to hers. His rancid breath slammed into her, and bitter bile gorged her throat. Instinctively, she swallowed it, then wished she'd had the foresight to spit it in his face.

The needle broke free, but the point was facing toward her palm. Without taking her gaze off the monster, she laid it on the table, turned it around, and secured a firm grasp on its shaft. His most vulnerable spot was his eye, which was on the side of his face opposite her left hand. Puncturing it, therefore, would be awkward, but she had no other choice. She'd have to be quick and accurate—and ready to run like the wind.

He seemed bent on taunting her with his foul breath and the promise of his wet, twisted lips descending on hers. Silently, she blessed his strategem, for it allowed her to absorb the rhythm of his swaying. She waited until he'd rocked all the way back and started forward again, then lashed out with her left hand and plunged the needle at his eye, hoping the dual momentum would increase the force of the blow.

She missed. Completely. The heel of her hand caught his nose and slid downward—and she dropped the needle.

He pinched at the spot where her hand had collided with his nose and pinned her with a wounded look. "How come ye to hit me?" he said. "I don' want to hurt ye. I love ye."

Control, Betsy reminded herself. *You've been through this before. You lost control then. Don't do it again. Don't faint. Don't scream. Don't show him any weaknesses. Don't give him the power.*

Footsteps bounded down the stairs and the two other men sauntered into the dining room. "Where d'ye keep the cash?" the older one demanded.

"Don't have any," she said, grateful they hadn't found what little bit she did have.

The older one pushed the monster aside and jerked her upright, his fist filled with the fabric of her bodice. "Liar!" he yelled. "Big, fine house like this—ye got t' have money."

She swallowed hard. "All gone," she managed.

He thrust her back into the chair, and she saw he'd found her father's pistols, which were shoved under the band of his britches. "Ye done kissin' her?" he asked the monster.

"Naw. Ain't started."

"Hurry up. Hit's time to git."

"But we ain't looked down here," the third one said.

"Go see what ye can find," the older one ordered, then to the monster he said, "Ye best git on with it."

I can't go through this again! she thought. *I'll die if he touches me.*

But she knew she wouldn't die. She'd survived before. She'd survive again.

Or would she? These men left no witnesses. They killed for the pure pleasure of seeing folks die. And then they set fire to the house . . .

Her gaze darted around the room, but she saw nothing worthy of this last final moment of her life. If only she could see Steele again—and Matt and Auntie Kee. Just one more time. Lord, just one more time.

Slobbery lips landed hard on her mouth, but she barely noted their pressure. Somehow, she'd divorced her living, breathing self from her soul, which these men couldn't touch. In her mind, she was in the meadow with Steele and he was telling her he loved her. *Her* . . . plain old Betsy Tyler. Crazy Betsy Tyler. That was the memory she wanted to take with her to the grave.

Someone grabbed her by the hair and yanked hard. Pain shot through her head and she screamed. An open palm smacked her cheek and a gruff voice told her to "shet it." The dull blade of a hunting knife flashed across her vision and she felt its cold steel against her throat.

"What're ye doin'?" the monster bellowed.

"Ye know what," the older one answered.

"She's my Betsy. Ye cain't kill her."

"We cain't leave her here to tell folks about us, now kin we?" He pulled harder on her hair, dragging her away from the chair, and the pressure from the blade increased. Fearful of the slightest movement in her throat, Betsy breathed shallowly through her nose and dared not swallow. But when a scream gurgled in her throat, she had no choice. Better to swallow than scream.

"We kin take her with us," the monster argued. "That's what we said."

"No, that's what ye said."

Golden flecks swam before her eyes and she fought back the panic threatening to engulf her. In quick succession, something brushed by her hip, the cold blade vanished, and a shot rang out.

I'm dying, she thought. *No, I'm already dead. There's no pain in death. There's only regret.*

"Ye see the sunball?" Auntie Kee said to Matt, her finger pointing at the blazing sun.

"Yes'm."

"When it gits halfway down that there ridge, ye come home. It don' make no diff'ernce if'n ye got a nibble on yore line. When it gits there, ye come home."

"Yes'm."

"I mean it," Auntie Kee said. "The onliest reason I'm lettin' ye stay is cause ye ain't ketched a fish yet."

There was another reason, too, but it was one she didn't think he needed to hear. For the last ten minutes or so, she'd had the strangest feeling something was wrong back at the house. If she was right, if Betsy was in danger, Matt would be safer right where he sat. If she was wrong, then she'd come right back. He ought to be all right by himself for the few minutes it would take her to walk home and back.

She was almost to the back door when the shot rang out.

When Rena's grandmother drew her last ragged breath, Steele placed her hand across her chest and comforted Mrs. Wakefield and Rena as best he could.

"We're beholden to ye fer comin'," Mrs. Wakefield

said, "fer easin' her last minutes. I'll stay and git her ready for the fun'ralizin'. Rena, ye go on back home now an' tell yore paw."

"I'd like to stay and help you," he said, sincerely meaning it yet more certain than ever that he needed to get back to Betsy as swiftly as possible, "but I need to get back to town. There's something . . . urgent."

"Preparin' bodies is wimmin's work," Mrs. Wakefield said. "Ye done what ye could."

"Of course, I'll preach the funeral sermon."

She nodded. "I'll send word."

"And I'll tell folks in town," he said, backing out the door and mentally kicking himself again for coming on foot.

"You gotta take care of Betsy for me, Lord," he murmured as he set off down the trail, "or give me wings to fly."

Twenty-six

His heart and mind in complete chaos, Hobe stared at the gaping black hole in Zero's side and the blood spurting out of it. He'd shot his brother, his own flesh and blood brother, but he wasn't sorry. Not even a little bit. Zero was bad. Always had been. Hobe supposed he was bad, too, but at least he had a little compassion left. Zero never had any.

That wasn't why Hobe shot him, though. He could a-gone right on living with Zero's evil nature if it hadn't a-been for Zero wanting to kill his Betsy, who had fainted dead away. Tears rushed to Hobe's eye as he dragged her limp body away from Zero. What if she was dead and not just asleep? Tenderly, he turned her head so he could look at her neck. Luckily, Zero's knife hadn't done any real damage, just a couple of scrapes that would heal up. If he hadn't taken the knife away when he did, though, Zero would have slit it open.

Assured now that she would live, he returned his attention to his brother. Zero's eyes stared right back at Hobe. They seemed to be asking why. He put one hand over the hole and blood oozed out between his fingers, while his other hand reached for the pistol still stuck in his waistband.

Hobe aimed the pistol he held at Zero's head and pulled the trigger. A tiny hole appeared in Zero's forehead, and his spine slid down the wall, leaving a wide bloody streak on the pretty flowered wallpaper.

Betsy's whimper snagged his attention. She was trying to sit up, her green eyes wide with terror. "Hit's all right," he told her, his voice as gentle as he could make it. "He cain't hurt ye now."

Lam came running into the room, stopped short and gawked at Zero. "How come ye to—"

Hobe turned the pistol on Lam. "Git!" he barked. Giving the orders for a change felt good. He hadn't ever liked Lam, just put up with him 'cause Zero said he had to. He didn't have to anymore.

Lam took another step toward Hobe, his arm raised and his eyes blazing with hatred. "Ye sorry sum-bitch—"

Aiming for Lam's head, Hobe squeezed the trigger again and laughed deep down inside when Lam's eyes opened as wide with disbelief as Zero's had. Neither of 'em had ever thought Hobe had any gumption. Well, he'd showed 'em. Now, they couldn't ever pick on him again about Betsy or about how slow he was or how ugly or nothing else. He'd showed 'em who was boss.

Now that he'd found his Betsy, no one was going to take her away from him. No one. He'd kill anyone else who tried.

When the second shot rang out, Auntie Kee hurtled her short, rotund body toward the back door, moving faster than she had in years. *It's jest Miss Betsy foolin' with them pistols again,* she tried to assure herself, but she didn't quite believe it. Not with the threat from the marauders hanging over their heads. She shouldn't a-ever gone off and left Miss Betsy alone. Recriminations, however, would only interfere with what had to be done.

She opened the door to a wave of black smoke, which stung her eyes and threatened to choke her, and the odor of burning cake, positive evidence that something was wrong. Betsy wouldn't have let it burn. She wanted to call out, to hear Betsy's voice in answer in return, but her instincts cautioned against it until she had a weapon in hand. Leaving the door open, both to prevent the noise of its closing and to allow another course of escape for the smoke, she made her way across the kitchen to the pantry.

With the loaded shotgun firmly planted against her shoulder, she stood with her back against the pantry door, which allowed her a clear view of both the back and dining room doors. It was to the dining room that she turned her attention—and the scatter-rifle. She grabbed the hammers with both hands, cocked them back, then curled the fingers of both hands around the triggers, which she'd learned had tight springs. When she'd practiced with the preacher, she hadn't been able to hold the heavy gun for more than a minute or so. She prayed her strength held out.

Footsteps pounded in the front hall and a man hollered, "How come ye to—" A second male voice ordered him to "Git!" Something else was said—Auntie Kee couldn't be too sure exactly what—then a third shot reverberated through the house.

Oh, Lord! she thought. *Lord, please tell me no.*

"Miss Betsy!" she cried then. Her pulse thrummed in her ears, her eyes swam with tears from the smoke and sweat from her brow, but her hands held the shotgun steady.

She moved away from the pantry door, toward the dining room, and hollered louder. "Miss Betsy!"

When there was still no answer, she fought back both the demons that haunted her and a vision of Betsy lying in a puddle of blood on the polished wood floor. If they'd hurt her Betsy—if they'd harmed one hair on her head, she'd kill every last one of them or die trying.

Suddenly, a creature appeared in the doorway, a bear of a man with the most hideous face she'd ever seen. When she looked closer, she realized that half his face was covered in thick, red skin.

The man with half a face! The one Matt had seen through the window. The one who'd kilt the boy's maw and more than likely Betsy, too.

She stepped out with her right foot, bent her knee, and leaned forward, angling the shotgun across her body and levering it up, gathering all her strength of both will and body as she moved. Refusing to think about what she was fixing to do, she pulled both hands toward her, squeezing first the forward trigger and then the back.

Ka-bam! Ka-bam! went the shots, much louder in the enclosed space than when she'd practiced outdoors, the noise ringing in her ears like the buzz of a thousand bees. The impact propelled the man backwards, his considerable weight crashing into chairs and the dining table. She barely felt the recoil, which pulled her upright, but her arms were shaking so much she couldn't hold the shotgun anymore. She laid it on the table, wiped the moisture from her eyes, and went looking for Betsy.

Matt heard the shots all the way to the branch.

At the first one, he dropped his pole and darted into the thick cover of the woods. With each successive shot, he inched closer to the house, terrified that he'd find Betsy and Auntie Kee lying near the woodlot, bullet holes in their backs, yet drawn to the scene nonetheless. If only he were a man . . . if only he had a gun . . . he'd get them men. He'd shoot 'em dead and leave 'em fer the buzzards.

But he wasn't a man, and he didn't have a gun. He was just a little kid hiding in the woods, shaking from head to toe and unable to keep himself from wetting his pants. He should've done something to help Maw, and he oughter do something now, though for the life of him, he didn't know what he could do that wouldn't get him killed right along with Betsy and Auntie Kee.

If something happened to them, if they died like Maw, he'd just as soon die right along with them. Nobody else wanted him anyway, 'cept maybe the preacher, but he'd made it plain as day that Matt couldn't ride the circuit with him. No, he might as well die, too. Then he could be in heaven with Maw and Paw and Betsy and Auntie Kee.

He was almost to the edge of the woods. He couldn't see anyone, and it was really odd that he didn't hear nothing. He reckoned they was there—the man with the ugly face and the other two, just waiting for him to show up. Squinching his eyes shut, he burst into the clearing behind the house and waited for the final shots, waited for the bullets to rip into his chest, waited for the angels to come take him to heaven.

But nothing happened. Nothing. He didn't hear a sound, not even a bird chirping.

He cracked open one eye and then the other. The clearing appeared to be empty. He chanced a glance to one side. Nothing but grass and a patch of pink lady's slippers. Feeling a bit more confident, he opened his eyes a little wider and glanced to the other side. Nothing there unusual either.

He knew he'd heard the shots. Five of them. There was no mistaking the report of a gun. Bewildered, he looked at the house. Little black clouds of smoke wafted out the open door. His heart fell to his knees. It was the bad men. They'd set far to the house.

Hope sprang within his breast. Since Betsy and Auntie Kee weren't in the clearing, maybe they were still alive. Maybe they were inside, knocked out or something. Energy and purpose surged through him. Maybe he *could* do something. Maybe he could save Betsy and Auntie Kee yet.

* * *

About halfway across the cove, a strange peace settled over Steele. The three marauders were dead. He knew this as surely as he knew the setting sun would shine again tomorrow. He knew, too, that Betsy had survived, that the threat to her life had passed. Nevertheless, he quickened his steps, ignoring the stitch in his side and the cramp in his left thigh. If his instincts were right, she needed him now more than ever.

As he walked, he wondered how the raiders had died. He was glad they were dead, but equally as glad he hadn't been the one to kill them. His destiny had never been to end their worthless lives, but rather to find the worth of his own. And that he had surely done.

The sun had completely set by the time he reached Begley's store. The windows gaped blackly, not even a hint of light burning within. So, Begley was with Betsy and Kee. That was good.

Or was he? The town was quiet. Too quiet. No one sat on a single porch. No mother called her children to supper. No lantern or candle burned anywhere.

In contrast, Betsy's house blazed with light. Golden light poured from every visible window, scaring him until he noticed that people moved about inside each room and heard the laughter of children chasing lightning bugs. So, this was where they all were. But why?

He looked closer and saw that several people huddled together on the front porch, their dark forms silhouetted against the dining room windows. He counted three, no, four heads, one much smaller than the others. Without breaking his pace, he opened the gate and headed up the walkway.

"Here he is!" Matt shouted. The smaller form separated itself from the others and tore off the porch. Steele caught Matt in his arms, picked him up, and hugged him close, all the while searching the darkness for a gleam of red hair, a familiar gesture, anything that would identify one of the remaining people on the porch as Betsy.

"We been worrit 'bout ye, Preacher," Matt said. "I shore am glad ye're all right."

"Worried about me? Why?"

"We didn' know but what the bad men got ye and Rena 'fore they come here."

Betsy moved out then and stood at the top of the steps, waiting for him. Love and pride and happiness coursed through him. He set Matt down and was in her arms before he knew he'd taken a step.

"We'll be back come mornin' soon," Imer Bailey called as she walked down the steps.

"Don't ye worry none 'bout doin' nothin' else tonight," Charlotte Patridge added. "We got yore rooms where ye kin sleep in 'em, and the kitchen where ye kin cook."

"Thank you," Betsy said from her spot on the porch floor. She supposed standing up and shaking all their hands as they left would be the polite thing to do, but her reluctance to leave the warmth and protection of Steele's arm kept her seated. They might be more comfortable elsewhere, but they'd be separated in chairs. She made a mental note to have Sam build her a swing so she and Steele could spend long hours cuddling on the porch if they wanted to. "Thank you all. I don't know what I would have done—"

Mary Snider cut her off. "Don' say no more. Ye'd a-done the same fer us. We're jest glad we could help."

As one family after another filed out of the house and down the flagstone walkway, Betsy waved good night and expressed her gratitude. What they had done at the Tyler house that night amazed and pleased her. Whatever doubts she'd clung to about acceptance, their cheerful help had washed away.

The gunshots brought folks running from every corner of town. As soon as they verified that Auntie Kee, Matt, and Betsy were all right, they set about hauling the dead bodies outside and cleaning up the blood and the mess the marauders had created when they ransacked the house. That two men could generate more havoc in a few minutes than fifteen or so adults could clean up in several hours dumbfounded Betsy. That Auntie Kee, who'd always walked the straight and narrow, had killed a man astounded her even more.

"I never did finish tellin' ye 'bout how I come to live here, did I?" Auntie Kee said, taking Betsy by surprise yet again. Perhaps the half-breed woman simply wanted to take her mind off the evening's events, Betsy reasoned. Then she remembered what Auntie Kee had said before: *I didn't think things could get worser. But they did.*

"No, you didn't," Betsy said, snuggling closer to Steele.

Auntie Kee and Uncle Begley were sitting as close together as their two rocking chairs allowed, his arm looped around her shoulders. Betsy decided to ask Sam to make a settee on rockers, too. Matt, who was softly snoring, lay on a folded quilt at their feet. Betsy suspected they looked for all the world like a normal family, merely taking in the cool night air. They would soon be a family, but there was nothing normal about them tonight, perhaps never would be again. For a long time to come, this night would be emblazoned in their memories, their hearts forever grateful and yet saddened by what had happened here.

Auntie Kee leaned forward and scrutinized Matt, apparently to assure herself he was really asleep, before she started to talk. "If I mem'ry right," she said then, her voice low, "I left off tellin' 'bout my maw dyin', but I spec' I best ketch Begley and the preacher up 'fore I go on."

As she talked, a hush fell over the night, as though even the insects and night birds were listening to her tale.

". . . So I give Dancin' Water a proper buryin' and then stayed the rest of the winter in that little cave. Ever' day, I'd go out a-lookin' fer food. They warn't much 'sides chestnuts, but I fount enough t' keep me alive. Come sprang, I thought, I'd go lookin' fer t'other Cherokees what was hidin' out in the mount'uns. I was hopin' agin hope they'd feel sorry fer me and take me in."

How much it must have hurt Auntie Kee to be shunned by her own people! Betsy thought, knowing at least partially how such treatment wounded. No wonder she and Auntie Kee had always been such kindred spirits.

"Finely, the snow started meltin' and I wandered farther and farther from the cave, but I never did see nobody else. Then one day, I come upon three men from the village. They was huntin' game and had a couple o' winter-scrawny rabbits a-hanging from thair belts. I looked at them rabbits and my mouth took to waterin'. I warn't thankin' 'bout nothin' else 'cept how good them rabbits'd eat. I don' recollect ever feelin' so hunger-bit afore or since. I was plumb weak from it."

She paused for a moment, taking several deep, audible breaths.

"Ye don' have t' tell us, Kee," Begley said.

"Yeah, I do. I ain't never tol' nobody, an' it ain't good to keep the past bottled up inside like I done. It makes ye all bitter-like."

Suddenly, Betsy didn't want to hear the rest of Auntie Kee's story. She'd bottled her own bitter memories up, wrote "poison" on the label, and put the jar on a shelf to collect the dust of time. And that was where it was going to stay. She didn't want to be told that opening it would be good. She didn't want anyone expecting her to recount the events of that night at the Confederate camp just because Auntie Kee was taking her memories off the shelf . . .

Auntie Kee took another deep breath, this one a bit ragged, before continuing. "Anyways, I was a-lookin' at them rabbits when I should a-been lookin' at the men totin' 'em. 'Fore I knew what was happenin', one of 'em grabbed me from behind and pulled me to the ground, and another one jumped on top of me. I don' spec' I have to tell ye what happened after that. Hit was horrible. I was too weak from hunger to fight 'em. All three of 'em took me 'fore they was done, then they went off and left me fer dead. I lay there fer a long time, thankin' I *was* dyin'. The night come, and I still didn't get up. Hit got cold, really cold that night. A wolf come sniffin' around and I figured—hit bein' at the back aidge o' winter—hit'd be as hunger-bit as me and would eat me alive. 'Stead, hit jest lay down beside me, then another wolf come and lay on t'other side. I reckon they's the reason I didn't die that night."

Matt roused then, sitting up on his pallet and rubbing his eyes. "Where'd everybody go?" he asked.

"Home," Betsy said. "It's past your bedtime." Surprisingly, he got up and went in the house without insisting she go with him. "I'll be up later to tuck you in!" Betsy called after him.

"Amazing," Begley said, shaking his head and leaving his observation open-ended, but Betsy figured he was referring to Auntie Kee's incident with the wolves rather than Matt's unusual compliance. For the most part, the boy obeyed his elders, but he thoroughly disliked sleeping in a room by himself and usually wouldn't go to sleep unless someone was with him.

Uncle Begley patted Auntie Kee's shoulder; his pale eyes shown with admiration and sympathy—and love. How long had he been in love with the half-breed woman? Betsy wondered. How sad that they'd wasted all those years.

"So you came to Peculiar Cove after that?" Steele asked.

"Not right then. I got off that mount'un quick as I could and fount a white fam'ly what agreed to take me in if'n I'd cook and clean fer 'em. That's when I learnt to speak 'Merican and when I got my name. They called me Cherokee, but this little 'un of theirn called me jest Kee, and it stuck."

"What was your Cherokee name?" Begley asked.

"*Gi-do hi-tlo-hi-hv.* It means, 'why do ye cry?' Dancin' Water said she named me for the night bird what cries for its home."

"The whippoorwill," Betsy whispered.

Auntie Kee nodded. "By the time I learnt the 'Merican word, I was use to bein' called Kee. They was nice enough, I s'pose, this fam'ly, I mean, but—well, I was jest a slave, fur as they was concerned. Soon's I got my strangth back, I left. Fer a long time, I jest went from place to place, till finely I come here. Yore folks was the first what treated me like I was somebody, so I stayed."

Begley pulled her closer. "And I fell in love with Kee the minute I seed her."

"Then why didn't you marry her?" Steele asked.

"Oh, he ast," Auntie Kee said. "I said no."

"Why?" The question was out of Betsy's mouth before she gave it any consideration. "I'm sorry," she hastily added. "That's your business."

"Ye 'member I started tellin' ye 'bout this 'cause ye ast me why I never married. If'n I didn't want ye to know, I'd a-told ye then." Auntie Kee put her hand on Begley's lower arm and smiled up at him. "I was afeared o' men," she said. "Afeared o' the marriage bed. Begley tried to tell me he warn't like them Injun bucks, but I wouldn't listen. Then today, when them men was here . . . well, it were like t'other time fer me all over agin. When them army men took Miss Betsy, I jest went all to flinders, couldn't do nothin' to help her a-tall. But today, when I kilt that man, it was like I got them bucks back."

She looked at Steele. "I know what the Bible says 'bout killin'. I know I done wrong. I'm sorry I had to do it, but I couldn't let that man hurt my Betsy."

"I'm sure God understands," Steele said.

"If'n Begley'll still have me . . ."

Betsy hadn't ever seen the storekeeper look so happy. Everything about him glowed. "Do ye mean it, Kee?"

She nodded, her dark eyes awash with tears of happiness. "I reckon I do."

Twenty-seven

As they'd promised, the townsfolk returned early Saturday morning. To Betsy's surprise and delight, Molly and Imer brought their mother's wedding gown for Betsy to wear.

"If'n this don' suit," Molly said, "we'll help ye finish sewin' t'other one, but we figured ye might just as soon borry this—with thangs goin' a bit crazy all of a sudden." She shook out a simple but lovely gown of pale peach satin, with an off-the-shoulder neckline, full sleeves, a tight bodice, and bell-shaped skirt.

"The color art to be perfect fer ye," Imer said, "and Maw was jest about yore size."

Betsy choked up and couldn't talk for a minute. This gown must be very special to them, too special to lend indiscriminately. That they were willing to let her wear it proved their friendship in a way little else could. She communicated her awe and gratitude with a smile they readily returned.

"Let's see if hit fits," Molly said, heading for the stairs.

Betsy wasn't at all surprised when it did. As Imer had said, the color was perfect for her—bringing out the creamy tone of her skin and making her eyes appear greener—as were the cut and fit. Nothing had to be adjusted, not even the length.

"Now, scoot," Imer said. "We're gonna press this gown and finish cleaning yore room." Betsy went straight to the kitchen, where the smell of charred cake lingered still, to tell Auntie Kee about the wedding dress.

Charlotte Patridge and her mother were there, sifting flour into large crockery bowls, while Auntie Kee was creaming butter and sugar together, surprising Betsy again.

"I thought we were almost out of flour and sugar."

"We was," Auntie Kee replied, "till folks brung us what they had. They brung eggs and butter and milk, too. We got enough now to make that big cake I done promised ye." She didn't mention what had happened to ruin the layers she'd made the day before, for which Betsy was grateful. The least said, the better, she thought.

"We couldn't let ye have a wedding without a cake," Charlotte said.

"I'm overwhelmed by everyone's generosity," Betsy said, telling them about the peach wedding gown.

Smiling, Mrs. Patridge dusted her hands on her apron and reached for a teacup. "Ye helped this town—more'n ye'll ever know. We're glad we can do sumpin to help ye back."

"And we're sorry we called ye Crazy Bets," Charlotte added. "Leastaways, I am. I'm plumb ashamed of myself."

Near tears, Betsy hugged Charlotte and her mother. "I wanted folks to think I was crazy. You could have gone right on thinking that, and with good reason. I appreciate your giving me a chance to prove I wasn't. Now, what can I do?"

"Nothing!" they all three said in unison.

"It's yore weddin' day, Miss Betsy," Auntie Kee explained. "Ye jest take it easy and let us worry 'bout workin'."

"But—"

"No argufyin'. Tonight, there'll be one less old maid in Peculiar Cove. And the way things is lookin', there might not be a single one left come fall."

This seemed to be a day for surprises. She knew about

Auntie Kee and Uncle Begley, but no one had said a word about Charlotte or Imer—and with Charlotte in the room, Betsy didn't want to ask. Thankfully, Mrs. Patridge enlightened her.

"Tom's ast Charlotte to marry him," she said, "and Sam Bartlett's gittin' awfully sweet on Imer."

"What wonderful news!" Betsy exclaimed. "Congratulations, Charlotte. Have you set a date?"

Charlotte grinned shyly. "We're thankin' on the end of the summer. I was wonderin' if maybe ye'd stand up with me."

"I'm honored. Of course, I will."

"Thank ye. Imer will, too." She looked down at the bowl, a look of pure misery on her face. "And I won't be teachin' at the school after the weddin'. Well, I will be, but not . . ." Biting her lip, she turned pleading eyes to her mother.

"What Charlotte's tryin' to say is that Tom's ast her to start a school for the grown-ups who never learnt t' read and write. I'm goin' to help her."

Betsy's heart soared. She almost told Charlotte how she'd wanted an adult school, but stayed her tongue in time. After all, Charlotte and Tom were the ones who were making it a reality; they deserved the credit. "That's wonderful news! If I can do anything, just let me know."

"Ye're goin' to be busy bein' a wife and a maw." Auntie Kee made a shooing motion with her wooden spoon. "Now git on out'n here and let us make yore cake."

Betsy wandered into the dining room, where Tom was repairing the wall and Sam was gluing a broken chair back together, but the memories of the previous day's events came flooding back and she fled to the front porch. Sitting in one of the rocking chairs, she looked off at the mist-covered mountains and let her mind wander back to the day Steele arrived in the cove. What a sight she must have made, with her jaw all swollen and probably looking as crazy as she was acting. How had he seen beyond the facade? She certainly hadn't even tried to see the person he really was. How had she ever thought he was the devil? No other man was as tender, as compassionate, and yet as strong as the Rev.

He'd let her get away with calling him that, let her rant and rave, let her come out of her shell in her own way. Outside of slapping her when she bit him, he'd allowed her total freedom of expression. Steele Montgomery was most definitely an unusual man.

And tonight he'd be her husband.

Tonight, he'd expect her to be his wife—in every way. Panic gripped her then. She didn't know if she could go through with it. She might know if she truly understood what "it" was, for an act of love couldn't possibly bear much relationship to the violation she'd suffered at the hands of the Confederate captain. If only there was someone she could talk to. Auntie Kee wouldn't know, nor would Charlotte or Imer. And she couldn't count on Lydia to arrive in time.

Molly! She could talk to Molly.

She jumped out of the chair and dashed into the house, hurrying up the stairs before she lost her nerve. She found Molly and Imer putting fresh sheets on her bed. Betsy stopped short in the doorway, her gaze fastened on the expanse of crisp white linen.

She must have looked as terrified as she suddenly felt, because Molly understood immediately. "C'mon in and close the door," she said. "It 'pears to be time we had us a little set-down."

"D'ye want me to leave?" Imer asked.

Molly smoothed her palm over the sheet. "Naw. I spect ye're gonna need the same talk 'fore too long. Might as well git it over with now."

* * *

While Molly quite frankly told Betsy what to expect that night, Steele was sitting on the outcropping of granite contemplating that very thing—and asking himself if maybe he and Betsy weren't making the biggest mistake of their lives.

Was she honestly ready for marriage? Was he?

They'd made the decision to marry in the midst of a crisis, when neither of them were thinking clearly. Now that the crisis had passed, maybe they ought to back up and give their fragile emotions time to heal.

He was skirting the issue, and he knew it. What really bothered him was the loss of her virginity to someone else. He simply didn't know if he could ever get past that hurdle. Nor was he sure she could get past the loss of his leg.

With faith and love and trust, all things are possible.

The voice came to him out of nowhere, as loud and clear as though someone standing right in front of him had uttered the words, yet he knew now that it was his own voice, his own instincts, talking—and that it always had been.

This realization caught him so completely by surprise that he verbally denied it. Not God's voice? But it had to be. The voice was always right. Without fail, it moved him in the right direction. The voice was calm when he was frantic, wise when he was foolhardy, forgiving when he was angry. Was it possible? Could he honestly possess those qualities along with his shortcomings?

He supposed he could. He supposed he did.

But, if it wasn't God's voice he'd been listening to all this time, then where was God?

Where was God when all the bad things were happening? Where was God when he lost his leg? Where was God when the Scoggins gang descended on the Montgomery farm? Where was God when the Confederate soldiers took Betsy back to their camp? Where was God when the Cherokee braves attacked Auntie Kee?

Did God even exist?

Yes, Steele affirmed. For him, at least, and for Betsy and Auntie Kee, for his mother and sisters, and for thousands of other good people who listened to their consciences, who tried to walk the straight and narrow path, who followed the Golden Rule. For all those people, goodness and love dwelt within. And what was God if He wasn't goodness and love and light?

But sometimes goodness wasn't enough to combat evil. Sometimes evil prevailed. And that brought him back to the question he couldn't answer: Why did God allow bad things to happen to good people? What possible purpose could such things serve?

To every thing there is a season, and a time to every purpose under heaven, Ecclesiastes said. *A time to be born, and a time to die . . . a time to kill, and a time to heal . . . a time to love, and a time to hate . . . a time of war, and a time of peace.*

Was it Maw's and Susan's and Sissy's time to die? What purpose did their deaths serve? If he'd come home to find them alive and well, where would he be now? What would he be doing?

He'd be living in his cabin on the ridge, that's where he'd be. He'd still be feeling sorry for himself, thinking of himself as a cripple, hiding from the world. If he hadn't lost his leg in the war, if the crutch hadn't slowed him down so much, he would have made it home several days, maybe even a week earlier. He would have been there when the marauders came—and then he would have either died along with Maw and Susan and Sissy, or he would have saved their lives.

Either way, he wouldn't have become a circuit preacher. He wouldn't have gone to Peculiar Cove. He wouldn't have met Betsy. He wouldn't have been there to rescue Matt.

MOUNTAIN MOONLIGHT

Heaven only knew what would have happened to the boy, alone at the isolated farm, but because Steele was there, Matt lived. And who was to say that he hadn't rescued Betsy as well? Rescued her from her own self-destruction, if not from the marauders? This was his purpose. He'd killed and he'd hated, but he'd also planted a seed. Now, it was time to harvest. Now, it was time to heal, to love, to be at peace.

Bad times would come again. They always did. There would always be threats from evil men. There would be another war. He could face those bad times alone . . . or at Betsy's side. The choice was his to make.

She was a vision of loveliness, the most beautiful woman he'd ever seen. So beautiful she took his breath away. And in a matter of minutes, she would be his wife.

He was a vision of grace, the most handsome man she'd ever seen. So handsome he took her breath away. And in a matter of minutes, he would be her husband.

Slowly, sedately, she walked toward him, her head held high, her green eyes focused directly on him, their heat, their intensity burning into his soul, melting away the last particle of ice.

Tall and proud he stood, waiting for her to take his hand, his brown eyes focused directly on her, their warmth, their compassion embracing her heart, dispelling the last fragment of shame.

Neither saw anything but the other's face smiling in faith and trust, nor heard anything but the dulcet tones of the other's voice vowing to love, honor, and cherish for as long as they both should live.

Their euphoria, their nearly total captivation with each other, continued throughout the reception at the Tyler house. It wasn't until the last guest left and Betsy and

Steele were on their way upstairs that reality began to penetrate.

He'd have to be careful. He knew that. But he refused to walk on eggshells. Somewhere deep inside Betsy, unleashed passion dwelled. The trick was in finding the key.

When he turned the key in the lock, a little gasp erupted from Betsy's throat. "I don't think anyone's going to come in," she murmured, visibly trembling in the dim light of a single candle someone had left burning on the bedside table.

He refused to look at the bed, depositing the key on her dresser instead. "I don't think anyone will, either, but let's not take any chances. It's right there, should you decide you want to escape." He closed the short distance between them and folded her into his arms, absorbing her quivers. "I love you, Betsy."

She nodded against his shoulder.

"And I won't hurt you."

He felt the movement of her head again, but he didn't think she believed him. Knowing something in your heart and believing it in your mind weren't the same. He vowed that before this night was over, she would believe him.

While he held her, his gaze traversed her room, which he'd never seen before outside of a few glimpses from the hallway. It matched her personality: feminine without being frilly, with an air of understatement, of simple elegance that appealed to him, much as her wedding gown did.

"You're beautiful," he whispered against her hair, cognizant, as she probably was, of the noise below as Auntie Kee, Lydia, and Ty cleared away the dirty dishes from the party. To ensure some privacy for the newlyweds, Ty and Lydia had taken Betsy's parents' room on the first floor, while Matt was sleeping on a pallet in Auntie Kee's room, which was also downstairs.

"No, I'm not. I'm just plain old Betsy Tyler." Surprisingly, there wasn't even a trace of bitterness in her voice, merely calm acceptance. "To everyone except you," she added.

"You *are* beautiful," he insisted. "Far lovelier than you realize. It's an ethereal beauty, one that would enhance the most hideous features." He took half a step backward and lifted her chin with his thumb and forefinger, forcing her to look at him. "But your features are not hideous. On the contrary, they're quite pleasing to the eye. Even before I fell in love with you, I thought you were pretty—a bit crazed, perhaps, but pretty."

"You did?"

"I did."

The corners of her mouth curved into a hint of a smile. "And I thought you were the Devil himself."

Steele laughed—so loud they probably heard him downstairs. "Why the Devil?"

Betsy's smile grew a bit. "Because you were dressed all in black. Because your hair's black and your eyes are dark. Because of that scar"—she traced it with her fingertip—"and your crooked nose. You frightened me. Of course, I was a bit crazed that day. I'm surprised you ever came to see me. Everyone must have told you about me."

He saw no point in denying the obvious. "I thought you were possessed of a demon and that God sent me to Peculiar Cove to exorcise it. Was I ever surprised to learn you had a toothache!"

"I never thought I'd be glad I had a toothache—or glad I'd done nothing about those rotten boards on the porch."

Her words called to mind the conclusions he'd reached that morning. One day soon, he'd tell her. But not now. They'd talked enough.

He smoothed his palms over her cheeks and upwards to her hair, where an ivory comb held a froth of creamy lace that cascaded down her back. This he removed, placing the simple headpiece on the chaise, when he wanted to yield to reckless abandon and toss it anywhere. Although he dared not take such rash action, he let her hairpins drop to the floor. One by one, he extracted them, until the pile of lush, auburn curls fell free. He drove his fingers into her hair, relishing its luxuriant softness, and drew her into his embrace.

She shivered, and he chastised himself for moving too fast. But when she put her hands on the back of his neck and pulled his head down, he forgot about everything except loving her. Lips and then tongues met in the dance of lovers, while his fingers slowly unhooked the back of the satin gown. She shivered again and pressed herself closer. He deepened the kiss, his hands caressing her bare shoulders and her back above her corset, all the while feeling himself grow long and hard.

This was going to be okay, he thought. She believed in him, trusted him.

Suddenly, however, she gasped and her spine gave a little jerk, dashing his hope of it being easy. Well, by golly, he'd make it okay, even if it took all night.

Although Molly had tried to prepare her, the length and rigidity of his manhood pressed against her stomach took her by surprise. He was a big man, in more ways than she'd thought.

She'd shocked Molly and Imer with her ignorance. They, like everyone else she was sure, thought her no longer a maiden. Steele must think the same! The realization startled her, and though she wanted to tell him, she was reluctant to take her mouth from his. Instead, she slipped her hands up his shirt and released the button at his throat. One by one, the buttons came loose beneath her nimble fingers, until the shirt gaped open, exposing his cotton knit undershirt.

Never had she dreamed that loving a man could be so wonderful, that making love to a man could make her feel so powerful. But when he shivered beneath her touch, when he moaned into her mouth and slipped the gown off her shoulders, she knew she affected him as much as he affected her. She'd expected to feel helpless, to feel victimized all over again, and had resigned herself accordingly. But Steele wasn't depraved—and he obviously had no problem proving his virility.

Despite her reluctance to interrupt the kiss, she took her mouth from his. "There's something I have to tell you," she said.

He kissed her forehead, the tip of her nose, her chin. "It can wait," he murmured.

She took his cheeks in her palms and set her unwavering gaze on his half-shuttered brown eyes. "Unfortunately, it can't, but it won't take long. Before we consummate this marriage, you need to know that I'm a virgin."

His eyelids flew open, and the measure of disbelief she saw in his face, though small, saddened her. But she would think the same, she told herself. Who wouldn't?

"He made me take all my clothes off, and he touched me all over, but he didn't do anything else. He . . . tried, but he couldn't." Without conscious direction, her gaze skittered downward to the bulge in his trousers, then back up again.

"And the other men?" His voice was harsh, the words torn from his throat. For an instant, she felt as though he'd slapped her. He was her husband now, and she supposed he had a right to know. Nonetheless, his apparent revulsion both rankled and saddened her.

"They never touched me. They took me only for their captain's pleasure."

She'd cried when she told Molly and Imer. It had all come back to her then—the humiliation, the degradation, the shame. This time, she felt only sorrow that an incident over which she'd had no control could taint her chance at complete happiness.

He took a ragged breath and pulled her back into his embrace, one hand moving tenderly over her hair, the other over her back. "I never thought I would know joy again," he said, "but I've found it in your arms."

There were tears in his voice, tears of shared pain, shared sorrow, shared love. But there was hope there, too. A whole lifetime's worth. Her fears and misgivings took flight, and from that moment on, she knew only bliss in his arms.

To Steele's delight, Betsy responded to his caresses with even more passion than he'd thought she possessed. Nevertheless, he continued to proceed slowly, to arouse her in small doses, even if his own arousal demanded surcease.

In degrees, he divested her of the peach gown and small clothes until she stood before him in naked splendor. He stepped back to admire her long, slender legs, the gentle curve of her hips, the narrow span of her waist, and the proud thrust of her breasts. She blushed beneath his scrutiny, her eyelids lowered demurely.

"You are so very beautiful," he said, his voice catching in his throat.

"It isn't fair," she whispered.

"What isn't?"

"You're still wearing your trousers."

He'd been so concerned with wooing her that he'd completely forgotten his wooden leg, but the thought of exposing himself to her, of allowing her to see him as the cripple he was mortified him. But she had overcome her fear, he reminded himself. If she could be so bold, so brave, he supposed he could, too. He reached for the button on his trousers, but her hands captured his. To his utter amazement, she led him to the bed and, when he was seated, she removed first his boots and socks, then his trousers, and finally his wooden leg. Not once did her eyes meet his. Instead, her gaze roamed his body, examining and inspecting it in much the same way he'd so recently indulged with hers—except that she couldn't possibly see in him what he saw in her.

It sickened him to think of what she saw. He lay back on the counterpane, his eyes closed against her revulsion, his cheeks flaming with humiliation.

"You are perfect," she whispered, the sincerity in her voice negating pity.

He couldn't believe it. He didn't dare believe it. And yet, when he opened his eyes and looked into hers, he did believe it.

With faith and love and trust, all things are possible, the voice had said.

Betsy had shown him her faith, her love, her trust. He could offer her nothing less.

Epilogue

May 17, 1867

"How long does it take to git a baby?"

Steele drove his fingers into his hair, which he still wore long, and stopped pacing to sit beside Matt on the parlor settee. He pulled the six-year-old onto his lap and hugged him tight. "I don't know, son. I've never been through this before."

"Ye reckon he'll be here 'fore dinner?"

Steele ignored the male reference, which Matt insisted on using, and concentrated on the supper part. He wasn't the least bit hungry himself, hadn't been since Betsy's pains had started near dawn, but he knew Matt was. Besides, eating would give him something to do other than worry. "Let's go see what we can find to eat."

To his surprise, he found Imer and Charlotte in the kitchen serving up plates. He hadn't even realized they were there.

"Ye didn' thank we was goin' to let ye go through this by yourself, did ye?" Imer asked, setting plates of fried squirrel and wild greens seasoned with fatback in front of Matt and Steele, while Charlotte brought a jug of milk and a pan of gritted bread to the table.

"I'm not thinking at all," Steele replied, sitting beside Matt at the kitchen table. "I'm much obliged."

" 'Tain't nothin', preacher," Charlotte said, her own stomach round with child. "Betsy'd do the same fer us."

That was the truth. Betsy amazed him with her energy and thoughtfulness. He couldn't have asked for a better helpmate in his profession—or a more understanding or passionate companion. He'd made the circuit one last time after the wedding, then assumed the ministry of the Peculiar Cove Methodist Church. In the fall, he'd taken Charlotte's place at the school and quickly discovered a natural talent for teaching he hadn't known he possessed. His life was rich and full of joy—and all because of Betsy. The thought of losing her in childbirth terrified him, but Granny Dunbar, James's mother and the resident midwife, assured him that Betsy was going to be fine.

"Kindly late to be havin' a baby," Granny said, " 'bout twelve year past most, I'd say, but she's a strong-'un."

Steele prayed she was right.

"It's li'ble to take a spell," Granny added. "Most first younguns does. 'Tain't no use in worryin'."

He did worry, nonetheless. He wasn't sure when he'd done quite so much worrying—or praying. As the day wore on, more and more folks showed up; by dusk, the house was full to overflowing, just as it had been the night of the wedding. He and Betsy had laughed later over her fear that no one would come. Over the past year, they'd shared many a happy moment. Every day, when Steele counted his blessings, he listed Betsy first, and he didn't want to spend another day of his life without her. From time to time, he marched into their bedroom, ignoring Granny's protests, just to assure himself Betsy was alive. Each time, she smiled and held his hand for a moment.

"This is awfully tiring," she said, "but otherwise I'm fine. The baby will be, too. You'll see."

Long about dusk, Ty and Lydia arrived. "Are we in time?" Ty asked.

Steele nodded in bewilderment. "How did you know?"

"I kin count!" Lydia quipped, cuddling her own baby against her bosom. They'd named their daughter Rebecca, after Ty and Betsy's mother, whom they'd learned was a member of the wealthy and politically powerful Pratt family of Boston.

Early that spring, Steele had answered the door to find a dapper gentleman of some fifty or sixty years standing on the porch. He introduced himself as Ethan Tyler, then proceeded to tell Betsy and Steele how he'd been searching for his brother Phineas, Betsy's father, for almost thirty years. The two brothers had had a terrible argument, he said, shortly after their father died. When their mother sided with Ethan, who was the younger by eleven years, Phineas took his inheritance and left, never to be heard from again. Later, Ethan said, he realized he'd been wrong, and he'd made it his life's goal to find Phineas and apologize. Although saddened by the fact that his brother was dead, he was thrilled to have found Betsy, whom he'd traced through the emerald ring she had used to pay for the repairs on her house.

Ethan's visit relieved Betsy of the burden of speculating about what her parents had been running from. Having also cleared up the matter of Ty's memory loss when he'd confessed everything late last summer, Betsy could finally put her family concerns to rest. She and Steele had offered their heartfelt understanding and their silence on the matter. Betsy and Ty were both working diligently at repairing their relationship and were growing closer all the time. Betsy would be thrilled to learn that Ty and Lydia were there when the baby was born.

If it ever was. He followed Lydia upstairs, then took up a post in the hallway right outside their bedroom, his nerves as tight as a new banjo string. When the wondrous cry of a newborn baby resounded from behind the door, he rushed in to find Auntie Kee laying a red-faced, screaming boy on Betsy's stomach. His heart lurched at the sight of her closed eyelids and peaceful face, but when he took her hand, she opened her eyes and smiled up at him.

"I can't go through this again," he said, planting a kiss on her forehead.

"I can," she whispered, joy in her voice, "and you can, too."

Together, they'd faced their demons—and won. Together, he supposed, they could do almost anything.

AUTHOR'S NOTE

While I was writing this book, my husband, two of our sons, and I spent a holiday with friends who live on a small farm in the hill country southwest of our home. We stuffed our faces with barbecued chicken and potato salad, then the men went off to the woods and the boys to the creek. Claudia, her mother Martha, and I spent a couple of lazy hours sitting on the side porch, swatting flies and talking. As I sat listening to Claudia's soft Southern drawl and country vernacular, I found myself thinking of ways I could incorporate her manner of speaking into my writing. When she told me about how their thirteen-year-old daughter Amanda and a charming young fellow named Jason, who was also there that day, had been friends for years but had just recently started "sparking eyes," I knew I had to use both her expression and the wonder of adolescent love in a scene somewhere in this book.

Later that week, such an opportunity presented itself in Steele's recollection of his first kiss. Even the blackberry picking sprang from that holiday, for my husband had planned to go back in a few days to pick blackberries that were getting ripe. He'd told Claudia he'd make her a cobbler. And I meant to call her to tell her about the scene she'd inspired. Events conspired to prevent the blackberry picking, and I didn't take time to call.

At the end of that week, Claudia and Amanda were dead, victims of a head-on collision.

Well before that lazy holiday, I'd had Betsy thinking about how tenuous is our hold on life, about how loved ones can be snatched away in the blink of an eye. But such things only happen in books or to faceless people you don't know. You feel for the family, you may even shed a few tears, but you don't truly grieve because you don't know those people. You don't expect it to happen to you or to anyone you know well. God wouldn't allow it.

When Steele arrived home from the war to find his mother and sisters dead, I had questioned (right along with him) why God allows such things to happen to anyone, why He allows good people to die young.

I'm still asking that question. I suppose I always will.